6/97

FIC
Wild women : contemporary
short stories by women
1994.

OCT 2 8 2000

97   98   00   01
10

ILL SEP 00
GAYLORD MG

0/97

Wild

Women

Wild

Women

Contemporary Short Stories by Women Celebrating Women

Edited by Sue Thomas

Introduction by Clarissa Pinkola Estés, Ph. D.

The Overlook Press
Woodstock · New York

First published in 1994 by
The Overlook Press
Lewis Hollow Road
Woodstock, New York 12498

Library of Congress Cataloging-in-Publication Data

Wild women / contemporary short stories by women
celebrating women / edited by Sue Thomas,
introduction by Clarissa Pinkola Estés, Ph. D.
p. cm.
1. Short stories, American—Women authors. 2. Women—United States—
Fiction. 3. Women—Psychological—Fiction. 4. Wild Women—Fiction
I. Thomas, Sue, 1951–
PS647.W6W53 1994
813′.01089287—dc20

Typesetting by AeroType, Inc.
Book design by Bernard Schleifer

CONTENTS ●

PREFACE ●

sue thomas

This collection of short stories by contemporary women writers brings together some modern examples of the various guises of the Wild Woman and presents an array of female protagonists as they catch a glimpse of her. Watch carefully. Somewhere inside every story in this anthology lurks the Wild Woman. She will jump out howling and you won't be able to miss her, or she will sneak around in the background, forever on the alert and watching for a chance to assert herself.

There is a breathtaking and heartening number of wonderful women writers today, and all of them, including the forty-six who are represented in this collection, give us all something to celebrate. They continue to add to a body of work that celebrates women's lives—their creativity, their sexuality, their spirits, their souls.

Ohba Minako's "The Smile of a Mountain Witch" traces the life story of a girl who has been a Wild Woman ever since she can remember. But as she grows up she discovers that her true nature upsets and disrupts the lives of her parents, husband and children, and she learns to conceal it. Subdued and acquiescent on the surface, in private she dreams of life alone in the mountains, naked in the sun-baked fields. In "Liking Men" Margaret Atwood asks "Who defines enemy?" A woman must always be alert to the possibility of predators, and her narrator is particularly sensitive to the threat of pain and entrapment. "How can you learn to do it?" she asks. "How can you like men?" and recommends retracing a man back to the day he was born in search of the time of innocence before he became dangerous.

Belisa Crepusculario in Isabel Allende's "Two Words" has a highly-developed wildish spirit which leads her to discover the power and mystery of language. She earns her living selling words, and the magic she invests in her wares brings her into the presence of the Colonel, the most powerful man in the region. Through him her wildish nature comes to fruition. Sometimes our wildish nature provokes the most atavistic imagery, as in Lisa Tuttle's "Birds of the Moon" and Leonora Carrington's "The Débutante."

It can be argued that Erica Jong's Isadora Wing is the prototype of the Wild Woman in modern literature. Exploring her sexuality through her search for the "zipless fuck," Isadora in *Fear of Flying* entered territory previously reserved largely for men, a heady region called by Henry Miller "the land of Fuck." In the selection from Jong's *How To Save Your Own Life*, female sexuality is raunchy, passionate, freewheeling and fun—and we see a fulfilling sex life as our due.

Anne Rice's "The Queen's Chamber" is a tantalizingly erotic combination of power and sexuality. The halls of this fairy tale palace, with its satin slippers, pink roses and sweet wines, echo to the sound of poor Beauty's cries as she bends to receive the lovingly administered royal punishment.

Melanie Tem's "Lightning Rod" and Kathy Page's "I Like to Look" both demonstrate how a woman can use her anger as a power to cook rather than destroy, but when a woman has a need she cannot fulfil, perhaps not even yet identify, she will try on different fantasies until she finds the one which seems to suit her best. In "Perma Red," Debra Earling describes the dilemma of young Louise who in this case is trying on whiteness for size. She has already lightened her hair and has tried several times to escape life on the reservation but each time she is caught in a circle of destiny which will not allow her to desert her own culture.

In Josephine Hart's "The Gift," a mother's sacrifice leaves scars that cannot heal her whole life long, and her tragedy, elegant in its symmetry, is at once breathtakingly noble and beautiful and inexpressibly terrible to bear.

• • •

My own most significant encounter with the Wild Woman was both amusingly bizarre and extremely empowering.

Ten years ago, and six months after my divorce, I built a poultry-house and bought half a dozen hens. I have always been fond of chickens, and one of my earliest childhood memories is of collecting eggs from the warm-smelling strawy nest-boxes. When after fourteen years of marriage my life finally became my own, the hens quickly became the symbols of my new independence, and soon I began to dream about chickens! They seemed somehow to represent my spiritual and intellectual freedom, and hens featured in a series of dreams, especially in the barren time following my father's death in 1987. Then, for example, I dreamed I'd found a cold and starving hen in the yard.

"I've been here all the time," it said, "You just forgot about me." I picked it up, brought it into the house and warmed it in my lap.

Several times, when things were going badly in the real world, I embraced these cold dream-hens and revived them. In my dreams people have tried to burn, freeze, and stab my chickens, but I rescued them every time. Meanwhile, I was working hard at becoming a writer, and as soon as my first book was published the dreams stopped. Well, of course they did. I no longer needed my chickens and now they've returned to the pool of the collective unconscious where they will remain until I need them again. But one thing's for sure—a dream about chickens is for me always a direct reference to my creative health, and a warning which I never ignore. At present I feel as if I have finally emerged into the light after so many years of wandering underground, and I look forward to spending the next cycle above ground enjoying my newly-replenished wildness.

INTRODUCTION ●

clarissa pinkola estés, ph.d.

When I first heard that I'd been given the opportunity to speak about my work on the instinctual nature of women for this anthology of short stories, I felt daunted about how to condense hundreds of pages into just a few. In the end, I must fall back on the most essential beginning I know. . . . *Once upon a time . . . a young woman sat at an old oak table to write . . .*

Women Who Run With the Wolves is the first part of a much larger body of work begun twenty-three years ago. The larger work encompasses one hundred fairy tales and myths about the inner life and the instinctual nature. *Women Who Run With the Wolves* is the first of five volumes, and is itself a multicultural work containing twenty tales accompanied by psychoanalytic commentary. The work was written in a blend of the scholarly voice via my training as a psychoanalyst, and in the voice of the traditions of healing and stories that reflect my ethnic origins as a mestiza Latina, who, as an older child, was raised by immigrant Hungarians.

I first began writing this work in 1971, because I found little in the modern psychoanalytic literature about women's real lives: the kind of women from my ethnic roots, we who were named the so-called "underclass," and "working class," the kind of women I knew as friends, and the kind of women who were my analysands (clients). The psychological literature of that time was almost completely bereft of material about the single mother, the widow, the working mother, the artist, the religious, the activist, the lesbian, the elderly woman, and on and on. The status quo material was particularly silent about one of my special interest areas: the inner lives of talented and gifted women.

Classical analytical psychology as postulated by Jung, although the second love of my life after poetry, had not done a very good job describing the varieties of women's psychological or spiritual experience. There were grave difficulties with some of the basic premises underlying classical depth psychology's view of women.

So, as the late sixties and early seventies were a time of maturing of many ideas, as a young activist, and in a burst of youthful enthusiasm, I decided I would attempt to make a contribution to these areas in which classical psychology determinedly had remained silent. In my clinical practice, I had used many stories given me in certain and special contexts by the old people in my family many years earlier. Now I used them in psychoanalytic context when and where indicated . . . according to rules and guidelines I'd learned, not only in psychoanalytic training, but equally from the old healers in our community who practiced a medicine of mind and soul themselves.

I'd been raised by old country people, most of whom could neither read nor write or who did so haltingly, and who therefore maintained an almost pure oral tradition. I had been taught as a child to recognize story as a quintessential medicine. I understood from years of being fed and groomed by the old women in my families, that story in all its many variations can, in right time and place, with proper application, give help to the hurts and wounds of simply having lived life.

In this regard, I could see that women's lives given such short shrift over the decades, needed the best sutures I could find. I felt the strongest suture I had were the stories I knew. I began to write and interpret the healing tales given me by my families, community and friends over the years.

In *Women Who Run With the Wolves*, there are fifty-two premises of instinctual life that I laid out as necessary in order that a woman be not just a surviving woman, but a thriving woman. Here are some:

- All women are born gifted.
- The gifted woman is an endangered species.
- Too often she is silent or silenced.
- The ability to speak one's own thoughts, know one's own mind, grow and develop according to one's own and most unique soul patterning is not a choice, but a psychological imperative.
- All creative life, emotional life, spiritual life, sexual life, relational life, moves in cycles of darkness and light, loss and return.
- There are feral women, who have been so long captured that when they are freed, their injuries to instinct cause them to no longer have

the proper radar to defend themselves from excesses and poor judgment. Their injured instincts must be assessed and repaired.
- The "normalization of violence," a phenomenon observed in animal studies, applies also to human women who seemingly volunteer to remain caged even though they are able to flee.
- Women become frail without the instinctual nature close by.
- Solitude is a psychological necessity.
- A woman's life is at its best when it is made by hand, when she refutes the latest fad in psychic shortcuts, when she surrounds her life and her art with those who support rather than oppose it.

As *cantadora* (keeper of the old stories), and an ethnic woman from two cultures, I recognize that humans are so very diverse culturally and otherwise, that it would be an error to think that any one way is *the* way. My work over these years is offered as a contribution to what is known and what is needed in a true psychology of women—one that includes all the kinds of women, and all the kinds of lives they lead. Regardless of a woman's state, stage, or station in life, she needs psychological and soulful strength to go forward. This is what my work is about.

• • •

Regarding women writers, I feel closest to those of most any stripe who are, in the main, what I call "psychologically extravagant." There are many such women writers in this book of short stories. They have developed characters who reflect diverse voices; some strident, many deeply erotic, some coiled as though ready to strike, some peering from the catbird seat, some very funny, endearing and compassionate. These writings are all impassioned, even those most languidly drawn.

The psychologically extravagant writer knows that there is a wild and vast territory in the psyche that belongs to her. Years ago, I thought this land of psyche was *terra incognita*, an unknown territory. But as I looked firsthand through the lenses of my own work as poet, and also through the eyes of those who came to me as psychoanalyst, I began to understand that wild continent of the female psyche is not undrawn, not unmapped, but one warmly recalled as though . . . as though what? Yes, as though women were in fact *born* there. And indeed women *are* born there, and more so, no matter how cut, pushed, pressed, or dragged away from there she might have been at whatever times of her life, she remembers her natural roots insistently, longs to return, struggles to proceed to that place as straight-away as possible, desires to stay there forever, and vehemently resists any re-development schemes regarding her most elemental home. The wild nature is her true natal site.

This darker ground of psyche is as necessary to a woman and to her art as water and air is to her body. If she is yet a fledgling, she will, in night dreams, and without wishing it so, dream herself there . . . home again. Those more experienced in that land, carry their own eye-witness accounts up from those zones and pour them into their art. No matter what laws or rules have forbade a woman to return to her own home country, she will risk many layers of emotional life to go there, stay for as long as she can or as long as she dares. She carries an exact map for the return in her arteries.

Why does she so yearn for that place? Because it is where the work, her work, her only work comes from. Work done elsewhere is thin like the shell of birds' eggs that have been poisoned by chemicals. Work done in her own home place is rich, sheltered while it is being writ, thick enough, lush and all other adjectives modifying goodness that begin with L's and S's.

So women writers, like those in this volume, who have returned to the home place, or who have never left it, have a peculiar quality to their work. Some would call it that old *Je ne sois pas*, an "I know not what." But here is the deeper truth: women who live there *do "know" what*, and here is what they know and share: The closer one comes to the great wild Self at the center of the psyche, the more one must change over from the ordinary mind to the extraordinary mind, and hence, from one's ordinary, often image-poor voice, to one's extraordinary metaphoric voice.

The closer one comes to the living Self—and it is represented in dreams, mythos, folklore and religions as a living, breathing being—the more impoverished ordinary and mechanistic language becomes in its ability to describe such. If one attempts to use ordinary language, that is, "a standard English," in order to describe the instinctual nature or the wild psyche, or any contents one derives from these, then one is assured of falling into unoriginal stutterings and paltry derivations—a kind of lexiconigraphic dumbness.

No, the leaps, required to convey both the bounty as well as the dangers of that instinctual world, rise on both a language and structure of another kind. And though anyone can develop or learn these, it is those who dedicate themselves to their art form, whichever it might be, who will have taken the greatest risks, for they attempt through daytime contemplations and nighttime dreams, to listen at the heart of it all, listen and translate, listen and attempt to draw forth something from one world to another.

Back in 1971 when I first began this work on the instinctual nature, I chose the words Wild Woman to delineate the powerful force, the heart, at the center of the psyche, because those very words, *wild* and *woman*, create *llamar o tocar a la puerta,* the fairy tale knock at the door of the deep female psyche. *Llamar o tocar a la puerta* is a form of *curandera* chant from my own heritage, one that means literally to play upon the instrument of the name in order to open a door. It means using words that summon up the opening of a passageway in the mind or heart. No matter by which culture a woman is influenced, she understands the words *wild* and *woman*, *intuitively* to mean more than just signs, but rather as living symbols which, when amplified, reveal layer upon layer of meaning and even direction.

When women remember through these words, an old, old memory is stirred and brought back to life. The memory of absolute, undeniable and irrevocable kinship with the wild feminine, a relationship which may have become ghosty from neglect, buried by over-domestication, outlawed by the surrounding culture, or no longer understood adequately.

In order to explicate the archetype of the Wild Woman, we must go even further and say that she, or rather She, has throughout the centuries been called by many names. Since this wild nature engenders every important facet of womanliness, she is named many names, not only in order to peer into the myriad aspects of her nature, but also to hold onto her, to retain this force in consciousness.

From my own people, in Spanish she is called, *Rio Abajo Rio*, the river beneath the river, *La Mujer Grande*, The Great Woman, *Luz del Abyss*, the light from the abyss. In Mexico, she is *La Loba*, the Wolf Woman, and *La Huesera*, the bone woman.

She is called in Hungarian, *Erdöben*, She of the Woods, and *Rozsomák*, The Wolverine. In Navajo, she is *Na'ashjé'ii Asdzáá*, the Spider Woman who weaves the fate of humans, animals, plants and rocks. In Guatemala among many, she is *Humana del Niebla*, The Mist Being, the woman who has lived forever. In Japanese, she is *Amaterasu Omikami*, The Numina who brings all light, all consciousness. In Tibet she is called *Dakini*, the dancing force which causes women to have clear-seeing through vitality. And it goes on. She goes on.

The comprehension of this instinctual nature of women is not a religion, but a practice. It is a psychology in its truest sense: *psych* soul, *ology* or *logos*, a knowing of the soul. The Wild Woman is the regulator, the same as a human heart regulates the physical body. Without this archetype, women are without ears to hear soul-talk or to register the chiming of their own inner rhythms. Without her, women's inner eyes are closed by some shadowy hand, and large parts of their days are spent in a semi-paralyzing ennui or else wishful thinking. Without her, women lose the sureness of their soul footing. Without her, they forget why they're here, they hold on when they would best hold out. Without her they take too much or too little or nothing at all. Without her they are silent when they are in fact on fire.

When we lose touch with the instinctive psyche, we live in a semi-destroyed state, and images and powers that are natural to the feminine are not allowed full development. When a woman is cut away from her basic source, she is sanitized, and her instincts and natural life cycles are lost, subsumed by the culture, or by the intellect or the ego—one's own, or those of others.

So you see, if a woman dries unto dust without this powerful force of psyche, then the Wild Woman must remain named. She must exist not only in the psyche, but above ground in the culture as well. And here is where all the trouble begins, for there are some who would like, just as a matter of fact, to silence this force, to silence any woman who derives from this force, in the main, because a woman connected here will have a steady and visionary mind of her own and far more importantly a voice that is *hers alone*.

She will be *an original*, meaning she will speak in original voice, act with original action. She will love fiercely, shelter what and who she loves, she will carry great weight, walk all night to get "there" by morning, she will bend and lift, heft and carry, and reach to extraordinary lengths emotionally, physically, and spiritually. And at her best psychic maturity, she will not easily be swayed from this "one place" in her life where she feels her strongest, knows the most, feels the most love. That is why a woman in her rightful wild mind is a force to be reckoned with. Her not being swayed is not a stubbornness. It is something far more exciting and daunting. It is pure conviction, from her very bones upward.

What is the Wild Woman archetype? It is an ancient force that *anyone* can observe, anyone who has ever read archeological texts about more than one culture, or examined the forms and shapes of icons, stelae, and other sculpture from times far past and across many cultures, or who has stood in the river of their own psyche for extended periods, or who has, as we do in psychoanalysis, seen the dreams of people from diverse parts of the world and found the same images repeated over and over in their dreams and artworks and spontaneous visions, regardless of the person's ethnic origin, education or any other categorizations.

Having seen such, one notes irrevocable feeling-toned images that are not personal, but rather, universal. These rise up over and over again, in dreams, and in the images and play of children, in the fears and hopes of adults, and yes in the paintings, writings and other representations of the life of the psyche, there too, these universal images rise. Whether representational images of the dark man, the lone wolf, the free nature, the sexual being, the captive woman, *la belle dame sans merci*, the beautiful woman who has no mercy, and the thousands of other symbols from this archetypal unconscious, they move us, and they require response.

By our interaction with these symbols, we find that the unconscious of humans carries all these myriad images in order to detail the wild nature, pointing to something fierce and very present in the psyche, something that has wind, has fire, can be torrential, can be like the palm of a lover's hand.

In my work as a clinician, I had to choose whether to define this force from the empirical point of view only, that is, standing outside of it, defining it from the outside and in the beautiful-in-its-own-way scholarly language I have studied and learned so well these past twenty-three years, or to transmit full bore and first hand from that wildish ground.

In essence I found that in order to give the matter full life and depth, and even though I shuddered to think of what some of my more traditional colleagues might say, I had to, and in fact dearly wanted to, not solely use the usual voice of psychology, but rather marry my personal voice as poet to the academic voice. Rather than stand on the outside of the wild psyche as has been the usual style of analyzing women for all one hundred years of classical psychoanalysis, I entered into the far older psychology, the one that is a million year old one, one that existed long before Freud, long before Jung, one that concerned itself with the spiritual and artful enterprise between ego, soul, spirit and outer life. Certainly there were other ways that others might use to proceed, but for me, there would be no rest unless I proceeded in as full wildish tone and timbre as possible.

Thusly, from the scholarly point of view, the wild nature would be called something like this: the elemental instinctual nature, a psychological and perhaps even biological drive that rests mostly in the unconscious and is often over-socialized by too stringent requirements to conform, and so on. This constructing of super-ego is necessary, but room must be left for the person to develop beyond the collective milieu as well. An overly harsh super-ego structure does not allow for such. In fact, it entirely blocks the aperture from which the instinctual nature flows. This in turn causes an ego distonic state and scrambles the meaning of the syntonic state. And so on such scholarly wordings go, and well enough.

But, what of describing this nature from the inside, from actual experience of it, for there are aspects of it that cannot be described by a sequential language alone. Understanding a bird comes not only from a schematic of the aerodynamics of its bone structure: to understand a bird absolutely requires poems so that a bird's essence might be known. A true description of a field flower requires that its color be presented as tastes, in both words and images, not only as a précis from the botanist.

So too, the psyche has its own idiosyncratic and symbolic language, one that is and has been used by mystics, poets, writers, artists, dancers, painters, and all those who want to describe, not just size and shape and duration, but depth, vitality and numinousity of matters that can never be justly counted by logistical words alone.

And so though relaying the descriptions of the archetype of the Wild Woman in clinical terms, I also brought the work of litanies, chants and poetics from my heritage. And in this way, I began to describe this force from the inside, from inquiring vision, and with enormous firsthand love, and most especially, in the strophes and rhythms of my mother tongue. So, the archetype of the Wild Woman is described thusly in *Women Who Run With the Wolves*.

How does the Wild Woman archetype affect women? With Wild Woman as ally, as leader, model, teacher, we see, not through two eyes, but through the eyes of intuition which is many-eyed. When we assert intuition, we are therefore like the starry night: we gaze at the world through a thousand eyes.

The Wild Woman carries the bundles for healing; she carries everything a woman needs to be and know. She carries the medicine for all things. She carries stories and dreams and words and songs and signs and symbols. She is both vehicle and destination.

To adjoin the instinctual nature does not mean to come undone, change everything from left to right, from black to white, to move the east to west, to act crazy, or out of control. It does not mean to lose one's primary socializations, or to become less human. Most of the time, it does not mean to refute all, and begin over. It means quite the opposite. The wild nature has a vast integrity to it.

It means to establish territory, to find one's pack, to be in one's body with certainty and pride regardless of the body's gifts and limitations, to speak and act in one's behalf, to be aware, alert, to draw on the innate feminine powers of intuition and sensing, to come into one's cycles and to protect them, to find what one belongs to, to rise with dignity, to retain as much consciousness as we can.

The archetype of the Wild Woman and all that stands behind her is patroness to all painters, writers, sculptors, dancers, thinkers, prayer-makers, seekers, finders—for they are all busy with the work of invention, and that is the Wild Woman's main occupation. As in all art, she resides in the guts, not in the head. She can track and run, and summon and repel. She can sense, camouflage and love deeply. She is intuitive, typical, and normative. She is utterly essential to women's mental and soul health.

So what is the Wild Woman? From the viewpoint of archetypal psychology as well as from the tradition of story, she is the female soul. Yet she is more, she is the source of the feminine. She is all that is of instinct, of the worlds both seen and hidden, she is the basis. We each receive from her a glowing cell which contains all the instincts and knowings needed for our lives.

She is the Life/Death/Life force, she is the incubator. She is intuition, she is far-seer, she is deep listener, she is loyal heart. She encourages humans to remain multi-lingual; fluent in the languages of dreams, passion, and poetry. She whispers from nights dreams, she leaves behind on the terrain of a woman's soul, a coarse hair, and muddy footprints. These fill women with longing to find her, free her, and love her.

She is ideas, feelings, urges, and memory. She has been lost and half-forgotten for a long, long time. She is the source, the light, the night, the dark and daybreak. She is the smell of good mud and the back leg of the fox. The birds which tell us secrets belong to her. She is the voice which says "This way, this way."

She is the one who thunders after injustice. She is the one who turns like a great wheel. She is the maker of cycles. She is the one we leave home to look for. She is the one we come home to. She is the mucky root of all women. She is the thing which keeps us going when we think we're done for. She is the incubator of raw little ideas and deals. She is the mind which thinks us, we are the thoughts that she thinks.

Where is she present? Where can you feel her, where can you find her? She walks the deserts, woods, oceans, cities, in the *barrios*, and in castles. She lives among queens, among *campesinas*, in the board room, in the factory, in the prison, in the mountain of solitude. She lives in the ghetto, at the university, and in the streets. She leaves footprints for us to try for size. She leaves footprints wherever there is one woman who is fertile soil.

Where does Wild Woman live? At the bottom of the well, in the headwaters, and in the ether before time. She lives in the tear and in the ocean. She lives in the cambria of trees which pings as it grows. She lives in the past and is summoned by us. She lives in the present and keeps a chair at our table. She stands behind us in line. She drives ahead of us on the road. She is in the future and walks backward in time to find us now.

She lives in the green poking through snow, she lives in the rustling stalks of dying autumn corn, she lives where the dead come to be kissed and the living send their prayers. She lives in the place where language is made. She lives on poetry and percussion and singing. She lives on quarter notes and grace notes, and in a cantata, in a sestina and in the blues. She is the moment just before inspiration bursts upon us. She lives in a faraway place which breaks through to our world.

People may ask for evidence, for proof of the Wild Woman's existence. They are essentially asking for proof of the existence of the psyche. Since we are the psyche, we are also the evidence. Each and every one of us is the evidence of not only Wild Woman's existence, but Wild Woman's condition in the collective. We are the proof of this ineffable female numen. Our existence parallels hers.

Our experiences of her within and without are the proofs. Our thousands and millions of encounters with her intra-psychically through our night dreams and our day thoughts, through our yearnings and inspirations, these are the verifications. The fact that we are bereft in her

absence, that we long and yearn when we are separated from her; these are the manifestations that she has passed this way.

from Chapter One, "Singing Over the Bones,"
from *Women Who Run With the Wolves*

• • •

Now you see why the voices in this volume of short stories are so expressive of what has been outlined thus far. I am, as always, less interested in the content of actual stories, whether they are old or new, than I am in the symbols of the story, and what these mean to the originator and to the listeners. But ultimately, I am most interested in the clearest possible connection to the creative force. In this volume of stories, the creative force is vastly present and immensely served.

The authors and the stories for this anthology were not chosen by myself, but by Sue Thomas and her editor, Tracy Carns, and the list is very fine. The voices I am most familiar with are those of my beloved Angela Carter who passed away last year, but her work, ah, it burns as brightly as ever, and also Anne Rice, and Andrea Dworkin, as well as those writers I know personally and count as friends, the also most beloved Alice Walker, Evelyn Lau, Dorothy Allison, Isabel Allende, and Erica Jong. What pleasure and treasure.

I know many writers in this book to be powerfully talented women who came from circumstances almost guaranteeing that they would be shorn of their voices at an early age. They endured much, and more so, danced and cackled their way upwards, eventually sassing back into the faces of some, but more so have been raised up into the hearts of literally millions world-wide. Many represented here truly claimed their own voices against the odds.

Here is a group of women writing from their own voices, from their own thousand eyes. We're all in the Baba Yaga's kitchen, or ought to be, don't you think? The wild nature, that is the deep instinctual nature of women, burns for whatever it is she truly loves, cares for, wishes to know, wants to exorcise, banish, deify, bring to the world.

There is far more to women's voices than the making of literature. We are still in a time when it is a historic act for women to think, feel, and say aloud, write in indelible ink, show right there on the page in broad daylight, what and how they perceive, think and create. So now, it is in this sense that I am honored to present to you—whether you be male or female, young or old, seasoned or just beginning and all in between—your sisters; your wicked, funny, sweet, merciful and merciless sisters. As you read the following stories by some of the best authors of the literate world, remember this: The words "oh, no," and "ah, yes," have existed far longer than any others.

Clarissa Pinkola Estés, Ph.D.

1

WHO IS THE
WILD WOMAN?

THE TIGER'S BRIDE ●

angela carter

MY FATHER LOST ME to the Beast at cards. There's a special madness strikes travelers from the North when they reach the lovely land where the lemon trees grow. We come from countries of cold weather; at home, we are at war with nature, but here, ah! you think you've come to the blessed plot where the lion lies down with the lamb. Everything flowers; no harsh wind stirs the voluptuous air. The sun spills fruit for you. And the deathly, sensual lethargy of the sweet South infects the starved brain; it gasps: "Luxury! more luxury!" But then the snow comes, you cannot escape it, it followed us from Russia as if it ran behind our carriage, and in this dark, bitter city has caught up with us at last, flocking against the windowpanes to mock my father's expectations of perpetual pleasure as the veins in his forehead stand out and throb, his hands shake as he deals the Devil's picture books.

The candles dropped hot, acrid gouts of wax on my bare shoulders. I watched with the furious cynicism peculiar to women whom circumstances force mutely to witness folly, while my father, fired in his desperation by more and yet more drafts of the firewater they call *grappa*, rid himself of the last scraps of my inheritance. When we left Russia, we owned black earth, blue forest with bear and wild boar, serfs, cornfields, farmyards, my beloved horses, white nights of cool summer, the fireworks of the northern lights. What a burden all those possessions must have been to him, because he laughs as if with glee as he beggars himself; he is in such a passion to donate all to the Beast.

Everyone who comes to this city must play a hand with the *grand seigneur;* few come. They did not warn us at Milan, or if they did, we did not understand them—my limping Italian, the bewildering dialect of the region. Indeed, I myself spoke up in favor of this remote, provincial place, out of fashion two hundred years, because—oh, irony—it boasted no casino. I did not know that the price of a stay in its Decembral solitude was a game with Milord.

The hour was late. The chill damp of this place creeps into the stones, into your bones, into the spongy pith of the lungs; it insinuated itself with a shiver into our parlor, where Milord came to play in the privacy essential to him. Who could refuse the invitation his valet brought to our lodging? Not my profligate father, certainly; the mirror above the table gave me back his frenzy, my impassivity, the withering candles, the emptying bottles, the colored tide of the cards as they rose and fell, the still mask that concealed all the features of the Beast but for the yellow eyes that strayed, now and then, from his unfurled hand towards myself.

"La Bestia!" said our landlady, gingerly fingering an envelope with his huge crest of a tiger rampant on it, something of fear, something of wonder in her face. And I could not ask her why they called the master of the place "La Bestia"—was it to do with that heraldic signature?—because her tongue was so thickened by the phlegmy, bronchitic speech of the region I scarcely managed to make out a thing she said except, when she saw me: "*Che bella!*"

Since I could toddle, always the pretty one, with my glossy, nut-brown curls, my rosy cheeks. And born on Christmas Day—her "Christmas rose," my English nurse called me. The peasants said: "The living image of her mother," crossing themselves out of respect for the dead. My mother did not blossom long, bartered for her dowry to such a feckless sprig of the Russian nobility that she soon died of his gaming, his whoring, his agonizing repentances. And the Beast gave me the rose from his own impeccable if outmoded buttonhole when he arrived, the valet brushing the snow off his black cloak. This white rose, unnatural, out of season, that now my nervous fingers ripped, petal by petal, apart as my father magnificently concluded the career he had made of catastrophe.

This is a melancholy, introspective region: a sunless, featureless land-scape, the sullen river sweating fog, the shorn, hunkering willows. And a cruel city: the somber piazza, a place uniquely suited to public executions, under the beetling shadow of that malign barn of a church. They used to hang condemned men in cages from the city walls; unkindness comes naturally to them, their eyes are set too close together, they have thin lips. Poor food, pasta soaked in oil, boiled beef with sauce of bitter herbs. A funereal hush about the place, the inhabitants huddled up against the cold so you can hardly see their faces. And they lie to you and cheat you, innkeepers, coachmen, everybody. God, how they fleeced us!

The treacherous South, where you think there is no winter but forget you take it with you.

My senses were increasingly troubled by the fuddling perfume of Milord, far too potent a reek of purplish civet at such close quarters in so small a room. He must bathe himself in scent, soak his shirts and underlinen in it; what can he smell of, that needs so much camouflage?

I never saw a man so big look so two-dimensional, in spite of the quaint elegance of the Beast, in the old-fashioned tailcoat that might, from its looks, have been bought in those distant years before he imposed seclusion on himself; he does not feel he need keep up with the times. There is a crude clumsiness about his outlines, which are on the ungainly, giant side; and he has an odd air of self-imposed restraint, as if fighting a battle with himself to remain upright when he would far rather drop down on all fours. He throws our human aspirations to the godlike sadly awry, poor fellow; only from a distance would you think the Beast not much different from any other man, although he wears a mask with a man's face painted most beautifully on it. Oh, yes, a beautiful face; but one with too much formal symmetry of feature to be entirely human: one profile of his mask is the mirror image of the other, too perfect, uncanny. He wears a wig too, false hair tied at the nape with a bow, a wig of the kind you see in old-fashioned portraits. A chaste silk stock stuck with a pearl hides his throat. And gloves of blond kid that are yet so huge and clumsy they do not seem to cover hands.

He is a carnival figure made of papier-mâché and crepe hair; and yet he has the Devil's knack at cards.

His masked voice echoes as from a great distance as he stoops over his hand, and he has such a growling impediment in his speech that only his valet, who understands him, can interpret for him, as if his master were the clumsy doll and he the ventriloquist.

The wick slumped in the eroded wax, the candles guttered. By the time my rose had lost all its petals, my father, too, was left with nothing.

"Except the girl."

Gambling is a sickness. My father said he loved me, yet he staked his daughter on a hand of cards. He fanned them out; in the mirror, I saw wild hope light up his eyes. His collar was unfastened, his rumpled hair stood up on end, he had the anguish of a man in the last stages of debauchery. The drafts came out of the old walls and bit me; I was colder than I'd ever been in Russia when nights are coldest there.

A queen, a king, an ace. I saw them in the mirror. Oh, I know he thought he could not lose me; besides, back with me would come all he had lost, the unraveled fortunes of our family at one blow restored. And would he not win, as well, the Beast's hereditary palazzo outside the city; his immense revenues; his lands around the river; his rents, his treasure chest, his Mantegnas, his Giulio Romanos, his Cellini saltcellars, his titles . . . the very city itself?

You must not think my father valued me at less than a king's ransom; but at *no more* than a king's ransom.

It was cold as hell in the parlor. And it seemed to me, child of the severe North, that it was not my flesh but, truly, my father's soul that was in peril.

My father, of course, believed in miracles; what gambler does not? In pursuit of just such a miracle as this, had we not traveled from the land of bears and shooting stars?

So we teetered on the brink.

The Beast bayed; laid down all three remaining aces.

The indifferent servants now glided smoothly forward as on wheels to douse the candles one by one. To look at them you would think that nothing of any moment had occurred. They yawned a little resentfully; it was almost morning, we had kept them out of bed. The Beast's man brought his cloak. My father sat amongst these preparations for departure, staring on at the betrayal of his cards upon the table.

The Beast's man informed me crisply that he, the valet, would call for me and my bags tomorrow, at ten, and conduct me forthwith to the Beast's palazzo. *Capisco?* So shocked was I that I scarcely did *capisco*. He repeated my orders patiently; he was a strange, thin, quick little man, who walked with an irregular, jolting rhythm upon splayed feet in curious, wedge-shaped shoes.

Where my father had been red as fire, now he was white as the snow that caked the windowpane. His eyes swam; soon he would cry.

" 'Like the base Indian,' " he said; he loved rhetoric. " 'One whose hand,/Like the base Indian, threw a pearl away/Richer than all his tribe . . .' I have lost my pearl, my pearl beyond price."

At that, the Beast made a sudden dreadful noise, halfway between a growl and a roar; the candles flared. The quick valet, the prim hypocrite, interpreted unblinking: "My master says: If you are so careless of your treasures, you should expect them to be taken from you."

He gave us the bow and smile his master could not offer us, and they departed.

I watched the snow until, just before dawn, it stopped falling. A hard frost settled next morning there was a light like iron.

The Beast's carriage, of an elegant if antique design, was black as a hearse, and it was drawn by a dashing black gelding who blew smoke from his nostrils and stamped upon the packed snow with enough sprightly appearance of life to give me some hope that not all the world was locked in ice, as I was. I had always held a little towards Gulliver's opinion that horses are better than we are, and, that day, I would have been glad to depart with him to the kingdom of horses, if I'd been given the chance.

The valet sat up on the box in a natty black-and-gold livery, clasping, of all things, a bunch of his master's damned white roses as if a gift of flowers would reconcile a woman to any humiliation. He sprang down with preternatural agility to place them ceremoniously in my reluctant hand. My tear-beslobbered father wants a rose to show that I forgive him. When I break off a stem, I prick my finger, and so he gets his rose all smeared with blood.

The valet crouched at my feet to tuck the rugs about me with a strange kind of unflattering obsequiousness, yet he forgot his station sufficiently to scratch busily beneath his white periwig with an oversupple index finger as he offered me what my old nurse would have called an "old-fashioned look," ironic, sly, a smidgen of disdain in it. And pity? No pity. His eyes were moist and brown, his face seamed with the innocent cunning of an ancient baby. He had an irritating habit of chattering to himself under his breath all the time as he packed up his master's winnings. I drew the curtains to conceal the sight of my father's farewell; my spite was sharp as broken glass.

Lost to the Beast! And what, I wondered, might be the exact nature of his "beastliness"? My English nurse once told me about a tiger man she saw in London, when she was a little girl, to scare me into good behavior, for I was a wild wee thing and she could not tame me into submission with a frown or the bribe of a spoonful of jam. If you don't stop plaguing the nursemaids, my beauty, the tiger man will come and take you away. They'd brought him from Sumatra, in the Indies, she said; his hinder parts were all hairy, and only from the head downward did he resemble a man.

And yet the Beast goes always masked; it cannot be his face that looks like mine.

But the tiger man, in spite of his hairiness, could take a glass of ale in his hand like a good Christian and drink it down. Had she not seen him do so, at the sign of the George, by the steps of Upper Moor Fields when she was just as high as me and lisped and toddled too. Then she would sigh for London, across the North Sea of the lapse of years. But if this young lady was not a good little girl and did not eat her boiled beetroot, then the tiger man would put on his big black traveling cloak lined with fur, just like your daddy's, and hire the Erlking's galloper of wind and ride through the night straight to the nursery and —

Yes, my beauty! *Gobble you up!*

How I'd squeal in delighted terror, half believing her, half knowing that she teased me. And there were things I knew that I must not tell her. In our lost farmyard, where the giggling nursemaids initiated me into the mysteries of what the bull did to the cows, I heard about the wagoner's

daughter. Hush, hush, don't let on to your nursie we said so; the wagoner's lass, harelipped, squint-eyed, ugly as sin, who would have taken
her? Yet, to her shame, her belly swelled amid the cruel mockery of the
ostlers and her son was born of a bear, they whispered. Born with a full
pelt and teeth; that proved it. But when he grew up, he was a good
shepherd, although he never married, lived in a hut outside the village,
and could make the wind blow any way he wanted to, besides being able to
tell which eggs would become cocks, which hens.

The wondering peasants once brought my father a skull with horns
four inches long on either side of it and would not go back to the field
where their poor plow disturbed it until the priest went with them; for this
skull had the jawbone of a *man*, had it not?

Old wives' tales, nursery fears! I knew well enough the reason for the
trepidation I cozily titillated with superstitious marvels of my childhood
on the day my childhood ended. For now my own skin was my sole capital
in the world, and today I'd make my first investment.

We had left the city far behind us and were now traversing a wide, flat
dish of snow where the mutilated stumps of the willows flourished their
ciliate heads athwart frozen ditches; mist diminished the horizon, brought
down the sky until it seemed no more than a few inches above us. As far as
eye could see, not one thing living. How starveling, how bereft the dead
season of this spurious Eden in which all the fruit was blighted by cold!
And my frail roses, already faded. I opened the carriage door and tossed
the defunct bouquet into the rucked, frost-stiff mud of the road. Suddenly
a sharp, freezing wind arose and pelted my face with a dry rice of
powdered snow. The mist lifted sufficiently to reveal before me an acreage
of half-derelict facades of sheer red brick, the vast mantrap, the mega-
lomaniac citadel of his palazzo.

It was a world in itself but a dead one, a burned-out planet. I saw the
Beast bought solitude, not luxury, with his money.

The little black horse trotted smartly through the figured bronze doors
that stood open to the weather like those of a barn, and the valet handed me
out of the carriage onto the scarred tiles of the great hall itself, into the odorous
warmth of a stable, sweet with hay, acrid with horse dung. An equine chorus
of neighings and soft drummings of hooves broke out beneath the tall roof,
where the beams were scabbed with last summer's swallows' nests; a dozen
gracile muzzles lifted from their mangers and turned towards us, ears erect.
The Beast had given his horses the use of the dining room. The walls were
painted, aptly enough, with a fresco of horses, dogs, and men in a wood
where fruit and blossom grew on the bough together.

The valet tweaked politely at my sleeve. Milord is waiting.

Gaping doors and broken windows let the wind in everywhere. We
mounted one staircase after another, our feet clopping on the marble.

Through archways and open doors I glimpsed suites of vaulted chambers opening one out of another like systems of Chinese boxes into the infinite complexity of the innards of the place. He and I and the wind were the only things stirring; and all the furniture was under dust sheets, the chandeliers bundled up in cloth, pictures taken from their hooks and propped with their faces to the walls as if their master could not bear to look at them. The palace was dismantled, as if its owner were about to move house or had never properly moved in; the Beast had chosen to live in an uninhabited place.

The valet darted me a reassuring glance from his brown, eloquent eyes, yet a glance with so much queer superciliousness in it that it did not comfort me, and went bounding ahead of me on his bandy legs, softly chattering to himself. I held my head high and followed him; but for all my pride, my heart was heavy.

Milord has his aerie high above the house, a small, stifling, darkened room; he keeps his shutters locked at noon. I was out of breath by the time we reached it, and returned to him the silence with which he greeted me. I will not smile. He cannot smile.

In his rarely disturbed privacy, the Beast wears a garment of Ottoman design, a loose, dull purple gown with gold embroidery round the neck, that falls from his shoulders to conceal his feet. The feet of the chair he sits in are handsomely clawed. He hides his hands in his ample sleeves. The artificial masterpiece of his face appalls me. A small fire in a small grate. A rushing wind rattles the shutters.

The valet coughed. To him fell the delicate task of transmitting to me his master's wishes.

"My master—"

A stick fell in the grate. It made a mighty clatter in that dreadful silence; the valet started, lost his place in his speech, began again.

"My master has but one desire."

The thick, rich, wild scent with which Milord had soaked himself the previous evening hangs all about us, ascends in cursive blue from the smoke hole of a precious Chinese pot.

"He wishes only—"

Now, in the face of my impassivity, the valet twittered, his ironic composure gone, for the desire of a master, however trivial, may yet sound unbearably insolent in the mouth of a servant, and his role of go-between clearly caused him a good deal of embarrassment. He gulped; he swallowed, at last contrived to unleash an unpunctuated flood.

"My master's sole desire is to see the pretty young lady unclothed nude without her dress and that only for the one time after which she will be returned to her father undamaged with bankers' orders for the sum which he lost to my master at cards and also a number of fine presents such as furs, jewels, and horses—"

I remained standing. During the interview, my eyes were level with those inside the mask, that now evaded mine as if, to his credit, he was ashamed of his own request even as his mouthpiece made it for him. Agitato, molto agitato, the valet wrung his white-gloved hands.

"*Desnuda*—"

I could scarcely believe my ears. I let out a raucous guffaw; no young lady laughs like that! my old nurse used to remonstrate. But I did. And do. At the clamor of my heartless mirth, the valet danced backward with perturbation, palpitating his fingers as if attempting to wrench them off, expostulating, wordlessly pleading. I felt that I owed it to him to make my reply in as exquisite a Tuscan as I could master.

"You may put me in a windowless room, sir, and I promise you I will pull my skirt up to my waist, ready for you. But there must be a sheet over my face, to hide it; though the sheet must be laid over me so lightly that it will not choke me. So I shall be covered completely from the waist upward, and no lights. There you can visit me once, sir, and only the once. After that I must be driven directly to the city and deposited in the public square, in front of the church. If you wish to give me money, then I should be pleased to receive it. But I must stress that you should give me only the same amount of money that you would give to any other woman in such circumstances. However, if you choose not to give me a present, then that is your right."

How pleased I was to see I struck the Beast to the heart! For after a baker's dozen heartbeats, one single tear swelled, glittering, at the corner of the masked eye. A tear! A tear, I hoped, of shame. The tear trembled for a moment on an edge of painted bone, then tumbled down the painted cheek to fall, with an abrupt tinkle, on the tiled floor.

The valet, ticking and clucking to himself, hastily ushered me out of the room. A mauve cloud of his master's perfume billowed out into the chill corridor with us and dissipated itself on the spinning winds.

A cell had been prepared for me, a veritable cell, windowless, airless, lightless, in the viscera of the palace. The valet lit a lamp for me; a narrow bed, a dark cupboard with fruit and flowers carved on it, bulked out of the gloom.

"I shall twist a noose out of my bed linen and hang myself with it," I said.

"Oh, no," said the valet, fixing upon me wide and suddenly melancholy eyes. "Oh, no, you will not. You are a woman of honor."

And what was *he* doing in my bedroom, this jigging caricature of a man? Was he to be my warder until I submitted to the Beast's whim or he to mine? Am I in such reduced circumstances that I may not have a lady's maid? As if in reply to my unspoken demand, the valet clapped his hands.

"To assuage your loneliness, madame . . ."

A knocking and clattering behind the door of the cupboard; the door swings open, and out glides a soubrette from an operetta, with glossy, nut-brown curls, rosy cheeks, blue, rolling eyes; it takes me a moment to recognize her, in her little cap, her white stockings, her frilled petticoats. She carries a looking glass in one hand and a powder puff in the other, and there is a music box where her heart should be; she tinkles as she rolls towards me on her tiny wheels.

"Nothing human lives here," said the valet.

My maid halted, bowed; from a split seam at the side of her bodice protrudes the handle of a key. She is a marvelous machine, the most delicately balanced system of cords and pulleys in the world.

"We have dispensed with servants," the valet said. "We surround ourselves, instead, for utility and pleasure, with simulacra and find it no less convenient than do most gentlemen."

This clockwork twin of mine halted before me, her bowels churning out a settecento minuet, and offered me the bold carnation of her smile. Click, click—she raises her arm and busily dusts my cheeks with pink, powdered chalk that makes me cough; then thrusts towards me her little mirror.

I saw within it not my own face but that of my father, as if I had put on his face when I arrived at the Beast's palace as the discharge of his debt. What, you self-deluding fool, are you crying still? And drunk too. He tossed back his *grappa* and hurled the tumbler away.

Seeing my astonished fright, the valet took the mirror away from me, breathed on it, polished it with the ham of his gloved fist, handed it back to me. Now all I saw was myself, haggard from a sleepless night, pale enough to need my maid's supply of rouge.

I heard the key turn in the heavy door and the valet's footsteps patter down the stone passage. Meanwhile my double continued to powder the air, emitting her jangling tune, but as it turned out, she was not inexhaustible; soon she was powdering more and yet more languorously, her metal heart slowed in imitation of fatigue, her music box ran down until the notes separated themselves out of the tune and plopped like single raindrops, and as if sleep had overtaken her, at last she moved no longer. As she succumbed to sleep, I had no option but to do so too. I dropped on that narrow bed as if felled.

Time passed, but I do not know how much; then the valet woke me with rolls and honey. I gestured the tray away, but he set it down firmly beside the lamp and took from it a little shagreen box, which he offered to me.

I turned away my head.

"Oh, my lady!" Such hurt cracked his high-pitched voice! He dexterously unfastened the gold clasp; on a bed of crimson velvet lay a single diamond earring, perfect as a tear.

I snapped the box shut and tossed it into a corner. This sudden, sharp movement must have disturbed the mechanism of the doll; she jerked her arm almost as if to reprimand me, letting out a rippling fart of gavotte. Then was still again.

"Very well," said the valet, put out. And indicated it was time for me to visit my host again. He did not let me wash, or comb my hair. There was so little natural light in the interior of the palace that I could not tell whether it was day or night.

You would not think the Beast had budged an inch since I last saw him; he sat in his huge chair, with his hands in his sleeves, and the heavy air never moved. I might have slept an hour, a night, or a month, but his sculptured calm, the stifling air, remained just as had been. The incense rose from the pot, still traced the same signature on the air. The same fire burned.

Take off my clothes for you, like a ballet girl? Is that all you want of me?

"The sight of a young lady's skin that no man has seen before—" stammered the valet.

I wished I'd rolled in the hay with every lad on my father's farm, to disqualify myself from his humiliating bargain. That he should want so little was the reason why I could not give it; I did not need to speak for the Beast to understand me.

A tear came from his other eye. And then he moved; he buried his cardboard carnival head with its ribboned weight of false hair in, I would say, his arms; he withdrew his, I might say, hands from his sleeves and I saw his furred pads, his excoriating claws.

The dropped tear caught upon his fur and shone. And in my room for hours I hear those paws pad back and forth outside my door.

When the valet arrived again with his silver salver, I had a pair of diamond earrings of the finest water in the world; I threw the other into the corner where the first one lay. The valet twittered with aggrieved regret but did not offer to lead me to the Beast again. Instead, he smiled ingratiatingly and confided: "My master, he say: Invite the young lady to go riding."

"What's this?"

He briskly mimicked the action of a gallop and, to my amazement, tunelessly croaked; "Tantivy! tantivy! A-hunting we will go!"

"I'll run away, I'll ride to the city."

"Oh, no," he said. "Are you not a woman of honor?"

He clapped his hands and my maidservant clicked and jangled into the imitation of life. She rolled towards the cupboard where she had come from and reached inside it to fetch out over her synthetic arm my riding habit. Of all things. My very own riding habit, that I'd left behind me in a trunk in a loft in that country house outside Petersburg that we'd lost long ago, before, even, we set out on this wild pilgrimage to the cruel South. Either the very riding habit my old nurse had sewn for me or else a copy of it perfect to the lost button on the right sleeve, the ripped hem held up with a pin. I turned the worn cloth about in my hands, looking for a clue. The wind that sprinted through the palace made the door tremble in its frame; had the north wind blown my garments across Europe to me? At home, the bear's son directed the winds at his pleasure; what democracy of magic held this palace and the fir forest in common? Or should I be prepared to accept it as proof of the axiom my father had drummed into me: that if you have enough money, anything is possible?

"Tantivy," suggested the now twinkling valet, evidently charmed at the pleasure mixed with my bewilderment. The clockwork maid held my jacket out to me, and I allowed myself to shrug into it as if reluctantly, although I was half mad to get out into the open air, away from this deathly palace, even in such company.

The doors of the hall let the bright day in; I saw that it was morning. Our horses, saddled and bridled, beasts in bondage, were waiting for us, striking sparks from the tiles with their impatient hooves while their stablemates lolled at ease among the straw, conversing with one another in the mute speech of horses. A pigeon or two, feathers puffed to keep out the cold, strutted about, pecking at ears of corn. The little black gelding who had brought me here greeted me with a ringing neigh that resonated inside the misty roof as in a sounding box, and I knew he was meant for me to ride.

I always adored horses, noblest of creatures, such wounded sensitivity in their wise eyes, such rational restraint of energy at their high-strung hindquarters. I lirruped and hurumphed to my shining black companion, and he acknowledged my greeting with a kiss on the forehead from his soft lips. There was a little shaggy pony nuzzling away at the *trompe l'oeil* foliage beneath the hooves of the painted horses on the wall, into whose saddle the valet sprang with a flourish as of the circus. Then the Beast, wrapped in a black fur-lined cloak, came to heave himself aloft a grave gray mare. No natural horseman he; he clung to her mane like a ship-wrecked sailor to a spar.

Cold, that morning, yet dazzling with the sharp winter sunlight that wounds the retina. There was a scurrying wind about that seemed to go with us, as if the masked, immense one who did not speak carried it inside his cloak and let it out at his pleasure, for it stirred the horses' manes but did not lift the lowland mists.

A bereft landscape in the sad browns and sepias of winter lay all about us, the marshland drearily protracting itself towards the wide river. Those decapitated willows. Now and then, the swoop of a bird, its irreconcilable cry.

A profound sense of strangeness slowly began to possess me. I knew my two companions were not, in any way, as other men, the simian retainer and the master for whom he spoke, the one with clawed forepaws, who was in a plot with the witches who let the winds out of their knotted hand-kerchiefs up towards the Finnish border. I knew they lived according to a different logic than I had done until my father abandoned me to the wild beasts by his human carelessness. This knowledge gave me a certain fearful-ness still; but, I would say, not much. . . . I was a young girl, a virgin, and therefore men denied me rationality just as they denied it to all those who were not exactly like themselves, in all their unreason. If I could see not one single soul in that wilderness of desolation all around me, then the six of us—mounts and riders, both—could boast amongst us not one soul either, since all the best religions in the world state categorically that not beasts nor women were equipped with the flimsy, insubstantial things when the good Lord opened the gates of Eden and let Eve and her familiars tumble out. Understand, then, that though I would not say I privately engaged in metaphysical speculation as we rode through the reedy approaches to the river, I certainly meditated on the nature of my own state, how I had been bought and sold, passed from hand to hand. That clockwork girl who powdered my cheeks for me—had I not been allotted only the same kind of imitative life amongst men that the dollmaker had given her?

Yet as to the true nature of the being of this clawed magus who rode his pale horse in a style that made me recall how Kublai Khan's leopards went out hunting on horseback, of that I had no notion.

We came to the bank of the river, which was so wide we could not see across it, so still with winter that it scarcely seemed to flow. The horses lowered their heads to drink. The valet cleared his throat, about to speak; we were in a place of perfect privacy, beyond a brake of winter-bare rushes, a hedge of reeds.

"If you will not let him see you without your clothes—"

I involuntarily shook my head.

"—you must, then, prepare yourself for the sight of my master, naked."

The river broke on the pebbles with a diminishing sigh. My composure deserted me; all at once I was on the brink of panic. I did not think that I could bear the sight of him, whatever he was. The mare raised her dripping muzzle and looked at me keenly, as if urging me. The river broke again at my feet. I was far from home.

"You," said the valet, "must."

When I saw how scared he was I might refuse, I nodded.

The reed bowed down in a sudden snarl of wind that brought with it a gust of the heavy odor of his disguise. The valet held out his master's cloak to screen him from me as he removed the mask. The horses stirred.

The tiger will never lie down with the lamb; he acknowledges no pact that is not reciprocal. The lamb must learn to run with the tigers.

A great, feline, tawny shape whose pelt was barred with a savage geometry of bars the color of burned wood. His domed, heavy head so terrible he must hide it. How subtle the muscles, how profound the tread. The annihilating vehemence of his eyes, like twin suns.

I felt my breast ripped apart as if I suffered a marvelous wound.

The valet moved forward as if to cover up his master now the girl had acknowledged him, but I said: "No." The tiger sat still as a heraldic beast, in the pact he had made with his own ferocity to do me no harm. He was far larger than I could have imagined, from the poor, shabby things I'd seen once, in the czar's menagerie at Petersburg, the golden fruit of their eyes dimming, withering in the far North of captivity. Nothing about him reminded me of humanity.

I therefore, shivering, now unfastened my jacket, to show him I would do him no harm. Yet I was clumsy and blushed a little, for no man had seen me naked and I was a proud girl. Pride it was, not shame, that thwarted my fingers so; and a certain trepidation lest this frail little article of human upholstery before him might not be, in itself, grand enough to satisfy his expectations of us, since those, for all I knew, might have grown infinite during the endless time he had been waiting. The wind clattered in the rushes, purled and eddied in the river.

I showed his grave silence my white skin, my red nipples, and the horses turned their heads to watch me also, as if they, too, were courteously curious as to the fleshly nature of women. Then the Beast lowered his massive head. Enough! said the valet with a gesture. The wind died down, all was still again.

Then they went off together, the valet on his pony, the tiger running before him like a hound, and I walked along the riverbank for a while. I felt I was at liberty for the first time in my life. Then the winter sun began to tarnish, a few flakes of snow drifted from the darkening sky, and when I returned to the horses, I found the Beast mounted again on his gray mare, cloaked and masked and once more, to all appearances, a man, while the valet had a fine catch of waterfowl dangling from his hand and the corpse of a young roebuck slung behind his saddle. I climbed up on the black gelding in silence and so we returned to the palace as the snow fell more and more heavily, obscuring the tracks that we had left behind us.

The valet did not return me to my cell but, instead, to an elegant if old-fashioned boudoir, with sofas of faded pink brocade, a jinn's treasury of Oriental carpets, tintinnabulation of cut-glass chandeliers. Candles in antlered holders struck rainbows from the prismatic hearts of the diamond earrings that lay on my new dressing table, at which my attentive maid stood ready with her powder puff and mirror. Intending to fix the ornaments in my ears, I took the looking glass from her hand, but it was in the midst of one of its magic fits again, and I did not see my own face in it but that of my father; at first I thought he smiled at me. Then I saw he was smiling with pure gratification.

He sat, I saw, in the parlor of our lodgings, at the very table where he had lost me, but now he was busily engaged in counting out a tremendous pile of banknotes. My father's circumstances had changed already; well-shaven, neatly barbered, smart new clothes. A frosted glass of sparkling wine sat convenient to his hand beside an ice bucket. The Beast had clearly paid cash on the nail for his glimpse of my bosom, and paid up promptly, as if it had not been a sight I might have died of showing. Then I saw my father's trunks were packed, ready for departure. Could he so easily leave me here?

There was a note on the table with the money, in a fine hand. I could read it quite clearly. "The young lady will arrive immediately." Some harlot with whom he'd briskly negotiated a liaison on the strength of his spoils? Not at all. For at that moment, the valet knocked at my door to announce that I might leave the palace at any time thereafter, and he bore over his arm a handsome sable cloak, my very own little gratuity, The Beast's morning gift, in which he proposed to pack me up and send me off.

When I looked at the mirror again, my father had disappeared, and all I saw was a pale, hollow-eyed girl whom I scarcely recognized. The valet asked politely when he should prepare the carriage, as if he did not doubt that I would leave with my booty at the first opportunity, while my maid, whose face was no longer the spit of my own, continued bonnily to beam. I will dress her in my own clothes, wind her up, send her back to perform the part of my father's daughter.

"Leave me alone," I said to the valet.

He did not need to lock the door now. I fixed the earrings in my ears. They were very heavy. Then I took off my riding habit, left it where it lay on the floor. But when I got down to my shift, my arms dropped to my sides. I was unaccustomed to nakedness. I was so unused to my own skin that to take off all my clothes involved a kind of flaying. I thought the Beast had wanted a little thing compared with what I was prepared to give him; but it is not natural for humankind to go naked, not since first we hid our loins with fig leaves. He had demanded the abominable. I felt as much atrocious pain as if I was stripping off my own underpelt, and the smiling girl stood poised in the oblivion of her balked simulation of life, watching me peel down to the cold, white meat of contract, and if she did not see me, then so much more like the marketplace, where the eyes that watch you take no account of your existence.

And it seemed my entire life, since I had left the North, had passed under the indifferent gaze of eyes like hers.

Then I was flinching stark, except for his irreproachable tears.

I huddled in the furs I must return to him, to keep me from the lacerating winds that raced along the corridors. I knew the way to his den without the valet to guide me.

No response to my tentative rap on his door.

Then the wind blew the valet whirling along the passage. He must have decided that if one should go naked, then all should go naked; without his livery, he revealed himself, as I had suspected, a delicate creature, covered with silken moth-gray fur, brown fingers supple as leather, chocolate muzzle, the gentlest creature in the world. He gibbered a little to see my fine furs and jewels as if I were dressed up for the opera and, with a great deal of tender ceremony, removed the sables from my shoulders. The sables thereupon resolved themselves into a pack of black, squeaking rats that rattled immediately down the stairs on their hard little feet and were lost to sight.

The valet bowed me inside the Beast's room.

The purple dressing gown, the mask, the wig, were laid out on his chair; a glove was planted on each arm. The empty house of his appearance was ready for him, but he had abandoned it. There was a reek of fur and piss; the incense pot lay broken in pieces on the floor. Half-burned sticks were scattered from the extinguished fire. A candle stuck by its own grease to the mantelpiece lit two narrow flames in the pupils of the tiger's eyes.

He was pacing backward and forward, backward and forward, the tip of his heavy tail twitching as he paced out the length and breadth of his imprisonment between the gnawed and bloody bones.

He will gobble you up.

Nursery fears made flesh and sinew; earliest and most archaic of fears, fear of devourment. The beast and his carnivorous bed of bone and I, white, shaking, raw, approaching him as if offering, in myself, the key to a peaceable kingdom in which his appetite need not be my extinction.

He went still as stone. He was far more frightened of me than I was of him.

I squatted on the wet straw and stretched out my hand. I was now within the field of force of his golden eyes. He growled at the back of his throat, lowered his head, sank onto his forepaws, snarled, showed me his red gullet, his yellow teeth. I never moved. He snuffed the air, as if to smell my fear; he could not.

Slowly, slowly he began to drag his heavy, gleaming weight across the floor towards me.

A tremendous throbbing, as of the engine that makes the earth turn, filled the little room; he had begun to purr.

The sweet thunder of this purr shook the old walls, made the shutters batter the windows until they burst apart and let in the white light of the snowy moon. Tiles came crashing down from the roof; I heard them fall into the courtyard far below. The reverberations of his purring rocked the foundations of the house, the walls began to dance. I thought: It will all fall, everything will disintegrate.

He dragged himself closer and closer to me, until I felt the harsh velvet of his head against my hand, then a tongue, abrasive as sandpaper. "He will lick the skin off me!"

And each stroke of his tongue ripped off skin after successive skin, all the skins of a life in the world, and left behind a nascent patina of shining hairs. My earrings turned back to water and trickled down my shoulders; I shrugged the drops off my beautiful fur.

WOMAN FROM AMERICA ●

bessie head

THIS WOMAN FROM AMERICA married a
man of our village and left her country to come and live with him here. She
descended on us like an avalanche. People are divided into two camps:
those who feel a fascinated love and those who fear a new thing.

Some people keep hoping she will go away one day, but already her big
strong stride has worn the pathways of the village flat. She is everywhere
about because she is a woman, resolved and unshakable in herself. To
make matters worse or more disturbing she comes from the west side of
America, somewhere near California. I gather from her conversation that
people from the West are stranger than most people.

People of the West of America must be the most oddly beautiful people
in the world; at least this woman from the West is the most oddly beautiful
person I have ever seen. Every cross-current of the earth seems to have
stopped in her and blended into an amazing harmony. She has a big dash
of Africa, a dash of Germany, some Cherokee and heaven knows what
else. Her feet are big and her body is as tall and straight and strong as a
mountain tree. Her neck curves up high and her thick black hair cascades
down her back like a wild and tormented stream. I cannot understand her
eyes though, except that they are big, black, and startled like those of a
wild free buck racing against the wind. Often they cloud over with a deep,
intense, brooding look.

It takes a great deal of courage to become friends with a woman like
that. Like everyone here, I am timid and subdued. Authority, everything
can subdue me; not because I like it that way but because authority carries

the weight of an age pressing down on life. It is terrible then to associate with a person who can shout authority down. Her shouting matches with authority are the terror and sensation of the village. It has come down to this. Either the woman is unreasonable or authority is unreasonable, and everyone in his heart would like to admit that authority is unreasonable. In reality, the rule is: If authority does not like you, then you are the outcast and humanity associates with you at their peril. So try always to be on the right side of authority, for the sake of peace, and please avoid the outcast. I do not say it will be like this forever. The whole world is crashing and interchanging itself and even remote bush villages in Africa are not to be left out!

It was inevitable though that this woman and I should be friends. I have an overwhelming curiosity that I cannot keep within bounds. I passed by the house for almost a month, but one cannot crash in on people. Then one day a dog they own had puppies, and my small son chased one of the puppies into the yard and I chased after him. Then one of the puppies became his and there had to be discussions about the puppy, the desert heat, and the state of the world and as a result of curiosity an avalanche of wealth has descended on my life. My small hut-house is full of short notes written in a wide sprawling hand. I have kept them all because they are a statement of human generosity and the wild carefree laugh of a woman who is as busy as women the world over about things women always entangle themselves in—a man, a home . . . Like this . . .

"Have you an onion to spare? It's very quiet here this morning and I'm all tired out from sweeping and cleaning the yard, shaking blankets, cooking, fetching water, bathing children, and there's still the floor inside to sweep and dishes to wash . . . it's endless!"

Sometimes too, conversations get all tangled up and the African night creeps all about and the candles are not lit and the conversation gets more entangled, intense; and the children fall asleep on the floor dazed by it all.

She is a new kind of American or even maybe will be a new kind of African. There isn't anyone here who does not admire her. To come from a world of chicken, hamburgers, TV, escalators, and whatnot to a village mud hut and a life so tough, where the most you can afford to eat is ground millet and boiled meat. Sometimes you cannot afford to eat at all. Always you have to trudge miles for a bucket of water and carry it home on your head. And to do all this with loud, ringing, sprawling laughter?

Black people in America care about Africa, and she has come here on her own as an expression of that love and concern. Through her, too, one is filled with wonder for a country that breeds individuals about whom, without and within, rushes the wind of freedom. I have to make myself clear, though. She is a different person who has taken by force what America will not give black people.

The woman from America loves both Africa and America, independently. She can take what she wants from both and say, "Dammit." It is a most strenuous and difficult thing to do.

THE ENGLISH DISEASE ●

nina fitzpatrick

FOR A DESCRIPTION OF location and general atmosphere you might like to look up Max Beerbohm's *Zuleika Dobson* or Jan Morris' *The Oxford Book of Oxford*. They're both out in paperback as far as I remember.

Everything that happened to Finnula confirmed my theory of *Puerophobia Brittanica*, the English disease. One of its symptoms is a fear of children. The other is a craving for the Dragon. As far as I can see, from the very first Saxon invasion, Englishmen have been given to tormenting children and slaying dragons. There must have been a bit of both in Finnula.

She took me by surprise. I read somewhere—maybe in Gustaw Alfons Bluszcz's *Celtowie: tragedia ginacego gatunku*—that Irish girls still went round on bicycles with one hand holding down their skirts and the other clutching their rosary beads. Finnula arrived at the College in a white Mercedes driven by a chauffeur who looked like Joseph Stalin at Yalta. I was checking my mail in the Lodge—bad news as usual—when I saw a skinny melusine swaying in the Front Quad. She was swaying and making bewildered grimaces while Stalin piled expensive trunks and leather suitcases beside her. She wore tomato-red pleated shorts over black tights, a black V-neck blouse showing a frilly black bra and a floppy red hat.

"You wouldn't by any chance know where staircase three is, now would you?"

The porter and I stared at her like cows at a painted gate. It took us a few seconds to answer her question.

Her voice was high and infested with elegant, half-swallowed diphthongs. The sound of those diphthongs filled me with respect and revulsion. At last a real Brit! I always wanted to improve my English by speaking to the English. But they wouldn't talk to me precisely because of my bad English. The only ones who talked to me were either American or Japanese or Welsh.

Apart from sharing the same staircase, Finnula and I had three things in common. We were bad Catholics, we hated to go back to our countries and we couldn't hold on to a man.

These things were of no use to me. I had counted on having an independent Protestant next door, somebody as self-righteous as mint tea and as uncomplicated as a table leg. Somebody who would lend me cigarettes, help correct my thesis and make phone calls for me in Queen's English. Instead there was this parasitic Catholic who was in the wrong country, the wrong clothes and maybe even the wrong body.

"I'm a virgin," she hissed at me with hysterical self-reproach in the bar on the same evening. "I've been a virgin since 1988."

She was dressed in crocodile boots, tight jeans and a pink bat-winged blouse which fell off her left shoulder. She smoked ferociously without ever inhaling and furtively inspected male crotches. She divided men into those who carried their penis on the left or on the right. The left-thigh men were the nice ones. It must be some sort of ancient Irish superstition.

I decided not to walk into the bogland of Finnula and lose my shoes in her. But it was impossible. She had invisible antennae which monitored my movements. I was hardly in the door when I would hear the clatter of her high heels on the stairs and her little voice calling out "Wisla, are you there?"

Flaming in a silk salmon-pink night gown she would burst into my room and fling herself on my bed. Then, with a pillow clasped to her serpent breasts she would talk about:

Her Moral Tutor
Her new Armani lipstick
Her irregular cycle
Her Moral Tutor
The advantage of contact lenses
The sexism of the English
Her Jungian dreams
Her oppressed childhood
Her Moral Tutor
Who was she?
Where was she going?
How to get there?

Was it worth going there anyway?
Who would know?
Did I know?
And such like.

She endlessly examined her reactions to things, testing her fears, petting her satisfactions, indexing her ennuis and anxieties, comparing the colors of her despairs, feeling the texture of her awakenings and probing the subtleties of her subtleties until she was pleased and perplexed with her own complexity. And I felt, not for the first time, that the sisterhood of women is a preposterous idea.

She loved me to oppose her. She was delighted when I said "Finnula, my dear, you are utterly perfidious." She pouted her lips and rolled her eyes and *was* perfidious. She gave me the mug of a mentor and advisor. I detested this role but found myself accepting it. In the same way I accepted my guilt when I was locked up during martial law. I was innocent, but it was enough that ZOMO treated me as a dissident and I became one.

There was only one thing I envied Finnula. Her family. I'm just a normal Polish Jew with the upper branches torched off the family tree. Finnula had real ancestors. They had been rotting away in the west of Ireland for seven hundred years. They were decayed and decadent, like a proper *szlachta*. There, near the bottom, were the syphilitic Plantagenets, over there, for balance, St Ferdinand, King of Spain. Near the top there was Finnula's grandmother. She had style. She gambled away the family castle—the lead from the roof, the great wooden staircase, fireplaces, chandeliers and all the trees of the estate. When she killed herself by eating a strychnine and cheese sandwich the wolves howled all night in the Burren mountains. Afterwards the family moved to the steward's house and stables. For years they had to pee behind the bushes and eat spare ribs and black pudding. But then a rich uncle died in South Africa and they were back to the candelabras and ponies. There were pictures of ponies with red rosettes on their bridles over Finnula's bed.

Finnula's father was a Protestant atheist, her mother a Catholic bigot. The mother's genes won out. All the children had mental breakdowns, all of them victims of victims. Finnula had her breakdown at some Catholic boarding school for rich girls in Connemara. The big girls stuck hairpins and swans' feathers up her orifices and threatened to throw her in the lake if she told on them. They called her Fishy Pussy and held their noses when she passed.

She spat out her childhood all over the Persian carpet in her room. I don't know why, but I felt no compunction about stealing perfume and nail varnish from her dressing-table. The last time such things were available in Krakow was under the Habsburgs.

The fall of the Soviet Empire meant that I had less and less time for Finnula. I spent sixteen hours a day at my typewriter trying to improve a chapter on my theory of the Patrimonial Pendulum in Soviet society. My thesis advisor had just returned the chapter to me for the third time with the same comment on every page: "How do you know this?"

As far as I could make out, Finnula spent most of the day in bed. Like all women who are unhappily but hopefully in love she was pouting in her boudoir. Sometimes, late at night, I caught her standing in front of a large mirror down the hall. She was pulling on endless blouses, skirts, dresses, shoes and underwear and shedding them just as quickly. She bristled with vexation. I had the same problem with my writing as she had with her clothes—taking up a sentence, changing it around, adding a clause, taking out a comma, throwing the whole lot away and starting all over again. Except that my stuff was cheaper.

Once she broke into my room for the loan of my feather earrings. She was wearing a shimmering ermine coat and when she sat down I saw that she was naked underneath. She was hungry for talk.

"I don't want to hear about anything," I said. "I'm working on the disintegration of the Soviet Empire and you are an adult woman. You know what you're doing."

"I'm really very unhappy," she moaned.

"I can't take the responsibility. Go and see a priest."

She kicked over my waste-paper basket and left like an angry child.

She returned an hour later in tears and still naked under her fur coat. She collapsed on the floor, so full of misery and grief that I felt sorry for her. I made her a cup of tea, gave her a cigarette and sat beside her. She was immediately consoled.

"Wisla, what's wrong with me? Should I see a doctor or something? I'm all right as a woman, amn't I?"

And she opened her fur coat. Her thigh bones were sharp as set squares.

"Why are you going around naked?"

"He ordered me to. My Moral Tutor. I think he doesn't love me."

It was no use my telling her she was stupid because she knew that already.

"Tell me about the Moral Tutor."

Her green eyes lit up. She catapulted everything at me in three passionate sobs.

Well, the poor dear had fallen ill, something to do with the prostrate and she sent him a get-well-soon card which made him invite her for tea and she found to her surprise and much to her pleasure that her card was pinned to his mantelpiece and that he was most grateful and he talked about the hell of being an intellectual in Oxford. "I am an island," he said, "within an island within an island," and he showed her his collection of masks and boomerangs and they were all from New Guinea and he told her he was a Jew, which gave her gooseflesh all over because she had this incredible weakness for the Jews who are a brilliant intellectual race, aren't they? so when he touched her shoulder she thought of a baby, not making love or anything but having a baby and wasn't that superbly irrational of her?

She knew he had tremendous power over her and all he had to do was lift the phone and tell her to come over and she would come no matter what and she always did exactly what he told her to do, can you believe it, he would ask her to put something on, knee-length white socks or a tennis skirt or fish-net stockings and she would, she would, even though it was so much beneath her.

Sometimes he would lecture her on Lévi-Strauss in front of the Radcliffe Infirmary beside the statue of Neptune having oral sex with the oyster, sometimes he would take down her knickers and give her a spanking because it was good for her, sometimes he would give her a bath, paying special attention to her toes and bum but never but never did he kiss her, like that evening he wanted nothing to be between him and her which meant that she was to come naked to his room but when she arrived he looked at her sadly and told her to go home.

Now what in the name of all that's high and holy was wrong with her?

"It's clear as crystal," I said. "You are a perfect English couple. You were both perverted by your boarding schools. It's a textbook case."

"But I'm Irish," said Finnula.

"I can't see any difference."

She was offended.

"For such a wise woman you can be very imperceptive. Of course there's a difference! No Irishman would ever get me to do what I did for my Moral Tutor."

As far as I was concerned Finnula had put herself in a very unrewarding position. She had the reputation of being a whore but none of the pleasures. She didn't seem to care that half the College was gloating over her supposed debauchery. Worse, she was totally oblivious to the effect that her long hair, short leather skirts, low neck lines and crocodile shoes had on men.

The effect was such that the dons invited her for dinner in the Senior Common Room at the end of term. She should have known not to go. The last person to receive that kind of invitation was a black professor of feminist studies from Tanzania.

Several lurid versions of this dinner circulated in the College. One maintained that it ended with Finnula dancing an Irish Jig on the table and the Fellows looking up her skirt. A second had them all playing doctors and patient until dawn. Still another described a game of strip poker over the port.

"Bastards and bitches!" said Finnula. "Nasty, vulgar lies! The truth is so much worse."

And she told me the truth.

When she entered the SCR she noticed that she was the only woman present. There were five of them against her in her green mottled dress and red stockings.

"Sit down," said the Senior Tutor, "and try not to fidget." He took her handbag with all her treasure in it and put it on the floor beside him. The others sat around in their gowns and evening suits looking at her drunkenly over the silver. She felt threatened by their clean-shaven red faces, piggy blue eyes and the sickly odour of tobacco, eau-de-Cologne and venom. The venom was dormant but somewhere in the room she could feel it becoming tumescent.

The Moral Tutor whispered in the Bursar's ear and looked at Finnula as if he were describing her anatomy. The Bursar whispered to the Dean, the Dean whispered to the Chaplain and the Chaplain said grace.

Soup was served by a dwarf with big red whiskers and no eyebrows. He barely reached to the top of the table. Nobody spoke. They just slurped and slurped away at their soup. Now and then one of the dons would stop, wipe his lips slowly and look at her with a question in his eyes as much as to say: Where did you come out of? The Bursar had a filthy habit of sticking his tongue out and licking his upper lip.

After the soup the Senior Tutor said: "Now Finnula, we are here to assess your standard of excellence, a quality in which I may say you're extraordinarily lacking. If we are severe with you, we mean it. If we are condescending, we mean it. Do not be under any illusion."

He gestured towards the Modern History Tutor who held out her term paper and dropped it page by page on the table in front of him.

"This – shall we call it prose? – has a hormonally determined character. I can find in it little by way of logic, argumentation or coherence. The comparison between De Valera and the Shah of Iran does little justice to the Iranian."

The dons he-hawed discreetly. The slayer in them was roused.

The dwarf came in with a huge silver tray of baked pigeons and chips. The table fell silent while he served the food. He did it awkwardly because of his height and the dons made no effort to make his task any easier. Finnula felt a sudden tide of sympathy for him; she said thank you several times in a sweet voice.

The pigeons were even more harrowing than the soup. Again, nobody spoke and all she could hear was gnashing and sucking and crunching. Suddenly it occurred to her that the dons, silence had a deeper meaning. And their voracity, it too had a meaning. They were telling her something. What could it be? But of course! The dons were devouring her! She felt her breasts and shoulders disappear down their gullets. They carved her expertly, carefully separating the bone from the flesh and chewing every last fibre with intense concentration. There was less and less of her.

"And now for dessert," said the Senior Tutor rubbing his hands. The dwarf wheeled in a tray with Grievous Angel and chocolate mousse. Finnula waved it away. She felt nauseous.

"Finnula, eat your dessert," barked her Moral Tutor.

"Yes," added the Bursar. "We do insist that you eat your dessert like a good girl."

All five of them put down their spoons until she started. She didn't have the strength to oppose them. Just as she was about to put a spoonful in her mouth she felt a hand slide along her thigh. Her horror subsided. Oh, God, she thought, at least somebody thinks I'm attractive. She looked around to see who it was but all hands were on deck. Then a second hand tried to pry apart her knees. As she leaned sideways to see who was molesting her, the table erupted with questions.

"Finnula," probed the Dean. "Isn't that a Scottish name? Macpherson and all that?"

"You've read 'Said on Celticism and Orientalism,' I presume?" asked the Chaplain.

"Hardly," said the Modern History Tutor. "She thinks the Iranians are Arabs, don't you, little Finnula?"

"I never," said the Bursar. "Now my dear child, the fact that the Irish are Catholic doesn't mean they're Italians, does it? You've certainly heard the comment of the Duke of Wellington?"

"Indeed!" cried the Dean. "Could you tell us, Finnula, who, in fact, was the Duke of Wellington?"

The face of the dwarf stared up at her from under the table. He looked like a sheik with the tablecloth draped around his head. He winked at her and made an obscene gesture with his index finger. Just then her Moral Tutor looked around the table and said: "Gentlemen, does anybody have anything good to say about our lady guest?"

There was silence broken only by the Dean who released a short energetic burp. Finnula felt immensely grateful to her Moral Tutor for his question.

"By the by, have you found what you were looking for under the table?" asked the Chaplain with a knowing lift of his eyebrows.

The dons collapsed in sniggers. Finnula stood up and pulled down her skirt. Excited by her confusion the slayers looked up and regrouped. Then they swooped on her, their swords drawn and lances erect. And Finnula ran out of the room forgetting her handbag.

That was the end of the dinner.

I enjoyed Finnula's story and she enjoyed it too.

"I'm going to write a novel about it, it was so awful," she said complacently.

I thought it was a very peculiar form of Irish revenge.

Finnula's passion for men who would defile her grew at every new encounter. She had no need to search them out. They came to her like passing dogs to a lamppost.

Roman Radziwill was one of them. Radziwill was the only person in the College with whom I could talk about the Eastern Bloc. He always had one hand on the pulse of Europe and the other on a girl's bottom. He was ruthless with both. His father was a count and his mother a baroness and his grandfathers had been hetmans in Lithuania. All of which, together with his hereditary ugliness and arrogance, made him more English than the English themselves.

Late in May Roman took to dropping in on me with a bottle of Crimean wine and we jeered at the science fiction of *glasnost*. Our raised voices lured Finnula down from upstairs.

"Why are you screaming at one another so much?"

"We are not screaming. We are having a discussion."

"You Slavs scream at one another all the time. But I like it. It's so spontaneous."

Roman was as predictable as John Paul II getting off a plane in a new country. He stood up, kissed Finnula's hand and begged her forgiveness in a Queen's English that squelched with sperm. She went limp as she listened to him.

I was too old for all that.

A few days later Finnula came to me with what she called a delicate problem.

"Roman wants to sleep with me," she said.

"I can't see any problem."

"But he's such an impossible reactionary. You're bad enough with your theories, but he's so much worse!"

"You're not going to sleep with his theories, I presume."

"Well, I suppose not. Besides, I think I can forgive him because he's from a communist country. But the real problem is something else. You see, I told him the truth. I mean I told him I'm a virgin."

"That, my dear, was a mistake. He must have been awfully distressed."

"He was disgusted. He said it was out of the question. He couldn't carry the burden. I would have to find somebody who would initiate me into that sort of thing and then come back to him. We spent hours and hours together last night wondering who might do it. Do you know anybody?"

I didn't. I imagined how stupefied Roman must have been. Led on by rumors he had doubtless been greasing his gun for an easy Kama Sutra with the Serpent of the Shannon. For a man of his experience in debauchery to make such a mistake was a terrible *faux pas*.

"What about the Captain of Boats?" I said in order to say something. "You know, the American with the beard. He looks at you with lust all the time."

"Oh Wisla, do be serious. It has to be an intellectual. And a European, I expect. What do you think I am? I want somebody with a mind."

"But he doesn't do it with his mind. You're not being logical, my dear."

I said it and I wondered if I was right. The trouble was that, as with many women, Finnula's genitalia were in her brain, somewhere in the region of the pineal gland.

She couldn't wait any longer to lose her pearl. For days she wore a hardened now-or-never look on her face. She stopped studying and sat in the College library staring into space with a book open in front of her. She took long baths, steeping her body in the oils of rosemary, pine and honeysuckle as if to lave her very entrails. Then she phoned her Moral Tutor. He was busy correcting examination scripts. But she called on him anyway with a punnet of fresh strawberries and a bottle of Bailey's Irish Cream. Then and there, as she bent to wash the strawberries in the wash hand-basin, he raped her.

She claimed he did it in three minutes flat without as much as a kiss or a cuddle.

"What are you doing?" she asked him again and again.

"I'm shoving my cock in your cunt," he replied like a true British empiricist.

He could not relinquish the habit of logical and cogent thinking even in this problematic situation.

"He took me like a heifer!" sniveled Finnula. "And then went back to his bloody exam scripts."

She was sitting on my floor again beside the divan which was her special misery zone. She wore a skimpy beige dress, green stockings and emerald earrings. For a woman who had been raped fifteen minutes earlier she looked very virginal with her bent head and her long hair sluicing down into her lap. To me she looked only half deflowered.

"How could he do it to me?"

"If he did it, it means that he could." I was only a little sorry for her. "The question is more how could you have let him?"

"What do you mean?"

"I won't say anything but I won't be silent either. I understand that you wanted to be relieved of your virginity and that is fine with me. What I don't understand is why on earth you chose an Englishman to do it. Can't you see that the whole thing is ideologically repugnant?"

"You just don't seem to understand. For me he is not an Englishman at all. He is a civilized, brilliant—"

I couldn't take it any more. I switched on Radio Free Europe, told her to grow up and go to bed with herself.

The following day a parcel arrived for Finnula. It was from her Moral Tutor. She opened it with trembling hands and a half expectant, half triumphant smile on her face. It died quickly. The package contained a green, white and gold garter belt and a pair of lace panties covered with shamrocks.

I was right after all. In the end it was pure ideology.

After defending my thesis on the Patrimonial Pendulum I went back to Poland and forgot all about Oxford, the easy life and the English disease. Then, one day, I received a postcard from Heidelberg with the picture of a statue of some Greek god or other from the classical museum. The statue was more or less intact except that the penis had fallen off. The postcard read: "Free at last. Staying in Heidelberg with Prof. Bloomenthal (*the* Bloomenthal). He's Jewish, brilliant and tender. What should I do? F."

I remembered Bloomenthal. He had been a visiting fellow at the College. He was tall, grey as a pigeon, and seventy-two years old.

I was very pleased that Finnula had written her address in full. People often omit it from postcards. I wrote back a registered, express letter to make sure that it got out of Poland.

Dear Finnula,

Great to hear from you. Forgive my importunity but I've run short of some basics since coming back. I wonder if you could send me the following:

(1) Package of Colombian coffee
(2) Bayer aspirin
(3) Raisins
(4) Vegetable stock
(5) Tampons (large)
(6) Tights (jasmine)

(7)   Package of Dunhills
(8)   Swiss army knife
(9)   Carton of matches
(10) Lancôme night cream (only if on sale)

Please send the package to my University address and mark it "Books."

Biodh rud agat féin, nó bí ina éamuis.

THE SMILE OF A ●
MOUNTAIN WITCH

ohba minako

I WOULD LIKE TO TELL you about a legendary witch who lives in the mountains. Her straggly gray hair tied with string, she waits there for a man from the village to lose his way, meaning to devour him. When an unknowing young man asks to be put up for the night, the owner of the house grins, a comb with teeth missing here and there clutched between her teeth. As he feels a cold chill run up and down his spine beholding this eerie hag of a woman, her yellowed teeth shining under the flickering lamp, she says, "You just thought 'What an uncanny woman she is! Like an old, monster cat!' didn't you?"

Startled, the young man thinks to himself, "Don't tell me she's planning to devour me in the middle of the night!"

Stealing a glance at her from under his brows, the man gulps down a bowl of millet porridge. Without a moment's hesitation she tells him, "You just thought in your mind, 'Don't tell me she's planning to devour me in the middle of the night!' didn't you!"

The man, turning pale, quickly replies, "I was just thinking that with this warm bowl of porridge I finally feel relaxed, and that my fatigue is catching up with me." But with his body as hard as ice, he thinks to himself, "The reason she's boiling such a big pot of water must be because she is preparing to cook me in it in the middle of the night!"

With a sly grin, the old witch says, "You just thought to yourself, 'The reason she's boiling such a big pot of water must be because she is preparing to cook me in it in the middle of the night!' didn't you!"

The man becomes even more terrified. "You accuse me wrongly—I was only thinking that I'm really tired from walking all day and that I ought to excuse myself and retire for the night while I'm still warm from the porridge, so that I may start early tomorrow morning."

But he thinks to himself, "What a spooky old hag! This monster cat of a woman must be one of those old witches who live up in the mountains I hear so much about. Or else she wouldn't read my mind so well!"

Without a moment's delay, the mountain witch says, "You just thought, 'What a spooky old hag! This monster cat of a woman must be one of those old witches who live up in the mountains I hear so much about. Or else she wouldn't read my mind so well!'"

The man becomes so frightened that he can hardly keep his teeth from chattering, but he manages to shuffle his body along on his shaking knees. He says, "Well, let me excuse myself and retire—"

Practically crawling into the next room, the man lays his body down on a straw mat without even undoing his traveling attire. The old witch follows him with a sidelong glance and says, "You're thinking to yourself now that you'll wait to find the slightest chance to escape."

Indeed, the man had lain down hoping to take her off her guard, so that he might find an opportunity to run away.

In any case, these old mountain witches are able to read a person's mind every time, and in the end the victim runs for his life away from her abode. The old witch pursues him, and the man just keeps running for his life. At least this is the form the classic mountain-witch tales assume.

But surely these old witches cannot have been wrinkled old hags from birth. At one time they must have been babies with skin like freshly pounded rice cakes and the faint, sweet-sour odor peculiar to the newborn. They must have been maidens seducing men with their moist, glossy complexions of polished silk. Their shining nails of tiny pink shells must have dug into the shoulders of men who suffocated in ecstasy between their lovers' plump breasts.

For one reason or another, however, we never hear about young witches living up in the mountains. It seems that the young ones cannot bear to remain in their hermitage, and their stories become transformed into stories of cranes, foxes, snowy herons, or other beasts or birds. They then become beautiful wives and live in human settlements.

These beasts that disguise themselves as human women invariably make extremely faithful spouses; they are very smart and full of delicate sentiments. Yet their fate somehow is inevitably tragic. Usually by the end of their tales they run back into the mountains, their fur or feathers pitifully fallen. Perhaps these poor creatures, with all their bitterness and resentment, turn into mountain witches. After all, devouring may be an expression of ultimate affection. Does not a mother in an emotional moment often squeeze her child and exclaim, "You're so dear to me I could eat you up!"?

Now, the woman about whom I am going to speak was a genuine mountain witch.

She died at the age of sixty-two.

At sixty-two, when her soulless body was cleansed with rubbing alcohol, her skin was bright and juvenescent like the wax figure of a goddess. Her hair was half-white, and on the mound at the end of her gently sloping belly were a few strands of silver. Yet around her calmly shut eyelids and her faintly smiling lips lingered a strange innocence and the bashfulness of a little girl who is forcing a smile even though she is about to burst out crying.

Indeed, she was the mountain witch of mountain witches. But even though she often longed for a hermitage on the mountains, she never lived in one, and she spent her entire life in the dwellings of a human settlement.

She had been a mountain witch ever since she could remember.

When she was still at a tender age and had not yet quite learned to use the bathroom, she would be so engrossed in play that she often had accidents. She would say to her mother who came running, "Oh you naughty girl. You've got to tell Mommy on time before it's too late. Oh dear, and today we don't have any change left for you—"

As her mother burst out laughing, she would go on, saying, "Really I'm no match for this child!—What can I say!"

At night, when her father was late coming home and her mother glanced at the clock on the wall, she would immediately say, "What in the world is he up to, coming home late night after night! He says it's work but I know he's really staying out as late as possible because it's so boring at home. As if he's the only one who feels that way!—Dear me—"

At that her mother would cast a wry grin and scowl at her. But before she could say anything, the little girl would exclaim, "You foolish girl! Come on, go to bed now. Little children who stay up late never grow, and they have to stay little for ever and ever."

The mother, utterly amazed at her daughter reading her mind time after time, would give in, saying, "This child is very bright, but she really tires me out!"

When she was a little older and her mother bought her a new toy, she would say, "This will keep her quiet for a while." Her mother, no doubt a little irritated, looked at her daughter, who would then say, "Why in the world does this child read other people's minds all the time. She's like a mountain witch. I wonder if people will come to dislike her like a mountain witch."

These are, of course, the kinds of things that her mother thought of often, and the child was merely verbalizing her mother's thoughts.

When she started going to school, the mother was, to a certain extent, relieved that she had times of separation from her daughter. But when she began to notice that her daughter ceased to read people's minds and became quieter each day, she asked, "How come you are so quiet now that you go to school?"

Her daughter replied, "When I say whatever is on my mind, people give me unpleasant looks, so I decided not to speak out any more. Grownups are happy when children act stupidly—as though they don't know anything. So from now on I've decided to keep grown-ups happy."

The mother responded firmly in a manner befitting one who had borne a mountain witch. "You say whatever is on your mind. You don't have to pretend. You're a child, remember?"

But the child merely regarded her mother with a disdainful smile.

All in all, the child performed well at school. On the occasions when she did not do well in a test, she would tear it up without showing it to her mother. Her mother would complain when she did not finish the lunch she brought to school, so on days when she did not have much of an appetite, she threw the remaining contents of her lunchbox into a trashcan on her way home. But so that her mother would not become suspicious, she left a little portion of it every now and then and showed it to her mother, saying, "The teacher talked longer today, so I didn't have enough time to finish it."

Time passed, and the child bloomed into maidenhood, but because her family was not well-to-do her mother could not afford to buy her expensive dresses. When the two went shopping together, the girl would purposely pick the dress her mother thought most adequate and pretended that she really liked it.

She would say instead of her mother, "I think this is really sweet. If I wore something extravagant at my age, I would give people the impression that I'm someone like the mistress of a rich old man."

On such occasions her mother would look at her with a slightly sad expression on her face. And on the way home, she would buy her daughter something way beyond her means. The girl would pretend not to notice her mother's impulse and showed a happy face to her as though she was genuinely pleased by her new acquisition.

The girl would assume whatever behavior was expected of her as though it was what came naturally to her, not only toward her family, but toward anyone by whom she wanted to be liked. When they wanted her to laugh, she read their minds and laughed. When they wanted her not to say anything, she remained silent. When talkativeness was desired, she chatted merrily. Toward a person who considered himself intelligent, she would act a little stupid—she did not overdo this, for usually this type of person thought it a waste of time to deal with stupid people—and as for those who were stupid, she appreciated their simplicity.

Perhaps because she demanded too much of herself and because she wanted too many people to like her, she had to spend an incredible amount of mental energy every day. So that before she realized it she had become antisocial, reading books in her room all day, avoiding being with others.

When her mother asked, "Why don't you go out with your friends?" she would answer with few words, "Because I get tired—"

The mother, too, began to feel fatigued when she was with her daughter. When she was not around her, she felt relieved. She began to long for the day when her daughter would find an adequate young man and leave her. In other words, the mother and daughter came to the natural phase of life when they would part from each other.

The daughter, too, knew that she was a burden to her mother—in fact, she had sensed that she was a burden to her as far back as she could remember—and she wanted to free her mother, as well as herself. At the same time, somewhere in her heart she held a grudge against her mother, a grudge which was sometimes so strong that she would feel surges of inexplicable rage. That is to say, she was going through the short, rebellious phase of puberty, but when she realized that her hatred and anger were directed at the cunning ways of her mother who had become her competitor of the same sex—that is, at her dishonest ways like taking advantage of her authority as a mother and avoiding direct competition— she became acutely aware that her mother had aged and that she herself had matured.

As a mature girl, she naturally came to know a man. He was an ordinary, run-of-the-mill type of man. Typical for one who had been doted on by his mother, he firmly believed that because his mother was of the opposite sex, he was allowed beyond all reason to express himself as freely as he pleased. When one such as he matures physically, the woman he marries has to be a substitute for his mother. For him, she has to be as magnanimous as a mother, as dignified as a goddess. She has to love him limitlessly and blindly like an idiot, yet at the same time have a spirit capable of being possessed by evil, like that of some sinister beast. Fortunately, however, he at least had the male characteristic of liking women.

Since the woman was gratified by the man, she came to think that she would not mind making all kinds of efforts to keep him happy. But this turned out to be very hard labor, for after all, every corner of his mind was transparent to her. If only one could not see another's heart, one would not become weary and would be able to live happily.

First of all, the man wanted the woman to be constantly jealous, so that she had to make every effort to appear that way. When another woman's shadow approached the man's life, she would act as though her presence made her competitive, and the man would be satisfied.

"Please don't go away from me. I can't live without you, you know that. I can't do anything by myself and I'm helpless when you're gone," she would cry as she sobbed and clung to him. And as she said the words, she would have the illusion that she really was a weak and incompetent creature.

Also, the man desired the woman to think of other men as something less than what they were, so that she had to close her eyes to the merits of other men and observe only their vices. But since the man was not excessively stupid, he did not allow her to denigrate others with idle speculation either. To please him, she had to make the right judgments, as well as be aware of all their vices, and indicate that even though they might have certain merits, these merits were certainly not to her liking. Thus every little opinion she expressed had to be well thought out.

On top of that, the man had the strange tendency of feeling pleasure in possessing all to himself a woman who was constantly being pursued by other men. Thus he tended to encourage rather than endure her affected flirtations. Perhaps deep down, all men long to become a part of the species of men we term "pimps."

To provide all the examples of this kind would take forever. In any case, at times the woman would forget to be jealous, or to flirt with other men. Or occasionally she was careless enough to express her true feelings about attractive men. At such times the man would become bored and think the woman lazy, thick-skinned, and lacking in sensitivity. Moreover, even when the woman succeeded in behaving perfectly to his liking, he would assert with the dignified tone of a sage who knew everything, "Women are utterly unmanageable creatures, so full of jealousy, capable of only shallow ideas and small lies. They are really just timid and stupid. In English, the word man refers also to human beings, but I guess women are only capable of being human by adhering to men."

Thanks to this irrational declaration of inequality, the two managed to live somewhat happily. Both the man and the woman grew old, and soon enough the man reached the age at which he would grumble all year long about something being wrong in this part of his body or that. He demanded that the woman worry about him all of the time and said that if anything happened to him he would be so concerned about her who would be left behind, that he would not die in peace. As she acted nervous and uneasy about him, she really became nervous and uneasy, until eventually she came to feel that he really was critically ill. For after all, unless she believed it he would not be at peace, and unless he were at peace, she could not feel that way either. Thus even though she hated nursing to such a degree that she thought she would die if she had to commit herself to it, she became a nurse just as a woman driven into a corner might sell her chastity. Observing the woman who now took up nursing, the man commended her, saying that nursing was an occupation truly in keeping with her instincts, and that as far as nursing was concerned, women were blessed with God-given talents against which no man could compete.

Around that time, the woman became exceedingly fat, so much so that when she walked just a little her shoulders would heave with every breath just like those of a pregnant woman. The main reason for this was that she was the possessor of exceptionally healthy digestive organs and consequently was constantly plagued by enormous appetites. But on top of that, she had the pitiful characteristic of wanting to make others feel good; even if she did not like it, she would eat up whatever was offered to her in order not to disappoint the person. Since other people thought that she just loved to eat, they would be terribly offended should she refuse the food that they offered her. On the other hand, her husband often boasted that he was a man of iron will. As she ate, saying, "Oh dear, here I go again—"he would cast a ridiculing glance at her; "You're such a weak-willed woman—" Even if someone put her heart into cooking something to please him, he would adamantly refuse if it was something that was not good for his health. In other words, his nerves were tenacious enough not to register shame at ignoring somebody else's feelings.

Because his use of words such as strength of will, insensitivity, and laziness so differed from hers, she would at times be overwhelmed by a sense of acute loneliness. She would come to fear not only her husband but many of the others around her as well, feeling as though she were surrounded by foreigners who did not speak the same language. Sometimes she thought she would rather live as a hermit in the depths of the mountains, just as she locked herself up in her room all day without playing when she was a little girl.

Far off in the midst of the mountains there would be nobody to trouble her, and she would be free to think as she pleased. The thought of extorting all those who tormented her in the human world made her heart beat with excitement: all those dull-headed, slow-witted people who could walk around with the looks of smug, happy heroes just because they were not capable of reading other people's hearts. If only she could say out loud like the legendary witches, "You just thought—didn't you!?" how relieved she would feel! It would be the sensation of slitting the skin around the temples in order to let horns grow, horns which are itching to grow out but cannot.

When she imagined herself living alone in the mountains, she likened herself to a beautiful fairy, sprawled in the fields, naked under the benevolent sun, surrounded by trees and grasses and animals. But once a familiar human being appeared from the settlement, her face would change into that of an ogress. He would stare at her, mouth open like an idiot, and utter coarse, incoherent, conceited words, making her fly into a rage.

On such occasions, her husband would appear, dressed shabbily like a beggar. He would wander about the abode of the woman who had now changed her appearance, and like a mischievous boy who had lost a fight he would mumble, "Without her to camouflage my unreasonable desires for me, I'd be done for—"

Listening to his voice, she would look at her face reflected in a clear spring. Then she would see that half her face was smiling like an affectionate mother, while the other half was seething with demonic rage. Blood would trickle down from half her mouth while it devoured and ripped the man's flesh apart. The other half of her lips was caressing the man who curled up his body in the shadow of one of her breasts, sucking it like a baby.

Now, as she became fatter, she began to develop arteriosclerosis, for her veins were put under increasing pressure. She found numbness in various joints of her body and suffered from headaches and the sound of ringing in her ears. When she saw a physician, he diagnosed that she was merely going through menopause. She was told in her early forties that she was suffering from menopause, and since then for over twenty years she had continued to receive the same explanation.

The man asserted that women were, as a rule, more durably constructed than men, their bodies and souls being more sturdily built. He pointed to a statistic that showed how women outlive men, and insisted that between the two of them, he would be the first to go. The woman thought that perhaps the reason women live longer has something to do with the fact that men end their lives on their own accord at youth, owing to war and other violent behavior, but since it was bothersome for her to prove this statistically, she just did not bring it up.

"That's right. Even though men are larger in build, they are actually sensitive at heart and more frail. That's why all women like men." As she said this, she told herself that the world would be a place of darkness without men, even though what she said was altogether fictitious, and continued stroking the man who complained that it hurt him here or there. In order to cook and feed him food as delicate as a little bird's, she spent hours day after day.

She knew that her own fat body did not have long to last with hardened arteries, but she could think of no other way to live than to provide food for the little bird of a man who believed that he was frail.

One morning, she examined herself thoroughly in the mirror. Her face was covered with wrinkles, giving her the appearance of a mountain witch. Her yellowed teeth were uneven and ugly like those of an aged cat. White frost had fallen on her hair and she felt chilling pain as though frost columns were noisily springing up all over her body.

She felt a slight numbness as though her body belonged to someone else. It was a stiffness related to the vague memory of her mother, long gone, far away. Somewhere, her flowing blood ebbed, and she felt dizzy. Suddenly a slight drowsiness attacked her, and when she came to herself her limbs were paralyzed and her consciousness dimmed as she felt various parts of her body gradually grow colder.

Customarily, she would have been up a long time ago preparing his meal. But finding her instead next to himself (they had slept alongside each other for forty years) face down and as stiff as a dead person, he became alarmed, and immediately straightening his body about which he had been complaining so much, he carried his wife to the hospital. Surprisingly enough, the physician who up until the day before had written her off as a case of menopause, now declared as if he were another man that she had the symptoms of cerebral thrombosis, and that if luck was against her she would only survive the next day or two. The man became totally confused, but he managed to pull himself together and decided that the first thing he should do was to send for their son and daughter, both of whom lived far away. The two children came immediately and with their father crouched around their mother who had now lost her speech.

Probably the next two days were the best two days of her life. The three of them took turns rubbing her arms and legs, and they would not leave it to the nurse to take care of even her most basic needs.

Even after two days, however, there was no drastic deterioration in their mother's condition; nor did it take a turn for the better. Her consciousness, however, became even dimmer, and she could no longer recognize the people around her. The uncertain physician said, "Considering her weight, her heart is strong. She may be able to hold on longer than expected." Soon the son claimed that he could not continue to stay away from work and that since it looked as though there would be no changes in the immediate future, he would return home for a while. With a gloomy look on her face, the daughter began to worry about her husband and children.

The poor man became anxious that he would not know what to do if his daughter left, so he pleaded with her to stay on. He sounded so helpless that the daughter, as worried as she was about her own family, reluctantly agreed to remain.

The daughter remembered the time when she had been critically ill as a child. Then her mother had stayed up for days watching over her. She thought that if not for this woman who lay in front of her unconscious, straying between life and death, she would not have been alive today. And this might be the last time she would be able to see her. Thinking through these matters, she hung on beside her. But when another two days passed, she began to wonder how long her mother would remain in her present condition, unable to converse and barely breathing, like a living corpse. She even thought that although the sixty-two years her mother had lived might be shorter than average, sooner or later everyone has to die, and that perhaps even if her mother went as she was from her present state, she would be considered fortunate that she could go watched over by her husband and daughter.

The daughter felt strangely uneasy when she remembered the story of the patient who survived for two years on intravenous feeding. She became worried whether her father's savings would be sufficient to pay the medical expenses should her mother survive as long. Even aside from the expenses, moreover, she thought that neither she nor her brother could afford to take care of her mother for such a long period of time, for they had their own families to consider.

She happened to think of her five-year-old daughter whom she had left behind with her mother-in-law. She remembered that at that age she herself had fallen ill and run a high fever for days, nearly contracting meningitis. Vividly, she envisioned her mother becoming frantic with worry and sitting by her bedside, cowering over her in their house which had become pitifully unkempt. Odd as it may seem, the impact of this memory led her thoughts away from her dying mother who lay moaning between life and death in front of her eyes, and made her concerned with the possibility of her own daughter falling ill while she was away. Unlikely as it may seem, she became plagued with fear at the thought of it.

Unaware of her daughter's worries, the mother survived another two days, occasionally staring into space with empty eyes and moaning something incomprehensible. The daughter woke up the third morning, too weary to climb out of bed after a week of intensive nursing. It was a dull, gloomy morning, typical of a cloudy day in the cherry season. She looked vacantly at the profile of her unconscious mother, who was also breathing quietly and who, with hollower cheeks, looked younger and beautiful.

When the morning round was over, the daughter, remembering that her mother's body was dirty, asked the physician if she could wash the patient. He instructed the nurse to do it and left the room. Soon the nurse came back, and in a very businesslike manner, carried out her duties as instructed, turning the patient over as though she were a log.

Timidly, the daughter helped her. Just when the patient was rolled over, stripped of her nightclothes soiled with perspiration and excrement, her eyes suddenly opened wide, staring at her daughter who happened to be standing right in front of her, holding her. She smiled faintly at her as light returned to her eyes. The radiance was like that of a firecracker, bright yet sad and ephemeral. Soon the firecracker died. The invalid lost the light in her eyes, and the saliva which had gathered trickled down the side of her mouth. Her throat went into a momentary spasm. The pupils of her eyes stopped moving, and then she was still. It all happened in a single moment.

At this sudden change, the nurse hurried off to call the physician. He rushed in and started to perform artificial respiration. He also injected cardiac medication through a thick needle into her heart. It looked more like shaking an animal that had failed in the middle of an experiment than dealing with a living human being. But in any case, it is certain that the people around her made various efforts to revive the pulse to her heart which had stopped.

The woman died.

No, it would be more truthful to say that she summoned up the last of her strength to suffocate her own self and body by washing down the accumulated saliva into her windpipe.

In the last smile she exchanged with her daughter, she clearly read her daughter's mind. Her daughter's eyes said to her that she did not want to be tied down by her any longer. "Mother, I don't need you to protect me any more. You've outlived your usefulness. If you have to be dependent on me, if you can't take care of yourself without being a burden to others, please, mother, please disappear quietly. Please don't torment me any longer. I, too, am preparing myself so that I won't trouble my daughter as I am being troubled by you. I'm willing to go easily. That's right. I ought to go easily. I never want to be the kind of parent who, just because she doesn't have the courage to come to terms with that resolution, continues to press her unwanted kindnesses upon her offspring." It seemed that her daughter, the product of her and her husband, possessed a strength of will that was twofold. Either she would overcome all temptation, exercise moderation, and live sturdily until the moment of her death at a hundred, or live haughtily and selfishly to the end, retaining the energy to kill herself at eighty. In either case, the woman was satisfied with the daughter she had borne and raised.

Through her daughter's face, she saw the son who was not there, walking among the crowds of the metropolis. He was talking to her with a crooked smile on his face. "Mother, I have incessantly chirping chicks at home. I myself don't know why I have to keep on putting food in their mouths. But when I catch myself, I'm always flying toward my nest, carrying food in my beak. Before I even think about it, I'm doing it. If I were to stop carrying food to them and stay close by you all the time, the human race would have perished a long time ago. In other words, for me to do as I do for them is the only way in which I can prolong and keep the blood you gave me—"

Next she looked at her husband, who was standing around absent-mindedly. This deranged old man, his head drooping, was touched by the beauty of his wife's naked body and absorbed self-righteously in the faithfulness that let him attend to his wife until the very end. The greatest happiness for a human being is to make another happy. She was satisfied with this man who had the capability to turn any situation into happiness, and she blessed the start of the second chapter of his life. At the same time, she thought she heard the pealing of her funeral bells.

With her own hands, she arranged her white shroud, left side under the right. In a dry riverbed, when she happened to look behind her, she saw somebody running away with his hair disheveled in the rushing wind. When she asked another deceased traveler whom she had not noticed before, the traveler answered, "He's being chased by a mountain witch."

Under the shroud which she had arranged, she felt the heartbeat of a mountain witch reviving, and she smiled. The heart of the mountain witch was throbbing as sturdily as ever. Only the blood vessels to transmit her vitality were closed, tightly, harshly, never to open again.

The time had come for the spirit of the mountain witch to return to the quiet mountains. The day had at last arrived when she would stand on a mountain ledge, her white hair swaying in the raging wind, sounding her eternal roar into the mountains. The transient dream of living in the human settlement disguised as an animal was now over.

The days she spent dreaming of living alone in the mountains, the sorrow she felt as a little girl when she first began to dislike humans, all came back to her and she shook her head. Had she lived up in the mountains, she would have been the mountain witch who devours humans from the settlement.

She wondered which would be the happier, to live in the mountains and become a man-eating witch, or to have the heart of a mountain witch and live in the settlement. But now she knew that either way it would not have made much difference. If she had lived in the mountains, she would have been called a mountain witch. Living in the settlement she could have been thought of as a fox incarnate or an ordinary woman with a sturdy mind and body who lived out her natural life. That was the only difference, and either way it would have been all the same.

Just before she took her last breath, it crossed her mind that her own mother must have been a genuine mountain witch as well. Strangely enough, when she died she had a mysteriously naïve face with the innocent smile of a newborn baby. Sobbing and clinging to this woman who died in peace, the daughter, with swollen eyes which told of her indescribable relief, said, "Such a beautiful death mask—Mother, you really must have been a happy woman." Her husband cried silently with wide open eyes full of tears like a fish.

TWO WORDS ●

isabel allende

SHE WENT BY THE NAME of Belisa Crepusculario, not because she had been baptized with that name or given it by her mother, but because she herself had searched until she found the poetry of "beauty" and "twilight" and cloaked herself in it. She made her living selling words. She journeyed through the country from the high cold mountains to the burning coasts, stopping at fairs and in markets where she set up four poles covered by a canvas awning under which she took refuge from the sun and rain to minister to her customers. She did not have to peddle her merchandise because from having wandered far and near, everyone knew who she was. Some people waited for her from one year to the next, and when she appeared in the village with her bundle beneath her arm, they would form a line in front of her stall. Her prices were fair. For five centavos she delivered verses from memory, for seven she improved the quality of dreams; for nine she wrote love letters; for twelve she invented insults for irreconcilable enemies. She also sold stories, not fantasies but long, true stories she recited at one telling, never skipping a word. This is how she carried news from one town to another. People paid her to add a line or two: our son was born; so-and-so died; our children got married; the crops burned in the field. Wherever she went a small crowd gathered around to listen as she began to speak, and that was how they learned about each others' doings, about distant relatives, about what was going on in the civil war. To anyone who paid her fifty centavos in trade, she gave the gift of a secret word to drive away melancholy. It was not the same word for everyone, naturally, because that would have been collective deceit. Each person received his or her own word, with the assurance that no one else would use it that way in this universe or Beyond.

Belisa Crepusculario had been born into a family so poor they did not even have names to give their children. She came into the world and grew up in an inhospitable land where some years the rains became avalanches of water that bore everything away before them and others when not a drop fell from the sky and the sun swelled to fill the horizon and the world became a desert. Until she was twelve, Belisa had no occupation or virtue other than having withstood hunger and the exhaustion of centuries. During one interminable drought, it fell to her to bury four younger brothers and sisters; when she realized that her turn was next, she decided to set out across the plains in the direction of the sea, in hopes that she might trick death along the way. The land was eroded, split with deep cracks, strewn with rocks, fossils of trees and thorny bushes, and skeletons of animals bleached by the sun. From time to time she ran into families who, like her, were heading south, following the mirage of water. Some had begun the march carrying their belongings on their back or in small carts, but they could barely move their own bones, and after a while they had to abandon their possessions. They dragged themselves along painfully, their skin turned to lizard hide and their eyes burned by the reverberating glare. Belisa greeted them with a wave as she passed, but she did not stop, because she had no strength to waste in acts of compassion. Many people fell by the wayside, but she was so stubborn that she survived to cross through that hell and at long last reach the first trickles of water, fine, almost invisible threads that fed spindly vegetation and farther down widened into small streams and marshes.

Belisa Crepusculario saved her life and in the process accidentally discovered writing. In a village near the coast, the wind blew a page of newspaper at her feet. She picked up the brittle yellow paper and stood a long while looking at it, unable to determine its purpose, until curiosity overcame her shyness. She walked over to a man who was washing his horse in the muddy pool where she had quenched her thirst.

"What is this?" she asked.

"The sports page of the newspaper," the man replied, concealing his surprise at her ignorance.

The answer astounded the girl, but she did not want to seem rude, so she merely inquired about the significance of the fly tracks scattered across the page.

"Those are words, child. Here it says that Fulgencio Barba knocked out El Negro Tiznao in the third round."

That was the day Belisa Crepusculario found out that words make their way in the world without a master, and that anyone with a little cleverness can appropriate them and do business with them. She made a quick assessment of her situation and concluded that aside from becoming a prostitute or working as a servant in the kitchens of the rich there were few occupations she was qualified for. It seemed to her that selling words would be an honorable alternative. From that moment on, she worked at that profession, and was never tempted by any other. At the beginning, she offered her merchandise unaware that words could be written outside of newspapers. When she learned otherwise, she calculated the infinite possibilities of her trade and with her savings paid a priest twenty pesos to teach her to read and write; with her three remaining coins she bought a dictionary. She poured over it from A to Z and then threw it into the sea, because it was not her intention to defraud her customers with packaged words.

One August morning several years later, Belisa Crepusculario was sitting in her tent in the middle of a plaza, surrounded by the uproar of market day, selling legal arguments to an old man who had been trying for sixteen years to get his pension. Suddenly she heard yelling and thudding hoofbeats. She looked up from her writing and saw, first, a cloud of dust, and then a band of horsemen come galloping into the plaza. They were the Colonel's men, sent under orders of El Mulato, a giant known throughout the land for the speed of his knife and his loyalty to his chief. Both the Colonel and El Mulato had spent their lives fighting in the civil war, and their names were ineradicably linked to devastation and calamity. The rebels swept into town like a stampeding herd, wrapped in noise, bathed in sweat, and leaving a hurricane of fear in their trail. Chickens took wing, dogs ran for their lives, women and children scurried out of sight, until the only living soul left in the market was Belisa Crepusculario. She had never seen El Mulato and was surprised to see him walking toward her.

"I'm looking for you," he shouted, pointing his coiled whip at her; even before the words were out, two men rushed her—knocking over her canopy and shattering her inkwell—bound her hand and foot, and threw her like a sea bag across the rump of El Mulato's mount. Then they thundered off toward the hills.

Hours later, just as Belisa Crepusculario was near death, her heart ground to sand by the pounding of the horse, they stopped, and four strong hands set her down. She tried to stand on her feet and hold her head high, but her strength failed her and she slumped to the ground, sinking into a confused dream. She awakened several hours later to the murmur of night in the camp, but before she had time to sort out the sounds, she opened her eyes and found herself staring into the impatient glare of El Mulato, kneeling beside her.

"Well, woman, at last you've come to," he said. To speed her to her senses, he tipped his canteen and offered her a sip of liquor laced with gunpowder.

She demanded to know the reason for such rough treatment, and El Mulato explained that the Colonel needed her services. He allowed her to splash water on her face, and then led her to the far end of the camp where the most feared man in all the land was lazing in a hammock strung between two trees. She could not see his face, because he lay in the deceptive shadow of the leaves and the indelible shadow of all his years as a bandit, but she imagined from the way his gigantic aide addressed him with such humility that he must have a very menacing expression. She was surprised by the Colonel's voice, as soft and well-modulated as a professor's.

"Are you the woman who sells words?" he asked.

"At your service," she stammered, peering into the dark and trying to see him better.

The Colonel stood up, and turned straight toward her. She saw dark skin and the eyes of a ferocious puma, and she knew immediately that she was standing before the loneliest man in the world.

"I want to be President," he announced.

The Colonel was weary of riding across that godforsaken land, waging useless wars and suffering defeats that no subterfuge could transform into victories. For years he had been sleeping in the open air, bitten by mosquitoes, eating iguanas and snake soup, but those minor inconveniences were not why he wanted to change his destiny. What truly troubled him was the terror he saw in people's eyes. He longed to ride into a town beneath a triumphal arch with bright flags and flowers everywhere; he wanted to be cheered, and be given newly laid eggs and freshly baked bread. Men fled at the sight of him, children trembled, and women miscarried from fright; he had had enough, and so he had decided to become President. El Mulato had suggested that they ride to the capital, gallop up to the Palace, and take over the government, the way they had taken so many other things without anyone's permission. The Colonel, however, did not want to be just another tyrant; there had been enough of those before him and, besides, if he did that, he would never win people's hearts. It was his aspiration to win the popular vote in the December elections.

"To do that, I have to talk like a candidate. Can you sell me the words for a speech?" the Colonel asked Belisa Crepusculario.

She had accepted many assignments, but none like this. She did not dare refuse, fearing that El Mulato would shoot her between the eyes, or worse still, that the Colonel would burst into tears. There was more to it than that, however; she felt the urge to help him because she felt a throbbing warmth beneath her skin, a powerful desire to touch that man, to fondle him, to clasp him in her arms.

All night and a good part of the following day, Belisa Crepusculario searched her repertory for words adequate for a presidential speech, closely watched by El Mulato, who could not take his eyes from her firm wanderer's legs and virginal breasts. She discarded harsh, cold words, words that were too flowery, words worn from abuse, words that offered improbable promises, untruthful and confusing words, until all she had left were words sure to touch the minds of men and women's intuition. Calling upon the knowledge she had purchased from the priest for twenty pesos, she wrote the speech on a sheet of paper and then signaled El Mulato to untie the rope that bound her ankles to a tree. He led her once more to the Colonel, and again she felt the throbbing anxiety that had seized her when she first saw him. She handed him the paper and waited while he looked at it, holding it gingerly between thumbs and fingertips.

"What the shit does this say," he asked finally.

"Don't you know how to read?"

"War's what I know," he replied.

She read the speech aloud. She read it three times, so her client could engrave it on his memory. When she finished, she saw the emotion in the faces of the soldiers who had gathered round to listen, and saw that the Colonel's eyes glittered with enthusiasm, convinced that with those words the presidential chair would be his.

"If after they've heard it three times, the boys are still standing there with their mouths hanging open, it must mean the thing's damn good, Colonel" was El Mulato's approval.

"All right, woman. How much do I owe you?" the leader asked.

"One peso, Colonel."

"That's not much," he said, opening the pouch he wore at his belt, heavy with proceeds from the last foray.

"The peso entitles you to a bonus. I'm going to give you two secret words," said Belisa Crepusculario.

"What for?"

She explained that for every fifty centavos a client paid, she gave him the gift of a word for his exclusive use. The Colonel shrugged. He had no interest at all in her offer, but he did not want to be impolite to someone who had served him so well. She walked slowly to the leather stool where he was sitting, and bent down to give him her gift. The man smelled the scent of a mountain cat issuing from the woman, a fiery heat radiating from her hips, he heard the terrible whisper of her hair, and a breath of sweetmint murmured into his ear the two secret words that were his alone.

"They are yours, Colonel," she said as she stepped back. "You may use them as much as you please."

El Mulato accompanied Belisa to the roadside, his eyes as entreating as a stray dog's, but when he reached out to touch her, he was stopped by an avalanche of words he had never heard before; believing them to be an irrevocable curse, the flame of his desire was extinguished.

During the months of September, October, and November the Colonel delivered his speech so many times that had it not been crafted from glowing and durable words it would have turned to ash as he spoke. He traveled up and down and across the country, riding into cities with a triumphal air, stopping in even the most forgotten villages where only the dump heap betrayed a human presence, to convince his fellow citizens to vote for him. While he spoke from a platform erected in the middle of the plaza, El Mulato and his men handed out sweets and painted his name on all the walls in gold frost. No one paid the least attention to those advertising ploys; they were dazzled by the clarity of the Colonel's proposals and the poetic lucidity of his arguments, infected by his powerful wish to right the wrongs of history, happy for the first time in their lives. When the Candidate had finished his speech, his soldiers would fire their pistols into the air and set off firecrackers, and when finally they rode off, they left behind a wake of hope that lingered for days on the air, like the splendid memory of a comet's tail. Soon the Colonel was the favorite. No one had ever witnessed such a phenomenon: a man who surfaced from the civil war, covered with scars and speaking like a professor, a man whose fame spread to every corner of the land and captured the nation's heart. The press focused their attention on him. Newspapermen came from far away to interview him and repeat his phrases, and the number of his followers and enemies continued to grow.

"We're doing great, Colonel," said El Mulato, after twelve successful weeks of campaigning.

But the Candidate did not hear. He was repeating his secret words, as he did more and more obsessively. He said them when he was mellow with nostalgia; he murmured them in his sleep; he carried them with him on horseback; he thought them before delivering his famous speech; and he caught himself savoring them in his leisure time. And every time he thought of those two words, he thought of Belisa Crepusculario, and his senses were inflamed with the memory of her feral scent, her fiery heat, the whisper of her hair, and her sweetmint breath in his ear, until he began to go around like a sleepwalker, and his men realized that he might die before he ever sat in the presidential chair.

"What's got hold of you, Colonel," El Mulato asked so often that finally one day his chief broke down and told him the source of his befuddlement: those two words that were buried like two daggers in his gut.

"Tell me what they are and maybe they'll lose their magic," his faithful aide suggested.

"I can't tell them, they're for me alone," the Colonel replied.

Saddened by watching his chief decline like a man with a death sentence on his head, El Mulato slung his rifle over his shoulder and set out to find Belisa Crepusculario. He followed her trail through all that vast country, until he found her in a village in the far south, sitting under her tent reciting her rosary of news. He planted himself, spraddle-legged, before her, weapon in hand.

"You! You're coming with me," he ordered.

She had been waiting. She picked up her inkwell, folded the canvas of her small stall, arranged her shawl around her shoulders, and without a word took her place behind El Mulato's saddle. They did not exchange so much as a word in all the trip; El Mulato's desire for her had turned into rage, and only his fear of her tongue prevented his cutting her to shreds with his whip. Nor was he inclined to tell her that the Colonel was in a fog, and that a spell whispered into his ear had done what years of battle had not been able to do. Three days later they arrived at the encampment, and immediately, in view of all the troops, El Mulato led his prisoner before the Candidate.

"I brought this witch here so you can give her back her words, Colonel," El Mulato said, pointing the barrel of his rifle at the woman's head. "And then she can give you back your manhood."

The Colonel and Belisa Crepusculario stared at each other, measuring one another from a distance. The men knew then that their leader would never undo the witchcraft of those accursed words, because the whole world could see the voracious-puma eyes soften as the woman walked to him and took his hand in hers.

The Débutante •

leonora carrington

WHEN I WAS A débutante, I often went to the zoo. I used to go there so often that I knew the animals better than the girls of my own set. In fact, I went to the zoo every day in order to get away from society. The animal that I got to know best was a young hyena. She got to know me, too; I taught her French and she taught me her language in return. So we passed many a pleasant hour.

My mother arranged a ball in my honor for the first of May; the very thought kept me awake at night; I have always detested balls, above all those held in my own honor.

I paid a visit to the hyena very early in the morning on the first of May. "What a bore!" I said to her. "I must go to my ball this evening."

"You're in luck," she said. "I'd love to go. I don't know how to dance but at least I could make conversation."

"There's going to be lots to eat," I said. "I've seen trucks full of stuff driving up to the house."

"And here you are complaining!" said the hyena disgustedly. "I get just the one meal a day and it's pigshit."

I had such a brilliant idea I almost burst out laughing. "You could go instead of me."

"We don't look enough like each other or I would, too," said the hyena rather sadly.

"Listen," I said, "nobody sees well in the twilight; nobody will notice you in the crowd if you are a bit disguised. Anyway, you are about the same size as me. You are my only friend. I beg you."

She thought about it, I knew she wanted to say yes.

"Done," she announced suddenly.

As it was so early, there weren't many keepers there. I opened the cage quickly and a few seconds later we were in the street. I took a taxi and everybody was asleep at home. In my room, I took out the dress I was supposed to wear that evening. It was a bit long and the hyena had trouble walking on the high heels of my shoes. Her hands were too hairy to look like mine so I found her some gloves. When the sun arrived in my room she walked all round it several times more or less straight. We were so preoccupied that my mother, who came to say good morning, almost opened the door before the hyena hid under my bed. "There is a bad smell in your room," said my mother as she opened the window, "take a bath perfumed with my new salts before this evening."

"Yes, of course," I said.

She did not stay long, I think the smell was too strong for her.

"Don't be late for breakfast," said my mother as she left my room.

The most difficult thing was, how to disguise her face. We pondered for hours and hours; she rejected all my proposals. At last she said, "I think I know the answer. Do you have a maid?"

"Yes," I said, perplexed.

"Well, then, listen. Ring for the maid and when she comes in we'll pounce on her and tear off her face; I shall wear her face instead of mine this evening."

"That isn't practical," I said. "She will probably die when she doesn't have a face any more; somebody is sure to find the body and we'll go to prison."

"I'm hungry enough to eat her," replied the hyena.

"What about the bones?"

"Those, too. Is it settled?"

"Only if you promise to kill her before you tear her face off, otherwise it will hurt her too much."

"It's all the same to me."

Rather nervously I rang for Marie, the maid. I would never have done it if I hadn't hated balls so much. When Marie came in, I turned my face to the wall so as not to see. I admit it was soon over. A brief cry and it was all done. While the hyena was eating, I looked out of the window.

After a few minutes, she said, "I can't eat any more; there are still the two feet left but if you've got a little bag, I'll finish them off later."

"You'll find a bag embroidered with fleur de lys in the chest-of-drawers. Empty out the handkerchiefs and take it."

She did what I told her. Then she said, "Turn around and see how pretty I am!"

The hyena was looking at herself in the mirror and admiring Marie's face. She had eaten all round the face very carefully so that only what she needed remained. "You've been really neat," I said. Towards evening, when the hyena was all dressed up, she announced, "I feel I'm in very good form. I think I'm going to be a big hit this evening."

When we'd been hearing the music from below for some time, I said to her: "Go down now and remember not to go near my mother, she'd be sure to know it wasn't me. I don't know anybody apart from her. Good luck!" I gave her a kiss as she left but she smelled very strong. Night had fallen. Exhausted by the emotions of the day, I picked up a book and relaxed beside the open window. I remember I was reading *Gulliver's Travels* by Jonathan Swift. After about an hour came the first sign of bad luck. A bat came in through the window uttering little cries. I am terribly frightened of bats. My teeth chattering, I hid behind a chair. Hardly was I on my knees before the beating of wings was drowned by a loud noise at my door. My mother came in, white with fury. She said, "We had just sat down at table when the thing that was in your place leapt up and cried out; 'I smell a bit strong, eh? Well, as for me, *I* don't eat cakes!' Then she snatched off her face and ate it. One big jump and she vanished out of the window."

THE DARK
INTRUDER/MATE

Like Bluebeard, the psychic predator, a fact of the psyche—whether symbolized internally or actualized externally—shows up in many fairy tales . . . shows up time after time in women's dreams. The predator can erupt in the midst of a woman's most soulful and meaningful plans. It severs a woman from her intuitive nature. When its cutting work is done, it leaves the woman deadened in feeling, feeling frail to advance her life. Her ideas and dreams lay scattered, drained of animation.

All creatures must learn that there exist predators. Without this knowing, a woman is unable to negotiate safely within her own forest without being devoured. To understand the predator is to become a mature animal who is not vulnerable out of naiveté, inexperience, or foolishness.

Psychologically, young girls and young boys are as though asleep about the fact that they themselves, because they are beautiful, they are considered by many and much, to be prey. Although sometimes it seems life would be much easier and much less painful if all humans were born totally awake, we are not. We are all born anlagen *like the potential at the center of a cell: in biology the* anlage *is the part of a cell characterized as "that which will become." Within the anlage is the substance which in time, will cause us to become a complete someone.*

from the chapter, "Stalking the Intruder, The Bluebeard Story,"
from *Women Who Run With the Wolves*

LIKING MEN ●

margaret atwood

I'T'S TIME TO LIKE men again. Where shall we begin?
I have a personal preference for the backs of necks, because of the word
nape, so lightly furred; which is different from the word *scruff*. But for most
of us, especially the beginners, it's best to start with the feet and work up.
To begin with the head and all it contains would be too suddenly painful.
Then there's the navel, birth dimple, where we fell from the stem, something we have in common; you could look at it and say, He also is mortal.
But it may be too close for comfort to those belts and zippers which cause
you such distress, and comfort is what you want. He's a carnivore, you're a
vegetarian. That's what you have to get over.

The feet then. I give you the feet, pinkly toed and innocuous. Unfortunately you think of socks, lying on the floor, waiting to be picked up and
washed. Quickly add shoes. Better? The socks are now contained, and
presumably clean.

You contemplate the shoes, shined but not too much—you don't want
this man to be either a messy slob or prissy—and you begin to relax. Shoes,
kind and civilized, not black but a decent shade of brown. No raucous two-
tones, no elevator heels. The shoes dance, with the feet in them, neatly,
adroitly, you enjoy this, you think of Fred Astaire, you're beginning to like
men. You think of kissing those feet, slowly, after a good scrubbing of
course; the feet expand their toes, squirm with pleasure. You like to give
pleasure. You run your tongue along the sole and the feet moan.

Cheered up, you start fooling around. *Footgear*, you think. Golf shoes,
grassy and fatherly, white sneakers for playing tennis in, agile and sweet,

quick as rabbits. Workboots, solid and trustworthy. A good man is hard to find but they do exist, you know it now. Someone who can run a chainsaw without cutting off his leg. What a relief. Checks and plaids, laconic, a little Scottish. Rubber boots, for wading out to the barn in the rain in order to save the baby calf. Power, quiet and sane. Knowing what to do, doing it well. Sexy.

But rubber boots aren't the only kind. You don't want to go on but you can't stop yourself. Riding boots, you think, with the sinister crop; but that's not too bad, they're foreign and historical. Cowboy boots, two of them, planted apart, stomp, stomp, on main street just before the shot rings out. A spur, in the groin. A man's gotta do, but why this? Jackboots, so highly shined you can see your own face in the right one, as the left one raises itself and the heel comes down on your nose. Now you see rows of them, marching, marching; yours is the street-level view, because you are lying down. Power is the power to smash, two hold your legs, two your arms, the fifth shoves a pointed instrument into you; a bayonet, the neck of a broken bottle, and it's not even wartime, this is a park, with a children's playground, tiny red and yellow horses, it's daytime, men and women stare at you out of their closed car windows. Later the policeman will ask you what you did to provoke this. Boots were not such a bright idea after all.

But just because all rapists are men it doesn't follow that all men are rapists, you tell yourself. You try desperately to retain the image of the man you love and also like, but now it's a sand-colored plain, no houses left standing anywhere, columns of smoke ascending, trenches filled with no quarter, heads with the faces rotting away, mothers, babies, young boys and girls, men as well, turning to skulls, who did this? Who defines *enemy*? How can you like men?

Still, you continue to believe it can be done. If not all men, at least some, at least two, at least one. It takes an act, of faith. There is his foot, sticking out from under the sheet, asleep, naked as the day he was born. The day he was born. Maybe that's what you have to go back to, in order to trace him here, the journey he took, step by step. In order to begin. Again and again.

SIMMERING ●

margaret atwood

IT STARTED IN THE backyards. At first the men concentrated on heat and smoke, and on dangerous thrusts with long forks. Their wives gave them aprons in railroad stripes, with slogans on the front—*Hot Stuff*, *The Boss*—to spur them on. Then it began to get all mixed up with who should do the dishes, and you can't fall back on paper plates forever, and around that time the wives got tired of making butterscotch brownies and jello salads with grated carrots and baby marshmallows in them and wanted to make money instead, and one thing led to another. The wives said that there were only twenty-four hours in a day; and the men, who in that century were still priding themselves on their rationality, had to agree that this was so.

For a while they worked it out that the men were in charge of the more masculine kinds of food: roasts, chops, steaks, dead chickens and ducks, gizzards, hearts, anything that had obviously been killed, that had visibly bled. The wives did the other things, the glazed parsnips and the prune whip, anything that flowered or fruited or was soft and gooey in the middle. That was all right for about a decade. Everyone praised the men to keep them going, and the wives, sneaking out of the houses in the mornings with their squeaky new briefcases, clutching their bus tickets because the men needed the station wagons to bring home the carcasses, felt they had got away with something.

But time is not static, and the men refused to stay put. They could not be kept isolated in their individual kitchens, kitchens into which the wives were allowed less and less frequently because, the men said, they did not sharpen the knives properly, if at all. The men began to acquire kitchen machines, which they would spend the weekends taking apart and oiling. There were a few accidents at first, a few lost fingers and ends of noses, but the men soon got the hang of it and branched out into other areas: automatic nutmeg graters, electric gadgets for taking the lids off jars. At cocktail parties they would gather in groups at one end of the room, exchanging private recipes and cooking yarns, tales of soufflés daringly saved at the last minute, pears flambeés which had gone out of control and had to be fought to a standstill. Some of these stories had risqué phrases in them, such as *chicken breasts*. Indeed, sexual metaphor was changing: bowls and forks became prominent, and *eggbeater, pressure cooker* and *turkey baster* became words which only the most daring young women, the kind who thought it was a kick to butter their own toast, would venture to pronounce in mixed company. Men who could not cook very well hung about the edges of these groups, afraid to say much, admiring the older and more experienced ones, wishing they could be like them.

Soon after that, the men resigned from their jobs in large numbers so they could spend more time in the kitchen. The magazines said it was a modern trend. The wives were all driven off to work, whether they wanted to or not: someone had to make the money, and of course they did not want their husbands' masculinity to be threatened. A man's status in the community was now displayed by the length of his carving knives, by how many of them he had and how sharp he kept them, and by whether they were plain or ornamented with gold and precious jewels.

Exclusive clubs and secret societies sprang up. Men meeting for the first time would now exchange special handshakes—the Béchamel twist, the chocolate mousse double grip—to show that they had been initiated. It was pointed out to the women, who by this time did not go into the kitchens at all on pain of being thought unfeminine, that *chef* after all means *chief* and that Mixmasters were common but no one had ever heard of a Mixmistress. Psychological articles began to appear in the magazines on the origin of women's kitchen envy and how it could be cured. Amputation of the tip of the tongue was recommended, and, as you know, became a wide-spread practice in the more advanced nations. If Nature had meant women to cook, it was said, God would have made carving knives round and with holes in them.

This is history. But it is not a history familiar to many people. It exists only in the few archival collections that have not yet been destroyed, and in manuscripts like this one, passed from woman to woman, usually at night, copied out by hand or memorized. It is subversive of me even to write these words. I am doing so, at the risk of my own personal freedom, because now, after so many centuries of stagnation, there are signs that hope and therefore change have once more become possible.

The women in their pinstripe suits, exiled to the livingrooms where they dutifully sip the glasses of port brought out to them by the men, used to sit uneasily, silently, listening to the loud bursts of male and somehow derisive laughter from behind the closed kitchen doors. But they have begun whispering to each other. When they are with those they trust, they tell of a time long ago, lost in the fogs of legend, hinted at in packets of letters found in attic trunks and in the cryptic frescoes on abandoned temple walls, when women too were allowed to participate in the ritual which now embodies the deepest religious convictions of our society: the transformation of the consecrated flour into the holy bread. At night they dream, long clandestine dreams, confused and obscured by shadows. They dream of plunging their hands into the earth, which is red as blood and soft, which is milky and warm. They dream that the earth gathers itself under their hands, swells, changes its form, flowers into a thousand shapes, for them too, for them once more. They dream of apples; they dream of the creation of the world; they dream of freedom.

In the Garden ●

darcey steinke

"Then the Lord God placed the man in the Garden of Eden to cultivate it and guard it. He told him, 'You may eat the fruit of any tree in the garden, except the tree that gives knowledge of what is good and what is bad. You must not eat the fruit of that tree; if you do, you will die the same day.'   Genesis 2: 15–17

"Wife," she whispered into her pillow, as she scanned the dark hotel room; she could just make out the desk, the chest of drawers, her bouquet of wilted white roses on top of the TV. And him sleeping beside her. His shoulders inched the blanket up with every thick breath. Eve envied how he could fall asleep quickly and anywhere like a child. She relaxed her weight into the mattress; there was a buoyant feeling like a ride on a late night bus.

She was conscious enough to know that her unconscious was opening like a toy chest. She saw his old girlfriend dressed in a spidery garter belt and platform shoes, sitting sideways on a horse. Beams of strong color circled like search lights behind her. The girlfriend put her cigarette holder to her lips and a gray snake of smoke rose from the tip. She sneered at Eve and threw back her head, vulgarly gulping wine.

Eve had the sensation of stumbling and started awake. Her mouth and neck were sore from smiling and there was a bitter taste of stale champagne in the back of her throat. What if they didn't get along? He could be stubborn. He could be selfish. What if her life reduced, as her mother's had, to a living hell? She imagined the mouth of hell, the flames, the lizards and snakes, the endless screaming. And that hot spot of frustration . . . her psyche in hideous and endless conflict with his.

She rolled onto her back, thought as she always did, whenever she tried to calm herself, of Jesus on the cross. She imagined him in tones of yellow and green, peaceful as a still life pear. *Have Faith*, she thought and moved over, pressed her stomach and hips into his back and rear. She felt his heart beating and knew in her own heart that her new husband was a reasonable man. She snuggled her face between his shoulder blades. His body's even pulse pulled hers towards sleep. Her mind lapsed into patterns, detailed as DNA chains in shades of blue and orange. She slid easily into her dream skin and landed deftly in the garden.

They walked together on grass so fine and cool it resembled water. He held her hand as they passed giant trees with huge purple blossoms big as a cat. At a fork in the path, he went off to check on something. She waited, watching a yellow bird jump from branch to branch on a tree heavy with apples. Apples that were more like succulent tomatoes and a little too, if the truth be known, like genitals, warm and red and throbbingly alive. She licked the sweat from her upper lip.

A snake came with a pattern of black skulls running all down its sinuous back. It rose up to Eve's eyes and swayed, like a charming snake. "What'ya doing baby?" the snake asked.

"Nothing," she looked down and noticed that her thighs were heavier than she remembered.

"Come on now," the snake said, bowing around so he looked again into Eve's tilted face. "I know you. All you want is everything."

Because it was true, her eyes teared.

The snake turned, licked the taut skin of an apple, still staring from the sides of its eyes. "Everybody's hungry. Ain't nothing to be ashamed of," he said wetly, and bit into the apple with his long crescent-moon fangs, yanking it violently from the tree.

And suddenly the sweet fruit was in her mouth and it was warm and delicious and better than she'd ever expected. But then just as quickly the wind blew up and her skin goose pimpled. Her husband stood beside her wearing his favorite shirt, carrying her dress for the honeymoon flight. She felt anxious and looked into his eyes which were blue-green like little worlds. For the first time she saw his raw and unfathomable need. She wanted to say something that would make everything better. So she touched the inside of his wrist and said, though where the words came from she didn't know: "Kneel down with me, know the sustenance of passion . . . take in the ALL, let us fall together into the WAY."

THE ODALISQUE, ●
EXTINCT

diana hartog

THE ODALISQUE RECLINES, rarely stands, and is never painted in stride. The feet do not support. The knees are sometimes bent akimbo as she lies at her length on a couch. This posture invites shadows to slowly approach.

The shadows of Paris are renowned—even more, perhaps, than its light. In April, fleet cumulus clouds sweep their shadows across the cobblestones; a broom leans its shadow against a wall at a pleasing slant; the shadows of strangers are trampled underfoot. These are the public shadows of Paris. To study the more private, one must move indoors, to the habitat of the Odalisque, circa 1923.

It is afternoon, after lunch and several wines. Angling in from the skylight, a shadow moves slowly across the floor of the studio; and will soon climb the shabby brocade of the couch and the fringe of black tassels dangling from a shawl.

All this takes time.

In the pose of the Odalisque, other shadows have already gathered. In the crook of her arm. In the hollow of her upturned palm. They nestle along her nakedness like privileged pets (the kind Parisiennes dine with on their laps, feeding them choice scraps from the table). Beneath her breasts smile two crescent moons of shadow. Her expression remains sober. Her nipples, impassive, return the turgid, unblinking stare of the voyeur. (The eyes of an Odalisque rarely meet one's gaze. There are exceptions—an "Olympia" for instance—but most glance away, in order to think, or read.)

High on the Odalisque's cheekbone is dabbed a mole—to balance the drop of shadow which pools in her navel and threatens to spill over her rounded belly if she moves. And if the pubis is shorn, and the Odalisque's hand is not in the way, the tip of the brush will be dipped into black: and a fine delicate stroke, applied with a slight tremor, will part the lips.

The bank of black encircling her throat is not a shadow but a black velvet ribbon, an artistic device implying the disjunction of head from body. It's a joke; in English it's called a choker.

A ribbon which, if missing from the canvas, Matisse has surely filched; and carries wadded in his pocket, fingering the velvet as he thinks about tomorrow, what he will change.

BLOODMANTLE ●

tanith lee

F EBRUARY, THE WOLF MONTH, is also the color of wolves. And through the pale browns and greys and whites of it, something so very red can be seen from a long way off.

In that fashion then, he saw her, coming down among the slopes of the damp and leafless woods. She passed by the old altar with its wrapper of ivy, the strips of hide hanging over it from the trees above. She crossed the stream by the old stones, carefully, so as not to get her little shoes wet. But the rain, which had earlier drenched the woods, beaded her long dark hair, and the fine palla she wore. The palla was so dense and rich a red, sight seemed to sink into it, it drowned and made vision drunk, as only natural colors were supposed to do. It was altogether of a hue that had no place in the wood, making everything else dim and unreal.

Having come over the stream, she could not avoid seeing him in turn as he emerged between the trees and stood there, looking at her. She was not apparently startled by him, though he was an interesting apparition, clothed, in the wintry day, only in hairy skins that were belted by a twisted briar. His own hair was long and shaggy, but his face clean-shaven and beautifully chiseled, as was his body. He too was the February color, silver-brown, his skin, his hair, and his eyes like brown water with a silver rim.

"Where are you going?" he said to her. "And why did you dye your cloak with blood?"

"Not blood," she answered haughtily. "Scarlet that the ships bring from the East."

"I serve the god in the woods," he said.

"I know you do," said she.

"You must submit."

"No," she said.

"Then you offend the god."

"I care nothing for your god. I have my own. I am a Christian," said the girl in the red palla.

"Yes, I have heard of him," said the young man who served Lycaean Pan. He spoke indifferently. The priests had marked him, he had a wolf soul that had shown itself during the ritual, grinning like a wolf with strong white teeth. He roamed through the woods, sacred to Faunus Lupercal, sleeping in dead trees, bathing in dew, shaving with slate, eating beetles, and hares with the life-hotness still in their meat, drinking from the fountains of the rocks, dancing under the full moon with wild hoarse howls and shrieks. It had always been this way, his kind in this place. And if she did not know it, the girl, she was a fool. And if she did know, why else was she here save to tempt her fate?

"Come now," he said, "submit. Or I can pull you down and have you anyway."

She neither ran nor trembled; she went no nearer to him.

So then he came up to her.

"What does the needle do with the pin?" he said. "The pin has a round knob and a piercing shaft. The needle has an eye. One goes through the other. Thread the needle with the pin."

"Very well," said the girl, "but you will be sorry."

Then she opened her scarlet mantle. She was naked under it. She lay down on the ground on her hair and the red stuff, and he lay down on top of her. No sooner had he possessed her—with difficulty, for she was a virgin, and hurt him—than something terrible occurred. The folds of the palla began to move and stretch and reach out, and before he knew what was happening, they had folded up over him and covered him and buried him, like the petals of some huge poppy.

The sensation was at first not unpleasant, then it became horrible and fearful. The great palla settled down on him and all his energy was drawn away into it, as into the body of the girl. They were together a blood-red plant that consumed him . . .

Later, much later, when the sun was going down through the woods, only a patch of rusty moisture showed on the earth, and by moonrise, this too was gone.

"The lupin is the wolf flower. Why?"

"Because it's hairy. And once there were blue wolves. They were born in nests high in the trees."

"Men," said my grandmother, "and wolves, were all one race, in the beginning. Then there had to be changes. There began to be a tribe that had only the heads of wolves, and the bodies of men, though they were shaggy-haired all over. But all wolves have human eyes. That's the difficulty. Men see it and they say, 'These are men disguised as animals.' Men have always been afraid of their own kind, but daren't admit it. Then they see the eyes of wolves and it gives them an excuse. That is why men hate wolves."

"I think wolves are handsome," said my young cousin, George. "I wouldn't mind being a wolf. Could I be?"

"Very likely," said my grandmother, spending her double meaning only on me.

"But you didn't finish the story," I said. "What happened to the wolf-boy? And the girl in the red cloak?"

My grandmother shrugged. "Where's your imagination gone? That was in the days when the beast gods were respected, although the Christians were driving the old ways out. That girl wasn't a girl, but a demon conjured up by some priest. The boy thought he had the protection of his own god, Wolfish Pan. But Pan was already dead. The Christians killed him. And that's another story. Now, off home, before it starts to get dark."

My smaller cousin, Bettany, began to cry. She said there would be wolves in the wood, and they would devour her.

George, a cruel, pretty child, sly, looking under his lashes, declared it was the demon girl who would cause us trouble.

Grandmother said there were no such things any more as demons, and that, otherwise, there had been no wolf seen in our countryside for fifty years. Besides, wolves ran away if you shouted at them. She had done this as a girl.

I held Bettany's hand, though it was wet from her snifflings. But George skipped ahead of us, slashing viciously at various bushes. The shadows were lengthening, but the wood was still bisected with broad avenues of light. It was April weather, not February, birds sang and waking squirrels sprang over the budding branches. We crossed the stream by the bridge, and I looked for an altar the other side but of course there was nothing left of it. It was easy to fancy, for all that, a slim brown shape now here, now there, between the tangle of trunks and sprays of wild vine.

Beyond the wood, the lane ran across the fallow fields, by the deserted park and the dilapidated houses of rich people long since dead and forgotten, and so uphill to the outskirts of our town. During the night, I dreamed that a wolf had given birth to me, high up in a tall tree of colossal boughs. By moonlight, the wolf was a soft milky blue, with wonderful sad eyes.

It was a melancholy, almost a mystical, dream.

Near morning, something very dreadful happened. I was roused by an awful crying note, over and over, so repetitious I thought it was something mechanical. The whole house seemed in uproar. Then, through the window, I saw one of the men rush out, and presently return with the doctor. George was very sick, my aunt told me, and put weeping Bettany, whom I was irritatedly powerless to comfort, with me into my room. Endless comings and goings next, we excluded from them, and finally silence.

A week later, I, with the rest, was dressed in black and taken to a graveside along the hill. Little George had died of an unpronounceable illness that years subsequently I discovered to be meningitis.

In the following months, the family cracked like a trampled eggshell. Soon I was sent away to school. Other things, events, and my maturity, drove me further and further off to exile, to the cities and the south.

I did not visit the town for many years, by which time not one of my kindred remained there, and my rather improper, story-telling grandmother had herself died. The ancient wood had been felled for the timber mills, and the encroaching roads and buildings of the town rolled over it.

"You've come back at a bad time," said the old man, who thought he remembered me, but in fact only remembered the little girl I had been. "Something going on now, not nice."

"What is that?"

But he would not tell a little girl. Later on, over midnight glasses of hot chocolate at the hotel, a sinister gossiping began between staff, regular guests, and the itinerants, among whom now I was numbered.

"There's been another."

"So there has."

"Oh, where?"

"The same area as last time. But worse, much worse, this one."

"Is it true that they—?"

"Oh, yes, quite true." Then, seeing me lean closer: "The throats are torn out and the bodies mauled. Dogs, you might say, or something escaped. But there's the other thing—they wouldn't do it. It's not an animal. Or if it is, then that's not all it is."

Although there are streets now, and hard concrete, over the wooded tracks, and the stream runs in a canal with seats on the banks and refuse in the water, and the trees have gone to copses on neat lawns, even so, the town keeps its dreams and nightmares of legends. They know what they think this is. Only the alien traveler would scoff.

"A month to the day they moved the cemetery. Lifting the stones . . . Everything was done properly, the priests saw to it. But there. The old Vaudron family, they were here from heaven knows when. The old lady, you knew her? Some of her tales, now, the children used to shake with fear for weeks—"

"And him only seven years of age, and dead in a night, calling out in pain. Awful cries, like something lost, or a whistle—"

The Vaudron family was my uncle's; they were talking about my little cousin, George.

"Well," said the receptionist, the doors being closed, coming to drink her own chocolate beside me. "There's a police patrol now every night, and a lot of good it does. Last month, they saw someone, a man, very late, along by the canal. They're not sure, he may be innocent, but they've found a dead woman—and there's something about him. They follow. Then he passes under a street lamp. Now there's a girl, looking out of her window, waiting for somebody, maybe. He goes by, across the street, under the lamp—and she starts screaming. He vanishes down an alley. The police run after him, can't find him. Some of them go up the stairs and hammer on the door of the girl's room. Was it a signal? It seems not. That girl, all she can say is, A man, but he had the *face of a wolf*. And they have to take her to the sanitarium, where she is to this minute. She lies there and screams that she saw a man with a wolf's head and a wolf's face."

"Do you believe she saw that, really, madame?" I said.

The receptionist shrugged. "Why not? Is it so strange? In my grand-mother's day it wouldn't have surprised a soul. Now we have television, which would have upset her no end."

I thought about my own grandmother, just young enough to have seen such witchcraft as television in. She was still renowned, it would seem, for her stories. I thought about little Cousin George, dying of meningitis. I couldn't accept that if any essence of us persists after death, it could degenerate into something so arcanely banal as a murdering ghost or werewolf. But on the other hand, perhaps some sort of subsidiary impression had been left over from the physical energy of the male child who liked wolves. Like a paw-print in wet cement.

A couple of nights later, I happened to run out of cigarettes, and so I walked down to the neon café and bought a packet, and drank a *fine*. Then, not wanting to go back to read or sleep, I began to stroll along by the canal. It was just after midnight, but the moon was high, completely round and slicked with white, so the street lights were nearly superfluous. A clear-edged bluish glow lay everywhere, and the shadows were only transparently black. Stars stung the sky. There was nobody about, not here, away from the cafés of the main street. It had occurred to me that, in the era of my childhood, this must have been the route to my grandmother's house in the wood: this the stream, though the old bridge was gone and I had already crossed over by the new one, and trees invisibly all round, in the blue light. Plowed under now, everything, house and all, along with the rich people's villas, and the concrete poured over, paw-marked or otherwise.

I smoked a cigarette, and when I finished, tossed the butt into the moon-lit water. Then, turning, I saw a man under one of the lamps, leaning there, watching me.

I walked over to him. Perhaps he was looking for company, but the prostitutes who might occasionally have touted here no longer did so. Then, without shock, I recognized him. It was not from the past, but the story.

Of course, I had never believed my little cousins would grow up, either of them, any more than I thought I would myself. This may be the reason why children are often not offended by the death of their peers. Five years older than he, I had found him easy to leave behind. Yet, there was a family resemblance; mostly he looked like the wolf-boy in the legend. Handsome and curious, those ash and amber colors, veiled by moonlight, and the pale, beautiful lupine eyes. It was a human head, if less human than anything I had ever seen before, less human than the face of an animal. Nor was he dressed in skins, but as one would expect of a poor young man, perhaps a student. Was he nineteen years old? Probably. I was twenty-four, that would be right.

I went up to him, and I said, "Good-evening, George."

He smiled, gorgeously. The hot eyes did not join in, but all the rest of the face, the body muscles, seemed to do so.

"You know me?"

"We're related, shall I say?"

"Is that," he asked, "why you're wearing red?"

It had happened, as it happened I had run out of cigarettes, that the coat I had brought with me was of the reddest, most scarlet wool, a coat of blood.

"Whatever do you mean?" I said.

"Remind me of your name, since you know mine," he said.

I told him, adding that until I was twelve, we had lived in the same house, with my uncle, his father. He looked uninterested rather than dismayed. He said, "Ah, that. But that's past. Well, will you come and have a drink with me?"

I said I would.

Naturally he did not, taking me lightly by the arm, walk me back towards the bright busy cafés, but away along the canal, and down a side-street. Soon we had reached some closed shops and then a rough empty lot with a ruined, boarded house, and many trees. He led me to the house, through the thickets, which were full of fallen stones. I had no notion who it belonged to, it had been built, and abandoned, after I left the town. Several had bivouacked there since. We crept through some loose boards into a cold, moon-stripped salon. A fire was ready-laid from branches, cones, newspapers, in the grate, regardless of the state of the chimney. This fire he immediately lit with matches. From under some bricks he took two bottles of wine, a cheese wrapped in oil-cloth, and a bag of apples. We feasted solemnly. We had done so as children.

"Didn't the police come here?"

"It goes without saying," he said.

"But you were away, and had left no trace."

He grinned at me slowly.

"And the smoke. Doesn't anyone see?"

He said: "There's always that." He seemed to think he was protected, and conceivably he was.

"Tell me," I said at last.

"Why should I?"

"I thought you might like to."

"Confession?"

"Or boast. Who else would listen?"

"Plenty of people would listen."

"Do you remember any childhood?" I asked him.

He looked at me a long while, as if gauging the limits of my understanding. Then he shook his head. His hair was a shaggy flamy thing in the firelight. His brown-silver eyes shone, when they were in the dark out of the fire, hard and flat and green. Human eyes do not do this. Wolf eyes, however human, do.

"Then, when did it begin? When they dug up the grave?"

"Yes." He moved closer—we were both seated on the floor. He touched my face gently, with his long-fingered, long-nailed hand. "After all," he said, "you remember your childhood, but you don't feel, do you, it was truthfully you? *That* was someone else."

"Yes, that's so."

"Well. I know he was a child. Another person. I simply recognize that it wasn't myself at all. I'm George here and now. I'm here, I'm now."

"And the grave—"

"Like lifting the lid of a kettle. The lid, down, gives the illusion of suppression. But I was there, underneath."

He said there was a darkness and he came out of the darkness in the way one comes out of sleep. There might have been dreams, or not. He asked, had I ever woken up and for a while not known where I was, or the day or date even, not minding it, knowing I would recall, but not yet recalling. I had, and said I had. Well, he said, it was like that for him. Then, he found himself walking through the town. It was quite unfamiliar, yet—

like days and dates—he realized it would *become* recollected, he had only to wait. And then he saw a girl, by the canal. Probably she was soliciting. He went up to her and asked her for a cigarette. (George had seen his father and brothers smoke. It would be normal for him to assume that he, when an adult, would smoke also.) The girl gave him the cigarette. (He asked me if I knew the prostitutes in Roman times had been called 'she-wolf'—not as an insult, but to indicate their honorable usefulness, linked to the motif of the wolf-mother of the city, and the werewolf festival of Lupercalia.) Then she suggested he might like to go with her, to a café, but instead he took her into an alley he had already found, and there he killed her. It seemed perfectly natural to him, he was excited but competent, knowing instinctively, as with sex, what should be done. In fact, it was like sex, and afterwards he was worried he had not possessed her before killing her. He did not abuse the corpse. The ethics of the bourgeois Vaudron family intervened. He found another girl to satisfy concupiscence, and then arranged to meet her again the next night. When he met this second girl this second time, he first made love to her and then tore her to pieces. He killed her in the middle of orgasm, both hers and his own. This was highly fulfilling, it seemed, and became thereafter his modus operandi. Sometimes he fed at these times. He also ate other food. The cafés and hotels threw things out, or gave them to him, or he stole them.

It came to me that the town had remained a wood for him, and in a way I wondered if he even saw the buildings and the roads as such, or if they were somehow caves and trees, and savage woodland glades. By this formula, too, he might have his uncanny protection, making himself in turn invisible to the town, and to its police force. Seeing him quite frequently, as they must do, they had never seen *him*.

The fire sank. It was cold in the boarded house, February weather.

"Sometimes I go to a church," he said. "Once, I did make confession. But not the killings. You see, for me, the killing is not a sin."

"No, I understand that."

As he moved to put more cones and branches on to the fading fire, I told him the dream I had had, the night he—no, George—had died. About the blue wolf who gave birth to me in the great tree, and her sad eyes. I mentioned the idea to him that the mother-birth is the second birth, that the ejection of the seed—the paternal birth—precedes it. I wanted to inquire after the metamorphosis he himself underwent, perhaps during this ejection, or directly before. Presumably, it did happen. But how did he accomplish it? He seemed totally physically real, and if he was, such a displacement of atoms must be impossible.

"Well, maybe the wolves did birth you," he said. "You arrived at the house an orphan."

"I don't remember my parents," I said.

"I remember mine," he said. "*His.*"

"Do you remember our grandmother?"

"A big mouth, always telling us things she shouldn't have. But you were a strange child. That's how I see you now. I wonder what happened to that other girl . . ."

"Bettany?" I paused. Bettany had married a banker, and become another woman who ate chocolates and produced children. I had not seen her for years. Neither of us now wanted to talk about Bettany. I think it was only some associative memory stirring in George's brief past, like a nerve. Eventually, I pushed her right away, and said, "And you remember the story our grandmother told us?"

"The girl with the mantle made of blood," he said. "Like you."

"Do you worship the old gods? Do you make sacrifices to Pan?"

He laughed. The laugh was wonderful. He sat back on his heels, laughing, warm February fire all over him. He ate life. It had filled him. He was unlike anything, human or beast.

"No. Pan? Pan is dead. Or is that a pun—*Pan*—*du pain*—bread—*peine*—pain—the body of Christ?"

"I meant, how do you effect the transformation?"

He lowered his eyes—with a dagger-green flash—like a modest girl who has been asked by a man if he may touch, very politely, her breast.

"What is that?" he said.

"Man into wolf. Is it possible?"

"Of course."

"How?"

"Do you want me to show you?" he said, looking at me now in the old sly way, under his lashes.

"No," I said. But I did want him to. "Could you not simply describe for me—"

"If I do it," he said, "you may be frightened. You may go mad. Or I may kill you."

"You would stop being yourself."

"I should become myself."

"There's no self to become," I said. "Whatever you are, not really. So, I suppose you could become anything. Is that what the answer is?"

"I remember the girl in the story," he said. "She wouldn't submit."

"Then she did."

"Yes. Then she did. Do you actually think," he said, "that any one of us is truly what we're pleased to call real? All matter, flesh, skin, trees, stone, bricks, blood—it's all illusory, fluid, non-existent, formed from nothing—therefore capable of any alteration, and of complete change. Wouldn't you say? Where else do the woods go to, when they turn into concrete? How else? And the bread that's a body, and children who grow up, or turn into a heap of calcium in the ground?"

"What about the needle and the pin?"

"There's no choice between them. They're the same. They both pierce and they both join together."

"Is that what it meant?"

"In the story she told us."

"Show me, then," I said.

"Look at me, then," he said.

So I did look. I looked hard, too hard. And then I let myself relax, even my eyes, I allowed them to unfocus a little, just a very little, and gradually, by the broad gusts of fire through the shadow, I began to see the wolf. There was no violence, no tearing or twisting, no flare up of pelt, the skull re-shaping itself, a howling frenzy. Frankly, it was all already there. By allowing myself to see, I merely saw it. Then again, the terror of it, for it was quite terrifying, was all because it was *not* a wolf at all, but some intrinsic fear-thing that was to do with man's phobia at wolves, primeval, matted, dark, fathomless. It was the head of a creature that was the head of fear, and with a man's body, a man's long wolfish hands, with which to work the horror out.

Presently I looked away, and opened my purse and took out a cigarette. When I had struck the match and lit it, I offered the packet to him, and he had become a young man again, a wolf-boy, much more wolf-like in his human form. The werewolf was only the image, the *icon* of the nightmare.

We smoked our cigarettes in silence, and then he lay down, his head in my lap. The fire played on the planes of his face. I watched him, trying to memorize his beauty, as one does with some work of art one may never see again. After a while, he said that he often slept here, but he was cold tonight, did I feel the cold as he did? He thought not. His blood was hotter than mine. So then I took off my red coat and laid it over him, drawing it up to his chin.

He slept after an interval, and I, my back propped against the rotted boards, also slept a few moments. I dreamed I was in the tree again, in the act of birth from the belly or the penis of the lupin-blue wolf. I thought, That's the riddle then. Not to find the bestial in humankind, but this constant thrust to be free of it, the coming out from the beast, the ancestor in his sheath of hair and hunger. Then I woke, and he slept, still. I got up carefully, not to wake him; I did not want to make him start. But as I moved to the fire, I half believed I caught the flash of his eyes, watching on under their lashes. Yet who goes in the wood, knowing the wood, is there to tempt his fate. He recalled, he had told me so. I pulled one of the last twigs out of the grate, and carried the bud of February fire back to him. I even still waited an instant, letting the glare and heat of the burning twig flicker above his face, as Psyche did, when she stared down on her shape-changer monster-god in the legend of love. But now he did not open his eyes, if he ever had.

I put the flame to the edges of my coat, all the way around, then threw the last smoulder of the twig down into his hair.

At first, there was nothing, just a ripple, sparks, smoke. Then suddenly, all of it went up, the coat, the wolf-mane, and he too, a spasm of fire, scarlet on the shadow, the color of blood, redness covering him, obliterating him. He gave no cry, and scarcely changed position, only rolling a little, as if to be one with the warmth and comfort.

I found it very cold outside, after the fire. The house was burning by the time I reached the canal. I could see the light on the sky, and the smoke going over the sinking moon.

My grandmother's grave, in the transported cemetery, has flowers growing on it, and ivy, but no lupins. I took photographs of that, and other Vaudron graves. That was really all modernization had left me. The dwellings and landmarks of my childhood were gone. There was some excitement in the town that day, about a derelict house which had caught on fire in the night. Tramps had been using it, and no one was astonished that the cooling clinker revealed the remains of a man. Then again, however, they were not sure it was a man, or anything, for that matter, ever alive. At the correct temperature, even bones will melt. You can rely on the constancy of nothing.

Having to buy a coat, I was disconcerted by the women in the shop. They were so interested in all the other aspects of their lives, that for them I hardly existed. I had become a sort of ghost. I left the town near evening, by the night train for the south. In the city I knew I would be recognized, and spoken to, I knew I should be perfectly alive and real.

SLEEPING BEAUTY, •
REVISED

jill mccorkle

IT'S LATE FALL and my refrigerator is covered in autumn leaves ironed between pieces of wax paper. Every day
Jeffrey brings something home from preschool, a treasure to be hung on
the wall or around my neck, like the food-colored pasta necklace he
presented me with today. On a Post-it alongside a bright yellow maple leaf
is the name of the man I'm meeting for dinner—Phil, who is in computer
sales, a friend of a friend, the first date I've had since I married Nick, which
means the first date I've had in nine years.

"He's getting a divorce, too," my friend Sarah, who teaches with me in
the junior high school, had said. Sarah is known for her matchmaking
attempts, quick to seize any common variables that two people might
have. "Three out of ten setups have resulted in marriage," she said.

What? You have two legs, a nose, and a mother? So does he!

Now I've done everything except remove the hot rollers from my hair
when our babysitter, a bubbling pepster of a girl, calls to tell me that she
can't come after all, that she dislocated her elbow while doing a back
handspring in gymnastics class.

"I have an ice pack," I say and then recognize the desperation in my
voice. I force a laugh. The girl is repeating what I just said to her mother.
"Of course I'm kidding," I say loudly when I hear her mother voicing
shock. "You tell your mother I was just kidding."

Our other sitter (also a high school senior) is at a *Cola Hour* being given
in her honor. I know because I declined the invitation with the excuse of a

previous engagement (I was still having trouble saying, "I have a date"). The party was being given by a circle of well-meaning matrons who never crossed the threshold leading from the nineteen-fifties to the sixties. A similar group of ladies had given *me* a Cola Hour back when I was just out of college and thrilled to be getting married. At the time, the most important thing had been to get at least eight place settings of every pattern chosen down at the local department store.

"I want my fine china more than anything," the girl had recently told me, her forehead glazed in acne. "Our pattern is Eternal by Lenox." She said the words in a dreamy way, a hypnotic way that suggested she wouldn't wake up until that first time she found her Eternal on the top shelf coated in dust. The happy ending comes if she can look at the dishes and laugh, and wonder why young couples don't ask for something like a washer and dryer, a car battery that never dies. If the dishes strike some distant unfulfilled yearning, then the future may not be so bright. I told her I also had picked a pattern by Lenox: Solitaire. She had squealed and clapped her hands. She knew my pattern. It had been one of her early considerations.

I call Sarah, who is responsible for this date in the first place, but there's just the cute little message on her machine, Sarah and hubby singing "Hey Ho Nobody Home." I hang up and dial the blind date's number, my mind void of pictures as the ring sounds in some unknown house/apartment/condo while some unknown man is stepping from the shower or pulling up his socks (cotton? nylon? black? white?) or driving to pick up his blind date. His machine answers but says nothing at all, just beeps.

"You be the giant," Jeffrey says, a rolled-up newspaper in his hand. "I'm gonna knock you out and steal the golden chicken."

"Fe, fi, fo, fum," I say for the hundredth time today and go stand on the hope chest (the giant's castle) at the foot of my bed. It's only been two years since I pulled that last brand-new set of wedding sheets from the chest. Now I use it as a storage place for cast-offs: baby blankets and squeaker toys, the hunting knife and heavy flannel shirt Nick forgot to pack. I'm thinking I'd like to climb in the chest and ignore the fact that any minute a complete stranger will be at my door.

Now Jeffrey is pretending to climb, head tilted back as he stares up at me. He's swinging a small tree limb he somehow smuggled into the house. "On guard!" He points to a stain on the carpet and says it's a crocodile. We've changed scripts just that fast. I'm Captain Hook and he's Peter Pan. I always get the sinister roles: witches and ogres and evil stepmothers. I give Snow White the poisoned apple and I make Sleeping Beauty touch the spindle and I talk Pinocchio out of going to school. I indulge my child's fantasy life despite the recent comments I've received about how this might not be healthy. My aunt Lenora has suggested that this is how he's (she leans close to whisper) *dealing with divorce*, these *violent* games.

Lenora is someone who got more education (one course here, another course there) than she could find room for in her head and has spent her whole adult life deleting whatever doesn't match her own opinion. "Give me a weekend and I could straighten him out," Lenora once told my mother, to which my mother simply replied, *Oh dear.* Lenora's own son has chosen a sort of evangelical route (having driven away a perfectly normal wife) and now spends his weekends in front of the Family Dollar store, handing out the religious poetry that he spent the rest of the week composing. I have always wanted to tell Lenora to go to hell. I can tell that, more than anything, my dear peace-loving mother wants to say, "Lenora, go to hell." But out of kinship or some distant childhood love, she just says things like, "Oh really, Lenora, he's just a little boy."

Still, in spite of my mother's loyalty, Lenora has planted the seed, and doubts are beginning to flourish. Just the other day my mother turned, her eyes narrowed in Lenora fashion, and said, "Doesn't it bother you that you always get the *negative* parts? You know, do you ever wonder if Jeffrey blames you, if he sees you as the *antagonist*?" That was Lenora's word for sure. Lenora had once made it perfectly clear that though Nick had left me, she thought I was the one to blame. *A man who is not well cared for will up and leave.*

I am being devoured by the crocodile when the doorbell rings. Jeffrey gets there first, his Ninja Turtle headgear in place. Phil is tall and fresh-looking, crisp as a stalk of celery. He extends his hand in a firm and cool shake and steps inside, navy wool socks and loafers, khakis and an oxford cloth shirt, narrow knit tie, circular brown frame glasses; he's the kind of man I always wanted to date in college, the kind of man Nick would size up quickly as a snob, a prep, a wimp. His eyes fix on me only a second and then he is looking around the room at the trophies and pictures and videotapes strewn about on the floor. I turn and catch a glimpse of myself in the hall mirror and quickly reach to pull the hot rollers from my hair.

"Sorry," I say and he looks at the rollers, nods and smiles; he thinks I'm apologizing for my hair. "But I don't have a sitter. She had an accident at school. There was just no way to get anyone else."

"Oh." He looks at Jeffrey, then looks back at me and shrugs. "So, we'll all go." He is wearing some kind of cologne which I don't recognize; Nick always said cologne was for somebody with something to hide. I'm not sure what else he is hiding but any disappointment is covered well.

"Yeah! Let's go. Let's go." Jeffrey runs and pulls his jacket from the low hook by the stairs.

"Are you sure?" I ask and he nods again. He is freshly shaven and not a scratch on his face. He looks like someone (a good guy or prince) out of one

of Jeffrey's books; I keep expecting him to turn to the side and become the
flat straight edge of a picture page or maybe just blow away and join the
ankle-deep leaves as we walk through the yard. "Fee, fi, fo, fum," Jeffrey is
saying as he crawls into the back seat. Phil holds open my door and I get in.
When I look at my house, porch light and living room light on, I have an
odd sense of guilt, like I'm breaking a rule or a law. It feels like *I'm* the one
running away from home, only it's not so easy with a thirty-four-pound
walking, talking superhero.

I imagine Phil had planned to take me somewhere else, maybe the tiny
dark Greek restaurant on the other side of town, a place for couples and
whispers. I imagine that with Jeffrey in the back, bumping against the seat
in beat with his rendition of "Fee, fi, fo, fum," that Phil has thought better
of disrupting that quiet dark meeting place for lovers and has made a quick
turn into Captain Buck's Family Seahouse. And so here we are, nets on the
ceiling and all furniture vinylized. I stir my iced tea round and round, the
red plastic tumbler wet against my hand.

"Rather violent, isn't it?" Phil asks, and I jerk to attention, certain that
he has seen my thoughts, my recounting of the final legal session that
granted me divorce and child custody. For a single dollar (truly a rare
bargain) I could have bought back my maiden name but declined since
Jeffrey was stuck with the married one. Phil is talking about Hansel and
Gretel and the way Jeffrey has delivered it, the mean ugly witch pushed
into the oven and gassed, charred to a crisp. I don't tell how many times in
the past week I've sat in the pantry, cackling and then screaming at the
victorious Hansel.

"It's the same old story," I say and nod when Jeffrey asks to go and look
at the aquarium on the far wall, a huge tank with glowing tropical fish. I
watch him dash through the restaurant, barely missing a waitress with a
tray piled high with fried food, oysters, shrimp, or clams, they all look the
same with the thick golden batter, *calabash style* it is called. "I mean, when I
was a kid, the witch landed in the oven."

"Yeah," Phil says and glances around, his fingers clasped loosely on
the grease-shined oilcloth. "I guess you're right, but they are horrible
stories, aren't they?"

"I don't know." I take a sip of tea and stare at the menu. Other than
today's special broil, everything is fried; the question is how much fried
can you take—small, medium, large, or deluxe? I can't imagine that Phil
will order anything fried; I can't imagine that he's ever even been here
before. "There are bad things that happen all over; why should fairy tales
be excluded?" Phil is studying me and with his cool glance, I hear Sarah,
the final advice/reprimand/instructions for this date: *Don't get all serious or*

maudlin, you know? The guy has never had kids so don't talk about Jeffrey the whole time and for God's sake don't talk about how the world is going to hell. Easy for her to say since her little *hey ho* world is not.

"What I mean is—" I force a laugh. "Well, it's just easy for things to go too far in either direction." And I begin telling him about taking Jeffrey to see a little production of "Jack and the Beanstalk," where the story was not even recognizable. The giant, instead of falling to his death, climbs from the beanstalk and upon reaching the bottom is struck with amnesia and becomes a big-time land developer while poor Jack the hero fights the infiltration of shopping malls. I had taken Jeffrey straight home and read him the *real* version. Then we spent the rest of the evening with me falling to my earth-shattering death from the cedar chest.

Phil nods and it looks as if he might want to compliment this new version of "Jack and the Beanstalk" when up walks our waitress with Jeffrey right behind her. "I thought he must belong to you," she says when Jeffrey crawls up beside me. "He's having a time with those fish." The waitress is probably right out of college, probably spending a care-free summer before graduate school or career planning. Her face is smooth as silk, her gestures animated as she stands there in her black stretch pants and nautical top. "Now what can I get you?" she asks, and I watch Phil take her in, from the wild dark tresses to the tiny white sneakers. He smiles at her and orders the broiled flounder. I ask if I can get boiled shrimp *just like it would be in the shrimp cocktail only bigger*, and she has to go to the kitchen and ask. Jeffrey realizes for the first time that the fish that swim around in aquariums or talk, like in *The Little Mermaid*, could just as easily be the fish that get eaten, so we finally settle on a hamburger.

"Haven't read any cow stories, I guess," Phil says and he and the waitress grin at each other. They have met before, it seems; it was at a big New Year's party hosted by a friend of his who is a relative of hers.

"You were about to go to France, I believe," he says, and she turns, her side to me as she talks to Phil.

"I went," she says. "It was great. Better than what I'm doing now, which is applying to law schools. How about you, still pushing computers?" Phil laughs and leans back in his chair. He is relaxed and amused.

"Small world, isn't it a small world?" they both keep saying and looking to me for confirmation. Yes, I say. Yes it is a small world.

"So," Phil and I both say when our waitress leaves us in a wake of silence. We go back to the one topic of conversation that is safe and certain, Sarah and Dave, the friends who arranged this date. I barely know Dave and he barely knows Sarah, but it is enough to get by. I tell him that I've known Sarah ever since I moved here, that our classrooms at the junior high are next door to each other. I met her in the parking lot the day I went for my interview. He keeps waiting, face animated as he anticipates some cute anecdote of it all: Sarah and I collide and our purses spill and our papers blow away or maybe I slip on a banana peel and land on the hood of her car. But nothing. It was a simple meeting where I said that I had grown up just thirty miles away and now my husband had been transferred here to oversee the construction of a new subdivision. Phil, it turns out, set up the computer system for Dave's podiatry clinic.

"I asked him," Phil says, our waitress within earshot, "why you'd ever choose feet for a living." Both of them burst out laughing, and I laugh out of beat, a little too late.

"So," Phil says when Betsy (the waitress) disappears behind the big bubbling aquarium. "I kind of like that new 'Jack and the Beanstalk.' "

"But what's next?" I ask. I look at him and keep thinking the words *perfect* and *manicured*. He is as clean and neat as a putting green, his fingernails rounded and filed to outline the balls of the fingers. I catch myself enjoying the clean brisk smell of his cologne, admiring the smoothness of his face. "How about," I say and take a sip of my tea, "if the evil witch in 'Hansel and Gretel' joins a support group?"

He laughs. "Then there's a spinoff group for daughters and sons of witches."

"The queen in 'Snow White' becomes a nice grandmotherly type?"

"It could happen," he says. I can't tell if his jolly mood is simply a part of him or spurred by his contact with Betsy. He's taking his time with his food, planning to stay awhile, it seems. Our booth looks out over the parking lot and the bypass. Jeffrey's face is pressed against the glass as he looks through the reflection of the room (a group of loud-talking middle-aged women behind us) and into the night. Heat spreads from his plump fingers, fogging the window.

An unbearable silence falls again (we've run out of cute ways to rehabilitate the evil characters), and it's difficult *not* to listen to the four women sitting across from us, their heads ringed in cigarette smoke as they pick through their mounds of batter and fries. They have already agreed at great length that anyone who burns the flag should receive the death penalty; they cannot imagine such a desecration happening, being *allowed* to happen in this country. "Let them just move in with the Communists," one of them is saying. "Just get out of our country if you disagree." I feel my chest tightening, my need to scream rising. Rewrite the fairy tales *and* the Constitution, I want to yell, go for the Gettysburg Address. Rewrite the Bible. I feel my grip tightening on my fork and I have that urge to drive it into the table, each tine sinking through the oilcloth with a pop. The Klan marches sixty miles from here. A five-year-old gets raped in a department store. There's about to be a war. Marriages fall apart like worn-out seams, and children's hearts get ripped along the edges where the threads won't give, and all you can talk about is a piece of cloth, a star-spangled *symbol*. If you burn your marriage certificate are you still married? If you burn your birth certificate are you still alive? If you lose your divorce papers is the decree null and void? Are you sentenced to return to that failed life?

I realize I've diced my food to bits but Phil doesn't notice; he smiles at Betsy as she fills the glasses of the women close by and then watches as she moves back towards the kitchen. Now the women are discussing with great fury the *hideous atrocity* which I soon figure out is Roseanne Barr and her rendition of the "National Anthem."

"Baseball, baseball," Jeffrey says and clicks his spoon against his milk glass, his voice an echo to one of the women who has told *where* it all took place. Phil raises his hand to Betsy and points to his empty water glass. She grins and steps out from the waitress station—a dark hall with a pay phone and a driftwood sculpture. Her stomach shows smooth and white as she reaches for the water pitcher. Phil is noticing, too. I hand Jeffrey a tissue and shake my head firmly, but he just laughs and goes back to what he was doing.

"Nose stuff," Jeffrey says when I shake my head again and pull his hand away. Betsy wrinkles her nose in disgust and then gives me a sympathetic smile, fills Phil's glass. "Ooh yuk," Jeffrey adds, and I encourage him to finish his meal or sit quietly, to count the cars that pass on the bypass, to see if he can name all seven dwarfs, all seven Von Trapp children, the past fifteen presidents, all the states and their capitals.

"She grabbed herself you know where," one of the women nearby says, while Phil and the waitress share a laugh. I feel the room closing in, the air getting thick. Phil is still looking at Betsy. He looks like he's in a trance, like the Prince when Cinderella enters the ballroom, the Prince when he finds Snow White in her glass coffin, the Prince when he makes his way to Sleeping Beauty's bedside.

"Crotch," I say and swing around to face the table of women. The volume of my voice surprises me and Phil sits back, knife raised. "She grabbed her crotch." I shake my fork with each word. "It is a common gesture in baseball. Men have been doing it for years."

"Well, it was disgusting," the woman continues and turns from me as if I weren't present. Her friends all nod, cheeks bulging with calabash goulash. "A man has to do that." She receives another round of nods and turns back to me. I feel Jeffrey slipping down to the floor of the booth and crawling past my legs. I feel helpless to stop him. "A man has to adjust hisself and it's not nice for the world to take notice."

"That's right," another swallows and says. "He can't go excusing himself each time he needs to adjust." Jeffrey has gone back to his spot by the aquarium now. His mouth is moving in mimicry of the fish. "Men have different needs. They always have."

"Well, what if I *need* to adjust myself?" I ask. "What if I have to keep adjusting my breasts all the time? Let's just say that I can't keep them properly housed inside my bra. What if my butt cheeks just will not stay in place?"

"Well, I *never*."

"I think we'll have the check," Phil says. The tips of his shiny ears are crimson. I watch Jeffrey, whose face is pressed against the aquarium glass on the opposite side. From here he looks immersed and misshapen, his face long and wavy. "Yo, fish," he says and licks the glass. Phil is watching me, his eyes pleading that I just let it all drop, while the table of women wait for me to make my move. Betsy has dashed off swiftly to Phil's rescue, her fingers rapidly figuring the bill for a hamburger barely touched and a plate full of mutilated shrimp I have rolled over and over in a cocktail sauce bath. My heart races as I watch Jeffrey twirling in the drapes. Betsy has signed the tab, "Have a wonderful evening. Come again soon!" in large rambling script, the loops of her letters as open as her young face. Phil smiles and hands her two twenties. He'll be back all right. There is electricity enough to light the building. She will give him excitement. He will give her stability. They will give each other warmth in a dark room.

I excuse myself to go untwist Jeffrey from the drapes. The women turn and watch, still expecting something from me. I want to swing around and grab my crotch but I keep walking, my hands reaching for my baby, his face and hands sticky with catsup. He says that the witch was behind the drapes and now he has got her locked in the oven and it's just a matter of time. The witch must burn. I pull him over to the door of the restaurant and wait for Phil, who is writing on what looks like a business card. He carefully tucks the card in his coat pocket and, after nodding to the table of women, joins me. I avoid looking at him for the time being. I know that I will apologize, that I will say *thank you for the meal*, that I will offer to pay for Jeffrey's, but for the moment I feel paralyzed. There is a sign in Uncle Buck's window advertising a Thanksgiving special and I toy with the thought of calabash-style turkey.

As soon as I step outside I feel sick, a cool sweat breaking out on my face and neck. I'd rather stretch out full length on the sidewalk and slip into a coma than to get in this man's car and try to carry on a conversation. Against my better judgment, I ease down and sit on the curb, head between my knees. Jeffrey spins around, a fake sword drawn and splitting the air. "I am Arthur! I am Arthur," he says. "I pulled this sword from that stone!"

"Are you okay?" Phil asks and after a few awkward moments, his feet shuffling beside me, he sits. He reaches inside his coat as if checking his pocket and then, reassured, he clasps his cool hands on his knees. "Dave told me you haven't had an easy year." I turn, startled. He is showing genuine concern. He has a pot on his back burner, a slow simmer of a phone number and so it's easier to be kind. I know that feeling; I remember it well. It seems I had more friends than I had ever had when I decided to get married just because I felt so confident that I had something. It wasn't threatening for me to be kind to someone. I didn't have to worry about what I'd do if that person took it the wrong way or wanted more from me, *I'm engaged*, or *I'm married*, that's all I had to say. For years, that's all I had to say, didn't even need to say it, it was obvious. And now that I'm single, legally free, everything seems threatening. I feel myself losing control, about to cry at this totally inconvenient moment.

"See if you can spin around like that again, Sir Arthur, see if you can count to twenty," Phil says, somehow knowing I need the extra time to get myself together.

"I'm sorry the night hasn't been more fun," he says.

"Well, it's not *your* fault." I force a laugh. "I'm certainly not the best company to keep."

"We all have our turns," he says and stands, offers me a hand. "Some of us abuse old women in seafood joints." He pulls me up.

"And some of us pick up young waitresses."

"You noticed," he says. I nod, reach for Jeffrey's hand, and pull him along. Phil apologizes over and over on the ride home but I tell him there's no reason. I shake his cool hand and thank him for dinner. I imagine his picture ripped from a storybook—a two-dimensional prince—as he stands and waits for us to get inside. I turn the lock as Jeffrey bounds down the hall to his room. He names a dwarf each time he slaps his hand against the wall.

I'm sure Phil will drive back to the restaurant or to a phone booth, little card clutched in his hand. He will certainly call Betsy within the next twenty-four hours. She is just starting out, probably uses plastic milk crates to support her bed, a soft mattress draped with mis-matched sheets and pillows. She doesn't trip over Ninja Turtles and Weebles in the middle of the night if she can't sleep and has to get up and walk around for a while. She doesn't feel herself needing to stick her head in the freezer and count to fifty. She's still waiting to begin, waiting to choose her patterns. There's no slate to wipe clean, no fears about having done (or doing) *irreparable damage to a young psyche*, and not just *a* young psyche, but *the* young psyche, *the* person you love more than anyone else on earth, the person who turns your mistake into something you wouldn't change.

It is very late when I hear Jeffrey get up. The night light glows behind him, and he looks so small as he scampers down the dark hallway to my room. Twice I have awakened to find him standing there staring at me, his hands on the edge of the mattress.

"Mom?" He is beside my bed now, his hand full of leftover candy from Halloween. "Who was that man?"

"Just a friend of Sarah's," I say, and he is totally satisfied with that answer. His trust in me is complete. If it weren't, he'd never give me the *bad* parts to act out. And what's wrong with acting out the bad parts? What's wrong with Jack getting rid of the giant? And why shouldn't Hansel and Gretel kill the witch in self-defense? Hooray for Dorothy, the wicked witch is dead. Then you just turn the page and start all over.

"You want to hear a story?" he whispers.

"Sure," I say. He crawls up, his breath like candy corn.

"It's a scary one."

"Scarier than 'Hansel and Gretel'?" I ask and he nods, moves in closer.

"This is about 'The Three Billy Goats Gruff,' " he says and begins, his voice a rapid whisper, his heart beating quickly each time he says *trip trap trip trap trip trap* and describes the old troll who threatens to eat the goats.

"Are you scared?" he asks, his sticky hand groping to find my face.

"A little," I say. "Are you?"

"Oh, no." He wiggles in closer. "I'm the biggest billy goat of all." His breath quickens as he repeats the verse, hand clutching my arm. I close my eyes and hug him tighter. *Who goes there? Trip trap trip trap trip trap.* I imagine a postcard scene, cartoon-green grass and a brilliant blue sky. Now all we have to do is cross the bridge.

ALL STRAPPED IN ●

sue thomas

IT DEPENDS UPON which direction you look. I can see quite a lot from here, but I still have to turn my head slightly in order to take in the full picture. I don't want to be seen to be staring however—I'm not a naturally nosy person—so I'm restricted to eye-movements rather than to turns of the head.

To readers of body-language I must appear to be pretty relaxed. I'm slumped in my seat so that my head rests upright on the back of the bench, allowing for a forward, rather than a skyward, view; and my spine sinks comfortably into the curved green slats. I have a magazine on my lap, and I'm holding down the pages with both hands because there's a slight breeze. I've read the Agony Column—nothing for me there—and now I'm reading the recipes.

If I look up from my magazine and gaze straight ahead I can see a wide expanse of grass dotted with small children running and playing. Beyond them, parents line the periphery of the paddling pool, seated like sentinels on a row of benches which face away from me, towards the water. In its shallow center there is a miniature light-house. It works. It lights up. And a little plastic keeper leans on the uppermost balcony. At his back, the miniature light spins, but the figure is fixed and cannot see it. Instead, he keeps watch over an ocean of grass. Has he noticed me, I wonder, run aground on this bench?

Behind the pool there are a few trees, mostly deciduous so very green at this time of year, and then the sky. Blue, with a few white puffy clouds.

There's an awful lot of it too, so much that I feel more comfortable looking for the edges.

I turn my head to find the sun, and a man comes into my line of vision. It's nearly twelve o'clock on a Thursday, and we women of the benches are not happy about a lone man wandering in the park at this time of day. As he crosses the grass he leaves behind him a wake of hastily re-formed groups—mothers calling in their children on a pretext of snacks. All eyes are upon him. We just need to check him out, then things will go back to normal again. Just natural cautiousness, that's all.

He is walking directly towards me, and even though I'm looking at the sun I don't wish him to think that he is the object of my stare, so I go back to my magazine—except, of course, I don't. I pull some sunglasses out of my bag and put them on so that I can keep an eye on him in safety. Head lowered towards the page, but eyes raised behind the glasses, I watch him. Now that I'm wearing the glasses he doesn't know that he has a spectator.

He's reached the gravel path now, and I can see him quite clearly. Let me tell you. I'll have to be quick though, because the muscles of my eyes are beginning to ache with all this clandestine movement. He has straight brown hair, and it's quite long. It kinks against his collar at the back, but at the front it has receded badly. He has heavy dark brows and he has obviously shaved very inefficiently, so that his face is streaked with darker patches of missed bristles.

He's wearing a white tee-shirt beneath a dark jacket, and faded jeans with the hems rolled up. His clothes are crumpled. The jacket is of soft cotton, deeply creased as though it has been recently confined to the bottom of a pile of laundry. The tee-shirt is clean, but the neck welt is coming away from the main body of the material and a long thread hangs from it. The jeans have no doubt kept company with the jacket in the laundry pile. I can't see his socks, but his running shoes were pale blue once.

The running shoes have come to a halt upon reaching the gravel, and above them he is looking southward then northward along the path. I cannot follow these directions because that would give the game away. I don't know if he has seen what he expects to see, but he saunters over and sits down on the bench next along from mine. I turn a page. It's the first chapter of a holiday serial: *'Jennifer had always longed to go to the Greek islands. . . .'*

It hurts quite a lot—a sort of ribbon pain across the eyebrows—but I manage to take a sidelong glance at the man. He's looking up and down, and then at his watch. A clue! He must be waiting for someone. We shall have to find out who it is. Jennifer has only just boarded the charter jet, so there's plenty of time. She is settling into her place and fishing for the ends of her seat-belt.

Then wheels crunch along the path, coming from my right. (The man is seated on my left). I strain my eyes his way—he's standing up. My magazine nearly slides off my lap, but I grab it just in time. The wheels come nearer.

Of course, as you'd expect at this time of day, it's a child's buggy. It contains a small girl, two-ish I should guess, and it is pushed by a very pretty lady. Very pretty. She has short white-blonde hair and a white summer dress. The child's hair is the same color, but longer, falling over her shoulders onto a pair of highly colorful dungarees. Both have a milky pale skin which is almost translucent. They must, of course, be mother and daughter.

I'm afraid this man intends to bother them, and indeed, as they approach a shadow of apprehension crosses the woman's face. I prepare to speak up and defend her. But it seems that this won't be necessary, because as they pass in front of me I hear them both say hello. I still feel rather concerned however, because even though they've spoken in greeting their voices have no expression in them whatsoever.

Then—"Hello Annie!" I guess from his tone that he's addressing the child now. I'm still pretending to read so the only view I have is of the blue running shoes, ten pink toenails in white sandals, and four small rubberized wheels. The child's feet rest on the bar of the pushchair, but at the sound of his voice they scramble up and I guess that she is climbing out and up into her mother's arms.

I must see. I raise my head a fraction and meet two blue eyes staring over a delicate shoulder. Chocolate fingers smear the back of the white dress. The adults seem to be unaware of my presence, but the child is looking straight at me. I'm sure that she can see me through my dark glasses. Our eyes meet, so I smile hesitantly. No response.

The couple are talking now—I can't help but hear, they're so close to me. His words come high and fast, but her tone remains low and slow, as though she's speaking through a vacuum. Emotion has somehow been sucked out of her voice on its way through the larynx. I imagine that her diaphragm is tight with all those unspoken thoughts booming around in there.

They're using legal words now—access, injunction, care and control. Neutral ground. Maintenance.

With the rise of his voice the child's arms tighten, but the little blue eyes remain fixed on mine. The smile hasn't worked, so I try to pass comfort across the gap instead. I do it invisibly. I don't know if it has arrived, but her gaze still clings to mine while her arms and legs hang on to her mother, monkey-style.

Suddenly, she grips even tighter, and panic flies across to me like a stream of small shining daggers. He is saying "Are you going to come with Daddy for a little walk now?".

Her head is shaking "no;" her whole body is shaking "no," but her mother is saying "It's only for a little while. Just so that Daddy can see something of you."

The child's head is twisting about but her eyes remain anchored on mine even as she is untangled and passed across. He holds her in his arms, but she drops her hands to her side. She will not embrace him.

"Are you going to ride in your buggy?"

He murmurs in her ear and the little fists clench negatively, so he simply takes the handles of the chair and turns to leave. He will have to carry her. The blonde woman calls "See you soon, honey. See you at four o'clock."

Her voice is brittle, and I wonder at her facility for containment. She walks rapidly away across the grass.

All this time, the blue eyes have not left mine for a moment. She clings now to the other neck, the firm dark neck, but as they move away her gaze still holds on to mine. I wave bye-bye. It's all I can think of to do. But she doesn't wave back.

As I watch them walk away I hear another set of wheels on the gravel— this time, more familiar. Laurie is with them. He's scowling and I expect that as usual I am the source of his irritation. I guess right.

"You are so ridiculous you know," he complains. "I've had to sit for an hour watching you from the van. Anything could have happened—you could have had a fit—you could have been mugged—and then what would you have done? Eh?"

I shrug my one-sided shrug. I know it always drives him crazy. And it does.

"You just don't care do you? I should never have let you talk me into it. What did you expect to happen? That someone would come and sit next to you and start up a polite conversation? I was watching, so I'll tell you. People didn't even come within a mile of you. They walked the other way."

He thinks he can break through my obstinacy by hurting my feelings, but I've developed a thick skin against insults, and anyway, he's wrong this time.

"You're wrong" I retort, peering up at him from my bench. There was, after all, the little girl.

"Oh what's the use?" he sighs, bending over me. "Let's get you back into your chair."

He slides an arm underneath my legs, and another behind my back. He's wearing Old Spice today. As he lifts me up my weight falls onto him— I can't help it, I just flop. I can feel my breast pressing against his chest. No matter how many years I have endured this, I still cannot help but feel embarrassed. I suppose lots of women fantasize about being carried off by all sorts of anonymous young men, but they should try it some time. The romance soon wears off.

My head drops heavily onto his shoulder, and as he steadies himself before placing me in the chair I stare past his broad back at the park beyond. Coincidentally, a woman is just passing by, and for a split-second I gaze straight at her from my lop-sided position across the back of Laurie's neck. But the moment our eyes meet she turns her head away and passes on. I get a good view of the gravel, then the grass, then the gravel again, as Laurie pivots me into my chair. He has forgotten to straighten my skirt, but I am too shy to mention it.

When I am all strapped in and under his control once more, he lightens up.

"Would you like an ice-cream, Wonder Woman?"

I wouldn't mind. He pushes me over to the van, and parks me to one side while he goes to buy two ninety-nines. My neck has started to ache, so I twist it from side to side to flex it, and that's when I see the little girl again. She too is parked in her chair, next to an old blue Cortina. Her father is in the ice-cream line just ahead of Laurie.

When we receive our treats we eat them simultaneously, and we never break eye contact once, even though we both have the same problems of co-ordination and aim resulting in two very messy faces. Her dad gets out his hanky, Laurie reaches inside the van for an enormous roll of all-purpose tissue, and we both receive a lick and a promise.

Then she and her dad continue their period of legal access, a stroll around the park. This time when she is pushed away she smiles goodbye to me, and I smile back. Then Laurie says

"I've just got to pay a visit to the gents'. Won't be long. Here, read your magazine till I get back."

I wonder how Jennifer's getting on in Greece? I return to the beginning of Page Two —

'Jennifer, her pale hair glittering in the Mediterranean sunlight, stepped off the plane into the arms of her lover.'

The illustration shows a couple embracing. Her arms are tight about his waist and a ring sparkles on her finger, but instead of gazing into his handsome face she's staring over his shoulder and out of the page, straight at me. She has that look in her eyes, one I seem to recognize from somewhere, a prisoner's look, and you know it may be surprising but there are times when I really count my blessings.

Because no matter how tightly I'm strapped in, no matter how disabled and fettered I might seem, inside I am sovereign and light-house keeper of my own spirit. And my mind, and my dreams, fly as free as seagulls.

3

EMPOWERMENT, SELF-ESTEEM

. . . These seasons were like important and holy visitors and each sent its harbingers: pine cones open, pine cones closed, the smell of leaf rot, the smell of rain coming, crackling hair, lank hair, bushy hair, doors loose, doors tight, doors that won't shut at all, windowpanes covered with ice-hair, windowpanes covered with wet petals, windowpanes covered with yellow pollen, windowpanes pecked with sap gum. And our own skin had its cycles too: parched, sweaty, gritty, sun-burnt, soft.

The psyches and souls of women also have their own cycles and seasons of doing and solitude, running and staying, being involved and being removed, questing and resting, creating and incubating, being of the world, and returning to the soul place. As children and young girls, the instinctive nature notices all these phases and cycles. It hovers quite near us and we are aware and active at various intervals as we see fit.

from the chapter: "Homing: Returning To Oneself,
Sealskin, Soulskin," from *Women Who Run With the Wolves*

ORCHIDS TO YOU, DEAR ●

fiona cooper

SHE DREAMED OF FLOATING up the aisle in frothy white, to stand beside a dark-suited figure. He slipped a golden band onto her finger, but when she turned to look at him, his face was never clear. It was her favorite dream, but she knew enough to keep it to herself.

"We all have our gifts, and yours is The Brain, Hilary," her mother had told her firmly, guiding her away from dates and dances and the like. Home and school had worn her success like a prize rosette, and she trotted off to university with a stack of leather-bound prizes and dire warnings about hard work, early nights and regular meals.

She saw him at the first lecture, and thrilled at his cultured voice. Black-jacketed on the podium, he was on a different plane from the student body, silent and scribbling at his feet. Everybody liked Professor Harrison.

"Call me Mark," he urged her in tutorials. She had been rapt at his every phrase, pen ready to score out any word or even a comma in her essays to please him.

A matter of months later, he chose her to be his wife. He told her she was beautiful. Her mother sniffed throughout the service. Her eyes said *mutton that wants to be taken for lamb* and *my poor impressionable baby*. She took the first train home.

Hilary put it all behind her. For she loved his dapper brilliance—my husband the professor. And now her heart anticipated his every wish, eager to change the slightest gesture, for how could he be wrong?

She had given up her hard-earned scholarship to make a home for them—she couldn't do both! He kept her in touch with the academic world, and she rushed the housework to type his lectures. He was so considerate when she lost the baby a year later, overlooking that she had failed in giving him what the nurse reluctantly told her would have been a son. The doctor said there were not likely to be others, and he assured her it didn't matter, so she must be all his family. He suggested she develop an interest of her own, generously allowing her space for something else, when all her heart and mind was his forever and ever, amen.

She opted for a sculpture class. He had guided her expertly around the monuments of Greece and Italy, the summer after the baby. But he knew nothing of the practical techniques of modeling and carving. He cleared the summerhouse so she would have a studio, and gave her the only key. How good he was!

At the class she dabbled: a dog, a horse, a ballerina. Pretty enough. But the summerhouse was for something special. She would make a bust of *him*. Perhaps it would even go to the faculty building when he retired, and they could take the world trip he dreamed of. She found the finest clay, built a web of wires to spread it on, and sat breathless at her bench.

It was the first day of spring when she began. The early light was damp and fresh as the clay when she slipped the wedding band from her finger, putting it carefully on the shelf, where it could not be lost. All day she shaped and softened the clay to build the great orb of his skull, working her fingers and palms in the heavy stickiness. Oh, she should have paid more attention to him when they lay close; she should have absorbed the hollows and smoothness of his brow and learned him by heart. Her fingertips had only fluttered around him in butterfly ecstasy. Evening found her in despair at the crude grey mass. It was a mockery.

She swathed the thing in damp cloths and plastic, and went indoors to make his supper. It was astonishing to her that he came in and told her his day, as usual, forking his food and waving the fork to show her when he had been his most witty and amusing. As if it were any day. She watched each gesture, scoring on her memory the slight frown, the pursing of his lips, and noticing with irreverent shock, for the first time, that his chin was rounded and weak. But she only loved him more.

"Are you listening to me?" he demanded when she failed to laugh at the right point.

"Every word," she said.

"Funny little thing," he said indulgently, rising to fill her glass. "I never know what women really hear. Sometimes I think—everything. Sometimes you don't seem to take anything in."

"Oh, but I do," she said intensely, and he looked puzzled. It was not the sort of thing she usually said.

When he asked her about her day, over coffee, she was vague.

"All day in the summerhouse?" he teased her. "Soon you won't have time for the old man."

He felt uneasy when she smiled at this: he had expected her to defend him from his accusation of age. No matter.

"I'll be in my study," he told her, and moments later she heard the phone click, and his low voice and laughter. How dull he must find her, to rush off and talk to someone else. She sighed and scraped a little dry clay from under her nails, letting the words of her book flow over her eyes.

When he came to bed, hours later it seemed, she was wide awake. She turned to him, and held his face on their moonlit pillow. Well, he thought, caressing her, such passion. And he was tender, and he was mighty, fueled by an illicit afternoon with one of his students. She'd thrown herself at him, of course. And he'd had her. Right on the carpet by his desk.

His wife took him into her body, and her eyes glittered in the half-darkness. She was unmaking all her day's work, making love with him as if they'd never been together before. She ran her palms and fingertips hard over his skull with joy.

God, he felt young again! Did she suspect? Apparently not. He was confident, anyway, that his words could talk her out of any ill-feeling.

Next morning, she smiled at him over breakfast, drinking him in, for she must toil alone all day and bring him from the clay. She touched him before he left—brow, nose, cheeks, ears, chin, lips. She would not bathe away the smell of him, and slipped an overall over her bare skin.

She went to the summerhouse. Like a child who cannot bear to look at the cupboard where the witch might live, she stared past the bench and its mummified shape. She shivered, and pulled on a jumper. Her golden wedding band gleamed on the shelf.

Ready!

The head was not as bad as she had thought. But it was not good enough by half. His wise brow in life was shallower than she had molded, and she leveled the clay with her new wisdom. The temptation to pause here and perfect his eyes! But no. She massaged the brow, standing back, closing her eyes to recall him better.

Her thumbs pressed symmetrical eye sockets, and she slung a lump of clay for his nose, patting, sheering . . . stopping herself from too much detail just yet. Time for coffee and—she hated to admit it, for he hated her doing it—a cigarette. She felt giddy with the first intake of smoke, but suddenly saw how to make a whole of the face. She smoked slowly, gulped the cooling coffee, and crossed to the bench.

The sun was high in the sky, mist burned from the chill lawn, when she stopped again. The face was there down to the mouth, and she was uneasy. No doubt that it was him. And would be more so when she could steel herself to pinch out the little chin and make it weak.

Petulant.

The word waved across her mind like a banner.

But he was not! Her mother had been petulant, shaking her head over her wasted talents. But her mother had the same sort of chin. Horrible! Nevertheless the chin would have to be done, although it loomed under his adored face like a wart, a boil. Such a teenager, she scolded herself. So he has a . . . weak chin.

And it was surely only her memory of her mother that made it repulsive. She kept the cigarette between her lips as she fashioned the dreadful thing, and her eyes watered in the stream of smoke. She thought of the chin as a thing apart, and ran her thumbs down the fold of flesh to the short neck. And stood back.

She walked around it, trailing smoke in the sunbeams. It was uncannily like him. The chin was as much part of him as his keen eyes, and her face softened at the thought. Enough for the day and, good God, it would have to be fish and chips. Suddenly she was flustered—she could smell her unwashed body, she hadn't even combed her hair today. She locked the door and flew over the lawn to the house and shrilling telephone. Perhaps there would be time to cook, to bathe . . .

"I've been calling all afternoon," he told her, "There's a faculty dinner. I won't be back until late. Where were you?"

"In the summerhouse. I'm so sorry. It's all right. I haven't done any supper, anyway." Poor man, he must have been frantic.

He sounded mildly disapproving.

"You must take care of yourself! 'Bye now."

Then he smiled, and dialed the student hall of residence. What a good thing, how well it worked out. He approved her new hobby.

A bath. Supper. But she wouldn't have stopped had he not been coming home. She felt daring at the thought of bread and cheese and a glass of wine alone in the dark garden. She could just see the mute grey head from the deckchair under the tree.

At her sculpture class, she was tentatively shaping a block of soapstone into something decorative, but her mind was away in the summerhouse.

"Now, has anyone been working at home?" the tutor asked at lunchtime. She looked away. He knew very well who her husband was and always deferred a little to her. None of his damn business!

Someone had been making clay ashtrays and abstract plant pots. How nice.

"I understand you have a little studio," said the tutor.

She flushed, the little wife with the little studio.

"Oh, it's very primitive," she apologized, and described their scullery as if it had been converted. Let him picture her pottering in the improvised chaos of a damp, windowless room . . .

• • •

But, in the summerhouse, she became dissatisfied with the slow growth of clay. He deserved the clean lines of polished marble! She would ask the tutor to get her a block—let him think what he liked. She applied herself to what she had decided was a prototype.

Which left her free to make mistakes, overdo the set of his features, and she grinned at the strange yet familiar creature, disdainful nose, full lips and ridiculous chin. Really she need only make the tongue loll a little and it could grace the pillars of any medieval church. She added fanciful satyr's curls—he enjoyed a good life, she thought fondly, and patted the damp cloth over it. In the kitchen she was cordon bleu, to make up for the neglect of the other evening.

In the middle of a frustrating béchamel sauce, the phone rang. Curse it! "Not sculpting?" his voice was tender mockery. "Only with flour and cream." "I'll be late this evening—damned tutorials. They're all panicking. Don't worry. It'll be before midnight!"

She swallowed her disappointment and told him she loved him. Then tipped the curdled sauce down the sink. She would surprise him with a picnic, and packed a wicker basket, pedaling through the streets face aglow with anticipation at his surprise. She stole up the staircase to his room, where she had not been since she was one of his students. Then she had brought her essays to be approved, now it was herself and her pannier of delicacies. The sign on his door said *Engaged*, and she smiled as she crept up to the next landing, where she knew the keyhole window that over- looked his study. How many hours had she spent here, drinking him in. She perched in the alcove and looked down.

There was his dear head, bent close to a tousled blonde mop over a pile of papers. A red-nailed hand flicked over the words as he nodded. He was so conscientious. She settled her back against the stone. And the hard chill crept through her bones as her husband's hand crept into the blonde student's blouse and they both smiled. He stood and the blonde head moved down his body, the scarlet nails deftly worked his trousers loose. She was petrified, and looked frantically at his face. Every professor was likely to be approached towards finals . . . But her husband was grinning, eyes closed as he collapsed into his chair, with the blonde mane moving between his legs. A moment later, he was lying on the student, pumping away, head buried in her neck, her pale face in a semblance of ecstasy on the rug. She wanted to go, but was frozen. They finished, and his red lips curled in satisfaction as he watched the student assemble papers and books and leave. Only then did he zip himself up and reach for the telephone. Whoever it was did not answer. Suddenly she knew he was ringing her.

I'm on my way home, darling.

He brought her a spray of orchids. She found a vase—his mother's wedding gift—and put them in his study.

At the sculpture class she expressed a wish to carve in hard stone. But not marble.

"I'm not ready for that!" she smiled.

Some grainy stone. Stone that the rain would wash over and wear away. The tutor found her an old block from a ruined church and brought it to the house. She lugged it to her studio in a wheelbarrow. She set it on the bench and raised hammer and chisel. What the hell.

And what the hell when it was suppertime. She had blinds on the window and said she wouldn't be long when he knocked at the locked door. With satisfaction she noticed how her dear little hands were becoming calloused. He told her his day. She added the blonde student, and who knows how many others. Was this jealousy? How could it be, when she didn't want him any more? Oh, there was still sex, but what astonished her in a distant way was that he didn't notice any difference.

And then he was leaving for the Devon summer school. He kissed her and pressed a list of phone numbers and dates and times into her hand. Other years, she'd gone with him. This year, he didn't seem to mind.

She fitted out the summerhouse with a sleeping bag and a change of jeans. When she went to the house to have a bath she used the back staircase, and walked through the garden afterwards with dripping hair.

She dreamed of him hurtling along in an open roadster, smiling at a blonde head and two scarlet-nailed hands spinning the wheel, reckless on the deep-banked lanes near the summer school.

And every waking hour she chipped at the ugly block, sanded, scored, chiselled, gouged gaping eye sockets. When the phone rang first, she paused, then shrugged. There was no time to lose. The finished brow and eyes leered at her and she imagined a bacchanalian wreath twined in the wisped locks of his hair.

The blonde student woke early in Devon, and shifted under the sleeping weight of his arm. How old he looked! His eyelids were pallid and wrinkled, and his red mouth was slack. His eyelids flickered and he put his sour unshaven mouth to hers. She closed her eyes and told him he was wonderful.

The clay prototype lay in shadow at boot level, dried to the color of ash. She stared down on it from time to time. He would be back in a matter of days and there was much to do. The fleshy mouth hanging from heavy folds of stone. And the chin, his chin. She had it dribble with solid drops of wine. In the still evening, she cleansed her mouth with sips of ice-clear water in the shade of the tree where dusk-grey birds rattled to roost.

• • •

Red velvet curtains closed out the Devon night, and the bar was awash with the drunken summer school intelligentsia. He had found an ancient leather wine-pouch and was boasting that he could drain it dry. His mouth stretched as he aimed the thin jet down his throat amid clapping and stamping. *Helluva fella!* they shouted as he thumped into the chair beside the student, one hand gripping round her shoulder, the other smearing red drops from lips and chin.

In her dream, they were still careering along the road. She floated above and ahead of them, and her eyes narrowed onto a shimmer of water at a hairpin bend. She swooped down and trailed her fingertips along the surface. Deep and cool, deep and cool. She smiled as she woke.

On the fifth day, she was almost done. Not quite. She paced around her gargoyle. The mouth. That pouting self-pleasure. She crumbled a slit between the lips, and knocked in broken teeth. Suddenly, she knew it was finished.

There he was. In stone. Frozen forever, gargoyle satyr. She was done with him.

Turning her back, she weighed the hammer and smashed it into the centre of the clay skull at her feet. She pounded the thing to grey dust and swept it through the open summerhouse doors. She cleared every surface and made coffee. But something was not complete: on her shelf, the band of gold lay in dust. She picked it up between thumb and forefinger and strolled into the garden. It made a high arc, vanishing against the sun as she flung it as far as she could.

She dreamed that night of the car they were in, the open-top funtime roadster, plunging towards that treacherous bend. The blonde hit the brakes too late and the wheels cut and thrust into the water, screaming. The car bucked and lunged against the flowered banks, shaking the two of them loose like dolls as it turned over and over. She woke with the tortured sound of ripped metal flailing against earth and stones.

The sun rose on the sixth day. She was sitting on the sill of the summerhouse and when the phone rang, she was ready to answer it.

REALLY, *DOESN'T* CRIME ● PAY?

alice walker

(Myrna)

SEPTEMBER, 1961

page 118

I sit here by the window in a house with a thirty-year mortgage, writing in this notebook, looking down at my Helena Rubenstein hands . . . and why not? Since I am not a serious writer my nails need not be bitten off, my cuticles need not have jagged edges. I can indulge myself—my hands—in Herbessence nailsoak, polish, lotions, and creams. The result is a truly beautiful pair of hands: sweet-smelling, small, and soft. . . .

I lift them from the page where I have written the line "Really, *Doesn't* Crime Pay?" and send them seeking up my shirt front (it is a white and frilly shirt) and smoothly up the column of my throat, where gardenia scent floats beneath my hairline. If I should spread my arms and legs or whirl, just for an instant, the sweet smell of my body would be more than I could bear. But I fit into my new surroundings perfectly; like a jar of cold cream melting on a mirrored vanity shelf.

page 119

"I have a surprise for you," Ruel said, the first time he brought me here. And you know how sick he makes me now when he grins.

"What is it?" I asked, not caring in the least.

And that is how we drove up to the house. Four bedrooms and two toilets and a half.

"Isn't it a beauty?" he said, not touching me, but urging me out of the car with the phony enthusiasm of his voice.

"Yes," I said. It is "a beauty." Like new Southern houses everywhere. The bricks resemble cubes of raw meat; the roof presses down, a field hat made of iron. The windows are narrow, beady eyes; the aluminum glints. The yard is a long undressed wound, the few trees as bereft of foliage as hairpins stuck in a mud cake.

"Yes," I say, "it sure is a beauty." He beams, in his chill and reassured way. I am startled that he doesn't still wear some kind of military uniform. But no. He came home from Korea a hero, and a glutton for sweet smells.

"Here we can forget the past," he says.

page 120

We have moved in and bought new furniture. The place reeks of newness, the green walls turn me bilious. He stands behind me, his hands touching the edges of my hair. I pick up my hairbrush and brush his hands away. I have sweetened my body to such an extent that even he (especially he) may no longer touch it.

I do not want to forget the past; but I say "Yes," like a parrot. "We can forget the past here."

The past of course is Mordecai Rich, the man who, Ruel claims, caused my breakdown. The past is the night I tried to murder Ruel with one of his chain saws.

MAY, 1958

page 2

Mordecai Rich

Mordecai does not believe Ruel Johnson is my husband. "*That* old man," he says, in a mocking, cruel way.

"Ruel is not old," I say. "Looking old is just his way." Just as, I thought, looking young is your way, although you're probably not much younger than Ruel.

Maybe it is just that Mordecai is a vagabond, scribbling down impressions of the South, from no solid place, going to none . . . and Ruel has never left Hancock County, except once, when he gallantly went off to war. He claims travel broadened him, especially his two months of European leave. He married me because although my skin is brown he thinks I look like a Frenchwoman. Sometimes he tells me I look Oriental: Korean or Japanese. I console myself with this thought: My family tends to darken and darken as we get older. One day he may wake up in bed with a complete stranger.

"He works in the store," I say. "He also raises a hundred acres of peanuts." Which is surely success.

"That many," muses Mordecai.

It is not pride that makes me tell him what my husband does, is. It is a way I can tell him about myself.

page 4

Today Mordecai is back. He tells a funny/sad story about a man in town who could not move his wife. "He huffed and puffed," laughed Mordecai, "to no avail." Then one night as he was sneaking up to her bedroom he heard joyous cries. Rushing in he found his wife in the arms of another woman! The wife calmly dressed and began to pack her bags. The husband begged and pleaded. "Anything you want," he promised. "What *do* you want?" he pleaded. The wife began to chuckle and, laughing, left the house with her friend.

Now the husband gets drunk every day and wants an ordinance passed. He cannot say what the ordinance will be against, but that is what he buttonholes people to say: "I want a goddam ordinance passed!" People who know the story make jokes about him. They pity him and give him enough money to keep him drunk.

page 5

I think Mordecai Rich has about as much heart as a dirt-eating toad. Even when he makes me laugh I know that nobody ought to look on other people's confusion with that cold an eye.

"But that's what I am," he says, flipping through the pages of his scribble pad. "A cold eye. An eye looking for Beauty. An eye looking for Truth."

"Why don't you look for other things?" I want to know. "Like neither Truth nor Beauty, but places in people's lives where things have just slipped a good bit off the track."

"That's too vague," said Mordecai, frowning.

"So is Truth," I said. "Not to mention Beauty."

page 10

Ruel wants to know why "the skinny black tramp"—as he calls Mordecai—keeps hanging around. I made the mistake of telling him Mordecai is thinking of using our house as the setting for one of his Southern country stories.

"Mordecai is from the North," I said. "He never saw a wooden house with a toilet in the yard."

"Well maybe he better go back where he from," said Ruel, "and shit the way he's used to."

It's Ruel's pride that is hurt. He's ashamed of this house that seems perfectly adequate to me. One day we'll have a new house, he says, of brick, with a Japanese bath. How should I know why?

page 11

When I told Mordecai what Ruel said he smiled in that snake-eyed way he has and said, "Do *you* mind me hanging around?"

I didn't know what to say. I stammered something. Not because of his question but because he put his hand point-blank on my left nipple. He settled his other hand deep in my hair.

"I am married more thoroughly than a young boy like you could guess," I told him. But I don't expect that to stop him. Especially since the day he found out I wanted to be a writer myself.

It happened this way: I was writing in the grape arbor, on the ledge by the creek that is hidden from the house by trees. He was right in front of me before I could put my notebook away. He snatched it from me and began to read. What is worse, he read aloud. I was embarrassed to death.

"No wife of mine is going to embarrass me with a lot of foolish, vulgar stuff," Mordecai read. (This is Ruel's opinion of my writing.) *Every time he tells me how peculiar I am for wanting to write stories he brings up having a baby or going shopping, as if these things are the same. Just something to occupy my time.*

"If you have time on your hands," he said today, *"why don't you go shopping in that new store in town."*

I went. I bought six kinds of face cream, two eyebrow pencils, five nightgowns and a longhaired wig. Two contour sticks and a pot of gloss for my lips.

And all the while I was grieving over my last story. Outlined—which is as far as I take stories now—but dead in embryo. My hand stilled by cowardice, my heart the heart of a slave.

page 14

Of course Mordecai wanted to see the story. What did I have to lose?

"Flip over a few pages," I said. "It is the very skeleton of a story, but one that maybe someday I will write."

"The One-Legged Woman," Mordecai began to read aloud, then continued silently.

The characters are poor dairy farmers. One morning the husband is too hung over to do the milking. His wife does it and when she has finished the cows are frightened by thunder and stampede, trampling her. She is also hooked severely in one leg. Her husband is asleep and does not hear her cry out. Finally she drags herself home and wakes him up. He washes her wounds and begs her to forgive him. He does not go for a doctor because he is afraid the doctor will accuse him of being lazy and a drunk, undeserving of his good wife. He wants the doctor to respect him. The wife, understanding, goes along with this.

However, gangrene sets in and the doctor comes. He lectures the husband and amputates the leg of the wife. The wife lives and tries to forgive her husband for his weakness.

While she is ill the husband tries to show he loves her, but cannot look at the missing leg. When she is well he finds he can no longer make love to her. The wife, sensing his revulsion, understands her sacrifice was for nothing. She drags herself to the barn and hangs herself.

The husband, ashamed that anyone should know he was married to a one-legged woman, buries her himself and later tells everyone that she is visiting her mother.

While Mordecai was reading the story I looked out over the fields. If he says one good thing about what I've written, I promised myself, I will go to bed with him. (How else could I repay him? All I owned in any supply were my jars of cold cream!) As if he read my mind he sank down on the seat beside me and looked at me strangely.

"*You* think about things like this?" he asked.

He took me in his arms, right there in the grape arbor. "You sure do have a lot of heavy, sexy hair," he said, placing me gently on the ground. After that, a miracle happened. Under Mordecai's fingers my body opened like a flower and carefully bloomed. And it was strange as well as wonderful. For I don't think love had anything to do with this at all.

page 17

After that, Mordecai praised me for my intelligence, my sensitivity, the depth of the work he had seen—and naturally I showed him everything I had: old journals from high school, notebooks I kept hidden under tarpaulin in the barn, stories written on paper bags, on table napkins, even on shelf paper from over the sink. I am amazed—even more amazed than Mordecai—by the amount of stuff I have written. It is over twenty years' worth, and would fill, easily, a small shed.

"You must give these to me," Mordecai said finally, holding three notebooks he selected from the rather messy pile. "I will see if something can't be done with them. You could be another Zora Hurston—" he smiled—" another Simone de Beauvoir!"

Of course I am flattered. "Take it! Take it!" I cry. Already I see myself as he sees me. A famous authoress, miles away from Ruel, miles away from anybody. I am dressed in dungarees, my hands are a mess. I smell of sweat. I glow with happiness.

"How could such pretty brown fingers write such ugly, deep stuff?" Mordecai asks, kissing them.

page 20

For a week we deny each other nothing. If Ruel knows (how could he not know? His sheets are never fresh), he says nothing. I realize now that he never considered Mordecai a threat. Because Mordecai seems to have nothing to offer but his skinny self and his funny talk. I gloat over this knowledge. Now Ruel will find that I am not a womb without a brain that can be bought with Japanese bathtubs and shopping sprees. The moment of my deliverance is at hand!

page 24

Mordecai did not come today. I sit in the arbor writing down those words and my throat begins to close up. I am nearly strangled by my fear.

page 56

I have not noticed anything for weeks. Not Ruel, not the house. Everything whispers to me that Mordecai has forgotten me. Yesterday Ruel told me not to go into town and I said I wouldn't, for I have been hunting Mordecai up and down the streets. People look at me strangely, their glances slide off me in a peculiar way. It is as if they see something on my face that embarrasses them. Does everyone know about Mordecai and me? Does good loving show so soon? . . . But it is not soon. He has been gone already longer than I have known him.

page 61

Ruel tells me I act like my mind's asleep. It is asleep, of course. Nothing will wake it but a letter from Mordecai telling me to pack my bags and fly to New York.

page 65

If I could have read Mordecai's scribble pad I would know exactly what he thought of me. But now I realize he never once offered to show it to me, though he had a chance to read every serious thought I ever had. I'm afraid to know what he thought. I feel crippled, deformed. But if he ever wrote it down, that would make it true.

page 66

Today Ruel brought me in from the grape arbor, out of the rain. I didn't know it was raining. "Old folks like us might catch rheumatism if we don't be careful," he joked. I don't know what he means. I am thirty-two. He is forty. I never felt old before this month.

page 79

Ruel came up to bed last night and actually cried in my arms! He would give anything for a child, he says.
"Do you think we could have one?" he said.
"Sure," I said. "Why not?"
He began to kiss me and carry on about my goodness. I began to laugh. He became very angry, but finished what he started. He really does intend to have a child.

page 80

I must really think of something better to do than kill myself.

page 81

Ruel wants me to see a doctor about speeding up conception of the child.
"Will you go, honey?" he asks, like a beggar.
"Sure," I say. "Why not?"

page 82

Today at the doctor's office the magazine I was reading fell open at a story about a one-legged woman. They had a picture of her, drawn by someone who painted the cows orange and green, and painted the woman white, like a white cracker, with little slit-blue eyes. Not black and heavy like she was in the story I had in mind. But it is still my story, filled out and switched about as things are. The author is said to be Mordecai

Rich. They show a little picture of him on a back page. He looks severe and has grown a beard. And underneath his picture there is that same statement he made to me about going around looking for Truth.

They say his next book will be called "The Black Woman's Resistance to Creativity in the Arts."

page 86

Last night while Ruel snored on his side of the bed I washed the prints of his hands off my body. Then I plugged in one of his chain saws and tried to slice off his head. This failed because of the noise. Ruel woke up right in the nick of time.

page 95

The days pass in a haze that is not unpleasant. The doctors and nurses do not take me seriously. They fill me full of drugs and never even bother to lock the door. When I think of Ruel I think of the song the British sing: "Ruel Britannia"! I can even whistle it, or drum it with my fingers.

SEPTEMBER, 1961

page 218

People tell my husband all the time that I do not look crazy. I have been out for almost a year and he is beginning to believe them. Nights, he climbs on me with his slobber and his hope, cursing Mordecai Rich for messing up his life. I wonder if he feels our wills clashing in the dark. Sometimes I see the sparks fly inside my head. It is amazing how normal everything is.

page 223

The house still does not awaken to the pitter-patter of sweet little feet, because I religiously use the Pill. It is the only spot of humor in my entire day, when I am gulping that little yellow tablet and washing it down with soda pop or tea. Ruel spends long hours at the store and in the peanut field. He comes in sweaty, dirty, tired, and I wait for him smelling of Arpège, My Sin, Wind Song, and Jungle Gardenia. The women of the community feel sorry for him, to be married to such a fluff of nothing.

I wait, beautiful and perfect in every limb, cooking supper as if my life depended on it. Lying unresisting on his bed like a drowned body washed to shore. But he is not happy. For he knows now that I intend to do nothing but say yes until he is completely exhausted.

I go to the new shopping mall twice a day now; once in the morning and once in the afternoon, or at night. I buy hats I would not dream of wearing, or even owning. Dresses that are already on their way to Goodwill. Shoes that will go to mold and mildew in the cellar. And I keep the bottles of perfume, the skin softeners, the pots of gloss and eye shadow. I amuse myself painting my own face.

When he is quite, quite tired of me I will tell him how long I've relied on the security of the Pill. When I am quite, quite tired of the sweet, sweet smell of my body and the softness of these Helena Rubenstein hands I will leave him and this house. Leave them forever without once looking back.

STONE-EATING GIRL ●

meena alexander

WHEN I WAS SEVEN, my cousin Koshy gave me a pile of Bata shoe boxes. I do not know where he got them from—perhaps the shoe store in Kottayam; or perhaps he had brought them from as far away as Bangalore where he went to boarding school. Koshy's mother was my appa's second sister and so we had the Kozencheri house and our Kannadical grandparents in common. Each summer when I returned from Khartoum for my Kerala season, three to six months of each year, Koshy and I would meet. He taught me how to prick holes in the shoe boxes and set sprigs of lily leaf inside. Then he showed me how to cradle the fat pupae he helped me pick off leaf and stone and place them inside the shoe box.

I loved butterflies and even after Koshy returned to Bangalore, I would often spend my afternoons in Kozencheri picking the ugly, shapeless pupae off the leaves of white lilies and sequestering them in the shoe boxes. When the wings seeped out, frail and wet, I would set the creatures free. I stared hard as they rose in the air, trying to fix in my mind the first fluttering motions that held the living creatures vibrating in blue air, in sunlight that bathed the low hills of Kozencheri.

A child of seven, crouched on a rock by the well side, I tried to figure out what it might mean to be a dark incipient thing. Struggling now to recapture what I felt then, I set the imprecision of these words to a child's fluid thoughts. Did the ugly pupa know it would become a butterfly? Where did the butterfly part exist, when the plump thing clung to a leaf in the darkness of a shoe box? Was there some secret that sustained it? Where did my Khartoum life go when I was in Kozencheri or Tiruvella? And what of this life of rock and stone, under the thick green leaves of Kerala, when I was living in a desert land so far away? Where was I at any one time? What was I?

I was transported from Tiruvella to Khartoum and back again each year. Cupped in the silver capsule of a DC-7 Air India plane, I crossed the rough winds and covered more space than a freed butterfly could. But if the part of me from Tiruvella were not already there, in invisible incipience in Khartoum, how could I be me? What was I when I was not quite in one place, nor in another, just in midstream? Was I like that ugly pupa, unfit to see?

I dropped the thoughts in confusion, picked up a tiny round pebble, wiped it on my sleeve, and set it to my tongue. Then, giving a little gulp, I swallowed hard. Fortunately my guts didn't hurt. Swallowing that stone gave me a sense of comfort, of power even. I felt I was a child who could accomplish certain feats, sustain something hard and solid inside her. It was a month later that summer, when I went to amma's house in Tiruvella, that I first saw the stone-eating girl.

She was sitting quietly underneath a tree, in the way that people do, doing nothing much, not fiddling or anything with her sari pallu. An ordinary-looking chit of a thing, one might have said, except for the unnatural pallor of her skin—no, not that prized Kashmiri, film star color, not that. Rather the muddiness of it, as if like a sadhu, she had smeared mud over her flesh.

"Should smear herself in garlic paste, that's what," Chinna muttered under her breath, as she caught me staring at the girl.

"So what's she doing there? Why not sell vegetables or go to school? Showing off, that's what. And she'll end up with more than coal dust on her face. See those stones?"

That's when I got closer, and got a good look. I squatted right in front of her and stared hard. No doubt about it. Her cheeks were filled with something. Not boiled sweets, for she didn't smell of that rancid taste, nor tamarind balls. She stared right back, and opened her mouth, and rolled one out. It was a pebble all right. I held it in my palm and gazed at it. It was beige but so clear you could see all the veins in it, blue and crimson, tumbling over yet never snarling up, stone skin licked clean with the saliva from the girl's mouth.

"Theru."

She wanted it back. That was the only word she ever spoke to me. I put it back in her hand. It looked a bit like mine, her hand. I wanted to look at her more closely, for it struck me that perhaps I could smarten myself up, dress like her. Her sari looked finer than those Dacca cottons amma prized so. By its side, my frock, with the embroidery and special smocking on it, looked quite dull. I felt ashamed of the pink roses, tiny green leaves, knotty stalks, on the fine cotton, stitched in by the nuns in Tholaseri to raise funds for the new orphanage. Then it struck me I should try a few words, or even bolder put out a hand and touch the girl under the tree.

But Chinna yanked me away, raced me down the dirt road.

"Enough? Enough? Satisfied?" she seemed quite irate.

"What's her name then?"

"Name? Who can tell. She's a shameless thing."

"Shameless? Why?"

"Making an exhibition of herself like that. Mark me now. In a few hours that area around the tree will be filled with youths, drunkards, and not searching for garlic either."

I was dumbstruck, then recovered my wits.

"Your tooth hurts, is that it?"

Chinna nodded and popped a clove out onto her tongue to show me. She had been chewing it hard all the while. Then suddenly she tightened her grip on my elbow and yanked me back. It was just as well, for otherwise we might have been run over by a black Ambassador car.

Inside the black car sat a girl utterly erect. She wore a dark silk blouse and her hair was edged with two silver clips set with pearls in the pattern of jasmine flowers. I knew she had bought them in Kottayam. Now this was Vatsala, a distant cousin. Whenever she visited us, she wore pearls around her neck that clashed with the brocade borders to the elaborate pavade she preferred. Once she had held up the pearls and said in a high pitched voice: "They're from Tokyo you know."

I couldn't bear Vatsala. Her hair was always perfectly in place and the pearls that hung round her neck, brought all the way from Tokyo, had a pale pinkish gleam to them, like the inside of the love apple fruit. She wouldn't let me touch them, nor would she tell where she had bought her new chappals in rainbow colors that she flaunted so elegantly on her feet. I knew, though, that chappals like those wouldn't last long on my feet, what with all the outdoor running I did, but it did not prevent me from feeling a sharp pang of envy when I looked at her.

Now there was mud on my skirt and on Chinna's chatta from that car wheel, and now the tiny malnourished children of the cobbler who lived by the train tracks were forced to crouch in the dirt to avoid the speeding vehicle. When the black car was well out of sight, and we had pulled ourselves forward and moved on to the garlic seller, Chinna, patting down her garments, expressed her approval of Vatsala's posture: "Such a good girl, now you should be like that, Mol," but having spoken out in this way, her own skepticism got the better of her thoughts, and she turned back to the stone-eating girl. "She'll never be a shameless thing like that one out there!" Chinna stabbed her thumb in the direction of the stone-eating girl.

The Malayalam word for *shameless* that Chinna used was the strong form of the word, the slang, the street use, *perachathe*, as in shameless-mad, as in mad dog, rabid, bitch, bitches being rabid, rabid dogs being known as bitches. I did not dispute her use, I just took it in. Amma had also used the word, not once, but twice, much to my shock. I wondered how she might have learnt such words from the Misses Nicholson's school to which she had been sent at an early age. Once amma had pointed at me when she said "shameless" in that way, but I was consoled since it was not quite what she had meant. In other words, it was not that I was shameless, but that, had I persisted in refusing to put oil in my hair and wear my skirts at a decent length so that they covered my kneecaps in the heat of Khartoum, I would become perachathe. It was a word that was to take on more and more importance in my life. *At times it has seemed to me that the price for being perachathe—shameless—was to have one's mouth filled with stones and perhaps the reparation was to perform, in the theater of cruelty that is our lives, all our lives together, choosing stones, filling one's mouth with them, ejecting them through the miraculous gut we call the imagination.*

Whenever I work at something hard, she comes to me, the stone-eating girl. It makes no difference whether it's a poem or rice and sambar, cucumber sandwiches, a torn hem, or a paper that must be graded. Or sometimes when I stand fumbling for keys for the double locks we use in Manhattan—though of course two locks will do nothing to prevent intrepid ones who might use a blow torch on the door and cut through the wood facades and the flimsy metal innards.

She comes through the doors, through the windows, through the walls of this apartment, sometimes keeping her body utterly still, sometimes gesticulating, mouth always filled with the small pebbles I first saw her roll around on her tongue over three decades ago in Tiruvella.

She comes to me in dark garments that seem to have been pieced together with bits from a Sudanese woman's tob, a Tiruvella woman's sari damp with monsoon rain, a Nottingham woman's schmatte—though of course she would not call it that as she hurries out of the local church in Beeston, into the pub—a New York City woman's scarf bought from the Korean vendor on the sidewalk, it jams in the metal subway doors and she tugs it out. It floats out, squeaking like oiled gold. And somewhere in that garment, I think, is a bit of silk from my grandmother Kunju's wedding sari, a frail pearly tissue, the most expensive silk you could buy in those days, amma said. But amma doesn't know the stone-eating girl, at least I think not, and the bit is so tiny that it is quite covered over by some rough stuff that hangs over her shoulder.

But when the stone-eating girl descends the steps to the subway—she frequents the Broadway local in Manhattan—that silk bit makes a manic flitter of light that catches the eye of the vendor of *Street News*, the mad saxophonist with antennae in his head, plastic, sprayed with glitter, bobbling. She hunches over in her garments of many colors, the stone-eating girl, eyeing it all.

Now all this is rather different, this bits-and-pieces covering, from the way she was dressed when I first saw her in Tiruvella, underneath a tree. She was dressed in a faded sari, washed so many times and bleached with sun, that the threads hung apart, letting her thin bones filter through. Surely the cloth had been of indifferent quality to start with, but with repeated washings with a few shavings of the cheapest soap, much water, much pounding on rock, the fabric became frail, the threads floated about her body, and were held in at the edges only by the stout handloomed borders.

At night, I lay under the cool white sheets in Tiruvella, staring through the barred window at the moonlight that flooded the bamboo grove, spilling over the speckled leaves of the gooseberry tree. The moonlight put me in mind of her frail sari. Asleep, I dreamt of the fine stuff, almost as fine as air spiked with moonlight, covering my own flesh, turning me into a magical thing. The next morning I sought out Chinna. She was sweeping out the ash in the ash room, shooing away the black hens with her big broom. I tugged hard at her hand so she was forced to stop:

"So?"

"Stop. Sit." I was choked up with the thought of asking her, even though I knew Chinna so well. She had come to work for us when I was born. At one stage she was my ayah. Now her only duty, as far as I was concerned, was to give me weekly oil baths and supervise my appearance. The rest of the time she hung around in the kitchen area, making sure the stoves were swept out so the ash didn't choke up the new flames, making sure the black hens that we bred in our compound in such profusion hadn't deposited another horde of eggs in the hole in the wall where the wood-burning fire for the outer bathroom was placed.

She was also in charge of making sure we had enough spices in the kitchen. The morning we sighted the stone-eating girl, Chinna had been in a tizzy. She had run around in little circles in the kitchen, scratching her head. Bhaskaran for some weeks now had been in a state of confusion. It was not entirely clear what ailed him. In any case, he had neglected to ask the boy who was bringing the vegetables home from the market to add an extra slew of garlic. Fish pickle was being prepared that morning for which the shiny cloves of garlic were always needed in great abundance. Chinna invited me to go shopping with her, so we set off down the road by the railway tracks towards the garlic seller's stall.

A sharp scent emanated from Chinna's mouth as she squatted by me. "Toothache?" I asked, just to calm me down.

She smiled back: "Garlic."

"What about her sari?"

"Whose, mol?"

"That girl's, the stone-eating girl's."

She laughed out loud, and as the black hens squawked about us, and in the middle distance Bhaskaran led out Susheela the cow to pasture, Chinna launched into her story. It came out in fits and starts, for she had to finish up work in the ash room, set the firewood in place, and then, purely as an act of kindness to help the cook, she started skinning some carrots—tiny finger-sized things, hardly larger than a big green chili. I held my nose as she worked on them, for I hated carrots, their color, their tepid flavor, even though Chinna insisted carrots would keep me from having brain fever. So as I sat at her feet, staring away into the tapioca leaves in the distance, Chinna told me the long, involuted tale of the stone-eating girl's sari.

The stone-eating girl's sari was woven by a woman in Pondicherry, long since dead of the exhaustion that can strike a poor middle-aged woman who has borne too many children, who is forced to fend daily for food. The weaver, whom Chinna called Ratna, was forced out of her work as a weaver by the new Hakoba Mills. Ratna had to make do as best she could, with a little housecleaning here, a little floor washing there, a few morsels handed out to her in charity, a few green mangoes a brother-in-law from the countryside passed onto her, which she was able to sell for a pittance in the marketplace and use for rice and a single vegetable, augmented with a few chilis for the evening meal. Her older children did what they could in terms of hiring themselves out for odd jobs, but the young ones simply waited for their mother, their dark eyes open.

One night as she watched the rice boil on the earthenware stove, the out-of-work weaver felt the skin on her palms, the fine colorless skin countless threads had run over, starting to vibrate, as if all the looms she had ever touched were whirring in her flesh. I huddled close to Chinna's ankles as her voice rose with the tale of poor Ratna of the vibrating palms. At night, the vibration grew unbearable and the fatigue rose within Ratna, a fever in all her limbs till she could scarcely breathe. By morning her mouth hung loose, then grew rigid, her eyes turned sightless, fixed into an eternity nothing in her could claim. At dawn, the youngest child rolled over on her mother, touched the cold flesh, and sat up in shock, hollering. Before they cremated her in the burning grounds reserved for those who are too poor to be sung over by priests or plenipotentiaries, they covered the weaver in a sari of the finest cotton they could find in her poor hut. The flames licked the cotton and burnt it into the same ash as wood and skin and bone.

The stone-eating girl never knew this Ratna who had once woven her sari. The sari that the stone-eating girl wore was given to her by Gomati, one of Chinna's associates. Gomati worked as a maid for a rich lady who lived over the hill, half a mile from the railway tracks in Tiruvella, and late one afternoon she had tossed the sari into Gomati's lap, tossed it just like that, without a single word uttered.

The rich lady collected handlooms and textiles, handicrafts and icons of ancient wood—ebony and teak—that were carved into likenesses of the ferocious goddesses of death and sexual regeneration, Kalimata with her string of human skulls, and Mariamma whose spirit causes the smallpox to come and pit the soft cheeks of infants with its dark stars. The rich lady had a husband who believed in yearly pilgrimages to the Aurobindo ashram at Pondicherry to cleanse the spirit. He was of the opinion that the spirit had to be cleansed in much the same way as the body. He knew that yogis swallowed yards of tape that they drew out of the mouth again, after it had entered the gut, so cleansing out the lower intestines. But this upstanding businessman and estate owner, given to acidity in his tummy, could never conceive of such rigors and decided instead that a spiritual path, of periodic abnegation from things of the flesh, worked much better for him, was more cost-effective in any case, taking up only one week in the year. And the cool air from the Arabian Sea that blew him into the arms of a certain air hostess on the Indian Airlines flight to and from Pondicherry, could more than make up for the mortification of the flesh required in the ashram.

It was on one of these trips that he passed through the village where Ratna the weaver lived, and came upon her selling a few saris under the banyan tree. He jumped out of his taxi, pushed a few rupees into her hand and made off with a striped handloomed piece. On his return to Tiruvella, he draped it over his wife's plump shoulders, and loosening her hair in a fit of passion that took him by surprise, murmured, "Ah, Sariamma, Sariamol, Sarikochu, how startling you are, my exotic coo-coo-coo. Wear this, wear this, little moo-moo-moo." Whereupon she, not displeased, pushed his hands away with as much gentleness as she could muster, wondering how she could extricate herself in time for the ladies Sevikasamaj meeting that was to discuss the building of a clinic for the poor beggars in the district. She undressed though and hurriedly put on the handloomed sari, sprayed some Chanel No. 5 over it—her brother-in-law had brought it back from his latest trip to Geneva—and waddled out to the car. All the way to the meeting she ran her hands over the coarse cotton and despised herself for wearing the rough crude thing. At the earliest opportunity she passed it on to Gomati, the maid. Gomati, who was terrified that a curse might be attached to the sari, handed it over to the stone-eating girl, who happened to be passing by the gates of Satyam Vilas, the house where the rich lady lived. The stone-eating girl, who made a living in those days by selling okra and brinjal in the marketplace, was delighted to accept the sari. And by the time her obsession came upon her, that was the only sari she would wear.

When I saw her, sitting cross-legged in a pile of dirt by the railway tracks, wrapped in Ratna's woven sari, now frail and threadbare, she had given up her trade in vegetables and now concentrated on stones. Her skin, which had been the same color as mine, a darkish brown, had grown pale with dirt. Her lips had turned the same color as the earth in the dry season.

One of the tales I like best about the stone-eating girl came from a visiting social worker taking tea with Ilya and amma one afternoon. According to her, the government was at fault. In order to construct the new railway line, government officials had evicted the stone-eating girl from the hut where she lived. Hearing that, during the Nationalist movement to get rid of the British, satyagrahis protested by sitting in one place and refusing to eat, the girl took it upon herself to do likewise. It was then that in sheer hunger she started cramming mud in her mouth, then stones, and when the stones rolled round on her tongue, they satisfied some hunger she did not even know had possessed her.

Bit by bit, even in its satisfaction, the hunger grew, and the means to consume it turned into a stern discipline. Hearing this tale, my admiration blossomed. Once an ordinary girl-child like me, she had taught herself whatever skills she had, learnt to use them in her own way, and set herself up as her own authority so that in her unmitigated gluttony—strictly directed at small rocks and stones and soil—she became a female icon, creator of a stern discipline, perfector of an art.

It's much harder to eat stone than to eat fire. I've tried both after a fashion. Fire consumes substance and you have to be careful it doesn't burn up your tongue, but that's about it. Otherwise you can close your mouth over a small match flame without too much hardship. My cousin Koshy showed me how. It was the summer after I had met the stone-eating girl. He had bought two beedis off Thoma the woodcutter and sneaked them into the attic in the Kozencheri house. We lay curled up in a pile of cut rice that was drying out, husks and all, and he showed me how to eat fire. First light the beedi, and, when you stop coughing, pick up the burning match and pop it into your mouth. Poof, the fire goes out. "Fire-eating girl!" he sang out at me, the time I singed my tongue. And I was so pleased to hear him, I quickly hid the sharp pain in my mouth, or tried my best to.

Then I heard of the fire-eating girl who worked in the Gemini Circus in Cochin. She became my other heroine. When I returned to Tiruvella, for my Indian summers were divided between the Tiruvella house and the Kozencheri house, I asked Chinna for more information. She told me the fire-eating girl was once as fearful as anyone else and had kept water in her cheeks to wet down the flames she had to swallow. At first she emitted flames that were so weak she almost didn't make the grade as a circus fire-eater, though in due course she became world famous, best known in Dubai where a filmstrip with her act has been circulated.

Years later it was rumored that a group of our people, Malayalees in Oklahoma, had raised money to invite her to come and perform after their Pentecostal church service, as if the Holy Spirit they had learnt to revere in their stern churches in Kerala might, in spite of their years of comfortable North American life—backyards with barbecues, Barbie dolls with blonde hair, acrylic suits, pantyhose, refrigerators that popped out ice at the touch of a button, dollars made of gold that could be given away as part of a girl's dowry—be placated, eased into the body of a gaunt young woman dressed in ocher sari and gold slippers.

I still remember Chinna wiping her hands free of the ash she had swept up in the ash room where I often hid out, telling me that the fire-eating girl, the world renowned Kameshwari, had been invited to America. I'm sure she told me this to take my mind off the fact that Ilya was very ill and in great pain from his heart condition. Also Chinna was a little nervous that I admired the stone-eating girl far too much:

"The *Manorama* ran an ad saying so. 'World Renowned Fire-Eating Kameshwari Travels to America!' "

I listened to her, but said nothing. I hoped I didn't look as bored as I felt. I had already sorted all this out at least a year earlier. While it might be a good thing to start on the fire-eating path—a way to make people notice me, even make my strict Scottish schoolteacher in Unity High School, Khartoum, sit up and grip her skirts and those odd socks she wore in her heavy shoes, even clutch her beads in dismay—I found that in Tiruvella, which was the only place I could think of practicing my arts, I was unable to filch a single coal from the kitchen or from the pile where the cashews were roasted in the harvest season. For I was constantly circled by guardians: three ayahs, four maids, five cooks, a cowherd, a goatherd, a boy who ran errands, and amma in the middle distance sitting silently in a corner, taking tea with her one hundred and one cousins, who on the slightest hint of anything fiery approaching my mouth could be guaranteed to raise a hue and cry and come tearing down to the kitchen in her katau sari.

Even Ilya, whom I thought I could count on in a pinch—he was forever encouraging me to try all sorts of things—might draw the line when it came to fire-swallowing. Though once, right after my morning perusal of "Mandrake the Magician," the cartoon that ran on the back page of the newspaper, he had called me into his study where he was working on an essay about the social gospel. He gazed at me through his silver-rimmed glasses and when he saw me running my hands over the dark-colored wood of the shelf that held the books by the great bearded Russian Lev Tolstoy, friend of Rabindranath Tagore, inspirer of Gandhiji, he leant over and pulled out the book I had touched last. I saw a glorious woman in Russian clothing on the cover, her hair dark as coals, her eyes the color of burning fire. I touched her eyes with my thumbs, trying to touch the flame, trying to close those eyes.

"That's Anna," he said gently, and when he saw my bewilderment, for that was the name of my baby sister, he added "Karenina, Anna Karenina. She was married to a man called Karenin and they lived in Russia. A great, passionate woman. If you want to go away child, take it away, anywhere you want. Or sit here if you like, but read it, read Tolstoy's book."

I took it away and read it, cover to cover. I read it hidden high in the love apple tree. I was ten years old by then. I used to hide the book under my skirts as I raced past the well to the love apple tree, for I did not want Chinna or Marya or amma to see the coal-burning eyes of the Russian Anna. And the thoughts of passionate love driven to despair, of church bells and snow in Russia filled me. The night I finished the book and crept back to put it on Ilya's shelf, the sound of the train driving hard over the tracks from the Palghat Pass left me breathless, almost choking, for I saw in my dreams the eyes of the Russian Anna and her snowy neck flat over the rusty rails.

A high wind blew down from the Vindhya Mountains. I was eleven by then. It blew all night as Ilya lay dying. The foxes flew out of their holes, crept into the kitchen, took fire in their tails and all that bushy fox hair burnt till the bodies were nuggets of solid flame and the foxes could not escape alive, not even by jumping into rivers or wells.

Lying on his deathbed, he asked me for water, "Meena, Meenamol, theru, velam theru." I shut my eyes so tight. I turned away, choking. I could not bear his gaunt hand, his eye moistened with tears, the harshness that life made for him as he lay struggling to breathe. Night after night, he groaned, the iron tightness in his chest making the sound come out as if spikes from the lightening conductor on the prow of the Tiruvella house were poking out the eyes of the parrot fish Paulos the fisherman brought in, and the fish, still alive, squirmed in its basket as the unseen hand prodded in, with the metal thing, so tall and pointed and proud, that rode atop the house that Ilya built.

At eleven in the morning, I heard the death rattle in his throat. I hugged my ears with both my hands and bit my tongue so I should never speak again. I turned away, my heart a soiled stone. I wrap up that stone now, in paper, in sand. It shivers in my hand. I do not have the tongue to spell it out, or the gut to swallow it up.

I hurt amma too. She could not understand why I did not bring him water. "You used to do it Meena, so faithfully. You were such friends.

Remember all the games you played with Ilya?" Then she hung her head. But little Anna, my sister, came racing up, a glass in her hand, and passed the cool cup to Ilya as he struggled to sit up. It was Anna who helped amma put a spoon with a few drops of water into Ilya's mouth, while I stood staring, my back against the oxygen cylinder, that rusty red thing they had wheeled in to give him a little relief so he could breathe. There were the daily shots of morphine too, and long, interminable prayers to God the Father and the Son and Holy Ghost and no one knew that God had closed up his heaven and forced the fish to swarm out of the Pamba River and lie breathless against cold sand.

And in those days all that was in my eleven-year-old mind, and out of it, grew bleak and flat and dry like the white wall against his bed where Ilya's shadow lay, unmoving, as he suffered his last days into death. And it's all unmoving for me, that death, the funeral I refused to go to, locking myself in the bathroom and watching through the bars of the wooden window frame as they carried his coffin to the church.

I think it was in those days too, though perhaps the thought had arisen in me earlier, that I felt I must refuse life, become a stone, a hard unmoving thing, no motion in it, no force, neither hearing nor seeing. It seemed unbearable as the hot skies unfurled themselves, the morning after Ilya's death, that I should go on living, unbearable too, that we should all be creatures that are born into bodies and subject to death. It was a knowledge I could do nothing to alter. In dreams my whole body seemed to me, then, buried under a pile of rubble. And the powers of the stone-eating girl were very far from me.

THE RAW BRUNETTES ●

lorraine schein

The Rushing, Raging, Trembling Ones

A CLOCK CHIMED MIDNIGHT in a small room. Its walls were all black; heavy swagged black curtains lined the wall at the far end. A glimpse of crowded black-blue evening sky was visible through a parting, over a busy New York City street. The sound of a siren scarred the silence. On the worn red Oriental rug before the window, a little girl was playing with her dolls. She was undressing them, one by one, very carefully. There was a small tidy pile of black, minute dolls' clothes next to her, on the left side of the carpet.

"And now we take off the *panties*," she said firmly to herself, removing the doll's last article of clothing, a tiny pair of black underpants, sliding it carefully off the long smooth plastic limbs of the anatomically correct doll, folding it neatly and placing it atop the pile.

On the top of the doll's left thigh was a small black mark, whose shape was indiscernible unless one looked more closely. Then would come the understanding of what that doll was.

On the opposite side of the room across from the girl, a group of women was gathered, sitting in a semicircle on small chairs facing the fireplace. All the women had dark hair of varying shades.

A tall, elegantly dressed woman with long black hair plaited into a single braid that hung well past her waistline entered the room.

There was an immediate silence. Then, one of the women rose and said to her, "We seek the sign, Feral."

Ms. Feral Darkness walked over to the big red brocade wingchair by the fireplace, sat down and gazed at the others. Raising her hands above her head, she made the infamous dread hand signal of the Raw Brunettes, cupping the air in a spiral.

The chant was spoken by the women in unison:

> Burnt hearts of umber
> Black hearts of umber
> Have the Raw Brunettes
> We rend all hearts asunder.

The women all continued. "We are the first principle of the universe and the last. We abide by and follow the sacred doctrine of Gynochaotics."

And so began the regular Monday night meeting of the Raw Brunettes.

Chanting over, the meeting came to order. "The first item on our agenda," said Feral Darkness, "is the approaching Hectic Red."

"Oh, the Hectic Red!" said a small, chestnut-haired woman with elfin features sitting on the far side of the circle. "I can't wait!"

Feral smiled affectionately, "I know it will be your first time, my dear. But believe me, this will be something worth waiting for.

"The reason we are here today," she went on, "is to prepare – this time we must try to pick out the secrets of the approaching universe."

"With a lockpick?" asked Tawn.

"With a toothpick?" asked Pink, ingenuously.

Feral laughed and said, "Nonsense, my dears!" with an aristocratic sweep of her hand that brushed all of their suggestions away. "We must throw ourselves into the middle of it. Then its secrets will be ours – ready to be coaxed out."

"Teased out?" said Pink hopefully. Her Pinkness, her royal Pinkness, with her pink teased hair.

"Yes, your Pinkness," agreed Feral. "Teased out skillfully by you."

Pink smiled, blowing out a large wad of pink bubblegum into a delicate thin perfect globe, and popped it, accepting it back into her mouth between fuschia lips.

Pink Clutter was descended from a long matrilineal line of Raw Brunettes. But she was an albino, with dead white hair that was tinted pale fuschia, and pale eyes whose corneas had been chemically stained pink. Her clothes were orchidacious and gauzy, her jewelry plastic. Her edges were jagged; she was always pinking – in out in out in out. She zagged zigged, zagged zagged or zigged zigged – but never zig zagged, not in public.

"Hey, Pink, who have you roseated today?"

"No-one at all, no-one for days," said Pink, tears starting. Pink snuffled into her gilt-edged mauve handkerchief. "Wah," she wailed, and on a higher note, "Waaaah! I want my dolly!" Her doll, a 1962 brunette Barbie with a bubble cut streaked palest pink, was kept in a secret hiding place and only brought out to bribe her into using her special talents.

"Oh, Pink Pink darling Pink, don't cry." Pink Pink oh darling Pink. Most exquisite of the Raw Brunettes.

"We must vote on who will go, and who will be back-up now," said Feral. "Let's start with Alfalfa . . . who I see is missing again." Hands were raised, the decision was made, and plans were put into motion immediately. "Then that settles it," said Feral with satisfaction and adjourned the meeting.

The Raw Brunettes sometimes run through the night, howling in their secret language at the moon. Or they ride on their black motorcycles, dark tresses flayed by the night air, skirts hitched up to show the dreaded thigh-tattoo under their silver mesh stockings. They have their own asteroid, a black chunk of rock on the edge of the galaxy. It is said to be tunneled throughout with labyrinthin tunnels, accessible only to special passwords.

The entrance to the headquarters of the Raw Brunettes is shaped like a giant eye. Through the open pupil women stream. Then it slowly, flirtatiously lowers its long lashes, forming a spiky, barricaded gateway as it closes behind them.

In the city, the Raw Brunettes are much like ghosts. They have the powers granted to them by their Magic Handbags. They drink shadows and cast moonlight. Every woman in her way is a spy, a secret agent working for the Raw Brunettes. Spying on the present and on men, looking for the hidden information which men don't see, are unable to see, secrets to transmit back to the others. I'm a spy for the Raw Brunettes myself.

Any woman is potentially more dangerous and anarchist than any man to the status quo. Because she isn't really part of it.

> There's a girl who lives a life of danger
> Everyone she meets is like a stranger
> For every love she makes
> Another heart she breaks . . .
> Secret agent woman. . . .

The cult of the Raw Brunettes has existed since the dawn of time, under many different names and guises. Men cannot perceive it. It also exists in the future, and sends back its members to assist women in the present.

The Black Mirror

Feral is standing before the Black Mirror, the Magic Mirror. She is unloosing her hair. There is a long crack, scarlike, across its surface. It is the mirror of Time and the crack is the line of History.

She is fomenting, fomenting always. Every minute she commits a thought crime, carries out a successful psychic assassination. Though twilight has fallen like her lover's dark hair over the bare curved back of the city, she has given up telling people—impossible to have them believe it, even more impossible for them to understand it, the occult knowledge, and only hints at it without revealing, works by indirection instead.

She lights a dark cigarette, and gazes out of the window, where her women walk, unnoticed, below, where the moon has turned dark too; the sky, a brilliant corrosive white.

Below me my women lurk lurk lurk. Hooded cloaks drawn up against their faces, hair flailed into a cornucopia of wind. Furled. Black Lightning signals their approach.

> Black hearts of umber
> Black hearts of umber
> Have the Raw Brunettes
> We rend all hearts asunder.

Clitoris, labia, vagina, urethral orifice, hymen, uterus, cervix, fallopian tube, ovary, bladder, urethra, vulva, anus. Dark curly hair covering the genitals.
Cross-section of a woman's breast.
Cross-section of a woman's mind.
Cross-section. Cross-section. Cross/Section.

Slice and examine the erotic. "If it is not erotic, it is not interesting," said a Surrealist once.

But, she thinks, turning from perusing twilight's soft body, away from the window, putting out her cigarette in a cup half-filled with water on the desk, where it hisses and gives off a strong burning odor, if a woman never had sex, remaining always a virgin, that would be interesting and fomenting also, fomenting always.

Black virgin. "She shines in the dark and is dark in the day". Black nail polish, once her uniform. Menstrual blood dries black, especially at the start of a period, when it is thickest, and has black clots. Black and Red. Lick it up from between my legs. Brush my hair when it was dark and long, like a mermaid's you said. The dark mermaid, not the blonde one. The blackness had entered her heart.

"What is that burning smell?" a woman in the room asks. But she does not answer.

For she is fomenting, fomenting always, fomenter/fomentee in a million invisible ways. Medial woman.

Below me my women lurk lurk lurk. Hooded cloaks drawn up against their faces, hair flailed into a cornucopia of wind. Furled. Black lightning signals their approach.

Wind. Women and Wind. Oya, the Yoruba goddess of wind, hurricane and fire. A wind feeling, a feeling caused by the wind, an intuition expressed in the wind. Wind Rendezvous and Wind Stations. Wind perfumes carry their unmistakable scent. The wind is a chaotic system that only the daughters of Chaos can ride. Buy a wind ticket for the West wind. O wild West wind.

The ticket that imploded.

When is a woman in History? She must find a way out of history. Where is the door that leads out of history? The Lost Door. The Forgotten Door, guarded by the faerie women on the Island of Avalon.

"I grow half sick of shadows/Said the Lady of Shalott."

But don't drown yourself yet. Search under the water. The water, where the mermaids live. O Angel of Anarchy. Where the Dark Mermaid with caliginous tail and chartreuse hair? The Black Virgin. The blackness has entered her heart. It's at sea. It's dark with sea water. See water. It's heading for a distant shore.

Psychic perfume invades the night, uncapped from a vial, an arcane potion. Blown glass for her wind perfume. The scent pervades the room.

We are the Raw Brunettes. We rend all hearts. Asunder. Asunder. Her psychic perfume. Her violet tattoo. The past never-ending. You can't get rid of it, only transmute and chaoticize. The nations of the earth surrender to her beauty. The Dark Mermaid rises up from Atlantis, raises Atlantis. Enormous crashing waves larger than cities gleam like giant crested skyscrapers, crash down on the evil nations.

Raw Brunettes! I seek the Isle of Avalon, before Arthur. Angel of Anarchy—fomenting always. Fomenting . . .

I seek the Isle of Avalon, before Arthur. Where Arthur is no more. I seek the Isle of Avalon, where Arthur is no more. Before Arthur.

Below me my women lurk lurk lurk. Their eyelids are wired for sound, hair adorned with synchronicity traps. Mouths with psychic lipstick and necks with psychic perfume. Their bodies are wired for multiple orgasms.

Hair flailed into a cornucopia of wind. Psychic water, fairies. Fairy must. Fairy dust. There are fairies at the top of my sky. Oooooh.

Look at her legs, her left thigh. There on the flesh is set the tattoo of the Raw Brunettes. Caliginous against the pale skin, under the dark fishnet stockings. The sign. Precognitive hand. Telepathic hips. Psychic sex. Psychic fish. Water flower. Japanese water flower paper thin as colored water thin paper colored water floating delicate as sleep.

Angel of Anarchy! Unwind into our brains across the centuries of dead time and space called History. Explode into our consciousness rushing water tidal wave tsunami. Drown our pasts and future. Hissing water slapping gigantically, white froth foaming into acid lace around women. Rising most around the Raw Brunettes.

Waves reach into space. An enormous sheet of water light-years across engulfs the solar system, advancing towards earth. Space tidal wave crashing over the planets, the galaxies. Cacophony of water. Raw Brunettes alert!

I LIKE TO LOOK ●

kathy page

I HADN'T SEEN OR HEARD of her for fifteen years. No one had. We sat in the garden, spaced equally around the circular table: she to my right and Bill, the man who brought her, to the left; in the middle a jug of lemonade. Their big red car gleamed in the drive. I wouldn't let them inside the house.

"I've been all around the world, some of it in a very small boat and some of it I even swam," said my sister Dee, folding her sunglasses away and examining the garden: walled, thick with shrubs and so much smaller than the world. "Listen. I've been in an *army*. I've lived with pigmies and Eskimos. I've—"

She was thinner than I remembered her, her skin darker, drier. Her ears had been pierced and she wore studs that looked like pearls and real gold, but it was her all right: her eyebrows still scattered across the bridge of her nose, her nails were still bitten close. I could see the right thumb, pointed from too much sucking as a child, the scar on her forefinger from the time she'd thrust it experimentally into a light socket. Me, Dee, Mother and our Idiot Brother: once we all lived here. Now Dee and I sat side by side in the garden of the yellow-stone house which she left, in which I still live. The window-panes are wartime glass, faulted so that the whole world can seem drunken-strange; on stormy days sea-spray lands on them, dulling my sight, like cataracts.

"I performed an appendectomy with a penknife," she continued. "I can speak eight languages. I've made love to nine people simultaneously— the men were all tied up and gagged. But best to begin at the beginning: I started off picking avocados, then I was on one of those trawlers that freeze the fish then and there. Herring. Once we were caught in the ice—"

"You always said that travel was what you'd like to do," I interrupted. "You always did like getting about."

"You . . ." She faltered, as if she couldn't quite remember me. "You didn't. You were odd. You used to sit and just stare into space."

"You haven't been there then?" I asked.

"Listen," said Dee, drawing herself up straight, "I just thought I'd look you up. The rest of them can go to hell, but you, I thought you'd be interested—" The man called Bill leaned over suddenly and kissed my sister on the lips. The pores around his nose were large and open. He had purple flecks on his cheeks and even on the lids of his eyes. His hair had been artificially streaked. Their lips squirmed wetly. My sister closed her eyes. A cobweb of saliva stretched between them, then suddenly broke as they pulled apart.

"What are you looking at?" Bill asked me angrily, wiping his mouth on his sleeve. I thought it was obvious. I saw that one of his teeth was chipped, and a line was beginning to cross the bridge of his nose, the flesh plumping up to either side of it.

"You're still doing it!" he said.

"I like to look," I replied. And then I thought: yes, that's what I do. Looking. I can look at anything, at a carpet: the patterns, repeats or complex geometry all stemming from a single point; even on a plain one the fibers sometimes lean all one way and other times they're a trampled chaos. I like to look, even at that. So I kept on looking at Bill, and saw how the ridge of his jaw was patchily shaved, the stiff hairs, just grey, growing through in clumps.

"For God's sake!" he said, turning his face away.

"Don't mind my sister," said Dee. "Listen. Bill's a director and he's going to make a film about me, the story of my life and my adventures. Aren't you? I dived for these pearls myself. There's so much to tell."

"I spent twenty-nine days alone in the Gobi desert; I've got a pilot's license; I've tickled the soles of the feet of the Dalai Llama for nearly an hour and, believe me, he didn't move a muscle. I've been in three movies, but you won't have seen them—it was in Turkey. I lost half a million dollars at cards—wasn't mine, but it would have been if I hadn't lost it. Easy come, easy go. Look at my arm, see? It was done in Hong Kong by a bearded lady. Took over forty hours. And look at the muscle too. I took cyanide in a hijack death-pact and came to just as they were about to bury me. I've got three passports. I didn't do much in the antipodes—too burnt out. Lived in a cave, had a baby, got it adopted, joined a theatre group. Then I met the Sheik—"

Bill refilled our glasses. The ice had melted into small shivers; it was old and made the drink taste faintly of metal. Dee paused to swallow.

"What about you, er—" Bill said, "do you share your sister's passion for adventure?"

"Yes," I replied, "but—"

"She was always the quiet one," Dee cut in. "It was the Sheik, you see, who gave me the half a million. He wanted to marry me, but I slipped out one morning and left for Canada. Now this might have got back: I killed someone in a bar in Montreal. Self-defense. I was tried, but I got off, of course. You didn't hear? After that, I went to the Soviet Union, in the summer, mind you. Left, my jacket padded with manuscripts, just before they kicked me out—"

Yes, I thought, I like to look. In trains, buses, gardens, at films, even those in languages I don't understand, on pavements and curbstones, in mirrors and water there's much to see and I look. I look at faces, the folds round eyes, the sculpture of flesh that grows with time to reflect habits of thought and feeling, the many textures and colors of skin. I look at litter, wet paper, September leaves. I look at the sea: sometimes the sky is darker than the water, a negative. Sometimes the beach is smooth and damp, and as the sun sets the sand blazes brazen-gold. On the rocks, mussels build themselves into tight black bouquets. I like to look at the fossils, exposed in shale that softens, blurring in a matter of hours the sharp record of past millennia, dissolving them within a day. I like to look at the shadows of twigs mingled with clots of leaves, just stirring in the wind. At sand blown round grasses and debris, at frost on windows, at gulls landing like a scattering of crumbs on the sea. I like to look at the wind seen through glass, at the flow of traffic, its motorway lights tailing into the distance, red retreat, oncoming white.

"Miles away," Dee said to Bill, meaning me. "We're twins, you know."

"You're not at all alike!" Bill said to Dee conspiratorially. No, we're not. She left, I stayed put. She has a story to tell; I sit and stare, look and see. While she was away I saw some sights. I saw our mother shrink. Her skin grew yellow, a damp envelope. A tumor burgeoned on her breast: it looked like a purple bubble but felt hard as iron. Layers of skin peeled away like tissue. I saw our Idiot Brother eat his own shit and handprint it on the walls. I saw the snowdrops each spring. I saw a last breath, and the skin growing luminously pale. I pulled back the sheet and looked upon our mother's bones, seemingly wrapped in bleached and shrunken cloth. I saw our Brother, taller than any of us and fitter too, trying to catch sparrows in his fat and useless hands. I looked at rainbows in soapsuds stretching and bursting, at a tangle of earthworms, wet, glistening; saw the scars where their ends had grown back. I saw the yellow stone of our house obscured by ivy, how the small dry roots pushed themselves into its pores and cracks. I looked at myself in the mirror and felt that it would break; I looked longer and the feeling went away.

Dee leaned closer towards me over the table.

"I spent three months in the Pacific Basin, stuck because of storms. I got married to an island chieftain, not that it counts now I'm back. Free as a bird—" She threw her head back and laughed. Dee, I thought, if I had been around the world, I would have seen a great deal more than you. That's but one of my bitternesses.

"I've dined with kings," she continued, "with shamans, beggars, gods incarnate, lunatics and transvestites. I've had more diseases than I can remember, unnamed fevers, various malarias, malnutrition, amoebic dysentery; in Nepal my liver grew so huge that it threatened to squash my lungs. My skin turned orange. I thought I would lose a leg . . ."

Looking. It isn't only a passive pleasure, a drinking in. Looking can be hard. Looking can vanquish time. Looking can change water to wine. It can wipe fear clean away: I have looked at entrails on the road until my gorge no longer rose and choked me, and now I can distinguish them and their circumstances. Looking can turn another's eyes away. Looking can strip skins, drain blood. Looking can abolish the other. There's a power in looking. I've discovered it over the years, and that day in the garden was the first day when I realized what I had, and the only time I dared its use.

Dee's glass was empty. She sighed, and smiled at us both. White flecks had collected at the corners of her mouth. Bill was sweating, the top of his collar grey and damp.

"Why did you come back here?" I said.

"To see you, of course," she lied, "and the house."

"Yes," said Bill, pushing back his chair, "I'd like to see the house."

"You can't film this house. It's mine until our Idiot Brother dies." I spoke without turning to look at him. "Perhaps you'd like to see him? Seeing as the garden is so secluded, I let him go naked in the summer. He can't speak. His face is slack, his brown body going the same way. He'll eat anything."

"Will you stop staring at me," snapped Dee, glancing down at the bracelet of pearls which she had dived for herself through a world of impossible color, blue and yellow fish, purple corals shimmering with refracted light. She was growing very pale. I looked, I looked hard for a very long time.

"I used to think you were beautiful," I said softly. She was about to continue her account of places been, not seen. And then she would have made her request again, more forcefully. Her eyes were glancing offside, to check that Bill was listening, her grainy tongue-tip poked through parted lips, moist with bitter lemonade. I looked.

"Dee?" Bill leaned forward, touched her arm, grasped her wrist. His fingers left no mark. Then he ran from the garden, and the red car sped off down the coast road, clashing with the sea and sky.

Those lips are dry now, Dee. Leaves whirl around your legs. Dirt collects in the crook of your arm. Rain runs clean tracks over your face. Saltspray ages you, scouring at the sharpness of your features. Sometimes our Idiot Brother pisses on you when I've locked him out; at other times he picks flowers and lays them at your feet. He at least, I think, can do what he wants. Dee, I am all eyes, and you are still and home at last, for ever in the garden: not flesh, nor bone, but stone.

PLANETESIMAL ●

keri hulme

I ONCE KNEW A girl who —
sat apart at the party, down on the floor. A small almost-woman in a
large blue overcoat, the kind sailors wear. She cringed within its folds. I sat
beside her on a sudden kindly impulse. I offered my roach in its glittery
skull holder. I was drowsed and calmhearted, gladly aware of all the
patterns of laughter and the brittle flowering color of the carpet. I wasn't
upset when she refused the smoke.

"Don't like it?"

"Don't smoke or drink," she said dully. Her head bowed. "Because . . ."

"Because?"

"I think I'm going mad. If I fuddle things more, if I."

Retreating into the midnight coat.

O dear. Another mixed-up strung-out febrile brain. I smiled, gently,
buddhalike. I said, charity of the smoke

"They say if you can think it," carefully between tiny exhalations, "you
are not going mad." Perfect curve of smile, perfect curve of smoke. I once
knew this girl who —

She looked back at me and winced.

"I can think what I like. The evidence . . . the evidence."

"What evidence?"

She peeled back the heavy coat sleeve. "Look."

I bent forward politely.

It was an ordinary female arm, pallid, slightly hairy, a little too thick at the wrist.

The roach smoke drifted between us.

She pulled the coat sleeve higher.

Needle tracks, I thought dreamily. There will be the footprints of needles and she will bore me with her tale of dirt and discouragement. Needle tracks.

"There," she said.

The inner cup of her elbow.

Except it wasn't there.

It was the most exciting tattoo I had ever seen in my life, and I exclaimed with delight. The connoisseur taken aback. I said so, exalted. With bitterness she said,

"It is not a picture. Touch, but only the very edge. Where there is still bone."

I leant my finger carefully over the outside rim of skin to touch that extraordinary black oval. The cancellation of her flesh. However with mere ink had an artist gotten—

I snatched the finger back.

"You see?"

Her smile was as crooked and hurt as her previous wince.

The lovely fog in my head bled away and I was left sitting, looking at a girl who—

gazed at her arm.

Where the tip of my finger had touched the black was a dead white patch like frostbite. It ached. And I had touched—nothing.

"The stars change," she said in a small voice. "Over the nights, they change. I watch them move in great circles."

I looked again.

Deep in the blackness was a myriad of intensely bright sparks. They made a far distant spiral.

"They are stars," she said, tiredly. "When I watch I feel as though I arch above, mother of the sky host."

A tired almost-woman, small, heavily bound in a coat.

"Like that Egyptian. Goddess. Thing."

She rolled the sleeve slowly down.

"Something even wants me there."

She looked at me. "Are you going mad too?"

I stood unsteadily. My eyes hurt from being kept too wide. My jaws hurt from being kept clenched. The unknowing laughter all around was harsh and raw and all the flowering colors had died. I wanted a glass a jugful a flagon of sherry to bring back the sweetness, to drown all the hurting, to believe in tomorrow again.

"You are not mad. Please wait. I am coming right back. Not mad."

I remember she didn't smile as I stumbled away. She stayed huddled against the wall, the upright collar of the coat at once frame and shelter for her pale forgettable face. I once knew a girl. Who?

I found my sherry. I drank too much too fast in a gay swirl of chatter. "Who's the girl?" I yelled. "A houri," said Anna, "a houri from the fragrant paradisiacal smoke." And Michael simpered, "Who cares, dear James? There are better things to do." And Big Molly looked at me carefully before saying, "She is one of my staff nurses. Sickleave. Nervous trouble y'know. You smitten?"

"No. Yes. I don't know."

Molly smiled. "Theresa Wyatt. Boards at Rossiter's. Y'know where?"

The sherry, the chatter, and inevitably, the nausea and the obligatory trip outside. When I returned inside, the girl had gone.

I went to Rossiter's in the dizzy morning after. Her landlady said she had not come home. "Which I expect you know about," she said grimly.

She never came home.

And here I sit, writing lines by a dead roach. I am doing it awkwardly, one finger swathed. I once knew a girl who—

the police believe committed suicide, jumped in the sea,

rendered herself bodiless.

Molly believes that. Her landlady believes that. Most times, I believe that. I meant to say, my dear, she was on six months sickleave *and* had gibbered openly about going to other worlds. So I believe that. I do.

Except when I take the bandage off my finger. My inquisitive forefinger. Where now, centered in the dead white like a strange intrusive wart, sits a tiny bluegreen jewel. I think. Staring at it.

I have wondered. If you sat among heartless strangers, with a universe within your reach, would you always stay, wallflower at the party?

Already the dark is growing round the jewel, and behind it in the depths of black the bitter stars wink.

PERMA RED ●

debra earling

S HE HAD BEEN WALKING on the highway for almost an hour. Last night's liquor was now just a cotton-dry whisper on her thick tongue, a faint buzz somewhere behind her head. The bastard had let her off outside of Ravalli on Highway 93, and now nearly an hour later, she was nowhere closer to Perma. The armholes of her blouse were tight and wet. The stiff blouse strained across her breast and had ribbed her nipples raw.

Her stomach rumbled. "No," she groaned. She looked for privacy. A lonely bush, a few scrub trees, sage, weeds, and dry grass. Rattlers? She looked to the pine trees a hundred yards or so further. "Hell with it," she said and ducked behind the nearest bush. When Louise stepped back onto the road the heavy August sun was clearing the Mission Range. Her knees felt a little weak, but she was now ready to walk a serious mile or two. A breeze cooled the sweat on her back and fluttered her thin skirt. She felt the hem wet on her calves and shivered. Although she tried to walk fast, she felt as if she were being pulled down. Each landmark she set her sights on remained distant, unobtainable. She shifted her gaze to the blonde hills.

The stiff grass rustled in the breeze. A gust of wind rattled the dry weeds, whirled a tumbleweed and threw a sheet prickle of dust up her legs. Grit stung her eyes. She stopped on the road's shoulder and watched the small whirlwind gather speed, twirling leaves, small twigs, powder dust. Under its path, thin rows of cheat grass collapsed like brittle sticks. She stood transfixed and watched until the swirling talcum dust disappeared in a steady cross-wind, becoming a faint wisp, a tendril of smoke, thin air.

Her grandmother believed whirlwinds were the souls of the dead, departing, becoming sky. Spirit winds. Louise had never really believed this. Now she swallowed a growing desire to run. She forced herself to walk slowly, but little by little, she began to quicken her pace.

She heard the hollow wind sound of an approaching car. She lifted her thumb, but the car swerved a perfect half moon to avoid her and whipped down the road. A glint of chrome and it disappeared over a hillswell. She raised a slender hand to her brow and blinked at the sun. It wasn't even close to noon and already the road was soft beneath her feet. She wasn't worried though; someone would pick her up, someone whom she knew and she would sit red-faced and silent on the way back home, wishing she had made it to Missoula, or Wallace, anywhere, off this reservation. The thought chewed her pride. This time it'd be different—she'd walk all the bitchin' way home. She stiffened her knees and her heart became her drumbeat homeward.

The shallow drone of an occasional passing car eased the monotony of the fields' humming. She listened to the steady flickering tick of the grasshopper and tried to block the image of her mother's fever-swollen face. She tried to think up an excuse for last night's drunk. But she knew excuses didn't matter now. She had come up with convincing alibis in the past. And Grandma would listen intently, nod politely, and excuse her. She would feel a little guilty at first, but later she would feel smug. But she was never sure she had fooled the old woman, only pride made her hold onto the thought that she had.

"Hey Louise! Red! Want a ride?" Behind her, grinning—cousin Victor hung out the window of his rusty '32 Ford pick-up. A slow cloud of dust billowed past her. He squinted at her, chewing on a tooth pick. His black-gray hair was butch block, bristled like a wire brush. Occasionally, he would get a crew-cut and when it grew out it made his head look square. He was wearing the maroon shirt he always wore, rolled up past his forearms, with a white tee shirt underneath. He looked hot.

Louise said nothing, walked to the passenger side and yanked on the door. Victor tried to roll down the window but it stuck. He yelled at her through the window crack. "Door don't open." He gestured with his fingers. "Gotta come around on my side." Louise noticed again the thin white scar that split his upper lip. It occurred to her that white men didn't have scars. He climbed out of the truck. And Louise crawled in. The dull leather seats were hot and she sat close to the passenger door on a seat rip that was sharp. It snagged her skirt.

The truck pulled out on the road and picked up speed until the window crack whistled and the stick shift vibrated. Victor spit out his toothpick.

"Whew," he said, "you smell like a white woman. Where you been?" Louise folded her arms across her sore breasts and looked at the dashboard. A bumper sticker sealed off the jockey box. She read its faded letters: "Pray For Me, I Drive Highway 93."

"Got any booze?" she said. He reached across her and pulled out a half-empty quart of beer. The bent bottle cap had been jammed back on and Louise pulled it off with her fingers. She took a long, easy swig of the flat warm beer and passed it to Victor. He chugged a few swallows. "Taste like dog piss!" he coughed.

"I wouldn't know," Louise said and gulped a quick swallow, then recapped it with her fist. She put the bottle between her legs. The seat poked her thighs.

"What'd you do to your hair, kid? It looks faded somehow."

"Got any gum?" she said.

He reached into his pocket, pulled out a stick of clove gum and tossed it in her lap. Last month she had heard you could lighten your hair with peroxide and water, so she had tried it. She stared out the window. "I like it," she mumbled and wiped her wet palms on her knees. Louise watched the clear shadow of a cloud as it moved over the hills. And it seemed to her that the hills were sleeping. She thought of her mother laying still beneath the clouds in the white heat of the day.

He spoke softly. "I heard Annie's been sick. Aunt Susy was up to your Grandma's house last night." Louise chewed the cuticle on her left thumb and busied herself smoothing her skirt. She looked at her brown shoes but said nothing. Her mother had been sick for only a week, but it was a different sickness. A sickness that pulled the muscles behind her eyes as tight as a blind strap and let go.

Now, every night Grandma listened for the owl and burned the thin strands of Annie's hair in the cook-stove. She also kept a tireless eye on Annie's lonely clothing flapping on the line. If she left her post she would call Louise to stand watch—so neither Annie nor her possessions were ever left alone.

Louise listened to the sound of the tires on the road and re-opened the beer. "Want a chug?" she pointed the bottle toward Victor. He shook his head. The truck hit a bump and beer splattered his lap. She gulped the rest, leaned over and tossed the bottle out his window. She heard a distant tinkle as it hit the ground.

"Aunt Susy says it's bad medicine." He looked at her.

"What?"

She had come from Hot Springs, the old medicine woman. Even in the bright sun, her clothes were black as the crows' wings. Louise remembered that the rattlesnakes buzzed her arrival. Rattlesnakes were blind this time of year. They hid in the grass with milk-white eyes. They struck at anything that moved.

"What?"

"Your mother's sickness."

"I don't know." She felt as if a cold, wet hand had just been placed at the base of her spine. She choked a gag.

Victor changed the subject. "Been a bad spell this summer. Road's too hot, even for snakes. You're lucky you have that spring."

Louise nodded, but said nothing.

The spring's creek was a slow mud trickle thick as blood. Grandma had milked the old cow for Annie and sent Louise down to the spring with a small jar of body-warm milk. The spring pool still bubbled, but it had receded and large mosquitos swarmed the cracked clay banks. Louise had slipped the jar in an old stocking and put it in the creek. For an hour she had sat holding onto the sock, slapping blood fat mosquitos.

They were slowly coming into Dixon. Victor shifted into second and the truck whined down. A few cars were parked at the Dixon Bar. Now it was early afternoon and shadows were short. A dirt gray dog slept in the shade of the Dixon Bar.

The milk was cool and sweet when they put it to her lips, but it dribbled through her hot yellow teeth and scummed the inside of her cheeks like phlegm; a gray paste too thick to swallow. Her ragged fingernails, thin and dry as paper.

"This sure is one hell of a town," Victor said. Louise looked over at the Dixon Bar and could see only darkness behind the ragged screen door. She placed her hand to the back of her neck and thought of sleep. Victor scuffed the palm of his hand over his hair and sighed. As they drove out of Dixon Louise noticed a small boy was playing near the edge of town. Louise turned to look back. A slow cloud of dust was passing over a few gray shingle houses built squat on the ground. The small boy had stopped playing. She saw him raise his hand as if to wave but he cupped his hand above his eyes then lifted his dark face to the sun.

Louise slumped back in the seat and crossed her arms. As she saw her Grandma's house in the distance she sat up suddenly and tugged at her door handle. "Let me out here, Victor." He started to protest but slowed down the truck and let her out. She stood squinting on the roadside and watched until Victor's pickup turned the first highway bend and slipped beyond the hill.

The weathered house stood among the weeds. Near the highway was a marshy stretch, thick with fuzzy cattails and cawing magpies. The rocky terrain of Grandma's land provided a haven for field snakes and rattlers. Louise walked slowly up to the house. She adjusted her skirt and wiped her mouth on the back of her hand.

For a while she stood, stoneblind and blinking in the doorway. She leaned into the queer hot darkness, straining to see. Her eyes gathered the dark room slowly, one inch at a time. Heavy blankets, smelling like singed hair hid the windows and suffocated the afternoon sun. Here and there pinholes of light poked the walls, illuminating golden particles of dust.

In the dim light, she saw the still shadow of Grandma standing near the cook-stove. Grandma opened the cast iron stove drawer and fanned the flames. Her face was washed with yellow light. She threw something into the flames and shut the drawer. Louise watched a thin flicker of fire lick the round edge of the stove lid and her nostrils were filled with the smell of burning sweet grass. Grandma pulled another grass braid from her deep pocket and touched it to the stove top. An orange flame smoked the withering grass. Grandma carried the smoking medicine to the bedroom where Annie lay. The door closed behind her with a quiet click. Louise clasped her hands to keep her fingers from trembling. And sat down in the sleepy heat and waited.

Annie's wake was held at Aunt Susy's house. The first day of the wake Louise waited outside of the small house. For a while she hid in the root cellar and listened to the sound of her heart. That evening Louise stood behind the pine tree in Aunt Susy's front yard. She cupped her hands to her ribs and watched the people who came to visit her mother for the last time. Even outside she could hear them praying. Sometimes she could hear them laughing and joking. And when they cried, Louise would sit on the porch and listen to the wind moving through the cheat grass.

Aunt Susy came out on the porch to sit beside her once. She had reached over and touched Louise's hand. Louise had looked at her in the darkness and thought the old woman's skin resembled the pickled tavern sausages at the Perma Bar. The old woman seemed small to Louise now. When Louise was a little girl she had been afraid of Aunt Susy. The old woman had a wizened hawk-face and a large dowager's hump. She always wore black garments. And some of her dresses had sleeves short enough to reveal the loose, olive flesh of her inner arms. Once Louise mentioned her Aunt Susy's skin color to Grandma. "Too much green tea," Grandma had said.

For three days and three nights they prayed for Annie. Louise watched Grandma in the kitchen sifting flour for fry bread. Louise could see the mouse turds like hard raisins grate the bottom of the sifter. Grandma would toss them out, scoop up another cup and dump it in the sifter.

Louise looked into the living room where her mother lay propped in a wooden box. She clenched her skirt up tight in her fists and stood still. "Go to her," Grandma said. Louise did not move for a moment. "Go on," her grandmother said. Louise walked slowly toward her mother. The candles flickered up on Annie's delicate waxen face. Annie's slender hands had been folded carefully across her bosom.

And Louise noticed that her mother's hands were still and dark. For a long time Louise gazed upon her, looking for signs of life. Twice, she saw her chest expand, gathering air. But looking again, it seemed to Louise that she had never seen anything so motionless. Even dust moved in the wind. And sometimes rocks seemed to shimmer in the heat. But her mother's stillness was uncomfortable to her. Louise passed her hand over her mother's face but did not touch her.

Louise looked above the casket where, haphazardly tacked on the gray wall, were pictures that Aunt Susy had cut out of magazines and catalogues. Fashion models smiled from the windows of their chauffeured cars. Hawaiian girls waved from a tropical paradise. Happy families sat down to dine in their immaculate kitchens.

Friends and relatives began to pray. Louise looked at their faces. Every face seemed distorted to her; continually changed by the candlelights' flickering. It seemed to Louise that they looked at her mother as though she were far away. Their eyes seemed vague and distant to her. Nervous fingers twisted rosaries. Some sang softly, almost inaudibly. Their chants became a low drone that buzzed like the hot fields. She looked at her grandmother in the kitchen. Louise wondered what caused this dark sadness. It seemed she had felt this way for a long time. Louise slipped out the door without a goodbye.

Louise returned home the next morning before the heat could dry the root-wet fields. She saw Victor's gray Ford parked out back. She held her breath, but she soon realized they had left sometime before.

When she opened the back door she called to her grandmother. She looked at the half empty coffee cups on the table. She sat down in the quiet kitchen; her skull felt thin as an eggshell. A meadowlark sang outside the window and she thought it was a lonely sound. She thought a while and went outside. Maybe Victor had left his keys in the truck. She peered in the window. No keys in the ignition. She opened the door and checked under the mat. She found an old gray key. She wondered if it would work.

The truck picked up speed, faster and faster, until the seats lurched and the rusted coil springs screeched with the rhythmic jar of the road's many potholes. Dust motes billowed behind the truck. Louise pressed the accelerator to the floor and gripped the steering wheel. The road gave way to a series of sharp bends that ended in a roller coaster hill. She sighed as the road gradually sloped to a straight tractor road.

Louise could see the small crowd at the burial ground so she began to slow down. She pulled the truck off on the roadside. Her tight chest felt empty and she was breathing hard. Louise rolled the window down and gulped a breath of air. She pressed her forehead to the steering wheel. Over the field, the wind carried the old songs. A warm breeze touched her damp hair. Louise looked over at the people gathered around the grave; eight or nine people she had known all her life. Grandma's red shawl flapped in the hot wind. She saw that all of them were wearing their best clothes. Victor stood close to Grandma in his stiff white shirt.

Louise twisted the mirror round so she could look at her face. In the sunlight she could see that the red color of her hair did not match her dark skin. She looked for something to cover her head. On the floor was an old bandana that Victor used to stuff the window crack. Carefully she tied the scarf over her hair. Louise looked at herself once more and slowly climbed out of the truck. She left the truck door open and walked a little closer. She waited until the small crowd departed. "Grandma?" she called. Grandma and Victor looked up at Louise.

"I'll meet you both at the truck," he said.

Louise moved slowly toward Grandma. "I know, Honey," Grandma said. "It's going to be fine."

Grandma lifted her palms to the sky and chanted in Salish. Her chant became a slow, meandering song that made Louise very sad. She sang to a part of Louise that was lonesome.

4

SEX

There is a being who lives in the wild underground of women's natures. This creature is our sensory nature, and like any integral creature, it has its own natural and nutritive cycles. This being is inquiring, relational, bounding with energy sometimes, quiescent at other times. It is responsive to stimulus which involves the senses; music, food, drink, peace, quiet, beauty, darkness.

It is this aspect of a woman that has heat . . . like a fire underground, that burns high, then low, and in cycles. From the energy released there, a woman acts as she sees fit. A woman's heat is not a state of sexual arousal, but a state of intense sensory awareness that includes but is not exclusive to her sexuality.

. . . There is an aspect of women's sexuality that in ancient times was called the sacred obscene, not in the way we use the word today, but meaning sexually wise in a witty sort of way. There were once Goddess cults devoted to irreverent female sexuality. They were not denigrating per se, but concerned with portraying parts of the unconscious that remain, even today, mysterious and largely uncharted.

. . . The very idea of sexuality as sacred, and more specifically, obscenity as an aspect of sacred sexuality is vital to the wildish nature. There were goddesses of obscenity in the ancient women's cultures—so called for their innocent yet wily lewdness . . .

from the chapter, "The Dirty Goddesses"
from *Women Who Run With the Wolves*

THE QUEEN'S CHAMBER ●

a.n. roquelaure (anne rice)

Hᴀʟꜰ ᴛʜᴇ ɴɪɢʜᴛ was gone before the Queen came.

Beauty had dozed, then awakened again and again, to find herself still chained in the ornate bedchamber as if in a nightmare. She was bound to the wall, her ankles cuffed in leather, her wrists up over her head, her buttocks pushed against the cold stone behind her.

At first the stone had felt good. Now and then she twisted to let the air touch the soreness. Of course the abraded flesh was much healed from last night's ordeal on the Bridle Path, but she still suffered, and she knew tonight she was surely destined for more torment.

Not the least of it, however, was her own passion. What had the Prince awakened in her that after one night of no satisfaction, she should feel so wanton? It was the stirring between her legs that first brought her out of sleep in the Slaves' Hall, and now and then she felt it as she stood waiting.

The room itself lay in shadow and unbroken stillness. Dozens of thick candles burned in their heavy gilded holders, the wax spilling in rivulets through the traceries of gold. The bed with its tapestried draperies appeared a gaping cavern.

Beauty closed her eyes. She opened them again. And when she was again on the verge of dream, she heard the heavy double doors thrown open and suddenly saw the tall, slender figure of the Queen materialized before her.

The Queen moved to the center of the carpet. Her blue velvet gown cleaved to her girdled hips before flaring gently to cover her black pointed slippers. She gazed at Beauty with narrow, black eyes tipped up at the ends to give her a cruel expression, and then she smiled, her white cheeks dimpling though an instant before they had seemed as hard as white porcelain.

Beauty had lowered her eyes at once. Petrified, she watched covertly as the Queen moved away from her and seated herself at an ornate dressing table, her back to a high mirror.

With an off-handed gesture she dismissed the Ladies who stood at the door. A figure remained there, and Beauty, afraid to look, was certain it was Prince Alexi.

So her tormentor had come, Beauty thought. Her heart pounded in her ears, becoming a roar rather than a pulse, and she felt the bonds holding her helpless so that she could not have defended herself against anyone or anything. Her breasts felt heavy, and the moisture between her legs greatly agitated her. Would the Queen discover it and use it to further punish her?

Yet mingled with her fear was some sense of her helplessness which had come over her the night before and never left her. She knew how she must appear, she was afraid, but she could do nothing and she was accepting it.

Maybe this was a new strength, this acceptance. And she needed all her strength, for she was alone with this woman who had no love for her. Without words, she evoked a memory of the Prince's love, of Lady Juliana's affectionate touch and warm words of praise, even of Leon's caressing hands.

But this was the Queen, the great powerful Queen who ruled all and who felt nothing but coldness and fascination for her.

She shivered against her will. The throbbing between her legs seemed to slacken and then to grow slightly more intense. Surely the Queen was staring at her. And the Queen could make her suffer. And there would be no Prince to witness it, no Court, no one.

Only Prince Alexi.

She saw him now, moving out of the shadows, a naked form exquisitely proportioned, the dark golden skin making him seem a polished statue.

"Wine," said the Queen. And he was moving to pour it for her.

He knelt at her side and he placed the two-handled cup in her hands, and as she drank, Beauty looked up and saw Prince Alexi smiling directly at her.

She was so startled, she almost made a little gasp. His large brown eyes were full of the same gentle affection he'd shown her last night when he passed her at the banquet table. Then he made his mouth into a silent kiss before Beauty looked away in consternation.

Could he feel affection for her, real affection, even desire, as she felt desire for him when she first saw him?

O, how she ached suddenly to touch him, to feel just once for an instant that silken skin, that hard chest, those dark, rose-colored nipples. How exquisite they were on that flat chest, those little nodules that seemed so unmasculine, giving him a touch of feminine vulnerability. How had the Queen punished them, she wondered? Were they ever clamped and adorned as her breasts had been?

They were piquant, those little nipples.

But the throbbing between her legs warned her, and it took an act of will for her not to move her hips.

"Undress me," the Queen said.

And from beneath her half-mast lids, Beauty watched as Prince Alexi obeyed the command skillfully and deftly.

How clumsy she had been two nights ago and how patient the Prince had been with her.

He used his hands but seldom. His first duty was with his teeth to unsnap the hooks of the Queen's dress and this he did, quickly gathering it as it fell down around her.

Beauty was astonished to see the Queen's full white breasts naked under a thin chemise of lace. And then Prince Alexi removed her ornate mantle of white silk to show the Queen's black hair hanging loose in ripples over her shoulders.

He took the garments away.

Then he came back to remove with his teeth the Queen's slippers. He kissed her naked feet before he took the shoes out of sight, and then he brought back to the Queen a sheer nightgown trimmed in white lace, the fabric a lustrous cream color. It was very full and pressed into a thousand pleats.

And as the Queen rose, Prince Alexi pulled down the chemise that she wore, and rising to his full height put the nightgown over the Queen's shoulders. She slipped her arms into the deep pleated bag sleeves, and the garment fell about her like a bell.

And then with his back to Beauty, Prince Alexi on his knees again tied a dozen little bows of white ribbon to close the front of the gown to its hem above the Queen's naked insteps.

As he bent over for the last of these, the Queen's hands played idly with his auburn hair, and Beauty found herself staring at his reddened buttocks where he had obviously been recently punished. His thighs, his tight, hard calves, all of this enflamed her.

"Pull back the curtains of the bed," the Queen said. "And bring her to me."

Beauty's pulse deafened her. It seemed there was a pressure in her ears, in her throat. Yet she heard the tapestries being drawn back. She saw the Queen recline on the coverlet amid a nest of silk pillows. The Queen looked younger now that her hair was free, and her face was without a trace of age as she stared at Beauty. Those eyes were as placid as if they had been painted in her face with enamel.

Then with a shock of unwelcome pleasure, Beauty saw Prince Alexi before her. He obliterated the vision of the menacing Queen. He bent to untie her ankles and she felt his fingers deliberately caress her. When he rose in front of her again, his hands up to free her wrists, she smelled the perfume of his hair and skin, and there seemed something utterly lush about him. For all his hardness, the squareness of his build, he seemed some great spicy delicacy to her, and she found herself staring right into his eyes. He smiled and let his lips touch her forehead. And they stayed secretly pressed to her forehead until her wrists were entirely free and he was holding them.

Then he pushed her gently down on her knees and gestured to the bed.

"No, simply bring her," said the Queen.

And Prince Alexi lifted Beauty and threw her over his shoulder as easily as a Page might have done, or the Prince himself when he took her from her father's castle.

His flesh felt hot beneath her, and thrown over his back as she was, she boldly kissed his sore buttocks.

Then she was laid down on the bed and realized she was beside the Queen, looking up into her eyes, as the Queen, who rested on her elbow, looked down at her.

Beauty's breath left her in rapid gasps. The Queen seemed quite enormous to her. And now she perceived a great resemblance to the Prince, only as always the Queen seemed infinitely colder. Yet there was about her red mouth something which might have once been called sweetness. She had thick eyelashes, a firm chin, and as she smiled dimples showed in her cheeks. Her face was heart shaped.

Flustered, Beauty closed her eyes, biting her lip so hard she might have cut it.

"Look at me," said the Queen. "I want to see your eyes, naturally. I want no modesty from you now, do you understand me?"

"Yes, your Highness," Beauty answered.

She wondered if the Queen might hear her heart beat. The bed was soft beneath her, the pillows soft, and she found herself staring at the Queen's great breasts, the dark circle of a nipple beneath the gown, before she looked at the Queen's eyes again obediently.

A shock passed through her, collecting in a knot in her belly.

The Queen merely studied her in great absorption. Her teeth showed perfectly white between her lips, and those eyes, slanted, long, were black to the core and revealed nothing.

"Sit there, Alexi," the Queen said without looking away.

And Beauty saw him take his position at the foot of the bed, with his arms folded on his chest, and his back to the bedpost.

"Little plaything," the Queen said under her breath to Beauty. "And now I understand perhaps why Lady Juliana is so enraptured over you."

She ran her hand over Beauty's face, her cheeks, her eyelids. She pinched Beauty's mouth. She smoothed back her hair, and then she slapped Beauty's breasts to the right and to the left and again.

Beauty's mouth quivered but she made no sound. She kept her hands still at her sides. The Queen was like a light that threatened to blind her.

If she thought about it, lying here so near the Queen, she would be overcome with panic.

The Queen's hand moved over her belly and her thighs. It pinched the flesh of her thighs and then the backs of her legs at the calves. And in spite of herself Beauty felt a tingling everywhere she was touched as if the hand itself had some dreadful power. She felt hatred for the Queen suddenly, more violently than she had felt it for Lady Juliana.

But then the Queen commenced to examine, slowly, Beauty's nipples. The fingers of the Queen's right hand turned each nipple this way and that, testing the soft circle of skin around it. Beauty's breath became uneven, and she felt the moisture between her legs as though a grape had been squeezed there.

It seemed the Queen was monstrously bigger than she, and as strong as a man, or was it only that to struggle against the Queen was unthinkable? Beauty tried to regain some calm, to think of her feeling of release on the Bridle Path, but it eluded her. It had been fragile all along. Now it was nothing.

"Look at me," the Queen commanded gently again, and Beauty realized as she looked up that she was crying.

"Spread your legs," the Queen ordered.

At once Beauty obeyed. "Now she will see," Beauty thought. "It will be as bad as when Lord Gregory saw. And Prince Alexi will see."

The Queen laughed. "I said spread your legs," she said, and gave Beauty's thighs fierce stinging slaps. Beauty spread her legs much wider and felt graceless as she did so. When her knees were pressed down to the coverlet on either side, she thought she could not endure the ignominy of it. She stared at the coffered ceiling of the bed above her and realized that the Queen was opening her sex as Leon had done. Beauty bit down on her cries. And Prince Alexi witnessed all of it. She remembered his kisses, his smiles. The lights of the room shimmered, and she felt her own shuddering as the Queen's fingers felt the moisture in this secret, exposed spot, playing with Beauty's pubic lips, smoothing the pubic hair, and finally catching a lock of it to pull and tease idly.

It seemed the Queen took both her thumbs and wrenched Beauty open. Beauty tried to keep her hips still. She wanted to rise to escape, like some miserable Princess in the Training Hall who could not endure being so examined. Yet she did not protest; her whimpers were faint and uncertain.

The Queen commanded her to turn over.

Blessed concealment, that she could hide her face in the pillows.

But those cool, commanding hands were playing with her buttocks now, opening them, touching her anus. "O, please," she thought desperately, and she knew that her shoulders shook with her silent crying. "O, this is dreadful, dreadful!"

With the Prince, finally, she had known what was wanted.

On the Bridle Path, finally, she had been told what was wanted. But what did this wicked Queen want of her, that she suffer, that she cringe, that she offer herself or merely endure? And the woman despised her!

The Queen massaged her flesh, prodding it, testing it as if for thickness, softness, resilience. She tested Beauty's thighs in the same manner, and then pushed Beauty's knees so far apart and high on the bed that Beauty's hips rose and she felt she was squatting, sprawled apart, over the coverlet, her sex protruding, hanging down, her buttocks surely split so that she resembled a ripe fruit.

The Queen's hand was under her sex as if weighing it, feeling the roundness and heaviness of the lips, pinching them.

"Arch your back," said the Queen, "and lift your buttocks, little cat, little cat in heat."

Beauty obeyed, her eyes flooded with tears of shame. She was trembling violently as she took a deep breath, and against her will felt the Queen's fingers commanding her passion, squeezing the flame so it burned hotter. Surely Beauty's pubic lips were swelling, their juices flowing, no matter how bitterly she struggled against it!

She did not want to *give* anything to this wicked woman, this witch of a Queen. To the Prince she would yield; to Lord Gregory, to nameless and faceless Lords and Ladies who showered her with compliments, but to this woman who despised her . . . !

But the Queen had sat back on the bed beside Beauty, and hastily she gathered up Beauty as if she were a floppy doll and threw her over her lap, her face away from Prince Alexi, her buttocks surely still exposed to his scrutiny.

Beauty gave an open-mouthed moan, her breasts rubbed against the coverlet, her sex throbbing against the Queen's thigh. It was as if she were some toy in the Queen's hands.

Yes, it was exactly like being a toy, only she was alive, she breathed, she suffered. She could imagine how she appeared to Prince Alexi.

The Queen lifted her hair. She ran a finger down Beauty's back to the tip of her spine.

"All the rituals," the Queen said in a low voice, "the Bridle Path, the stakes in the garden, the wheels, and then the Hunts in the Maze, and all the other clever games devised for my pleasure, but do I ever know a slave until I have this intimacy with the slave, the intimacy of the slave over my lap ready for punishment? Tell me, Alexi. Shall I spank her with my hand only to sustain this intimacy? Feel her stinging flesh, its warmth, as I watch it change color? Shall I use the silver-back mirror, or one of a dozen paddles that are all excellent for the purpose? What do you prefer, Alexi, when you are over my lap? What is it you hope for even as you are crying?"

"You may hurt your hand if you spank her that way," came Prince Alexi's calm answer. "May I get you the silver mirror?"

"Ah, but you do not answer my question," the Queen said. "And do get me the mirror. I shall not spank her with it. Rather I shall see her face with it as I spank her."

In a blur, Beauty saw Prince Alexi move to the dressing table. And then before her, propped against a silk pillow, was the mirror, tilted so she could see the Queen's smooth white face in it distinctly. The dark eyes terrified her. The Queen's smile terrified her.

"But I shall show her nothing," Beauty thought desperately, shutting her eyes, the tears squeezed out down her cheeks.

"Surely, there is something superior about the open hand," the Queen was saying, her left hand on Beauty's neck, massaging it. She slipped it down under Beauty's breasts, and pushing them closer to one another, touched both nipples with her long fingers. "Have I not spanked you with my hand as hard as any man, Alexi?"

"To be sure, your Highness," he answered softly. He was behind Beauty again. Perhaps he had taken his place against the bedpost.

"Now clasp your hands in the small of your back and keep them there," said the Queen. And she closed her hand over Beauty's buttocks just as she had closed her other hand over Beauty's breasts. "And acknowledge my commands to you, Princess."

"Yes, your Highness," Beauty struggled to respond, but to her further shame her voice broke into sobs and she shivered trying to restrain them.

"And be quieter than that," said the Queen sharply.

The Queen commenced to spank her. One great hard slap after another fell on her buttocks, and if a paddle had ever been worse she could not remember it. She tried to be still, to be quiet, to show nothing, nothing, as she repeated that word over and over in her mind, but she could feel herself writhing.

It was as Leon had said with the Bridle Path; you always struggle as if you could escape the paddle, squirm away from it. And she heard herself crying out suddenly in gasps as the slaps stung her. The Queen's hand seemed immense and hard and heavier than the paddle. It shaped itself to her as it spanked her, and she realized she was frantic, full of tears, and cries, and all of this for the Queen to see in her cursed mirror. Yet she could not stop it.

And the Queen's other hand pinched her breasts, stretched her nipples one at a time, letting them go, and stretching them again, as the spanks went on and on until Beauty was sobbing.

Anything would have been better. Rushing through the hall at the end of Lord Gregory's paddle, the Bridle Path, even the Bridle Path, was better for there was some escape in the movement, and here there was nothing but the pain, her enflamed buttocks laid bare for the Queen who now sought out new spots, spanking on the left buttock and then the right, and then covering Beauty's thighs with smacks while Beauty's buttocks seemed to swell and throb unbearably.

"The Queen must tire. The Queen must stop," Beauty thought, but she had thought this only moments before and it went on, so that Beauty's hips were rising and falling, and she found herself squirming to the side only to be rewarded with sounder blows, more rapid blows, as if the Queen were growing ever more violent. It was as when the Prince had beaten her with the strap. It was becoming more frenzied.

Now the Queen worked on the very bottom of her buttocks, that portion which Lady Juliana had so deliberately lifted on her paddle, and she spanked hard and long on either side before moving up again and to the side, and then to Beauty's thighs and back again.

Beauty clenched her teeth to stifle her cries. She opened her eyes in frantic silent pleas seeing only the Queen's hard profile in the mirror. The Queen's eyes were narrowed, her mouth twisted, and then suddenly she gazed through the mirror at Beauty though she never ceased punishing her.

Beauty's hands broke their firm clasp and struggled to cover her buttocks, but the Queen at once moved them aside.

"You dare!" she whispered, and Beauty clasped them tight again, sobbing into the coverlet as the spanking continued.

Then the Queen's hand lay on the burning flesh without motion.

It seemed the fingers were still cold, yet they burned. And Beauty could not control her racing breath or her tears, and she would not open her eyes again.

"You shall tender me your apology for that little slip of decorum," said the Queen.

"I . . . I . . ." Beauty stammered.

" 'I am sorry, my Queen.' "

"I am sorry, my Queen." Beauty whispered frantically.

" 'I deserve only your punishment for it, my Queen' "

"I deserve only your punishment for it, my Queen."

"Yes," the Queen whispered. "And you shall have it. But all and all . . . " The Queen sighed. "Was she not good, Prince Alexi?"

"Very well behaved, your Highness, I should think, but I await your judgment."

The Queen laughed.

She pulled Beauty up roughly.

"Turn around and sit in my lap," she said.

Beauty was astonished. She at once obeyed and realized she was facing Prince Alexi. But he did not matter to her in these moments. Shaken, sore, she sat shivering on the Queen's thighs, the silk of the Queen's gown cool under her burning buttocks, the Queen's left arm cradling her.

The Queen's right hand examined her nipples, and Beauty looked down through her tears to see those white fingers again pulling the nipples.

"I had not thought to find you so obedient," said the Queen, pressing Beauty to her ample breasts, Beauty's hip against the Queen's smooth stomach. Beauty felt tiny as well as helpless, as if she were nothing in this woman's arms, nothing but something small, a child perhaps, no, not even a child.

The Queen's voice grew caressing.

"You are sweet, sweet as Lady Juliana told me you were," she said softly in Beauty's ear.

Beauty bit her lip.

"Your Highness . . ." she whispered, but she did not know what to say.

"My son has trained you well, and you show great perception."

The Queen's hand plunged down between Beauty's legs and felt the sex which had never grown cold or dry during all of the worst of the spanking, and Beauty shut her eyes.

"Ah, now why are you so afraid of my hand when it touches you gently?"

And the Queen bent and kissed Beauty's tears, tasting them on Beauty's cheeks and on her eyelids. "Sugar and salt," she said.

Beauty broke into a fresh shower of sobs. The hand between her legs massaged the most moist portion of her, and she knew that her face was flushed, and the pain and the pleasure mingled. She felt overpowered.

Her head fell back against the Queen's shoulder, and her mouth went slack, and she realized the Queen was kissing her throat, and she murmured some strange words that were not words to the Queen, some plea.

"Poor little slave," said the Queen, "poor little obedient slave. I wanted to send you home to get rid of you, to rid my son of his passion for you, my son who is now as enchanted as you were before, under the spell of the one whom he released from the spell, as if all life were a series of enchantments. But you are as perfect in temperament as he said you were, as perfect as more trained slaves, and yet you are fresher, sweeter."

Beauty gasped as the pleasure between her legs washed through her, mounting and mounting. She felt her swollen breasts might burst, and her buttocks, as always, throbbed so that she felt every inch of the abraded flesh relentlessly.

"Now, come, did I spank you so very hard, tell me?"

She took Beauty by the chin and turned her so that Beauty looked into her eyes. They were huge and black and fathomless. The lashes curled upwards, and there seemed a great casing of glass over the eyes, so deep they were, so brilliant.

"Well, answer me," said the Queen with her red lips, and she placed her finger in Beauty's mouth and tugged on her lower lip. "Answer me."

"It was . . . hard . . . hard, my Queen . . . ." Beauty said meekly.

"Well, yes, perhaps for such fresh little buttocks. But you make Prince Alexi smile with your innocence."

Beauty turned as if bidden to do so but when she gazed at Prince Alexi she did not see him smiling. Rather he was merely looking at her with the strangest expression. It was both remote and loving. And then he looked to the Queen without haste or fear and let his lips lengthen in a smile as she seemed to wish of him.

But the Queen had tipped back Beauty's head again. She kissed Beauty. The Queen's rippling hair fell down around her, full of perfume, and for the first time, Beauty felt the velvety white skin of the Queen's face, and she realized the Queen's breasts were pressed against her.

Beauty's hips moved forward, she started to gasp, but just before it became too much for her, this shock penetrating to her wet, throbbing sex, the Queen suddenly pushed her down and drew back smiling.

She held Beauty's thighs. Beauty's legs were open. And the hungry little sex wanted for all the world for the legs to be crushed closed against it.

The pleasure subsided slightly, back into that great never ending rhythm of craving.

Beauty moaned, her brows knit in a frown, and the Queen suddenly pushed her off, slapping Beauty's face so hard that Beauty cried out before she could stop herself.

"My Queen, she is so young and tender," said Prince Alexi.

"Don't try my patience," the Queen answered.

Beauty lay facedown on the bed crying.

"Rather ring for Felix and have him bring Lady Juliana. I know how young and tender is my little slave, and how much she has to learn, and that she must be punished for her small disobedience. But that is not what concerns me. I should see more of her, more of her spirit, her efforts to please, and . . . well, I have promised Lady Juliana."

It did not make any difference how hard Beauty cried, they would proceed, and Prince Alexi could not stop them. Beauty heard Felix come, she heard the Queen walking about the room, and finally when Beauty's tears were now a steady silent flow, the Queen said, "Get down from the bed, and prepare yourself to greet Lady Juliana."

HER THIGHS ●

dorothy allison

I WAS THINKING ABOUT Bobby, remembering her sitting, smoking, squint-eyed, and me looking down at the way her thighs shaped in her jeans. I have always loved women in blue jeans, worn jeans, worn particularly in that way that makes the inseam fray, and Bobby's seams had that fine white sheen that only comes after long restless evenings spent jiggling one's thighs one against the other, the other against the bar stool.

After a year as my sometimes lover, Bobby's nerves were wearing as thin as her seams. She always seemed to be looking to the other women in the bar, checking out their eyes to see if, in fact, they thought her as pussy-whipped as she thought herself, for the way she could not seem to finally settle me down to playing the wife I was supposed to be. Bobby was a wild-eyed woman, proud of her fame for running women ragged—all the women who had fallen in love with her and followed her around long after she had lost all interest in them. Hanging out at softball games on lazy spring afternoons, Bobby would look over at me tossing my head and talking to some other woman and grind her thighs together in impatience. The woman was as profoundly uncomfortable with my sexual desire as my determined independence. But nothing so disturbed her as the idea other people could see both in the way I tossed my hair, swung my hips, and would not always come when she called. Bobby believed lust was a trashy lower-class impulse, and she so wanted to be nothing like that. It meant the one tool she could have used to control me was the very one she could not let herself use.

Oh, Bobby loved to fuck me. Bobby loved to beat my ass, but it bothered her that we both enjoyed it so much. Early on in our relationship, she established a pattern of having me over for the evening and strictly enforcing a rule against sex outside the bedroom. Bobby wanted dinner—preferably Greek or Chinese take-out—and at least two hours of television. Then there had to be a bath, bath powder and toothbrushing, though she knew I preferred her unbathed and gritty, tasting of the tequila she sipped through dinner. I was not supposed to touch her until we entered the sanctuary of her bedroom, that bedroom lit only by the arc lamp in the alley outside. Only in that darkness could I bite and scratch and call her name. Only in that darkness would Bobby let herself open to passion.

Let me set the scene for you, me in my hunger for her great strong hands and perfect thighs, and her in her deliberate disregard. When feeling particularly cruel, Bobby would even insist on doing her full twenty-minute workout while I lay on the bed tearing at the sheets with my nails. I was young, unsure of myself, and so I put up with it, sometimes even enjoyed it, though what I truly wanted was her in a rage, under spotlights in a stadium, fucking to the cadence of a lesbian rock-and-roll band.

But it was years ago, and if I was too aggressive, she wouldn't let me touch her. So I waited, and watched her, and calculated. I'd start my efforts on the couch, finding excuses to play with her thighs. Rolling joints and reaching over to drop a few shreds on her lap, I scrambled for every leaf on her jeans.

"Don't want to waste any," I told her, and licked my fingers to catch the fine grains that caught in her seams. I progressed to stroking her crotch. "For the grass," I said, going on to her inseam, her knees, the backs of her thighs.

"Perhaps some slipped under here, honey. Let me see."

I got her used to the feel of my hands legitimately wandering, while her eyes never left the TV screen. I got her used to the heat of my palms, the slight scent of the sweat on my upper lip, the firm pressure of my wrists sliding past her hips. I was as calculated as any woman who knows what she wants, but I cannot tell you what magic I used to finally get her to sit still for me going down on my knees and licking that denim.

It wasn't through begging. Bobby recognized begging as a sexual practice, therefore to be discouraged outside the darkened bedroom. I didn't wrestle her for it. That, too, was allowed only in the bedroom. Bobby was the perfect withholding butch, I tell you, so I played the perfect compromising femme. I think what finally got to her was the tears.

Keeping my hands on her, I stared at her thighs intently until she started that sawing motion—crossing and recrossing her legs. My impudence made her want to grab and shake me, but that, too, might have been sex, so she couldn't. Bobby shifted and cleared her throat and watched me while I kept my mouth open slightly and stared intently at the exact spot where I wanted to put my tongue. My eyes were full of moisture. I imagined touching the denim above her labia with my lips. I saw it so clearly, her taste and texture were full in my mouth. I got wet and wetter. Bobby kept shifting on the couch. I felt my cheeks dampen and heard myself making soft moaning noises—like a young child in great hunger. That strong, dark musk odor rose between us, the smell that comes up from my cunt when I am swollen and wet from my clit to my asshole.

Bobby smelled it. She looked at my face, and her cheeks turned the brightest pink. I felt momentarily like a snake who has finally trapped a rabbit. Caught like that, on the living room couch, all her rules were momentarily suspended. Bobby held herself perfectly still, except for one moment when she put her blunt fingers on my left cheek. I leaned over and licked delicately at the seam on first the left and then the right inner thigh. Her couch was one of those swollen chintz monsters, and my nose would bump the fabric each time I moved from right to left. I kept bumping it, moving steadily, persistently, not touching her with any other part of my body except my tongue. Under her jeans, her muscles rippled and strained as if she were holding off a great response or reaching for one. I felt an extraordinary power. I had her. I knew absolutely that I was in control.

Oh, but it was control at a cost, of course, or I would be there still. I could hold her only by calculation, indirection, distraction. It was dear, that cost, and too dangerous. I had to keep a distance in my head, an icy control on my desire to lose control. I wanted to lay the whole length of my tongue on her, to dribble over my chin, to flatten my cheeks to that fabric and shake my head on her seams like a dog on a fine white bone. But that would have been too real, too raw. Bobby would never have sat still for that. I held her by the unreality of my hunger, my slow nibbling civilized tongue.

Oh, Bobby loved that part of it, like she loved her chintz sofa, the antique armoire with the fold-down shelf she used for a desk, the carefully balanced display of appropriate liquors she never touched—unlike the bottles on the kitchen shelves she emptied and replaced weekly. Bobby loved the aura of acceptability, the possibility of finally being bourgeois, civilized, and respectable.

I was the uncivilized thing in Bobby's life, reminding her of the taste of hunger, the remembered stink of her mother's sweat, her own desire. I became sex for her. I held it in me, in the push of my thighs against hers when she finally grabbed me and dragged me off into the citadel of her bedroom. I held myself up, back and off her. I did what I had to do to get her, to get myself what we both wanted. But what a price we paid for what I did.

What I did.

What I was.

What I do.

What I am.

I paid a high price to become who I am. Her contempt, her terror, were the least of it. My contempt, my terror, took over my life, because they were the first things I felt when I looked at myself, until I became unable to see my true self at all. "You're an animal," she used to say to me, in the dark with her teeth against my thigh, and I believed her, growled back at her, and swallowed all the poison she could pour into my soul.

Now I sit and think about Bobby's thighs, her legs opening in the dark where no one could see, certainly not herself. My own legs opening. That was so long ago and far away, but not so far as she finally ran when she could not stand it anymore, when the lust I made her feel got too wild, too uncivilized, too dangerous. Now I think about what I did.

What I did.

What I was.

What I do.

What I am.

"Sex." I told her. "I will be sex for you."

Never asked, "You. What will you be for me?"

Now I make sure to ask. I keep Bobby in mind when I stare at women's thighs. I finger my seams, flash my teeth, and put it right out there.

"You. What will you let yourself be for me?"

FOUR BARE LEGS ●
IN A BED

helen simpson

WHEN YOU DRAW the curtains in the morning you stand in front of the window like a black dog. I am brought down to earth with a bump. It isn't fair.

"Where were *you* last night?"

You ask, even though you *know* we were sitting side by side over a shepherd's pie in front of *World in Action*. I sip my tea and blink at the little azure Chinaman fishing from his pagoda.

"*Well?*" you insist.

I channel vertically under the sheet to hide my blushing neck, muttering demulcent nothings. Goats and monkeys.

What can I say, after all? I can hardly admit that I had a most colorful and stimulating night, thank you, lying bear-hugged with your squash partner skin to skin, dissolving in an exchange of slow damp kisses.

Don't let on to the Old Man, but I think I can safely say I have slept with all the men and boys of my acquaintance, including the grey-beards and one-way homosexuals and those towards whom I had not thought I felt an iota of oestrus.

Only two nights ago I was lying on a riverbank with the other girls, and beside me knelt a boy of about fourteen or fifteen, a childish little chap. A boatload of his schoolfriends in their uniforms drifted past. They wore straw hats, but the sun beat up from the river to make crescents of light flick like sticklebacks over their faces. As they floated by, their smarmy teacher unleashed on us a particularly obsequious grin. His teeth were snaggled and tarnished. Ooh, we all giggled, revolted, and my little boy showed himself in sympathy. I gave him a kiss and a hug; there was a beam of envy from the schoolmaster. I gave him more hugs and kisses, and a generous warmth spread through me, tantalizing and lovely.

"You're only fourteen, aren't you, darling," I teased, pressing his head to my bosom, pretending to be motherly. I woke describing circles, and I was laughing.

When we were first married, all of six months ago, he used to bring home large men in suits who laughed loudly, drank beer from tins and said outlandish things in suddenly solemn voices: for example, "It's time to put your cock on the block," and, "We are talking serious megabucks." After a couple of months he stopped inviting them. I missed the flick of their eyes, but by then of course we were talking serious monogamy.

A couple of nights before the wedding we met for a drink on Eel Pie Island. We stood in the long grass staring upstream, watching the Thames flow by on either side, dividing just before it reached us and meeting again behind us. I looked back down half-a-dozen years and saw my secret self at thirteen or fourteen. I had never felt incomplete alone, nor had I ever trembled for security. Now I had a premonition that my privacy and self-possession, which harmed nobody and were my only important treasures, would be things of the past the day after tomorrow. My saying yes to a wedding appeared in this illuminated instant as self-betrayal. A tide of shame and terror crept over my skin, moving fast like spilt wine. I stammered some thin wedge of these thoughts to my future husband, thinking (with an early marital shudder at the predictability), he will say no man is an island.

"No man is an island," he said.

Incidentally, marriage gave his words the lie, since it made an island of every man except himself. Conjugal life correctly conjugated reads: libido libidas libidat libidamus libidatis libiDON'T. Goodbye to the pure uncomplicated glee which can spring up between strangers, leading them out of their clothes and towards each other in a spirit of, among other things, sunny friendship.

The girls at school had a quasi-religious conviction that once you felt the right way about a man, that was *it*. He was the other half who would make you whole, he was the only possible father of your children. I meet Rhoda every once in a while for a slice of cauliflower quiche, and she still subscribes to all that.

"Either it's Animal Lust, which doesn't last," says Rhoda, "or it's the Real Thing, which means Marriage." Rhoda likes things cut and dried. Recently she became engaged to the only possible father of her children. She took him shopping for a ring, hauled him past the windows of Hatton Garden, and he expressed nothing but ridicule at the prices. Next time he went to tea with Rhoda's parents, he was sitting on the edge of the sofa balancing a plate of flapjacks on his knee when his prospective mother-in-law produced a tray of unpriced rings and demanded that he choose one.

She said her daughter Rhoda was not to be shamed by a naked finger. He chose, and of course it turned out to be the second most expensive, over a thousand. There is a moral in that somewhere.

Sometimes I slide my ring off before we go to a party, but he makes me put it on again. That left-handed ring finger is the weakest of the ten, always the first to let you down during a vigorous scherzando; there are sets of arpeggios based exclusively round strengthening its feebleness. It is also the most sensitive, the one women use when following such instructions as, Pat this featherweight creme lightly into the fragile skin tissue which surrounds the eye area.

Lily-livered, swathed in white from head to foot, I said, "I will." Willing and waking may come to the same thing, but sleep is another matter. I am only properly alone now when I'm asleep, such is the encroachment. Well, sleep is a third part of life so I suppose I mustn't grumble.

You don't even have a right to your own bed when you're married. There is no escaping the mildmint breath toothpasting its way across the pillows. I am lying cool and straight in my bed when *he* climbs in with a proprietorial air, and I catch myself thinking, "How dare you." I never achieve the old full secrecy now, I never properly escape him, not until I've lost consciousness altogether. And even then . . . The other night as I lay waiting for sleep—almost there—I felt his fingertips on my eyelids, and I knew he was testing whether the eyeballs were moving in order to tell whether I was dreaming or not.

My husband is older than me; not so much older that he thanks his lucky stars for me, but sufficiently older to create the distance of a demi-generation gap between us. He is a Management Consultant and he thinks he's got me taped. He probably has, except for my nocturnal life. He has a square leonine head with icy blue-green eyes. I don't know what he thinks about—"If only he could talk," as old people say of their pets.

You could say we rushed into it, but then, why *not* repent at leisure. How dismal are those long-term liaisons where, the seven years and a day being up, no nerve is left to take the plunge. On our honeymoon near St. Ives, there was one late wordless picnic down on the beach when I stared at his cleanly minted profile against the night sky and worshipped the silence. Out last week at some busy new restaurant, however, we sat dumbly over plates of chili-spiced pomfret fish until in the end, to stop the water-drops leaping, I lowered my eyes, staring hard at his tee-shirt, on which was traced a detailed map of half a square mile of the Outer Hebrides, and savagely wished myself there.

His worst failing so far is jealousy. The last time I rang him at the office, his secretary said earnestly, "I haven't seen hare nor hound of him." But if *he* rings *me* and I don't answer, there is likely to be an inquisition. Last week it got beyond a joke. I had taken the phone off the hook because Mr.

Pembleton had come round to give me my clarinet lesson and at nine pounds an hour I don't like to take any chances on being interrupted. Anyway, towards the end of the lesson we were deep into a passage of Albinoni, quite transported by its bosky rills, and Mr. Pembleton's eyebrows were leaping in time to the rhythm as always, when in burst my bellowing pinstriped husband. It was very embarrassing. I was furious. Mr. Pembleton was almost crying as he slunk off, not even given enough time to pack away his clarinet properly.

I shall have to be more careful in future.

Sometimes I have a dream that tears through me like a hurricane and leaves me shaking, the sort of dream that used to be explained away as the work of devils. There were sleepy female demons who gave out such heat that even in midwinter the soporific lettuce seeds sprouted when they walked by, the mere rustle of their skirts made frosty rosebushes blossom into full-blown crimson. Such a succuba would descend in a hot dream upon a sleeping man with an appetite so violent that by the time she had finished with him even the densest-bearded would wake quite exhausted and feeling as though his bones had been dislocated. My own hurricanes would no doubt have been described as the work of that cocky male devil the incubus, whose nocturnal interference was held responsible for the births of mutants and monsters.

Occasionally, at the end of some mad sparkling quarrel, he clubs me down at last with that spiteful threat: "What *you* need is a baby. *That* would sort you out." Oh yes, that would be the end of this road and no mistake. They're all on his side, of course: First it was ordained for the procreation of children, etc.

Do you think it possible that a dream confluence—put it more bluntly, fusion with a chimera—might result in a phantom pregnancy? Or does the waking self give up the ghost?

My dreams have been with me from the edge of childhood, mostly the sort of dream in which every courtesy is maintained and every permission given; but I never knew before I married what it was to be a quarreller. Our rows are like the weather, there is no control over them and very little warning, sometimes none at all. We might be basking in the sunshine when a squall appears from nowhere and within seconds develops into a howling tornado. At the same time and with equal speed we hurtle back down the decades, transformed into giant infants stamping and frowning and spouting tears of rage.

"*Don't* talk to me then! See if I care!" rings out with playground simplicity.

I slap his arm and burst into tears of rage and disappointment. I follow him into the next room. "What about the time you left me stranded by the Albert Memorial," I yell.

"You sound just like a scratched old record," he hisses. He follows me upstairs. Insults cramp my throat. I find the best one and aim it carefully like a dart. I watch the pupils disappear to pin-points in the great excited aquamarine irises of his eyes.

"Go away! Go away!" I shout, turning to the wall as he approaches and whamming my forehead against it.

Every time this happens I am astonished at the pack of devils let loose.

We fall into bed like two nasty children. He says things so hard that I feel little shooting spasms in sexual places, so then I feel they *must* be true. I am quiet. I think about them. Then I slap out at him and he thumps me, so I scratch and bite. He says my name after I've turned out the light but I don't answer. We lie awake in that sort of long dead silence when all future life is Arabia Deserta.

We still behave fairly normally in public, avoiding the little bitternesses which longer-established married couples automatically bat to and fro without self-consciousness. Recently we had to go to a dinner party given by one of my husband's grateful clients. Towards the end of the meal, the client's wife ran in from her kitchen bearing a Baked Alaska alight with blue rum-based flames. In case you don't know about Baked Alaska, it is a nightmare of a pudding which only a fool would try to make, a large lump of ice cream covered with heavily whipped sugar-stiffened raw egg-whites sitting on a sponge cake. This structure is cauterized in a scorching oven for three minutes, during which time the ice cream is supposed to stay frozen while the meringue bakes to brown peaks. It is what you might call the Ur-recipe for disaster.

The client and his wife were a fairly tense couple anyway, but the stealthy sniping with which they had seasoned the early part of the meal was now given culinary fulfillment.

"Knife, darling." His voice rose to shrillness. "*Sharp* knife."

"I *know*, darling, but cut it faster than you did last time," she urged. "You remember what happened *then*."

"It's *melting*, darling," he barked.

"You're not cutting it *fast* enough," she said. A slice shot across the waiting tea-plate, and ice cream slopped onto the tablecloth.

"Come on, come *on*!" Her brows were knitting furiously, and she was dancing a little jig at his side.

"It's been in too long," he said as the second slice collapsed.

"Three minutes and not a second more, on my mother's grave," she said with hatred. "It's *you*. You're so *slow*."

The table had fallen silent, no chit-chat being possible at the borders of such a scene. I looked on with what I thought of as a sort of Olympian compassion at first, until, like a tuning fork, I shuddered, catching certain unmistakably *married* reverberations.

This morning when I wolf-whistled him as he emerged shaggy and glistening from the shower, he clapped his hands over himself and said, "That's not exactly very feminine, is it." He has beautiful hands, fine as earth, rough and warm like brown sand. Sometimes he lets me wash his back and shoulders, which is when I get the *marvelling* feeling most strongly. I have never told him about this.

I first felt helpless admiration when I watched him come off the court after a game of tennis, pulling off his shirt as roughly as a child would, his sweat drops white and pearly in the sun. His face was brighter than silver, sunburnt to coppery patches on the cheekbones, his florid shoulders weathered almost to the color of claret. Let me love you, I said silently as we went to bed that night for the first time, let me stroke your shadows with my fingers and inhale your skin's smell of honey and air; let me love you before you heave ho my hearty.

At night, in pajamas (which did not appear until after the wedding), he curled to me like a striped mollusk, with the long curving back of a prawn. My little crocodile, I said maliciously as he draped his length against me in bed. When he whispered in my ears (which he still does sometimes) then he caused trembling while my fingers and toes turned to sparklers. It made him groan like a wood-pigeon before falling asleep, though usually I was chortling away for some time afterwards.

Then, my mind was a sunny prairie of contentment; my body was quick, god-like, with a central line of stars. There was the scarcely-dare-believe-it hope that marriage might even mean years of this ahead, safe-guarding a life of such subterranean holiday in perpetuity. Yes, yes, there is more to marriage than *that*, I know that now; but surely there is nothing as good.

About six months ago, a week or two after the marrying event, we were walking along the edges of some stubbled corn-fields when we came to a solitary house in a field of its own. We looked through the windows—some of which were broken—and there was no furniture inside, so we didn't feel like intruders when we lifted the latch of the garden gate. Concealed by its hedge from the gaze of idle ramblers was a menagerie of topiary, wild-looking peacocks, boars sprouting long leafy green bristles, one or two blurred heraldic hounds. It was hot, late in the afternoon, and we lay down on a bed of box clippings at the end of the garden. I could see horse-chestnut trees nodding beyond the hedge. The densely knit noise of bees came from a nearby tangle of blackberries. I slipped out of my clothes, we lay together on his shirt, we concentrated suddenly for a while on a time of intense and escalating delight. Afterwards I was wicked with pleasure, and we shared the bread roll and apples saved from our pub lunch. I remember noticing the red and green striations on the apples' skins and the miraculous honey-combed structure of the bread. Then we fell asleep.

I dreamed an urgent heated dream of the sort which sometimes follows hard on the heels of satisfaction.

I was walking down the High Street in Bakewell with a modest strong young man. He was quite tall; as he talked to me, he turned his head slightly and tipped his glance down to shoulder level. He was telling me how he made all his own bread, how easy it was, just two or three loaves a week, or four when he felt unusually hungry.

"How on earth do you find the time," I said. "All that kneading and proving."

"Oh, you can fit that in round other things in the odd few minutes here and there," he assured me.

He showed me his current mass of dough, throwing it lightly from hand to hand like a goal-keeper. Then he wore it as a vast damp pliable boxing glove, deftly pulling at it and pummelling it with his other hand.

"You try," he said. I found the glove-trick manipulation too difficult, so instead I kneaded away enthusiastically. It grew and grew, elastic and cirrus-streaked, until I felt worried.

"Have I spoiled the loaf?" I asked anxiously.

"Not at all," he said. "It'll be even better than usual." We continued our walk, his arm round my shoulder as friendly as could be.

When I woke up it was almost evening, warm and still. I watched his crumpled face a foot away coming out of sleep, the lids flickering, light clearing the eyes and then a wreath of smiles.

We used to be *friends* then.

He upends me, he takes no notice of anything above the waist. How would *he* like it, that's what *I'd* like to know. And after some farmyard activity, while *I'm* still inside my nightdress, very often, he cages me in his big arms and legs and disappears with a snore.

"How did you sleep?" My husband has started to make casual enquiries. "Did you have any interesting dreams?" I found a rubbishy paperback calling itself a Dictionary of Oneirology in his briefcase the other night when I was looking for *The Times*. How fascinating to learn that in Islam dreams of shrews are always related to faithless wives; I wonder if that works the other way around. And dreams of being infected with vermin are often the equivalent for pregnancy, it says here. No flies on *me*. Soon he will be cross-questioning me about the possible appearance of daggers, snakes, nail-files and umbrellas in my night pictures.

What does worry me is that I am finding it increasingly difficult to tell the difference between dreaming and awake. I often feel quite astonished when I turn out of a dream into the morning. I shout or laugh in dreams and wake my husband. I dream I am dreaming; or I dream I have woken up. I try to test whether a dream is a dream by cutting a plate of sardine sandwiches; I scoff the lot and am none the wiser. Recently I tried biting my hand in a dream to see if I was awake. Next morning there were toothmarks, so where does that leave me?

I was very late back one night last week, and crept up the stairs hoping he would have fallen asleep. No such luck. He was propped up against the pillows, and closed *Anna Karenina* with a bang as I came into the room.

"It took ages to find a taxi," I said. "They seem to dry up after eleven."

. "Why didn't you catch the train? The last one doesn't go until eleven-thirty."

"I know, but Rhoda and I were having such an interesting discussion in the wine bar. The film was very thought-provoking."

"What was it again?"

"*Battleship Potemkin*." Surely he wouldn't have seen that. *I* certainly hadn't.

"Ah. What was it about?"

"Oh, you know, the nature of war, particularly at sea."

"And you and Rhoda sat till past midnight discussing naval tactics over the Liebfraumilch."

"Along with related matters. Look, you can just stop being so suspicious. I'm sick of your bullying. I'm going to get changed." I stormed off to the bathroom with my nightdress.

"Stay here," he called. No fear, I thought as I bolted the bathroom door. That way he would see that, at the particular request of Mr. Pembleton, I had uncharacteristically left off my bra. I took a quick cold shower using Coal Tar soap, and went back into the bedroom with an innocent smile.

"Where did you find a taxi," he said.

"Oh, don't start again."

"I want to know."

"Waterloo Bridge."

"But you say you met Rhoda at the Barbican."

"Yes, I did, but the wine bar was a little way off, and then there are no taxis in the City late at night. So we carried on walking because we knew there are always taxis on Waterloo Bridge."

"It's miles to Waterloo from the Barbican."

"I *know*, and that's why I'm so tired and cross and longing for bed. And if that's all the sympathy you can show, I wish I'd never married you." I burst into tears at last, and finally convinced him of my blamelessness, so much so that he apologized and kissed me goodnight.

Then I woke up, and the crocodile tears were still trickling down my cheeks. I looked at the clock—five a.m.—and at the sleeping bulk beside me, remembering how we had spent the previous evening in front of the fire playing chess. You see how confusing it can be.

He beat me at that game of chess as he usually (though not invariably) does. When I was putting the pieces away, thinking about them one by one, I said, "I like the knight best. I like his L-shaped hopping."

"You would," said my husband, *bitterly*. The funny thing was, I understood exactly how he felt.

When I catch him in some detail of his body, whirling his little finger round an ear rim or squeezing a pore on the wing of his nose, our eyes meet coldly and he looks away. These fugitive glimpses of hatred between us are frighteningly hearty.

Yesterday, on my way to the shops, I was standing waiting to cross at the busy corner by Marchmont Drive, when a blue plumber's van flew by. The driver's window was open and, although he must have been doing fifty, I caught a long moment of his burnished shoulder and beautiful naked arm with the underarm tuft like the beard of a mussel. There was a blast of music—"Get Out of My Dream and Into My Car"—as potent as a rogue whiff of jasmine, then it was all gone. I almost cried; I still had a lump in my throat by the time I reached the dry-cleaners. You're not saying that means nothing.

Recently I have noticed a disturbing change. Disapproving of my keeping any secrets from him, my husband has started appearing at precisely the wrong moment in places where he doesn't belong. Last night I was lying in a tipped-back chair while the dentist puffed some sort of dizziness around me until I was only half-conscious. He approached and stroked me, removing his white coat, holding me, pressing me to him; and then my husband appeared in the doorway and said, "Excuse me, I'll take over now."

I woke furious to his unconscious weight at my side. I felt like hitting him, but subsided, snarling. When I got back again I was by the sea and it was warm luminous evening. The light was so rare, the sky and sea of such a strange icy blue-green, that I knew I was further north than usual. I walked a few steps along sibilant shingle and quietly plosive bladder-wrack, noticing that both a red sun and a yellow moon were in the sky, though the sun was very low. Now, running lightly down the dunes of marram grass appeared some sort of fisherman or sea-gypsy; I was only able to take in the black eyes with their oblique gleam.

He was beside me and the sides of our faces touched; his felt like the skin of a starfish and mine like the lining of a shell. I was both aware of existing in my own body—the mild drumming of my pulses, the gentle maritime roar in my ears—and of being able to see myself and this other figure standing on the shore.

He took a small mother-of-pearl box from his trouser pocket and gave it to me, watching intently as I nodded my thanks. Then his arm lifted at the elbow and he slid his finger under a strand of hair which had stuck to my forehead. I saw my face and neck flood with color just as the disappearing sun set fire to a stripe of sea. He slid his hand suddenly through the deep armhole of my dress and his fingers curled to the shape of my breast. I lost all power and was beached onto his shoulder.

Time makes a little leap. We are in a house built of driftwood and pine branches. The windows show oblongs of brine-blanched aquamarine; there are bubbles and knots in the glass. He is stoking the sea-coal fire. I stand waiting and hot salt tears brim up. He draws me gently into him again. I feel the extreme heat of his body; it radiates through his clothes like the sun. The middle of my own body bucks softly, gratefully. We stare at each other with reluctant half-smiles, and from our stiff breathing you might think we are about to fight.

We lie down together on the bed by the wall. I close my eyes, curiously at rest now, floating. His violent hand plucks me from my suspension in the middle air and I hug him with equal violence. We rock together as though it seems our ribs must crack.

But when at last it comes to it, clipped in the warm frame of his arms, thighs enfolded in his tangle, at this moment I happen to glance across his shoulder and so spoil everything. It has been going swimmingly but now there will be no conclusion. I sit up, spit words of refusal, glare across the room.

He has done it again. This second invasion *proves* he has broken my cover. Now I will never more be private, even in the slumbering third part of my time. There at the window, his face like a censorious turnip, my husband is staring in.

FROM HOW TO SAVE ● YOUR OWN LIFE

erica jong

Now, THERE ARE TIMES when the very air is sexual, when it's dusk and the moon is hanging low over the rooftops, and the temperature of your blood is the same temperature as the air and you look at a man—any halfway decent-looking man—and you know you could go right to bed with no questions asked at all. This was *not* that sort of night.

It was cold, the participants were all rather constrained and strange to each other, and sex was not in the air. But here we all were together—and Rob was a practical fellow. An opportunity like this might not arise again. At such time, pot is invaluable. Pot and the Beatles. How many orgies might have faltered without pot and the Beatles! That clitoral trill, that thumping bass. And sweet smoke filling the lungs, the head, the cunt . . . and the Beatles singing *'because the world is round . . . it turns me onnn.'*

Goddamn, I *missed* the sixties. When everyone was dropping acid and their pants every two minutes, I was in Germany with boring Bennett being a "good wife," cooking gourmet meals, breaking my leg in penance for wanting the most natural thing in the world—my freedom. I wanted to go to parties in town with the students at the University of Heidelberg. I wanted to get stoned and fuck and act my age. But Bennett, who was routinely fucking Penny in my study twice a week, pronounced all that *"infantile"* and sent me to a shrink to "work it out." Then, at the dangerous age of twenty-nine I took one fling with Adrian Goodlove and came back— not dutiful this time—but, worse, cynical. Formerly submissive, I was now independent—independent but resigned to never communicating with my husband, to never finding any love that lasted, to patching up my aching emptiness with silly meaningless midday affairs . . .

Damn, damn, damn—if only I hadn't missed the sixties! If only I had sown some wild oats like Josh did.

Josh. I shut my eyes and saw Josh. I was lying on the couch, wineglass in one hand, joint in the other, when Josh's funny, warm, furry face swam into my field of vision. "I love you too—but is it *enough?*" he was saying. He was standing at the airport, at the end of the boarding ramp. And I would never get back through that tunnel and into his arms again. Like Alice, having drunk the wrong potion, I was too big, too old, too sad, too disillusioned . . .

"Want to dance?" Hans said, taking me by the hand. He had a nice bony European face—but it wasn't Josh's.

What the hell, I thought. Hans pulled me up out of the deep couch. The music had now changed to 1967 psychedelic—*Sgt. Pepper's Lonely Hearts Club Band*—and it was taking me back, back, back to those years in Germany when I felt so guilty for being young, for being horny, for wanting what *every*one wants at twenty-five—while my middle-aged husband (who was *born* middle-aged) had his cake and ate it too, telling me all the while I was "infantile." Unforgivable!

Damn. It wasn't too late to be twenty-five! I would rather be twenty-five at thirty-two than never be twenty-five at all!

Dancing. I had almost forgotten how much I loved dancing. With a little pot and some good music and a pinch of despair as the kicker, I can get into dancing as if dancing were the only thing I ever did. My body moves right into the music as if the music were its home. And I dance—not like someone who thinks and frets and worries all the time, not like someone who analyzes and re-analyzes everything—but like someone who listens to no beat but the beat between her legs. And in a way I *become* that person.

Hans and I danced and danced until we danced into the bedroom. "Someone has to start an orgy," I said to him, "and it might as well be us."

"Agreed!" he said, laughing. Hans said *everything* laughing. Hans was jolly and clever and if I closed my eyes and forgot his bony body, his strange face, his strange laugh, his death's-head skull, his funny accent—I could almost pretend it was Josh taking off my clothes, Josh running a slick finger between the wet lips of my cunt, Josh unzipping his fly, Josh's big cock coming into me, Josh's face covering mine with kisses . . . I looked up at Hans and through his face I could see—in that special way only possible to the very stoned—all the faces of the men I had loved or lusted for blending into each other. Josh melted into Bennett, Bennett into Adrian, Adrian into Charlie, Charlie into Brian, Brian into my father. They were all one man. There was no difference between them at all. I dug my nails into Hans's back and came screaming and crying and shrieking at the top of my lungs, 'It isn't fair, it isn't fair, it isn't fair!'

Hans had gentle instincts. He didn't get angry or frightened. He stroked my hair.

"*What* isn't fair, Isadora?" he asked.

But I was too stoned to explain, and by now my screams had attracted the rest of the party, who appeared, dancing like bacchantes—some wishing to comfort me, others to join in the fun. I was bleary-eyed and stoned. The music was loud ("*I'd love to turn you on* . . .") and I scarcely remember who inaugurated the first combination or the second or the third—or indeed how one could *tell* one from the other.

Somewhere at the hazy beginning of it all, I was being fucked in the ass by Hans while Rosanna ate me and Rosanna's husband sucked my nipples. (Then Kirsten of the gigantic knockers appeared and preempted me in the breast department.) At a later, wetter, and sweatier point in the evening, Robert was fucking me and Rosanna was behind him encouraging him and holding his balls helpfully. I couldn't help but notice that Robert never did get very hard—and it momentarily flickered through my mind that maybe this was really the secret of *most* of the sex people—the sexual emissionaries; they really weren't very potent without (what you might call) all this peer-group pressure. At some point Robert fucked Rosanna—and I had the distinct sense that it took all the *rest* of us being there as observers for them to accomplish the simplest missionary mating.

"But was it *fun*?" my friends always ask. And the truth is, I can hardly even *remember*. Of course it was engrossing. And of course there were lots of orgasms—mine, his, hers, theirs, everybody's. And there was the added pleasure of feeling superior, liberated, special—above the common bourgeois run of uptight people, fucking two by two.

I kept thinking, Oh gee, I'm eating a *woman* while another woman eats *me*, while a man fucks her, while a man sucks him! Oh *golly*, this is certainly a first! And yet the dominant feeling of it all was that we should have had someone there directing traffic, possibly with a megaphone—because it was all so much like *rush hour*. There was a good deal of rearranging bodies so that our various human chains would be unbroken, and the positions we found were not the kind that were easy for your average amateur nonpracticing yogin or yogina to master. But we persevered—valiantly. A kind of group greediness took over—and those of us who were normally sated after one, two, three orgasms felt it incumbent upon us to have dozens of orgasms—in all positions, with everyone present.

I was astounded at my own stamina. This (by now) virtually anonymous pile of bodies became like one organism, stretching, contracting, eating, excreting, moving onto drier ground when we had soiled the last. It had ten arms, ten legs, two penises, three vaginas and six breasts—of assorted sizes—not to mention ten eyes, ten ears, and five mouths (that were practically always full). Something was always in eruption—as in a region of volcanos. Something was always being gobbled by some orifice or other. When at last Kirsten got up and went into the living room to bring wine for us, it felt like an amputation.

And yet there was also a wonderful feeling of closeness, of sheer physicalness, of being nothing but a body and that being *enough*. It was almost like the way I'd felt in California, looking at the waves roll in, feeling the balmy air, and thinking that nothing could possibly be wrong with the world if the sky was so clear you could see all the way to Japan—or Catalina.

Thinking of California made me fix on Josh again, and I was overcome with sadness. I felt I'd betrayed him. I remembered the orgy we hadn't had with Ralph Battaglia, and I felt incredibly guilty to have participated in this one. These weren't people I loved—they were *bodies*. The closeness I'd felt a minute before shifted to revulsion. The others were drifting off to sleep in various position on the bed and floor. I got up and wandered into the bathroom, where I stared at myself for a long time in the mirror over the sink, wondering what on *earth* to do now.

5

EXTREME BEHAVIOR

Women trick themselves this way. They've thrown away the treasure, whatever it might be but they're sneaking bits and pieces anyway they can . . . Are they writing? Yes, but secretly, so they have no support, no feedback. The student, is she going for her edge? Yes, but secretly so that she can have no help and no mentor. What about the ambitious woman who is pretending to be not ambitious, but who is heartfelt toward accomplishments for herself, her people, her world? She is the powerful dreamer, yet consigns herself to struggle forward in silence. It is deadly to be without a confidante, without a guide, without even a tiny cheering section.

It is difficult to sneak little shreds of life this way but women do it every day. When a woman feels compelled to sneak life, she is in minimal subsistence mode. She sneaks life away from the hearing of "them," whoever the "them" are in her life. She acts disinterested and calm on the surface, but whenever there is a crack of light, her starved self leaps out, runs for the nearest life form, lights up, kicks back, charges madly, dances herself silly, exhausts herself, then tries to creep back to the black cell before anyone notices she is gone.

You see, there is something in the wild soul that will not let us subsist forever on piecemeal intake. Because in actuality, it is impossible for the woman who strives for consciousness to sneak little sniffs of good air, and then be content with no more . . . go slowly if you have been a feral woman, starved for the wild, broken in instinct for a time. Go slowly and learn your way back, know the difference between snuffling up all things in excess and savoring your reclaimed life . . . Nothing is leaving the planet. Even though you've not had real life for a time, it is all still here. Go easy . . .

from the chapter, "Identifying Leg Traps and Self Preservation— The Red Shoes," from *Women Who Run With the Wolves*

IT'S BAD LUCK TO DIE ●

elizabeth mccracken

MAYBE YOU WONDER HOW a Jewish girl from Des Moines got Jesus Christ tattooed on her three times: ascending on one thigh, crucified on the other, and conducting a miniature apocalypse beneath the right shoulder. It wasn't religion that put them there; it was Tiny, my husband. I have a Buddha round back, too. He was going to give me Moses parting the Red Sea, but I was running out of space. Besides, I told him, I was beginning to feel like a Great Figures in Religion comic book.

He got dreamy-eyed when he heard that. "Brigham Young," he said. "And some wives."

I told him: "Tiny, I've got no room for a polygamist."

Tiny himself had been married three times before he met me, one wife right after the other. I only had him, the one, and he's been dead six months now.

I met Tiny the summer I graduated high school, 1965, when I was eighteen and he was forty-nine. My cousin Babs, who was a little wild, had a crazy boyfriend (the whole family was worried about it) and he and some of his buddies dared her to get tattooed. She called me up and told me she needed me there and that I was not to judge, squawk, or faint at the sight of blood. She knew none of that was my style, anyhow.

We drove to Tiny's shop over on East 14th because that's where Steve, the crazy boy, had got the panther that had a toehold on his shoulder. The shop was clean and smelled of antiseptic; Babs and I were disappointed.

Sheets of heavy paper in black dime-store frames hung on the walls—flash sheets—arranged by theme: one had Mickey Mouse and Woody Woodpecker; another, a nurse in a Red Cross cap and a geisha offering a drink on a tray. A big flash by the door had more ambitious designs: King Kong and Cleopatra on the opposite sides of one page, looking absentmindedly into each other's eyes.

Tiny was set up on a stool in back, smoking a cigarette, an itty-bit of a man next to a Japanese screen. He was wearing a blue dress shirt with the cuffs turned back, and his hands and arms were covered with blue-black lines: stars across the knuckles, snakes winding up under the sleeves. The wide flowered tie that spread out over his chest and stomach might've been right on a big man, but on Tiny it looked like an out-of-control garden. His pants were white and wrinkled, and there was a bit of blue ink at the knee; a suit jacket, just as wrinkled, hung on the coat rack in back.

He eyed our group, scowled at Steve and his two friends, and solemnly winked at me and Babs.

"So," he said. "Who's the one?"

"Me," Babs said, trying to sound tough. She told him what she wanted: a little red-and-black bow on her tush. He asked her if she were old enough; she got out her wallet and showed him her driver's license.

Steve and his friends were buzzing around the shop, looking at the flash and tapping the ones they really liked.

"Keep your hands off the designs, boys," said Tiny. "I can't tattoo a fingerprint." He turned to Babs. "Okay. Come back of the screen." There was something a little southern in his voice, but I couldn't pick out what it was. He jumped off the stool, and I saw that he was about a full foot shorter than me. I'm six feet tall, have been since eighth grade. I looked right down on top of his slick black hair.

We all started to follow him. Tiny looked at us and shook his head.

"You boys have to stay out here."

"I'm her boyfriend," said Steve. "I've seen it before, and I'm paying."

"If you've seen it before, you'll see it again, so you don't need to now. Not in my shop, anyhow. You—" he pointed at me "—come around to testify I'm a gentleman."

He beckoned us back of the screen to a padded table, the kind you see in doctors' offices, only much lower. Tiny turned around politely while Babs lowered her blue jeans and clambered up. He spun back, frowned, pulled down just the top of her yellow flowered underwear like he was taking fat off a chicken, and tapped her. "Right here's where you want it?"

"That's fine."

"Honey, is it fine, or is it what you want?"

Babs twisted to look, careful not to catch his eye. "That's what I want."

He squirted her with antiseptic, got a razor and shaved the area good. I sat on a folding chair across from them.

Tiny loosened his tie, slipped it off, and hung it, still knotted, on a peg on the wall. "Hey Stretch," he said, looking at me. "What's your name?"

"Lois."

"Lois. Like Louise?" He rolled his shirtsleeves up further. Babs was holding on to the table like a drowning sailor, and Tiny hadn't even got the needle out yet.

"Lois," I answered, and fast, because I had to talk to him over Bab's hindquarters and that made me a little self-conscious, "after my Uncle Louis. I was going to be named Natalie, after my Uncle Nathan, but then Louis died and Mom liked him better anyhow."

"My name is Tiny. No story there but the obvious." He picked up an electric needle from a workbench and hunted for the right pot of color.

"I'm Babs," said Babs, reaching around for a handshake. Tiny was looking elsewhere, and he dipped the needle in some black ink and flipped it on. "For Barbara?" he asked, setting into her skin.

"A-a-a-a-bigail. Ouch." She gripped the table.

"Honey," said Tiny, "this doesn't hurt. I got you where you're good and fleshy. Might sting a little, but it doesn't hurt."

"Okay," said Babs, and she sounded almost convinced.

"For Abraham," I said suddenly. "Abigail after Abraham."

"Pretty girls named after men," said Tiny, taking a cloth and wiping some ink off of Babs so he could see what he was doing. "Thought that only happened in the South."

Looking back, it seems like he took an hour working on Babs, but now I know it couldn't have been more than ten minutes. He looked up at me from time to time, smiling or winking. I thought that he was just one of those flirty types, one of those bold little guys, and that if he had been looking at Babs in the face instead of where he was looking at her, he would've flirted with her the same. Years later he told me that he was bowled over by all those square inches of skin, how I was so big and still not fat. "I fell for you right away," he said.

Up until then, I'd always thought it was only sensible to fall in love with tall men so that I wouldn't look like so much of a giantess. That way we could dance in public, in scale, no circus act. It didn't matter, though: I never had a date all through high school, couldn't dance a step. I spent my time in movie houses, because most movie stars looked pretty tall, even if it was only a trick of the camera, a crate under their feet in love scenes.

Tiny, no doubt, no tricks about it, was short, but he charmed me from the start. His charm was as quick and easy as his needle, and he could turn it on and off the same way. On the Tuesday afternoons I visited him before we got married, I saw all types jangle the bell on the front door as they pushed it open: big men, skinny kids, nervous couples gambling on love forever. Most of them asked the same thing: "Does it hurt?" To people who rubbed him wrong, he'd say, "If you're worried about it, I guess you don't really want one"; to those he liked, chiefly the women, he'd drawl, "I could make you smile while I do it." He could, too; he could tell your background by the feel of your skin, and would talk about ridiculous things—baseball scores, recipes for homemade beer, the sorry state of music—anything but the business at hand.

He could even charm my mother, who, on meeting Tiny, this little man only two years younger than her, was grieved to discover she liked him.

When he was finished with Babs, he put on a bandage and handed her a little white card that said *How To Take Care Of Your New Tattoo*. It had his name and address at the bottom. She read it and nodded. He turned and gave me a card, too.

"Anything for you today?" he asked me.

"No, no. I'm a chaperon, that's all."

"Too bad. You'd tattoo great. You're pale—high contrast." He reached up and tapped me on the collarbone.

Babs looked a little white herself now, standing up, zipping her pants. Tiny got his tie and put it back on, tightened it as we walked around front.

"I like to look natty," he told me. Then he said to Steve, all business, "Eight dollars."

The boys crowded around Babs, who was suddenly looking pleased and jaunty, shaking her head: no, it didn't hurt; no big deal; no, not now, I'll show it to you later. I'm still the only member of the family that knows she has that tattoo.

"You wanna stick around and chat awhile?" Tiny asked me, pocketing Steve's money. "Tuesday's my slow day."

The boys turned and looked at me, like I was the tough one all of a sudden; I could see Babs was jealous.

"Sure," I said.

"Careful, Lois," said Steve. "By the time that character gets through with you, you'll be the tattooed lady."

But he didn't give me my first tattoo till a year later, the day after we were married: a little butterfly pooled in the small of my back. Five years later, he began referring to it as his "early work," even though he'd been tattooing for twenty-five years before he met me. That didn't rankle me as much as you might think—I liked being his early body of work, work-in-progress, future. That little butterfly sat by itself for a while, but in five years' time Tiny flooded it with other designs: carnations, an apple, a bomber plane, his initials.

• • •

When I told my mother about that first tattoo, she said, "Oh Lord. Is it pretty?" Like all good mothers, she always knew the worst was going to happen and was disappointed and relieved when it finally did. But she didn't ask to see that tattoo, or any of the ones that followed. Sunday afternoons, when I went to have lunch with her, I dressed very carefully. I covered myself whenever I left the shop, anyhow: I hated nosy women in the grocery store trying to read my arm as I reached for the peas; I suspected all waitresses of gossiping about me in the kitchen. On my visits to my mother, though, I was extra wary. Through the years, my sleeves got longer, the fabrics more opaque. I never wore white when I visited her: the colors shimmered through.

How could I explain it to my mother? She has always been a glamorous woman, never going anywhere without a mirror, checking and rechecking her reflection, straightening, maintaining. When I was a teenager, there were days that I didn't look in a mirror at all; I avoided my shadow passing in shop windows. Makeup hated me: mascara blacked my eyes, lipstick found its way onto my teeth and chin. At best, on formal occasions, I would peer into the rectangle on my lipstick case, seeing my mouth and nothing more. Tiny changed that. He caught me kneeling on the bathroom counter trying to get a glimpse of part of my back between the medicine chest and a compact, and he went on a campaign, installing mirrors, hiding them. He put a triple mirror from a clothing shop in our bedroom, put a full-length mirror over the bathtub. Once, I opened the freezer and saw my own reflection, chalked up with frost, looking alarmed in a red plastic frame in front of the orange juice.

Most of Tiny's own tattoos were ancient things that he'd done when he was just starting out. He learned the art traveling with the circus in the thirties, could only practice on himself or a grapefruit, and sometimes there wasn't a grapefruit around. The top of his left thigh was almost solid black with experiments.

When we were first married, he revealed a different tattoo every night, all of them hidden away: one night, a rose on a big toe; next, a banner that said E PLURIBUS UNUM half-furled in the hinge of his armpit; the next, his own signature, crooked and ugly, on the inside of his lip. One night, he said, "Are you ready?" and before I could answer he turned his eyelids inside out, and there was a black star floating on the back of each one, isolated, like a scientific experiment.

"Flipping them up," he said, turning them back, "hurts more than the needle does. I was young and drunk and crazy when I had those done, and the guy who did them was younger and drunker and crazier. I'm lucky he stopped there, didn't tattoo my eyeballs scarlet red."

He showed me all these designs like he was performing magic tricks, and sometimes I expected him to wave his hand over his toe and the rose would disappear and end up cupped in his palm; or the banner would finish rolling out from under his arm straight into the air, and go up in a flash of fire; or his name would unwrite itself; or I would fall asleep and find, in front of my own eyes, those floating stars, as black and unruly as Tiny's hair.

It didn't take me long to get used to the feel of the needle. I learned to love it. Tiny gave me maybe two tattoos a year for our first four years of marriage. Little ones. The bigger ones took form over several months, or even longer. He sometimes did sketches for them on his own knee. I started sitting in the shop in a halter top and high cut, low slung shorts, ready to get up and turn a thigh this way or that, showing the customers how the colors went. I saw the same sorts of people I'd seen Tuesdays before I married Tiny, plus others: businessmen, priests, telephone operators, school-board members. Now they started asking me: "Does it hurt?" I told the truth. Of course it hurts, about the same as a vaccination, a lightly skinned knee, but less than a well-landed punch, a bad muscle cramp, or paying the bills. And look what you get: something that can't be stolen, pawned, lost, forgotten, or outgrown.

In the late sixties, when Tiny was still working on a small scale, every time I got a new tattoo, I'd steal a daily touch—I would feel the scab starting, covering the colors, and I'd get impatient and think about peeling it off myself. Tiny'd read my mind and bawl me out, so I'd just run my finger over the tattoo, feeling the outline raised up like it always is when fresh. Then it'd peel by itself, and one day I'd put my finger down and not be able to tell the difference in skin: it'd really be a part of me. And that's when I started wanting another one.

After we'd been married ten years, Tiny got interested in art. Mother had given me a big book called *Masterpieces of the Renaissance*—she wanted me to latch on to something, to go to college, and she figured art history, all things considered, might appeal to me. It was a beautiful book—the gloss of the paper made all the paintings look just finished; the pages gave off the scent of brand new things. I read it the day I got it, and set it aside. The next afternoon, I picked it up and all the reproductions had been taken out with a razor blade. No Raphael, Michelangelo—just a tunnel of empty frames where they'd been, front of the book to back.

I ran down to the shop, grumbling. The plates from the book were tacked up on the wall; Tiny was eyeing an El Greco and sketching.

"What do you think you're doing?" I asked, hands on my hips, the way my mother stood when she started a fight.

"Take off your pants," he said.

"You ruined my book."

"I saved your mom's inscription. When I'm finished, we'll tape all the pictures back in. Come on, Lois, I want to try something."

"I don't feel like getting tattooed today, thank you very much."

"Pen and ink, that's all. I just want to sketch something."

"Sketch it on paper."

"Paper doesn't curve as nice as you. It'll only take a minute. Please?"

So I gave in, and Tiny sketched something on my hip in ballpoint pen. He didn't like whatever he'd done, and wiped my hip clean with rubbing alcohol. The next day he tried again. He took his time. I got a book to read while he was working (I couldn't get interested in something that wasn't permanent), but I couldn't figure out how to arrange myself. I leaned this way and that, holding my book at arm's length, and Tiny told me to stop squirming. Every night for a week he sketched and erased. At the end of the sessions, my hands would be dead asleep from trying to hold the book steady, and when I hit them on the edge of the table, trying to rouse them, they'd buzz like tuning forks. He never let me see what he was doing.

One night at the end of the week, after closing, Tiny said he had achieved what he wanted. He planned to tattoo it on my hip as a surprise.

I balked; my hip was my own, and I wanted to know what was going to be there. He promised that it would be beautiful and decent and a masterpiece.

"You'll love it," he said. "I've got this painting racket figured out."

"Okay," I said.

He decided to do the work upstairs at home. I stretched out on the bed, and he put on some Bing Crosby. Tiny loved Bing Crosby and at one point wanted to tattoo his face on me, but I put my foot down on that one. He gave me a glass of wine; he often let me have a glass, maybe two, when he was working on me. Never more, because it was against his strictest principles to tattoo a drunk.

He started at eight and worked until eleven. Tiny had a light touch, and by the end of the evening I had a little bit of El Greco. The colors weren't quite right, but it was mostly wonderful, the face of a Spanish monk blooming on my hip: Fray Felix Hortensio Paravacino. Tiny was good, believe it.

He adapted a lot of paintings from that book, did them up in flash and hung them in his shop. Few people asked for those designs—he thought of them mostly as eye-catchers, anyhow—but one skinny lady had the Mona Lisa put on her back, all those folds of fabric, the little winding roads in the background.

"Lucky she's built like a boy," Tiny said, meaning the woman, not Mona Lisa. "Otherwise, the picture woulda been all lopsided."

We went to the Art Center every now and then and wandered through one square room after another. I tried to get Tiny to look at my favorite thing there, a little Van Gogh landscape, but he always shook his head.

"That guy," said Tiny. "He's not a painter, he's a sculptor."

All those paintings and little descriptions made me sleepy; I would sprawl on a bench while Tiny practically pressed his nose to the oldest canvases.

We made the guards very nervous.

Tiny started to work bigger all the time, and put designs on my arms, down my legs. Eventually, he left only my hands, my feet, my neck, and face blank—I can still get dressed and look unmarked. But look at me undressed, see how he got better over the years: his patriotic stage, his religious stage. He liked greens and reds especially, and fine single-needle outlines, which he called "rare and elegant." I've got George Washington on one arm and Lincoln freeing the slaves on the other; I've got a garden planted between my breasts, Japanese peonies and daisies, reds and faded yellows; I've got a little pair of arms sinking into my belly button captioned HELP LET ME OUT.

My life drove my mother crazy. All she wanted was for me to become miraculously blank. I broke her heart—that was my job. She let me know her heart was broken—that was hers. She loved me, loves me. She has had a thousand lives: as a girl, she was pretty and could dance and flirt; her mother died, and she learned to take care of her father and older brother, and still she was happy, poised, and courted. She worked her way through college cleaning houses; she went to law school and New York and had a practice for a while; she married the owner of a women's clothing store and moved to the Midwest; she went to Indianapolis to learn how to fit women's underwear, and has her G.C. (Graduate Corsetiere) from the Gossard School. When my father died in 1955, she took over the shop herself and ran it for twenty years. She has taught ballroom dancing, travels to foreign countries; she is a small-business consultant, the vice-president of her temple, and president of the sisterhood. She used to paint, sculpt, needlepoint, and knit, and there is a table in the front hall of her apartment that she made sixty years ago. My mother believes in being able to start fresh whenever life demands. Tattoos confound her.

One Sunday when I was thirty and just beginning to become the tattooed lady (Tiny had started the Ascension the week before), my mother poured me a cup of coffee and said, "Sweethearts carve their names on trees, not each other. Does it ever occur to you that you are not leading a normal life?"

"Yes," I said. "Thank you." I adjusted my pants and peered at my ankle to see whether I had embarrassed myself, whether a tattoo had managed to come loose and slip to the floor. My cousin Babs, who had just had a baby, was coming to lunch, too, and my mother and I sat on the brocade sofa waiting.

"I just feel that you're painting yourself into a corner," Mom said to me. "How's Tiny?"

"Doing very well," I said. "Business is up." My mother winced.

The doorbell rang. Mom answered the bell and ushered in Babs, still a little thick around the middle, but elegant in her suit, stockings of just the right color, curled hair.

Mom sat her down on the sofa.

"Honey," she said. "How's the darling baby?"

"A baby, all the way," said Babs. "No, he's fine, he's sweet."

"Well," said Mom. "Look at those nice clothes."

Babs had calmed down in the passing years; her parents had offered her a car if she stopped seeing Steve, and it was a better-than-fair deal. After college, she met and married a high school principal turned local politician, and she seemed to have lost every drop of wildness in her.

The sight of a well-dressed Babs never failed to surprise me. "No one would ever suspect you had a reckless youth," I told her.

"It's true," said Babs. She looked at me with some regret and sighed. "Now I'm a nice married lady who sometimes has one too many glasses of whiskey at one of my husband's parties and then tells the truth." She sighed and shifted her weight on the sofa cushion. I imagined her bow tattoo pricking her skin, an old war injury kicking up.

The three of us sat there and chatted about local news, babies, recipes. We covered ourselves. Looking at my mother, I realized how little I knew of her. Recently, I had gone through her desk, trying to unearth a phone book, and found a doctor's bill for a mammogram, detailing two suspicious spots, the next appointment. My heart jumped whenever I thought of it. Did her body show what happened next? Her face didn't, and nobody—especially me—asked my mother such things. Babs, too—besides that bit of color, what else: stretched-out stomach, the zipper of a surgical scar?

I knew myself under my green pantsuit, could tap George Washington on the chin, prick a finger on the thorn of a rose, strum an apocalyptic angel's wing, trace the shape of a heart Tiny'd given me after our first fight.

Anyone could read me like a book.

When my mother took the dirty dishes to the kitchen, I leaned toward Babs.

"Watch that whiskey," I told her, "or sometime you'll drop your pants to show a visiting dignitary the colorful result of a misspent youth."

She looked sad and understanding. "Oh," she whispered, "I *know*."

That night, after Babs left, my mother took me to her bedroom closet to give me some of her old clothing. She was almost as tall as I was and very fashionable, her hand-me-downs nicer than my new things.

"Here," she said, handing me a pile of skirts and dresses. "Try them on. Don't take what you can't use."

I started for the bathroom to change.

She sighed. "I'm your mother," she said. "I used to fit girdles on women with stranger bodies than yours. You don't have to be modest."

So I undressed there and tried on the clothes, and my mother looked at me and frowned. Afterward, I sat down on her bed in my underwear and lit a cigarette.

"Wouldn't you like something to eat?" she asked me.

I did, but couldn't. I had just taken up smoking because I had put on a few pounds, and Tiny told me I better cut it out before I changed the expressions of all the tattoos. If I wasn't careful, Washington and Jesus and Fray Felix would start to look surprised or, at best, nauseated.

"No thanks," I told her.

My mother, who only smoked in airports and hospital waiting rooms ("All that cleanliness and worry gets to me," she'd say), slid a cigarette from my pack, took mine from my hand, and lit the end of hers. She looked at all of me stretched along the bed, started to touch my skin, but took her finger away.

"Well," she said, blowing out smoke, "you've finally made yourself into the freak you always thought you were."

I looked at her sideways, not knowing what to say.

"Actually," she said, "you look a little like a calico cat."

My mother was wrong. I never felt like a freak because of my height: I felt like a ghost haunting too much space, like those parents who talk about rattling around the house when the kids move out. I rattled. It's like when you move into a new place, and despite the lease and despite the rent you've paid, the place doesn't feel like home and you're not sure you want to stay. Maybe you don't unpack for a while, maybe you leave the walls blank and put off filling the refrigerator. Well, getting a tattoo—it's like hanging drapes, or laying carpet, or driving that first nail into the fresh plaster: it's deciding you've moved in.

When Tiny turned seventy, he retired. His hands were beginning to shake a little, and he hated the idea of doing sloppy work. We still had the apartment over the shop, and Tiny kept the store open so that people could come in and talk. Nobody took him up on the tattooing lessons he

offered; after a while, he tried to convince me to learn. He said I'd at-
tract a lot of business. I told him no, I didn't have the nerves, I wasn't brave
like him.

I took a job at the public library instead, shelving books. I worked in the
stacks all day, and when I came home, Tiny'd be asleep. I'd know that he'd
been napping all day so that he'd be awake enough to stay up and chat. He
was getting old fast, now that he wasn't working.

I pulled the dining room table into the shop's front window, because
Tiny liked to see who was coming and going. He knocked on the glass and
waved, even to strangers. One night, a week before his seventy-sixth
birthday, his arm started hurting halfway through dinner.

"I'm calling an ambulance," I said.

"Don't," he told me. "It's like saying there's something wrong. It's
bad luck."

"It's bad luck to die," I said, and phoned.

He was surprisingly solid in that hospital bed, unlike his roommate, who
looked like he had withered away to bedding. After a week, that roommate disappeared and was replaced by a huge man, a college professor
with a heart problem.

One day, Tiny asked me an impossible favor. He wanted me to bring in
the needle and put my initials on him.

"Ah, Tiny," I told him. "I'm not ready to sign you off yet."

"You have my initials on you, but I don't have yours. It's bad luck."

"I don't know how."

"You've seen it a million times."

The college professor was eavesdropping, and he looked a little queasy.

"We'll get caught," I whispered.

"We'll be quiet."

"This is a hospital," I said, like maybe he hadn't noticed.

"Sterile conditions," he answered.

So I brought the needle and some black ink the next day, rolled up my
sleeves, got to work. We had to bribe the professor quiet, but he was easily
bought. All he wanted was quart bottles of Old Milwaukee and the sort of
food that would kill him. We turned on the television set to drown out the
needle's hum. The professor pretended to sleep, so that if a nurse came in
he could plead innocent.

We lived in terror of those nurses. One of them might walk in on us or
notice something new on Tiny's arm. Tiny might die while I was working
on him, and the hospital would conclude tattooing was some weird form
of euthanasia. The professor might raise his price and demand fancier
food, imported beers I couldn't afford.

I started with a G, and put an E on the next day. That afternoon, when I was just sitting there watching Tiny sleep, he raised his eyelids to half mast and muttered, "I wish I woulda finished you."

"I thought I was finished, Tiny," I said.

"Nope," he said. He put a hand on my arm; his nails were rippled like old wood. "A tree, for instance. You don't have a tree."

"Where's room?"

"Soles of feet, earlobes. There's always room. Too late now. But you'll change anyhow, needle or no. For instance, when I put that George Washington on you, he was frowning. By the time you're my age, he'll be grinning ear to ear." He yawned, then suddenly pulled himself onto his elbows, squeezing the one hand on my arm for support. "I mean, tell me," he said. "Do you feel finished?"

"Yes," I said, and although I was thirty-nine, it was true: it hadn't occurred to me until that minute that I'd have to exist after he was gone.

The next day I was putting a T on his arm when Tiny said, "Do me a favor, Lois, huh? Don't forget me?"

The professor began to giggle in bed and ended up laughing, hard. "Do you think she'd be able to, even if she wanted? Look at her—she's a human memo board."

I really thought that I would keep on going, that I'd put a letter a day on him for a year, more. I hoped it would keep him going, because he seemed to be giving up a little.

By the end of the week, Tiny's arm said GET WELL in letters of all different sizes.

"Well," he said. "It's a little boring."

"It's going to get more interesting."

"It better," he told me, smiling. "Tomorrow you can put on a horseshoe for luck. Get fancy. Put on a heart for love."

"Okay," I said. But he died in the night, left without my name or love, with only my good wishes on his arm.

"What's going to happen to you now?" my mother asked me. "What if you want to get married again? What man will want you when someone else has been scribbling all over you?"

A month after Tiny died, Mama told me she was going to start inviting nice young men to our Sunday lunches. She bought me new outfits, unrevealing ones, and told me that we should keep my figure secret—she always referred to it as my figure, as if, over the years, I had put on a few things that could easily be taken off. I go to keep her happy, and sit on one side of the sofa while the fat divorced sons of her friends flirt with her instead of me, knowing that'll get them further. Sometimes I eat fudge and don't say one word all afternoon.

Every day I get up and go to work at the library, dressed in short skirts, short sleeves, no stockings. The director has told me that I'm frightening people.

"I'm sorry," I told her. "These are my widow's weeds."

Three weeks ago I got a letter from a young man on the coast, a tattooist who said that Tiny was a great artist and that I was proof of it. He wanted to take my photo, see the whole gallery. I packed him a box of Tiny's things, old flash sheets and needles and pages of El Greco, and told him to study those. He called me and said I was better than any museum. I told him that I apologized, that I understood, but really: I am not a museum, not yet, I'm a love letter, a love letter.

MINDMOVIE ●

christine slater

MET IN A VALIUM fog on the plane to Antigua; at least I was in the Valium fog and feigning a coma when Irving sat next to me. I was pleasantly strung having been on a major coke binge in the days leading up to my gathering the guts, and the desire even, to get on the plane. From under thin, veiny lids, I saw him glance briefly at me and then take a heavy-looking sheaf of paper, bound in grey cardboard, from a leather briefcase. We may have met before, or perhaps I was hallucinating, because in my condition everything looked familiar and nothing looked the same and if that sounds nonsensical, think about it because it's called growing older. It turned out to be true anyway—the part about having met because when I made a shambling sort of effort to rouse myself when the drink trolley lunged up the aisle, he turned to me and smiled, passed the requested Coca-Cola (I needed the caffeine) and said, "We've met, you know. You were with Rainer Hofgren at Doubleday once. My name is Irving Reisman."

I shook his hand.

"Yes," I said, struggling. "I remember. You're a literary agent."

"Yes."

"I'm Anita Asher."

"Yes," he said. "I remember too."

We smiled. Friendly skies and all that.

It turned out that we were both only going to Antigua to make a connecting flight to Montserrat. An odd coincidence. I said as much, adding that Montserrat was off the beaten track and not too many people knew about it.

"You know about it," Irving said, as if that meant anything. "How did you find it?"

"I went with Rainer once about five years ago. He made an album there."

"It's not overrun with pop stars, is it?" Irving asked smiling.

"No. Nor with writers."

Our eyes met; instead of smiling again, we began to laugh.

The day drifted more pleasantly than most of my days and to stretch odd coincidence stiff, we were booked into the same hotel. Well, the island's small. We said goodbye at the front desk and then I went to my room to excavate the Valium. I needed to feel foggy again. In the end, I slept.

I went down shortly after 11 the next morning for coffee. The patio overlooking the water was nearly empty. I was bored already. I could have been back in New York, I could have been working, I could have been with Rainer (not really, but the thought had found a home in my cluttered head), I could have been anywhere but there, shipped off by the warm and woolly urges of concerned friends and assorted acquaintances who hoped I wouldn't have the nerve to transport drugs across an international border and would spend 10 days going cold turkey. They were wrong; as always, in a pinch, I found the nerve. In spades.

I walked the beach. Irving waved to me from the patio. When I got there, retracing my steps a little, shaking sand from the cuffs of my pants, he was sitting, watching, perched on the low, rocky wall that divided the hotel from the escarpment.

"Hello," he said. "How are you?"

"I'm fine . . ." I answered, hesitant, lying. "How are you?"

"I feel great."

"Good for you."

"Would you join me in a juice?"

"You're very healthy. . . ."

"Well, something stronger if you'd like. . . ."

"No, a juice would be very nice."

They served us passion fruit which made me laugh: Irving was tall, skinny, stooped and spectacled, and couldn't, I thought, induce passion on a bet. I could be wrong; I so often was. He was nice to talk to, though. And we talked for a while, skirting the serious and the silly.

"Can you have dinner with me tonight?" he asked.

I could.

Inevitably we spent the 10 days together. Fate etc. In the island sunlight, he began to look quite beautiful to me as if his intellect and self-effacement, which were so much a part of his charm, had made him handsome. I began to find the kinks in his hair attractive. And perhaps too, the clarity of the light had removed some ugliness of my own—the shallowness, for example, with which I sought to see things because I couldn't bear to be perceptive anymore. I needed tranquilizing less and less as the days passed and when I did take them it was because I was almost embarrassed to admit that being with Irving had stirred me, excited me even. Even excited me. I would go to bed, alone, for he never really came near me, and think, in wonder almost, "I could give up a lot of things, even the bad stuff, for this man." And then the Valium would take hold and I would sleep.

When I awoke, I was home again and alone. Irving was staying for two weeks, but promised to call. I hoped he would but held out for nothing, things being easier that way. He phoned from the island the day before he was supposed to leave, something crackling through the line between us.

"I thought if you weren't doing anything, we could have dinner tomorrow?"

"When does your flight get in? I could meet you at the airport."

"Oh," he said with some pleasure, "you don't have to do that."

"I don't mind at all."

Of course I didn't. Without meaning to in the least, I had fully attached myself to him. I had been feeling so awful, so empty and so frightened of both. Irving was solid and Irving was smitten and I had taken what he had so far so shyly offered me with a greediness I rarely summoned for anything—much less love.

When I saw him that evening, with four more days' worth of tan than I had, I just stood there, as if rooted by my expectations, and watched him approach. He smiled tentatively. I held out my arms, and he came to them quickly, happily. We seemed to hug for a long time and then, with impatience, I took him home.

We all but made love in the limo. I was wearing a long sable (when I did my second album cover for Rainer, he paid me a pittance, just for a joke, but gave me an imperceptible percentage of the profits. The album was a huge hit, and that imperceptible percentage bought me the coat) and a man's shirt underneath pinned at the collar. The coat fell open, Irving's hand had found a home.

"Good," I whispered when we parted for air. "I want to know what your tongue feels like when it's inside me. . . ." His hand reached further. It stayed.

I met Rainer once at Kennedy, wearing an old trenchcoat and this purple sweater—I still remember the sweater because he said he liked me in mauve—coughing, throwing myself into a paroxysm of phlegm, my skin turning pale, shiny, green.

"Darling," he said, throwing an arm around me. "You've changed your hair.

"Much of what I remember about the years I spent with Rainer is wiped clean by a terminal glare—airport glare, that is. We were always in airports in those days. Friends in New York told me that they saw me more frequently in pictures taken at Heathrow or in Frankfurt than they did in person. It satisfies a bizarre, but intensely enjoyable human need to be able to walk through the arrival gates wearing sunglasses. It was in an airport, too, that Rainer said he loved me. We re-enacted the fadeout of *Casablanca*, only this time Bogart went off with Bergman and was so saved the speech about human insignificance: we found out about that stuff soon enough anyway, as if we already didn't know it. When I think about Rainer I see such absorbing brightness, but with Nick, with Nick, it's nearly black—shadows and dim, cheesy restaurant booths and endless black coffees. The only whiteness in his life came from the purity of the cocaine he sold so lovingly.

He lived in a succession of terrible rooms, didn't mind in the least, and for a long time said the whole business of playing poor kept his soul clean. I didn't buy it then—when I was starting out and fairly skint—and I don't go for it much now that I have the opportunity to emulate him. I laugh about it, you know, because Nick was the first person to say "make the money first and the art will come later," and that is how I got involved in doing commercial stuff—album covers and concert posters—and how, in the end, I met Rainer. For a long time, in my mind, Nick played Fate for me. He welcomed all extravagant possibilities and I loved him for it. He made me feel as if there existed within what was then such a fractured personality and self-conscious soul the opportunity of being anything imaginable. So I became a junkie.

"Why do you paint?" he asked me, as we walked shoulder to shoulder in the Village one summer night. Nick had his sunglasses in his pocket, ever at the ready despite the lack of direct light, as if called upon, they could become an irresistible urban armor.

"How the hell should I know?" I replied.

But I did, you see, I just couldn't tell him. After a lifetime of gargling the outlaw blues in capital letters and in fancy dress, what else could I have done? How else could I give all those feelings a life beyond my own body— feelings of such happy misfortune, high life on a low planet? That awesome, rankling joy of finally knowing that words and colors and notes on a page can actually connect you with people who don't have to know you to understand you . . . the best kind of friends in the end, I thought. The ones you never actually have to meet.

On a similarly warm New York night, unchanged save for the uptown address, I had the same conversation with Irving. He sat watching me rearrange debris: clearing the easel, stacking frames, looking like hell with my hair up, wearing a pair of black jeans violated by smears of incompatible paint.

"Do you like doing this?" Irving asked. "Do you *like* being an artist?" I was feeling somewhat playful and chose not to be hurt by the question, so I picked up a couple of small mounted posters and held them the way girls on game shows do, trying to look helpful but sexy at the same time.

"What do you think?"

Irving smiled, his eyes shining indiscriminately.

"Oh, I think you're a genius."

I went over to him.

"Oh, you're very helpful," I said. "You know bugger all about art."

He laughed, reaching out to me.

"But," he said. "I do know that I love you."

"I love you," Nick said, laying me down on the bed, kneeling over me, a hulking blond-pink presence. He had everything ready. First, he kissed me, slowly, slowly, slower. He held the needle haphazardly to the light, then smiling, his hand caressed the knot above my elbow.

"Oh, yes," he whispered, "I really do love you." He put his arm around my shoulders and raised me a little so that I was balancing on the bloated arm. He put my fingers around the syringe. "Feel it," he whispered, "feel it. . . ." His fingers folded around my own, dwarfing them, until I couldn't feel where Nick ended and I began, a mass of bony flesh huddled around the plastic. Before we thrust, he smiled again.

"See Anita," he said. "See all the pretty pictures?"

The pictures weren't pretty any more, of course—they were condemned to be familiar and grotesque—but for a long, long time the colors grew more splendid until it seemed my life, up to that point, had been lived entirely in black and white. I should have known better and stayed there. But all of my life, as long as this mind can remember, I have been, as someone once said, a rolling stone. I thought movement was freedom, but I took the greatest trips without going anywhere; as long as I can remember too, my mind has been in acute overdrive. Often I've wanted to stop it, but not often enough.

I have this friend, a girl I more or less grew up with. I don't see her much now; she's married to a decent guy and has a fun job and is basically living a nice life and I have to wonder, what is it in me that insists it must be different? Why do I envy her in a puny way but end up being grateful for having had the big downtown loft and the famous lover and the spaced-out notoriety? Sometimes I think she pities me. Most of the time so do I.

Irving hasn't a shred of it, self-pity that is, which makes him rare and wondrous. I see him jollying me out of it every now and then—probably more often than that—and though I don't tell him, I'm happy he does it.

He's a nervous man, one of the worst, but his core is calm. I'm the opposite: so fucking cool on the outside and an utter wreck in the depths. Once I was in a flap and had a couple of Valium in hand (if I didn't have even the most pitiable possibility of self-control, I would chew them like breath mints: they both conned you into thinking that, as far as the outside world was concerned, all you had to do was take them to be perfect). Irving saw them and frowned.

"You shouldn't take that stuff," he said.

The radio in the kitchen was playing "Satisfaction" and though I don't think I really *heard* it, an answer shot out of me, unattended:

"They're 'Mother's Little Helpers.' "

He looped a long arm around my shoulders—the long arm of the law, I guess. I leaned against him for a minute and closed my eyes. His arm was hard and all-enclosing. His head bent forward until his face was close, very close, to mine.

"If you ever have a problem," he said quietly, "we'll talk about it, okay?"

I nodded into his chest. I couldn't even argue.

It was odd for me to face such concerted opposition towards the worst of my bad habits. I have always found people quite encouraging. I know I was invited to parties simply because my reputation for being an entertaining oddity, a famous freak, preceded me. It didn't bother me really—we all hit the streets in disguise. I lived in California for a couple of months, helping out the art director on a big-budget adventure flick (it turned out that Irving was on the same lot at the same time, negotiating the movie rights for a novel he represented. I doubt we even saw each other) and accepted all and sundry social invitations as a sacred duty. It got to be a joke, this A-B-C list shit, and so I laughed about it; what else can you do? You pay for your fame. You pay for everything.

And I love all that raw, raunchy, bloated cash. Art as sacrament; art as a con job. I can, when I have to, verge on the blasphemously commercial, and though there are moments, long ones, when I try to avoid it altogether, a starving artist could never find a home in these bones. It has always been to me a meaningless mark of valor.

"Don't be afraid of your money," Rainer told me. "It gives you the freedom to work as you want." He said this in his sweet guttural whisper, each word sheared by the accent. I have always had a good ear—and a pretty good eye, too: right place at the right time stuff. It amuses me because it's a phoney kind of power—it doesn't mean anything, but it kicks the shit out of that tango with paranoia you do every once in a while. How often *do* you do it, huh? How often?

Rainer and I lived in a villa in northeastern Switzerland, near Lake Constance. All told, I stayed in Europe seven years, coming back to the States to lick my wounds: it left a very bad taste. In the end, it was the career, of all things, that saved me, which I found comforting because for some time I harbored the not-unfounded suspicion that people thought I had been bankrolled by Rainer—every paint drop bought and paid for by his ever-present wad of cash.

By the time I met Irving, I was in the single-minded pursuit of my reputation, the venture assuming proportions that left little room for the acceptance of other things and other people. I realize now that it kept me going because I wanted it to. I didn't know that what I had been excising from my life was really essential to it: when I returned to New York, I was alone and for three years, stayed that way. Nick was a help then—and not in the way people might expect. He was living upstate in a place so unlike him, pretty grey colonial clapboard, that I couldn't believe he actually *paid* for it. He came into town "for business," he'd say, but as he turned up more often, I think he just wanted the company. Nick never married, couldn't bear, as he put it, "sharing my thoughts with someone else" (harkening back, I suppose, to a strange, otherworldly childhood with two deaf-mute parents), and although he really did seem to like living alone, his cool, white, implacable exterior hid a wild craving for conversation and camaraderie and silliness. I spent many years pretending to be his best friend, as he spent many years pretending not to need one. Once I took up with Rainer, our contact became, predictably, sporadic until I called him one day and told him to get his ass on the next plane to London where we spent a long, crazed weekend. He came, of course. Again and again. Rainer joked about it when he was planning on being home for a long stretch:

"Is this all right," he would inquire, "or were you going to be tied up with your junkie boyfriend?" Oh, fuck it, Rainer, do let's be liberal.

Too many years depending on men, saying I love you to too many people. Not quite wasted maybe, but maybe better spent. Maybe not.

Irving, of all of them, was my best friend: the best friend I ever had in my life. He was the loveliest person I ever spoke to—his depth cooling and very comfortable. He fretted like a Yiddish mama—fussing over everything, clearing the crumbs off the table while you ate—but he only fussed because he loved so totally. I had never looked into somebody's face before and seen myself so beautiful.

I fell in love with Irving faster than I had with anyone. I needed it more at the time, I think; timing being so crucial. When I met Rainer, we sparred for a while—he trying to charm me and I trying not to notice. I was in a weird sort of superficially independent mood too; I wanted to be won over. When he pulled out the big guns, of course, I didn't have a chance; the impact was incredible. He kept rejecting my mock-ups for the album design—only later did he say that he had done it to keep me there. With Nick, this silent, faintly erotic deal we had lurked undisturbed in the background. Never noticed much, but never allowed to leave. We were close because of it, oddly, but, then, we tried so hard to be odd.

I nearly dismissed Irving because he was so obviously normal—normal men not ever having rated much with me. He was too eclectic in a sense. I seemed to like single-minded types with a streak of sloth. Irving wasn't a time waster. But he could be quiet and pensive too. He didn't always need to be on the go and so much of his job simply involved sitting down with a book. Next to him I felt, at times, as if I were corrupting my life by not getting on with things, by procrastinating, by evasion. I could so often get into the sort of mood in which absolutely nothing appealed to me and that's a bad thing to even brush up against because all you want to do is sit on your ass in front of the TV. I remember feeling so offended when I would look through curriculum guides and see nothing, out of hundreds of possibilities, that remotely interested me. How can the world outside of yourself be so boring?

"I'm terrified of dullness," I told Irving once as we were lying in bed. He hit the nail on the head, as was his wont.

"Terrified of dullness in general, or of being dull yourself?" he asked.

I turned on him. "Do you think I'm dull?"

He smiled. He looked six-years-old.

"No. You're the least dull person I've ever met."

Settling back into the pillows, I felt absurdly vindicated. How could I not help it? You grow into a little nothing, hitting 18 or 19 and feeling, idiotically maybe, that you've got basically nothing to show for two decades of living, so you transform yourself into a personality: joining a hip underground kind of milieu, making yourself a little too happy by the snortful, drawing, always drawing, rating an *Interview* cover, living with a famous guy, everything you touched tainted by the drive to be anything other than yourself. I even went to the Grammy Awards, for God's sake.

When I became pregnant, I wanted to fall off the face of the earth, if only because my parents would have killed me. I took the easy way out and killed the baby, which was, without a doubt, the most shameful thing I have ever done, that sort of competition being fierce in my life. If it had been anybody else's—Rainer's, for instance, or Nick's even, I probably would have kept it, but this one—this dirty little artist with whom I fell in and out of love, quite efficiently, over the Labor Day weekend. . . . I am embarrassed to remember that I once would have slept with somebody like that. I was on my own at the time, 23 years old; no one would ever find out and no one ever did. It was done very cleanly in a bright room with a motherly woman holding your hand while you were silencing the motherhood in yourself. I almost resented it happening to me so neatly. And when I went home, they pressed packages of Valium into my palm, the way you were rewarded with candy as a child for having a proper check-up. I knew, when I told Irving about it—every detail as raw as it had been 20 years ago—that I must love him very much.

I killed so much in my life, slaying anything that dared inconvenience me. I danced around trouble all the time, drawing myself in colors that were amiable, amusing, dangerous and intensely shallow. Friends fell by the wayside.

"It's life," I used to think. "People aren't supposed to stick around each other forever," and maybe it was true. I think about the weddings I forgot to attend, the phone calls never returned. I wouldn't go near the phone if I could possibly help it. An interviewer once commented on Rainer's accessibility—how he had to be the world's only major rock star to take his own calls. He smiled slyly, shrugged and said, "Well, I have to, you see; Anita won't do it."

The scenarios of life change, so the characters must too. It's only as you get older that you begin to notice the same people turning up in different costumes. I worried when all my friends started to look like David Crosby. After about six months with Irving, the wild unconventional rags were loose enough to reveal a woman in what could kindly be called early middle age who thought she wanted nothing more than to be a harmlessly eccentric housewife.

"You mean he actually asked you to marry him?" my mother, a woman of epic prejudice, asked, her voice quietly level. I had kept it brief, didn't tell her that, at 39, I had received my first real proposal one night on the way home from the deli from which we frequently scavenged dinner. Yes, mother, on the street, for God's sake. Right there on the street.

"It doesn't matter that he's Jewish, I suppose . . ." she murmured again, turning her head from me. I laughed. I knew it would offend her. She hated it when I laughed at her. But what else could I do? Out of a past so checkered it could have doubled as a chess board: the drugs, the inappropriate boyfriends, the bohemian life, she had to object to the fact that my fiancé, solid, humane, gentle, civilized Irving was, as she would delicately put it in her Bostonian brahmin way, "of the Hebraic persuasion." She couldn't make it to the wedding.

Irving and I stood at the window of Van Cleef and Arpels.

"What do you like?" he asked. This was, it turned out, a couple of weeks before he proposed.

I laughed and looked and pointed to a diamond eternity ring—ordinary glitter amid the excess. It was very nearly closing time, he couldn't have done anything about it.

"Wrapped," he inquired. "Or unwrapped?"

"Oh, wrapped, definitely. Having the box is half the fun."

After he asked me to marry him, that night we walked along 57th Street, we came back to the apartment. Sitting on my pillow was the box, wrapped in complex and infuriating folds. And inside—that ordinary glitter. Then I remembered that, earlier, we were out of the door and heading towards the elevator when Irving said he'd forgotten a letter he wanted to mail and went back to get it. That entire evening is almost a breathing entity for me: that night, I knew bliss. When I die, when I die, you can say that I knew bliss. There is nothing either good or bad but thinking makes it so. We went to Montserrat for our honeymoon.

"Congratulations to you both," the telegram read. "My very best thoughts wishing you the happiness you deserve." Hell, Rainer, I could take that in more ways than one. God bless you for it, though. I could find that telegram in 10 seconds if I had to.

ANITA ASHER: THE ROLLING STONE INTERVIEW

Q: You're 40 now, you recently married Irving Reisman and you've just had a very successful showing of your concert posters. It seems to be a time of intense productivity for you after something of a fallow period. . . . How has your life changed?

A: The outward stuff has been a determining factor, obviously. I have had some very nice things happen to me in the last couple of years, but the most positive things are how I feel in here (touches head) and in here (touches gut).

Q: You were quoted recently as saying you were feeling human again.

A: That's it exactly.

Q: How did you feel before then?

A: I'm not sure what it was, but it didn't seem particularly human.

"Do you think it's a good idea to give interviews like that?" Irving asked, looking worried.

"What do you mean?"

"Well, you know, they'll only ask you the personal things. . . . In the end it could be a little exploitative."

"I don't mind talking about those things, though. Let's face it, I've got the kind of past people like to hear about."

"Only because you're willing to tell them."

"Are you suggesting I shouldn't give the interview then?"

"No, of course not. I don't have the right to tell you that. I just want you to be careful; I don't like the idea of your being wounded by this."

"I've given interviews before, I don't have a problem with them. It takes a lot more than that to hurt me."

He got up muttering something incomprehensible.

"What did you say?" I asked.

He stood above me, looking mournful.

"I said I think that you can be stung by a good deal less."

Q: Do you still see Rainer Hofgren?

A: Once in a while. . . . We keep in touch, after a fashion.

Q: Do you miss him?

A: Sure. You can't help but miss someone you were once close to.

Q: It must have been hard for you to leave then. You had acquired a very specific lifestyle that must have been difficult to abandon.

A: You do what you have to, you know. You can't think about whether you're going to miss the furniture.

"Darling," he whispered, smiling. "I read the interview in *Rolling Stone*. It seems so long ago, doesn't it?"

"No, not really," I replied. "It was only the issue before last."

Q: For a few years your career was definitely subjugated to that of Rainer's and indeed, most of the work you did during that time had some connection to him. Do you regret that now? Do you wish you got more involved in other things?

A: Not really. The opportunities, for one thing, didn't exist for me in Europe, at least not in the way they did here, so I had to make a choice: do I stay here and work on my own, or do I live in Europe with the people I want to be with and accept limited prospects? I was very happy with the work I did during that time even if, by earlier standards, I wasn't prolific. Hey, man, you know how it is: the door's open but the ride it ain't free.

It's a town full of losers, and I'm pulling outta here to win. . . . Pulling outta here to win . . . only, shit, I never went anywhere. My body may have moved, but where in hell did my head go? Feeling human, who needs to feel human when all you feel is such incredible pain?

"The needle loves you," Nick said. "He's there when you need him." I want the color back so bad. I want my veins clean. Was I ever even remotely pure? I don't think so; some people come out of the womb corrupt.

Q: Do you think your work has ever been adversely affected by the drugs?

A: No. Never.

"You have to stop," Rainer shouted, jerking me hard by the shoulders. I flailed against him, helpless against the contempt more than anything.

"You just don't understand," I cried. Suddenly he let me go, his face broken by heavy lines of disgust.

"Anita," he said, turning away. "Get a grip."

Gripping the brush, I painted for days until my fingers grew twisted, almost arthritic.

"Slow down," Irving said. "You're working too hard."

"You don't have a clue, do you?" I said, not even looking at him. "I *have* to do it."

Q: You've been described as a brilliant, but lazy artist. How do you respond to that?

A: I don't. It's true.

At the beginning of the ninth day, Irving called the doctor.

"Get the fuck away from me," I screamed, suddenly roused. "Can't you bastards leave me alone?"

Obviously desperate, he got hold of Nick, who arrived bearing gifts. On the 12th day I got up and passed for human. Nick was there, having coffee in the living room.

"Are you okay?" he asked. He looked older than I'd remembered, or had my eyes merely aged?

"Yeah. Tired."

The apartment felt empty, as if abandoned by an essential presence. "Where's Irving?" I asked.

"He went out for a while. He asked me to stay in case you got up."

He stood before me then, his bony fingers pulling at the buttons of my shirt. I could feel his long, blond hair slither across my cheek, my throat, my shoulder. Involuntarily, I put my arms around him. He propelled me into the hallway.

"Anita honey," he said, "let's go to bed."

"But Irving . . ." I protested weakly, shamefully.

"Fuck Irving. Fuck me instead."

Nick left when Irving came back. Nick always left when Irving came back.

Irving and I went to Martha's Vineyard a while later. Neither one of us found the sea air bracing. It rained.

"Maybe you should come to LA with me," Irving said one night in a downpour. Maybe I should.

We stayed at an uncelebrated hotel. Irving was in meetings all day, every day; I sat out by the pool in a little orange grove. I saw a couple of friends and thought I had relaxed. Pretended to be, at least. Rainer came by.

"I'd give you a couple of tickets for the concert," he said, his eyes hidden by mean-looking shades. He had lost weight. "But I don't think you'd want them."

"No," I said. "Thanks anyway."

"Perhaps you and your husband could join us for drinks later."

I gave him a pitying smile. "Well, perhaps. But I don't think so."

Pangs of nostalgia and temptation. I went to the concert anyway, trying to remember what it had been like to always be backstage, the dressing room as a second home. Rainer smiled when he saw me—one more same old face. He had left the latest girlfriend in London on a modelling assignment. I cautioned him against being too trendy—all those goddamn rockers and their model girlfriends. Rainer laughed, wrapped me tightly and said,

"Oh God, Anita, when we broke up I lost my originality."

For reasons too selfish to enumerate, this was a terrible pleasure.

Back in New York, I had another show (the bad results of sleeplessness)—" insubstantial" they said.

Asher's knee-jerk acquiescence to pop kitsch leads
one to believe that there is a seriously talented
artist hidden behind a larger than life cult
heroin(e) who is simply out to make a buck.

Irving said he was very sorry. I told him not to bother.

"Hey," I said, "when you've been hiding as long as I have, somebody's bound to find you out."

"You shouldn't say that," he replied. "It isn't true. You just think it is."

"That's half the problem."

It didn't bother me as much as people feared it would. Even Nick, for God's sake, approached me as if treading on splinters. No one seemed to understand how people like me need a great and glorious kick in the ass once in a while. It's like putting Pachelbel's *Canon* on when you are excruciatingly depressed; it doesn't make you feel better, but you feel worse with nobility.

I stayed in New York for a long time after that. Irving and I finally began acting like a married couple or maybe I'd begun to act like a wife. At any rate, I stayed away from a paint brush.

Someone told me once that they mentioned to a friend that they had been to dinner at our place and this friend had said, "You don't mean that Anita Asher has gone establishment?" Well, maybe in my own way, I had. One day Nick and I met for lunch and when we laid eyes on each other, we actually began to laugh; we had become so buttoned-down.

"Not completely," I said to him. "We still have crazy eyes."

"Let's make them crazier," he whispered, pressing a flat little box into my hand under the table.

I said let's.

I walked. Everywhere. There was no desire to leave the Big City Womb. It occurred to me that this might be a lazy way of running from something, but with so much of what I walked through deadening and apocalyptic, it often felt as if I was heading straight into burning Rome and almost relishing it. So much tacky frivolity and sadness: paint stores becoming decorating centers, parking lot sparrows, pathetic neighborhood restaurants nearly always empty except for the one or two elderly widowers, places set for the non-existent, sad, dusty cups no one will ever touch, paper placemats beginning to curl with age.

I came home one night and almost as an afterthought, started sketching an old guy I'd seen in one such place—a face I had pretended not to notice—old eyes struggling through an old window. Irving picked it up and sat with it awhile, laying it on his lap like a baby.

"What do you think?" I finally asked.

"I think," he said, his voice strange and different, "it's beautiful."

Suddenly life loosens the leash enough for you to be able to see things, if not as they should be, at least how they were meant to be. Meeting Irving was such a moment for me, and so was getting back to work again. It's as if I had found something terribly close to patience after four decades of not being very comfortable inside my own flesh. Who owns this skin anyway? Well, I do. That last cocaine binge, when I painted frenzied garbage for a week and didn't have the sense to see it—it seemed to be a totally different person, as if the memory was akin to looking at a photograph of yourself taken so long ago or under such different circumstances that you scarcely recognize it as being you. But I had wasted enough time in my life to realize that some day, whenever, all the people you've been come back to haunt the hell out of you.

So I floundered, did drugs, got a weird haircut, saw more of the worst kind of people and less of the best, probably made Irving's life more than moderately miserable. I still did some good work though. It's an ineffable part of human nature not to take your own best advice and I had never believed in the longevity of perfect situations anyway. Made it easier to do nothing.

"You have to be more careful with things," Irving said. "With your work, with yourself, with me. . . ."

"I'm sorry," I said and really meant it. "I do love you though, you know."

"Some day that's not going to be enough."

And it was then that I became frightened.

Sometimes I wouldn't be able to sleep and I'd sit up in bed and watch him, tracing the folds of his face, the wiriness of each hair, and never going near him. My husband, I would think, the fact barely registering. Did I feel any sort of responsibility at all? Was all that feel-good guilt and languishing concern enough to make me change? I knew that Irving wasn't out to remake me, but had I become a disappointment to him?

Unravelling, my mind is unravelling and there's nothing left on the spool now. For once the body's caught up to the brain. The color has been building for so long—flashy images of a flashy past—that it feels almost as if I've exploded and all the colors are draining out of me and I am left here, in black and white—Nick and Rainer—smudged and blended and splattered into grey, into Irving, into nothingness. All I see are tiny drizzles down my arm, every moment worth remembering tracked in bloodied pinpricks—nothing left to talk about now, nothing left of me.

A DAY AT THE PEEP SHOW ●

veronica vera

THE WALRUS CARRIES A brown paper bag into the glass booth. I call him the Walrus because his face is covered with long, shaggy hair, sideburns and a scraggly beard. The Walrus is not very attractive and he shows it by dressing like a slob. But armed with his brown paper bag and a pocket full of tokens, he is about to treat himself to a fantasy fuck.

He takes his jar of Vaseline out of the brown paper bag and drops a coin in the slot. The window shade rises very, very slowly to reveal me grinning at him from the other side of the glass. My body is covered in stretchy black lace that displays every curve.

The Walrus unzips his baggy pants and pulls his big red cock through his fly. He spreads the Vaseline over his penis and works his hand up and down, up and down, over a familiar path. I lean back in a high chair and plant a shiny stiletto pump on either side of the window. The Walrus extends his left hand to pick up the telephone. "Hello," he purrs, sounding much better than he looks. I cradle the phone under my chin, reach into my blouse and lift out my breasts. He stares at me from behind his thick glasses. I stare at the Walrus from behind my hard, dark nipples.

It's 1985, four years since the publication of my first explicit story, three years since I popped my porn cherry in a fuck film. I enjoy the sex biz but there's been this little gnawing fear that one day I'd wind up a side-show attraction, a girl in a peep show. When I decided to write about the 42nd Street Show World Sex Emporium, I knew that I would put myself inside this cage, a tiny glass booth, where men would drop their tokens and their pants to pay for the pleasure of seeing me naked. I guess what I want more than anything is to jump through this ring of fire, to live out this experience. The story is just an excuse.

The peep show is a seductive, rock & roll, neon cave that promises to all who enter some longed-for satisfaction. The customers look for an end to their frustrations. Most walk around like zombies, their hands in their pockets, while through the disco dazzle, the hawkers promise: "Hard core action upstairs in 10 minutes! Girls, girls, girls. Wall to wall pussy." The people who work here are attracted, at first, by the money. It's a job, a way to pay the rent and put food (sometimes drugs) on the table. But there are other hungers. Yes, each action is determined by the dollar, but there is desire for affection, the need for a basic, one-to-one, human connection that motivates every person who walks through the door.

I learned a lot about the Walrus before he entered my booth. I interviewed him upstairs after we watched a strip show in the Triple Treat Theater. He is a bridge player. He reads a lot—one of those unwashed intellectuals. He even tells me about his preference for Vaseline as an aid in jerking off. When he hears that I plan to spend a few hours working a booth, he runs across the street to Wahlgreen's and buys himself a king-sized jar of petroleum jelly.

The Walrus spends $50 in my booth, pumping in one $2 token after another. He wags his big tongue in circles up near the glass and pretends that we are kissing. His hairy mouth gobbles desperately at the phantom kisses. I am sorry for him for just an instant, but then enjoy a surge of power as I lick my lips and watch his tongue perform tricks in the air. He seems to relish the kisses even more than the creamy explosions he leaves on the glass.

Damian comes to work in a three-piece suit. He could be a cocky young clerk on the floor of the Stock Exchange or a bright guy from a tough neighborhood who has decided to work his way up in a bank. Like any guy just starting out, he doesn't quite have his look all together. A Brooklyn accent, patchy mustache, and the curls that creep over his shirt give him away. What Damian does have plenty of is ambition. His body jumps with it. You might say that he is perfecting his craft, tightening his act while he fucks on stage upstairs in the Triple Treat Theater, for twenty-five minutes, six times a day, sometimes six days a week. Damian wants to be a porno movie star.

His partner is Baby Doll, a slim Haitian girl with a tomboy quality. Her stiff black hair is cropped real short and her body is lithe like a bow. "We have some show-stoppers," Damian tells me. "There's the 69 we do with me standing up eating her and holding her upside down while she sucks my cock. We also have the 'wheelbarrow'—she bends over and puts her hands down on the floor, I stick my cock in her and wheel her around the room."

"Don't call them 'teams'" warns Ron Martin, the manager of Triple Treat Theater. "You don't hitch them up to a wagon. These are 'performers.' " These performers, these teams, these women and men are engaged in a very unusual and controversial occupation—the Love Act. They do it for money.

Ivory and Major Motion have been working together for two years. Ivory calls herself that because she isn't quite black and she isn't quite white. She is very beautiful, the color of strong coffee with cream. Ivory hopes one day to live on the island of Jamaica. When Ivory met Major Motion, she was a virgin. They went out together for four months before they made love. Major Motion took his time with Ivory. He knew that she would be worth the wait. He was not exactly starved for sex because he followed the family tradition established by his older brother and got a job fucking on stage. Shortly after Major Motion and Ivory became lovers, they began performing the Love Act in public.

The men in the theater sit in quiet anticipation when Ivory enters the room. She dances on stage in a tight black dress. She is very tall, at least 5'10", and most of that is leg—gorgeous long legs that come to perfect points at the tips of her toes. Her arms, legs and back show a hint of muscle from her workouts at the gym. Ivory's perfect body wraps around the shabby black sofa on the stage. Soon, she is completely naked. Her thick, curly hair forms a lush mane around her face. Her eyes are big dark almonds that avoid the hypnotized stares of the audience.

Ivory pours herself like golden rum over the couch. She lifts her ass high in the air and her dark bush becomes the focus of every eye in the house. Her cunt looms up larger than life. It's a gateway to Paradise and Major Motion is about to slide in.

He saunters in from the side of the stage to join his partner. While he casually strips, she lies on her back, twists her long legs toward the ceiling and plays with her nipples. The Major's thick black tool pops out of his shorts. It is swollen with excitement, filled with the Major's spunk and with the horny desire of every man in the house. The Major fucks Ivory gently. He fucks her hard. He kisses her nipples, her belly, her thighs. The Major buries his face between her legs. Ivory, the serpent, coils around her man.

They are careful to make sure the audience can see every move, can watch every inch of cock as it is swallowed by cunt. My pussy muscles twitch as I feel the Major's cock sliding in and out of my hole. A man a few seats to my left masturbates vigorously. "Touch it, please touch it," he begs. Well, you'll never know if you don't ask. I admire his opportunism but ignore his request.

Major Motion and Ivory hold back on the orgasm. They still have four more shows to do today. The Major, like every stage stud, has to conserve some of his strength. Like the nutritionist in the health store up the block told Damian: "You've got to replenish your seminal fluids. If you don't take care now, by the time you are sixty you'll have shot your load."

Ivory knows exactly how much money she can make from a full week of shows. She and the Major each make $10 for every twenty-five minute performance. They work six days a week, six shows a day, and sometimes double shifts. It's the money, she says, that keeps her coming back. Her grandmother left her a house and she has to pay off the mortgage. The men in her family have all disappeared. But now there's Major Motion and he's daddy and brother and lover. She tells me of her dream to open a body-building gym in Jamaica. "There's so much I want to do," she says, "but I just don't know how to get started."

For Baby Doll, the money, too, is important. Baby Doll is twenty-one and the mother of a three-year-old daughter whom she raises alone. I ask her if she ever regrets having a child without a husband. "I used to feel bad," she tells me, "when I had nothing to give my little girl. But I don't feel bad anymore because now I earn the money to take care of her." Another dancer passing through the dressing room overhears her and adds, "Right on, sister."

Zoila or 'Z' worked for a year in the booths before she was promoted to manager on the first floor, a position she takes pride in. When I tell her that I want to spend a few hours in a booth, she looks at me like I've got glory holes in my head. She has seen me all week, dressed in a conservative skirt and blouse as I interviewed her and all the other people in the three-tiered emporium. She is delighted, dollar signs dancing in her eyeballs, when I come downstairs in my black lace lingerie.

"The split is 60/40," she tells me. Sixty for the house, forty for the booth baby. Each $2 token buys 90 seconds of time. I mentally calculate that in one hour's time, if the booth is never empty, the customers could deposit $90 worth of tokens in the coin slot. That's $36 for every hour of taking off my clothes, playing with myself, talking to the customers, spreading my legs, sticking my fingers inside my pussy, spreading my cheeks . . .

The men enter in a steady stream. One is a whitebread college boy who wears a Princeton sweatshirt. Another is a young black man who spends twenty minutes dancing with me: by the time he leaves I am ready to collapse. Clink, clink, clink, clink. I love the sound of those deposits. The money inspires a Pavlovian reaction. Up in the chair, out with the tits, hand in the panties, stand up, strip down, start all over again. An eighty-year old regular has a neat gimmick. He carries a big box of flimsy lingerie and offers to sell it to the performers real cheap. I met him upstairs when he sold me a bra and then copped a feel when I tried it on. Now he's in the booth pulling out his nearly hundred-year-old dick. It's got a few hairs growing out of it that probably weren't there when he was forty, but the thing still works and he's real happy with it. When he exits, the lingerie salesman presses a buck tip into my palm. It's nice to be appreciated. Another man with a gruff voice and gold chains around his neck barks orders at me through the glass. He is the only one of a dozen men who chooses not to use the two-way telephone. He wants only to see my asshole. "Turn around. Spread your cheeks. Wider. Wider!" He doesn't seem to understand that I'm a fucking goddess. I can't wait for him to get out. "You want to see an asshole, mister, look in the mirror!" Lines like that are made for guys like him. He is one of the few who goes without coming. And he's definitely the one who could use it the most.

I get along well with the other women in the row of cubicles. Only one is pissed because until I showed up, she was the only white woman on the block. The others all work upstairs on the main level. She walks off the floor and for this she will be fined by Z.

Z runs a tight ship. She is protective of the women who work for her, but she believes in nipping trouble in the bud. When she does not have enough women on duty, she has to fill in herself and this manager has no desire to rejoin the labor force.

In the two hours I stay in the booth, I take in $112 out of a possible $180. My end is approximately $45, not bad for a couple of hours of work. But could I do it for six or eight hours a day, five or six days a week? A lip-licking wind-up doll. Not all of the women can. The most reliable workers have well-lighted spots on the main floor in a place called 'the hill.' The women who show up only when they feel like it work in a dark corner referred to charmingly as 'death row.'

When I return a few days later to pick up my check, I stop in to see Ron, the boss of the Triple Treat Theater. He tells me that he's sorry he missed me in the booth and offers me ten dollars to show him my tits. He lays a ten on the table and I unbutton my blouse. I give him a look at my naked breasts and scoop up that ten in my greedy little fist. Now I am starting to get the hang of this place. The boss sees the big smile on my face and decides that he's parted with his ten too easily. "Now, how about paying ten bucks to see my cock?"

Is he crazy! Maybe he thinks I'm really cockeyed! I've seen enough dicks that week to last me quite awhile and every one of them got whipped out for free. It does not take long to learn that in the game of sex and money, it's the man who comes up with the cash.

But do they really know what to do with their money? It's been several years since my first visit to Show World. I've made it my business to do considerable research in the field. The Love Act is currently forbidden but except for technological changes, the peep shows remain the same. As we approach the new millennium, why not have erotic emporiums reflect a new attitude? I propose the creation of one or more SEC's in cities across the country. This does not stand for the Securities and Exchange Commission that governs Wall Street, though it is an interesting coincidence. No, these SEC's would be Sexual Evolution Centers, conceived in liberty and dedicated to the proposition that sex is a nourishing, life-giving force and that sex work is of benefit to humanity. Let's begin with the practical considerations, how to make the SEC's accessible to both the clients and performers. On-premise child-care facilities are a must. Professionals like Baby Doll would welcome this convenience as would prospective clients, particularly housewives. SEC's would be for the female as well as male clientele.

No one would have to go without sexual nourishment for want of funds. We could issue fuck stamps the way we do food stamps. Or access to sexual nutrition could be incorporated in our desperately needed national health care plan. The government, however, would not be allowed to legislate the libido. For the guiding principle of SEC's would be the concept of sexual evolution. We are all at different stages in our sexual development. In terms of each individual's experience, nothing is bizarre, kinky or perverse. It all makes sense. Or, more succinctly, 'different strokes for different folks.' The prevalent atmosphere would be one of ecstasy and experimentation.

Working in SEC's would be an enviable position and the sex professionals would be revered for their expertise and the potent sensuality that keeps them strong and vibrant. Wages would reflect a grateful society.

Scientists could develop ways to channel the tremendous energy generated in SEC's so that it could be used to fuel entire communities.

The very first time I entered a Times Square burlesque house, a pretty blonde with a pony tail came dancing out, wearing only a pair of high heels. She bobbed around for a while, then sat on the edge of the stage, leaned back on the floor and spread her legs. The men in the theater left their seats and formed a line, single file, in front of her cunt. Each one of the men clutched a bill in his hand. I looked at that scene through my Catholic girl eyes and I knew this was a form of Holy Cumm union, another ironic coincidence of words. After ten years of explicit research, I see sex more than ever as a sacrament. A powerful and intimate connection with the universal energy, no matter where it is performed, or for how long, or with whom. And I also believe that what you see is what you get.

ROSES ●

evelyn lau

THE PSYCHIATRIST CAME into my life one month after my 18th birthday. He came into my life wearing a silk tie and dark eyes half-obscured by lines and wrinkles. He brought with him a pronounced upper class accent, a futile sense of humor, books to educate me. *Lolita*. *Story of O*. His lips were thin but when I took them between my own they plumped out and filled my mouth with sweet foreign tastes.

He worshipped me at first because he could not touch me. And then he worshipped me because he could only touch me if he paid to do so. I understood that without the autumn leaves, the browns of the hundreds and the fiery scarlets of the fifties, the marble pedestal beneath me would begin to erode.

The first two weeks were tender. He said he adored my childlike body, my unpainted face, my long straight hair. He promised to take care of me, love me unconditionally. He would be my father, friend, lover—and if one was ever absent, the other two were large enough on their own to fill up the space that was left behind.

He brought into my doorway the slippery clean smell of rain, and he possessed the necessary implements—samples of pills tiny as seeds, a gold shovel. My body yielded to the scrapings of his hands.

He gave me drugs because, he said, he loved me. He brought the tablets from his office, rattling in plastic bottles stuffed to the brim with cotton. I placed them under my tongue and sucked up their saccharine sweetness, learning that only the strong ones tasted like candy, the rest were chalky or bitter. He loved me beyond morality.

The plants that he brought each time he came to visit, baby's breath, dieffenbachia, jade, began to die as soon as they crossed the threshold of my home. After twenty-four hours the leaves would crinkle into tight dark snarls stooping towards the soil. They could not be pried open, though I watered his plants, exposed them to sunlight, trimmed them. It was as if by contact with him or with my environment, they had been poisoned. Watching them die, I was reminded of how he told me that when he first came to Canada he worked for two years in one of our worst mental institutions. I walked by the building once at night, creeping as far as I dared up the grassy slopes and between the evergreens. It was a sturdy beige structure, it didn't look so bad from the outside. In my mind though I saw it as something else. In my mind it was a series of black and white film stills, with a face staring out from behind a barred window. The face belonged to a woman with tangled hair, wearing a nightgown. I covered my ears from her screams. When he told me about this place I imagined him in the film, the woman clawing at him where the corridors were grey and there was the clanking sound of tin and metal. The way I used to lie awake as a child on the nights my father visited my bed and imagined scenes in which he was terrorized, in pain, made helpless. I could smell the bloodstains the janitors had not yet scrubbed from the floors. I could smell the human discharges and see the hands that groped at him as he walked past each cell, each room. The hands flapped disembodied in the air, white and supplicating and at the same time evil.

He told me that when he was married to his first wife, she had gone shopping one day and he had to bring their baby with him on his hospital rounds. I didn't know where to put him when I arrived, he said. So I put him in the wastepaper basket. When he returned the child had upended the basket and crawled out, crying. Glaring at his father. I had no other choice, he said, and he reached into his trenchcoat and gave me a bottle of pills. I love you, he said, that's why I'm doing this.

I believed that only someone with a limitless love would put his baby in a trash can, its face squinched and its mouth pursing open in a squawk of dismay. Only someone like that could leave it swaddled in crumpled scraps of paper so he could go and take care of his patients. I could not imagine the breadth of the love that lay behind his eyes, those eyes that become as clear as glass at the moment of orgasm.

He bought a mask yesterday from a Japanese import store. It had tangled human hair which he washed with an anti-dandruff shampoo, carefully brushing it afterwards so the strands would not snap off. It had no pupils; the corneas were circles of bone. He took it home with him and stared at it for half an hour during a thunderstorm, paralyzed with fear. It stared back at him. It was supposed to scare off his rage, he said.

After two weeks his tenderness went the way of his plants—crisp, shrivelled, closed. He stopped touching me in bed, but grew as gluttonous as dry soil. I started to keep my eyes open when we kissed and to squeeze them shut all the other times, the many times he pulled my hand or my head down between his legs.

He continued to bring me magazines and books, but they were eclipsed by the part of him he expected me to touch. Some days, I found I could not. I thought it was enough that I listened to his stories. I fantasized about being his psychoanalyst and not letting him see my face, having that kind of control over him. I would lay him down on my couch and shine light into his eyes while I remained in shadow, where he could not touch me.

His latest gift, a snake plant, looks like a cluster of green knives or spears. The soil is so parched that I keep watering it but the water runs smartly through the pot without, it seems, having left anything of itself behind. The water runs all over the table and into my hands.

Tonight I did not think I could touch him. I asked him to hit me instead, thinking his slim white body would recoil from the thought. Instead he rubbed himself against my thigh, excited. I told him pain did not arouse me, but it was too late. I pulled the blankets around my naked body and tried to close up inside the way a flower wraps itself in the safety of its petals when night falls.

At first he stretched me across his knees and began to spank me. I wiggled obediently and raised my bottom high into the air, the way my father used to like to see me do. Then he moved up to rain blows upon my back. One of them was so painful that I saw colors even with my eyes open; it showered through my body like fireworks. It was like watching a sunset and feeling a pain in your chest at its wrenching beauty, the kind of pain that makes you gasp.

How loud the slaps grew in the small space of my apartment, like the sound of thunder. I wondered if my face looked, in that moment, like his Japanese mask.

The pain cleansed my mind until it breathed like the streets of a city after a good and bright rain. It washed away the dirt inside me. I could see the gutters open up to swallow the candy wrappers, newspaper pages, cigarette butts born along on its massive tide. I saw as I had not seen before every bump and indentation on the wall beside my bed.

And then he wanted more and I fought him, dimly surprised that he wasn't stronger. I saw as though through the eye of a camera this tangle of white thighs and arms and the crook of a shoulder, the slope of a back. I scraped his skin with my fingernails. I felt no conscious fear because I was the girl behind the camera, zooming in for a close-up, a tight shot, an interesting angle. Limbs like marble on the tousled bed. His face contorted with strain. He was breathing heavily but I, I was not breathing at all. I knew that if I touched his hair my hand would come away wet, not with the pleasant sweat of sexual exertion but with something different. Something that would smell like a hospital, a hospital without disinfectant to mask the smells underneath.

And when he pushed my face against his thigh, it was oddly comforting, though it was the same thigh that belonged to the body that was reaching out to hit me. I breathed in the soft, soapy smell of his skin as his hand stung my back—the same hand that comforted crying patients, that wrote notes on their therapeutic progress, that had shook with shyness when it first touched me. The sound of the slaps amplified in the candlelit room. Nothing had ever sounded so loud, so singular in its purpose. I had never felt so far away from myself, not even with his pills.

I am far away and his thigh is sandy as a beach against my cheek. The sounds melt like gold, like slow Sunday afternoons. I think of cats and the baby grand piano in the foyer of my father's house. I think of the rain that gushes down the drainpipes outside my father's bathroom late at night when things begin to happen. I think of the queerly elegant black notes on sheets of piano music. The light is flooding generously through the windows and I am a little girl with a pink ribbon in my hair and a ruffled dress.

I seat myself on the piano bench and begin to play, my fingertips softening to the long ivories, the shorter ebony keys. I look down at my feet and see them bound in pink ballerina slippers, pressing intermittently on the pedals. Always Daddy's girl, I perform according to his instruction.

When it was over he stroked the fear that bathed my hands in cold sweat. He said that when we fought my face had filled with hatred and a dead coldness. He said that he had cured himself of his obsession with me during the beating, he had stripped me of my mystery. Slapped me human. He said my fear had turned him on. He was thirsty for the sweat that dampened my palms and willing to do anything to elicit more of that moisture so he could lick it and quench his tongue's thirst.

I understood that when I did not bleed at the first blow, his love turned into hatred. I saw that if I was indeed precious and fragile I would have broken, I would have burst open like a thin shell and discharged the rich sweet stain of roses.

Before he left he pressed his lips to mine. His eyes were open when he said that if I told anyone, he would have no other choice but to kill me.

Now that he is gone, I look between my breasts and see another flower growing: a rash of raspberry dots, like seeds. I wonder if this is how fear discharges itself when we leave our bodies in moments of pain.

The psychiatrist, when he first came, promised me a rose garden and in the mirror tomorrow morning I will see the results for the first time on my own body. I will tend his bouquets before he comes again, his eyes misty with fear and lust. Then I will listen to the liquid notes that are pleasing in the sunlit foyer and smile because somewhere, off in the distance, my father is clapping.

JULIA AND THE ● BAZOOKA

anna kavan

J ULIA IS A LITTLE girl with long straight hair and big eyes. Julia loved flowers. In the cornfield she has picked an enormous untidy bunch of red poppies which she is holding up so that most of her face is hidden except the eyes. Her eyes look sad because she has just been told to throw the poppies away, not to bring them inside to make a mess dropping their petals all over the house. Some of them have shed their petals already, the front of her dress is quite red. Julia is also a quiet schoolgirl who does not make many friends. Then she is a tall student standing with other students who have passed their final examinations, whose faces are gay and excited, eager to start life in the world. Only Julia's eyes are sad. Although she smiles with the others, she does not share their enthusiasm for living. She feels cut off from people. She is afraid of the world.

Julia is also a young bride in a white dress, holding a sheaf of roses in one hand and in the other a very small flat white satin bag containing a lace-edged handkerchief scented with Arpège and a plastic syringe. Now Julia's eyes are not at all sad. She has one foot on the step of a car, its door held open by a young man with kinky brown hair and a rose in his buttonhole. She is laughing because of something he's said or because he has just squeezed her arm or because she no longer feels frightened or cut off now that she has the syringe. A group of indistinct people in the background look on approvingly as if they are glad to transfer responsibility for Julia to the young man. Julia who loves flowers waves to them with her roses as she drives off with him.

Julia is also dead without any flowers. The doctor sighs when he looks at her lying there. No one else comes to look except the official people. The ashes of the tall girl Julia barely fill the silver cup she won in the tennis tournament. To improve her game the tennis professional gives her the syringe. He is a joking kind of man and calls the syringe a bazooka. Julia calls it that too, the name sounds funny, it makes her laugh. Of course she knows all the sensational stories about drug addiction, but the word bazooka makes nonsense of them, makes the whole drug business seem not serious. Without the bazooka she might not have won the cup, which as a container will at last serve a useful purpose. It is Julia's serve that wins the decisive game. Holding two tennis balls in her left hand, she throws one high in the air while her right hand flies up over her head, brings the racket down, wham, and sends the ball skimming over the opposite court hardly bouncing at all, a service almost impossible to return. Holding two balls in her hand Julia also lies in bed beside the young man with kinky hair. Julia is also lying in wreckage under an army blanket, and eventually Julia's ashes go into the silver cup.

The undertaker or somebody closes the lid and locks the cup in a pigeonhole among thousands of identical pigeonholes in a wall at the top of a cliff overlooking the sea. The winter sea is the color of pumice, the sky cold as gray ice, the icy wind charges straight at the wall making it tremble so that the silver cup in its pigeonhole shivers and tinkles faintly. The wind is trying to tear to pieces a few frostbitten flowers which have not been left for Julia at the foot of the wall. Julia is also driving with her bridegroom in the high mountains through fields of flowers. They stop the car and pick armfuls of daffodils and narcissi. There are no flowers for Julia in the pigeonhole and no bridegroom either.

"This is her syringe, her bazooka she always called it," the doctor says with a small sad smile. "It must be twenty years old at least. Look how the measures have been worn away by continuous use." The battered old plastic syringe is unbreakable, unlike the glass syringes which used to be kept in boiled water in metal boxes and reasonably sterile. This discolored old syringe has always been left lying about somewhere, accumulating germs and the assorted dirt of wars and cities. All the same, it has not done Julia any great harm. An occasional infection easily cured with penicillin, nothing serious. "Such dangers are grossly exaggerated."

Julia and her bazooka travel all over the world. She wants to see everything, every country. The young man with kinky hair is not there, but she is in a car and somebody sits beside her. Julia is a good driver. She drives anything, racing cars, heavy trucks. Her long hair streams out from under the crash helmet as she drives for the racing teams. Today she is lapping only a fraction of a second behind the number one driver when a red-hot bit of his clutch flies off and punctures her nearside tire, and the car somersaults twice and tears through a wall. Julia steps out of the wreck uninjured and walks away holding her handbag with the syringe inside it. She is laughing. Julia always laughs at danger. Nothing can frighten her while she has the syringe. She has almost forgotten the time when she was afraid. Sometimes she thinks of the kinky-haired man and wonders what he is doing. Then she laughs. There are always plenty of people to bring her flowers and make her feel gay. She hardly remembers how sad and lonely she used to feel before she had the syringe.

Julia likes the doctor as soon as she meets him. He is understanding and kind like the father she has imagined but never known. He does not want to take her syringe away. He says, "You've used it for years already and you're none the worse. In fact you'd be far worse off without it." He trusts Julia, he knows she is not irresponsible, she does not increase the dosage too much or experiment with new drugs. It is ridiculous to say all drug addicts are alike, all liars, all vicious, all psychopaths or delinquents just out for kicks. He is sympathetic toward Julia whose personality has been damaged by no love in childhood so that she can't make contact with people or feel at home in the world. In his opinion she is quite right to use the syringe, it is as essential to her as insulin to a diabetic. Without it she could not lead a normal existence, her life would be a shambles, but with its support she is conscientious and energetic, intelligent, friendly. She is most unlike the popular notion of a drug addict. Nobody could call her vicious.

Julia who loves flowers has made a garden on a flat roof in the city, all around her are pots of scarlet geraniums. Throughout the summer she has watered them every day because the pots dry out so fast up here in the sun and wind. Now summer is over, there is frost in the air. The leaves of the plants have turned yellow. Although the flowers have survived up to now the next frost will finish them off. It is wartime, the time of the flying bombs, they come over all the time, there seems to be nothing to stop them. Julia is used to them, she ignores them, she does not look. To save the flowers from the frost she picks them all quickly and takes them indoors. Then it is winter and Julia is on the roof planting bulbs to flower in the spring. The flying bombs are still coming over, quite low, just above roofs and chimneys, their chugging noise fills the sky. One after another, they keep coming over, making their monotonous mechanical noise. When the engine cuts out there is a sudden startling silence, suspense, everything suddenly goes unnaturally still. Julia does not look up when the silence comes, but all at once it seems very cold on the roof, and she plants the last bulb in a hurry.

The doctor has gone to consult a top psychiatrist about one of his patients. The psychiatrist is immensely dignified, extremely well-dressed, his voice matches his outer aspect. When the bomb silence starts, his clear grave voice says solemnly, "I advise you to take cover under that table beside you," as he himself glides with the utmost dignity under his impressive desk. Julia leaves the roof and steps onto the staircase, which is not there. The stairs have crumbled, the whole house is crumbling, collapsing, the world bursts and burns, while she falls through the dark. The ARP men dig Julia out of the rubble. Red geraniums are spilling down the front of her dress, she has forgotten the time between, and is forgetting more and more every moment. Someone spreads a gray blanket over her, she lies underneath it in her red-stained dress, her bag, with the bazooka inside, safely hooked over one arm. How cold it is in the exploding world. The northern lights burst out in frigid brilliance across the sky. The ice roars and thunders like gunfire. The cold is glacial, a glass dome of cold covers the globe. Icebergs tower high as mountains, furious blizzards swoop at each other like white wild beasts. All things are turning to ice in the mortal cold, and the cold has a face which sparkles with frost. It seems to be a face Julia knows, though she has forgotten whose face it is.

The undertaker hurriedly shuts himself inside his car, out of the cruel wind. The parson hurries toward his house, hatless, thin gray hair blowing about wildly. The wind snatches a tattered wreath of frost-blackened flowers and rolls it over the grass, past the undertaker and the parson, who both pretend not to see. They are not going to stay out in the cold any longer, it is not their job to look after the flowers. They do not know that Julia loves flowers and they do not care. The wreath was not put there for her, anyhow.

Julia is rushing after the nameless face, running as fast as if she was playing tennis. But when she comes near she does not, after all, recognize that glittering death-mask. It has gone now, there's nothing but arctic glitter, she is a bride again beside the young man with brown hair. The lights are blazing, but she shivers a little in her thin dress because the church is so cold. The dazzling brilliance of the aurora borealis has burnt right through the roof with its frigid fire. Snow slants down between the rafters, there is ice on the altar, snowdrifts in the aisles, the holy water and the communion wine have been frozen solid. Snow is Julia's bridal white, icicles are her jewels. The diamond-sparkling coronet on her head confuses her thoughts. Where has everyone gone? The bridegroom is dead, or in bed with some girl or other, and she herself lies under a dirty blanket with red on her dress.

"Won't somebody help me?" she calls. "I can't move." But no one takes any notice. She is not cold any longer. Suddenly now she is burning, a fever is burning her up. Her face is on fire, her dry mouth seems to be full of ashes. She sees the kind doctor coming and tries to call him, but can only whisper, "Please help me . . . ," so faintly that he does not hear. Sighing, he takes off his hat, gazing down at his name printed inside in small gold letters under the leather band. The kinky-haired young man is not in bed with anyone. He is wounded in a sea battle. He falls on the warship's deck, an officer tries to grab him but it's too late, over and over he rolls down the steeply sloping deck to the black bottomless water. The officer looks over the side, holding a lifebelt, but does not throw it down to the injured man; instead, he puts it on himself, and runs to a boat which is being lowered. The doctor comes home from the house of the famous psychiatrist. His head is bent, his eyes lowered, he walks slowly because he feels tired and sad. He does not look up so he never sees Julia waving to him with a bunch of geraniums from the window.

The pigeonhole wall stands deserted in the cold dusk. The undertaker has driven home. His feet are so cold he can't feel them, these winter funerals are the very devil. He slams the car door, goes inside stamping his feet, and shouts to his wife to bring, double quick, a good strong hot rum with plenty of lemon and sugar, in case he has caught a chill. The wife, who was just going out to a bingo session, grumbles at being delayed, and bangs about in the kitchen. At the vicarage the parson is eating a crumpet for tea, his chair pulled so close to the fire that he is practically in the grate.

It has got quite dark outside, the wall has turned black. As the wind shakes it, the faintest of tinkles comes from the pigeonhole where all that is left of Julia has been left. Surely there were some red flowers somewhere, Julia would be thinking, if she could still think. Then she would think something amusing, she would remember the bazooka and start to laugh. But nothing is left of Julia really, she is not there. The only occupant of the pigeonhole is the silver cup, which can't think or laugh or remember. There is no more Julia anywhere. Where she was there is only nothing.

6

CREATIVITY, LIFE PHASES

Since Wild Woman is Rio Abajo Rio, the river beneath the river, when she flows into us, we flow. If the aperture from her to us is blocked, we are blocked. If her currents are toxified by our own negative inner complexes or by the environs of persons around us, the delicate processes that craft our ideas are polluted also. Then we are like a dying river. This is not a slight thing to be ignored. The loss of clear creative flow constitutes a psychological and spiritual crisis.

Some say the creative life is in ideas, some say it is in doing. It seems in most instances to be in simple being. It is not virtuosity, although that is very fine in itself. It is the love of something, having so much love for something—whether a person, a word, an image, an idea, the land or humanity—that all that can be done with the overflow is to create. It is not a matter of wanting to, not a singular act of will, one solely must.

We can first of all not entertain the fantasy land as shown in the fairy tale of the "The Little Match Girl," who freezes to death while lighting matches in order to see beautiful, cloudy fantasies arise. There are three sorts of fantasies. Some are for our pleasure, like day-dreams. Some are vehicles to take us forward—all successes— psychological, spiritual, financial and creative—begin with a fantasy. Then there is the third kind of fantasy, the kind that brings everything to a stop.

This is the kind the Match Girl spins. It is a fantasy that has nothing to do with reality. It has to do with feeling nothing can be done, so one might as well sink into a dream. What will reverse this and restore soul-esteem and self-esteem? Action, acting in one's behalf, pure and simple . . .

from the chapter, "Clear Water, Nourishing The Creative Life,
The *La Llorona*," from *Women Who Run With the Wolves*

SILVER WATER ●

amy bloom

MY SISTER'S VOICE WAS like mountain water in a silver pitcher; the clear blue beauty of it cools you and lifts you up beyond your heat, beyond your body. After we went to see *La Traviata*, when she was fourteen and I was twelve, she elbowed me in the parking lot and said, "Check this out." And she opened her mouth unnaturally wide and her voice came out, so crystalline and bright that all the departing operagoers stood frozen by their cars, unable to take out their keys or open their doors until she had finished, and then they cheered like hell.

That's what I like to remember, and that's the story I told to all of her therapists. I wanted them to know her, to know that who they saw was not all there was to see. That before her constant tinkling of commercials and fast-food jingles there had been Puccini and Mozart and hymns so sweet and mighty you expected Jesus to come down off his cross and clap. That before there was a mountain of Thorazined fat, swaying down the halls in nylon maternity tops and sweatpants, there had been the prettiest girl in Arrandale Elementary School, the belle of Landmark Junior High. Maybe there were other pretty girls, but I didn't see them. To me, Rose, my beautiful blond defender, my guide to Tampax and my mother's moods, was perfect.

She had her first psychotic break when she was fifteen. She had been coming home moody and tearful, then quietly beaming, then she stopped coming home. She would go out into the woods behind our house and not come in until my mother went after her at dusk, and stepped gently into the briars and saplings and pulled her out, blank-faced, her pale blue sweater covered with crumbled leaves, her white jeans smeared with dirt. After three weeks of this, my mother, who is a musician and widely regarded as eccentric, said to my father, who is a psychiatrist and a kind, sad man, "She's going off."

"What is that, your professional opinion?" He picked up the newspaper and put it down again, sighing. "I'm sorry, I didn't mean to snap at you. I know something's bothering her. Have you talked to her?"

"What's there to say? David, she's going crazy. She doesn't need a heart-to-heart talk with Mom, she needs a hospital."

They went back and forth, and my father sat down with Rose for a few hours, and she sat there licking the hairs on her forearm, first one way, then the other. My mother stood in the hallway, dry-eyed and pale, watching the two of them. She had already packed, and when three of my father's friends dropped by to offer free consultations and recommendations, my mother and Rose's suitcase were already in the car. My mother hugged me and told me that they would be back that night, but not with Rose. She also said, divining my worst fear, "It won't happen to you, honey. Some people go crazy and some people never do. You never will." She smiled and stroked my hair. "Not even when you want to."

Rose was in hospitals, great and small, for the next ten years. She had lots of terrible therapists and a few good ones. One place had no pictures on the walls, no windows, and the patients all wore slippers with the hospital crest on them. My mother didn't even bother to go to Admissions. She turned Rose around and the two of them marched out, my father walking behind them, apologizing to his colleagues. My mother ignored the psychiatrists, the social workers, and the nurses, and played Handel and Bessie Smith for the patients on whatever was available. At some places, she had a Steinway donated by a grateful, or optimistic, family; at others, she banged out "Gimme a Pigfoot and a Bottle of Beer" on an old, scarred box that hadn't been tuned since there'd been English-speaking physicians on the grounds. My father talked in serious, appreciative tones to the administrators and unit chiefs and tried to be friendly with whoever was managing Rose's case. We all hated the family therapists.

The worst family therapist we ever had sat in a pale green room with us, visibly taking stock of my mother's ethereal beauty and her faded blue t-shirt and girl-sized jeans, my father's rumpled suit and stained tie, and my own unreadable seventeen-year-old fashion statement. Rose was beyond fashion that year, in one of her dancing teddybear smocks and extra-extra-large Celtics sweatpants. Mr. Walker read Rose's file in front of us and then watched in alarm as Rose began crooning, beautifully, and slowly massaging her breasts. My mother and I laughed, and even my father started to smile. This was Rose's usual opening salvo for new therapists.

Mr. Walker said, "I wonder why it is that everyone is so entertained by Rose behaving inappropriately."

Rose burped, and then we all laughed. This was the seventh family therapist we had seen, and none of them had lasted very long. Mr. Walker, unfortunately, was determined to do right by us.

"What do you think of Rose's behavior, Violet?" They did this sometimes. In their manual it must say, If you think the parents are too weird, try talking to the sister.

"I don't know. Maybe she's trying to get you to stop talking about her in the third person."

"Nicely put," my mother said.

"Indeed," my father said.

"Fuckin' A," Rose said.

"Well, this is something that the whole family agrees upon," Mr. Walker said, trying to act as if he understood or even liked us.

"That was not a successful intervention, Ferret Face." Rose tended to function better when she was angry. He did look like a blond ferret, and we all laughed again. Even my father, who tried to give these people a chance, out of some sense of collegiality, had given it up.

After fourteen minutes, Mr. Walker decided that our time was up and walked out, leaving us grinning at each other. Rose was still nuts, but at least we'd all had a little fun.

The day we met our best family therapist started out almost as badly. We scared off a resident and then scared off her supervisor, who sent us Dr. Thorne. Three hundred pounds of Texas chili, cornbread, and Lone Star beer, finished off with big black cowboy boots and a small string tie around the area of his neck.

"O frabjous day, it's Big Nut." Rose was in heaven and stopped massaging her breasts immediately.

"Hey, Little Nut." You have to understand how big a man would have to be to call my sister "little." He christened us all, right away. "And it's the good Doctor Nut, and Madame Hickory Nut, 'cause they are the hardest damn nuts to crack, and over here in the overalls and not much else is No One's Nut"—a name that summed up both my sanity and my loneliness. We all relaxed.

Dr. Thorne was good for us. Rose moved into a halfway house whose director loved Big Nut so much that she kept Rose even when Rose went through a period of having sex with everyone who passed her door. She was in a fever for a while, trying to still the voices by fucking her brains out.

Big Nut said, "Darlin', I can't. I cannot make love to every beautiful woman I meet, and furthermore, I can't do that and be your therapist too. It's a great shame, but I think you might be able to find a really nice guy, someone who treats you just as sweet and kind as I would if I were lucky enough to be your beau. I don't want you to settle for less." And she stopped propositioning the crack addicts and the alcoholics and the guys at the shelter. We loved Dr. Thorne.

My father went back to seeing rich neurotics and helped out one day a week at Dr. Thorne's Walk-In Clinic. My mother finished a recording of Mozart concerti and played at fund-raisers for Rose's halfway house. I went back to college and found a wonderful linebacker from Texas to sleep with. In the dark, I would make him call me "darlin'." Rose took her meds, lost about fifty pounds, and began singing at the A.M.E. Zion Church, down the street from the halfway house.

At first they didn't know what to do with this big blond lady, dressed funny and hovering wistfully in the doorway during their rehearsals, but she gave them a few bars of "Precious Lord" and the choir director felt God's hand and saw that with the help of His sweet child Rose, the Prospect Street Choir was going all the way to the Gospel Olympics.

Amidst a sea of beige, umber, cinnamon, and espresso faces, there was Rose, bigger, blonder, and pinker than any two white women could be. And Rose and the choir's contralto, Addie Robicheaux, laid out their gold and silver voices and wove them together in strands as fine as silk, as strong as steel. And we wept as Rose and Addie, in their billowing garnet robes, swayed together, clasping hands until the last perfect note floated up to God, and then they smiled down at us.

Rose would still go off from time to time and the voices would tell her to do bad things, but Dr. Thorne or Addie or my mother could usually bring her back. After five good years, Big Nut died. Stuffing his face with a chili dog, sitting in his unair-conditioned office in the middle of July, he had one big, Texas-sized aneurysm and died.

Rose held on tight for seven days; she took her meds, went to choir practice, and rearranged her room about a hundred times. His funeral was like a Lourdes for the mentally ill. If you were psychotic, borderline, bad-off neurotic, or just very hard to get along with, you were there. People shaking so bad from years of heavy meds that they fell out of the pews. People holding hands, crying, moaning, talking to themselves. The crazy people and the not-so-crazy people were all huddled together, like puppies at the pound.

Rose stopped taking her meds, and the halfway house wouldn't keep her after she pitched another patient down the stairs. My father called the insurance company and found out that Rose's new, improved psychiatric coverage wouldn't begin for forty-five days. I put all of her stuff in a garbage bag, and we walked out of the halfway house, Rose winking at the poor drooling boy on the couch.

"This is going to be difficult—not all bad, but difficult—for the whole family, and I thought we should discuss everybody's expectations. I know

I have some concerns." My father had convened a family meeting as soon as Rose finished putting each one of her thirty stuffed bears in its own special place.

"No meds," Rose said, her eyes lowered, her stubby fingers, those fingers that had braided my hair and painted tulips on my cheeks, pulling hard on the hem of her dirty smock.

My father looked in despair at my mother.

"Rosie, do you want to drive the new car?" my mother asked.

Rose's face lit up. "I'd love to drive that car. I'd drive to California, I'd go see the bears at the San Diego Zoo. I would take you, Violet, but you always hated the zoo. Remember how she cried at the Bronx Zoo when she found out that the animals didn't get to go home at closing?" Rose put her damp hand on mine and squeezed it sympathetically. "Poor Vi."

"If you take your medication, after a while you'll be able to drive the car. That's the deal. Meds, car." My mother sounded accommodating but unenthusiastic, careful not to heat up Rose's paranoia.

"You got yourself a deal, darlin'."

I was living about an hour away then, teaching English during the day, writing poetry at night. I went home every few days for dinner. I called every night.

My father said, quietly, "It's very hard. We're doing all right, I think. Rose has been walking in the mornings with your mother, and she watches a lot of TV. She won't go to the day hospital, and she won't go back to the choir. Her friend Mrs. Robicheaux came by a couple of times. What a sweet woman. Rose wouldn't even talk to her. She just sat there, staring at the wall and humming. We're not doing all that well, actually, but I guess we're getting by. I'm sorry, sweetheart, I don't mean to depress you."

My mother said, emphatically, "We're doing fine. We've got our routine and we stick to it and we're fine. You don't need to come home so often, you know. Wait 'til Sunday, just come for the day. Lead your life, Vi. She's leading hers."

I stayed away all week, afraid to pick up my phone, grateful to my mother for her harsh calm and her reticence, the qualities that had enraged me throughout my childhood.

I came on Sunday, in the early afternoon, to help my father garden, something we had always enjoyed together. We weeded and staked tomatoes and killed aphids while my mother and Rose were down at the lake. I didn't even go into the house until four, when I needed a glass of water.

Someone had broken the piano bench into five neatly stacked pieces and placed them where the piano bench usually was.

"We were having such a nice time, I couldn't bear to bring it up," my father said, standing in the doorway, carefully keeping his gardening boots out of the kitchen.

"What did Mommy say?"

"She said, 'Better the bench than the piano.' And your sister lay down on the floor and just wept. Then your mother took her down to the lake. This can't go on, Vi. We have twenty-seven days left, your mother gets no sleep because Rose doesn't sleep, and if I could just pay twenty-seven thousand dollars to keep her in the hospital until the insurance takes over, I'd do it."

"All right. Do it. Pay the money and take her back to Hartley-Rees. It was the prettiest place, and she liked the art therapy there."

"I would if I could. The policy states that she must be symptom-free for at least forty-five days before her coverage begins. Symptom-free means no hospitalization."

"Jesus, Daddy, how could you get that kind of policy? She hasn't been symptom-free for forty-five minutes."

"It's the only one I could get for long-term psychiatric." He put his hand over his mouth, to block whatever he was about to say, and went back out to the garden. I couldn't see if he was crying.

He stayed outside and I stayed inside until Rose and my mother came home from the lake. Rose's soggy sweatpants were rolled up to her knees, and she had a bucketful of shells and seaweed, which my mother persuaded her to leave on the back porch. My mother kissed me lightly and told Rose to go up to her room and change out of her wet pants.

Rose's eyes grew very wide. "Never. I will never . . ." She knelt down and began banging her head on the kitchen floor with rhythmic intensity, throwing all her weight behind each attack. My mother put her arms around Rose's waist and tried to hold her back. Rose shook her off, not even looking around to see what was slowing her down. My mother lay up against the refrigerator.

"Violet, please . . ."

I threw myself onto the kitchen floor, becoming the spot that Rose was smacking her head against. She stopped a fraction of an inch short of my stomach.

"Oh, Vi, Mommy, I'm sorry. I'm sorry, don't hate me." She staggered to her feet and ran wailing to her room.

My mother got up and washed her face brusquely, rubbing it dry with a dishcloth. My father heard the wailing and came running in, slipping his long bare feet out of his rubber boots.

"Galen, Galen, let me see." He held her head and looked closely for bruises on her pale, small face. "What happened?" My mother looked at me. "Violet, what happened? Where's Rose?"

"Rose got upset, and when she went running upstairs she pushed Mommy out of the way." I've only told three lies in my life, and that was my second.

"She must feel terrible, pushing you, of all people. It would have to be you, but I know she didn't want it to be." He made my mother a cup of tea, and all the love he had for her, despite her silent rages and her vague stares, came pouring through the teapot, warming her cup, filling her small, long-fingered hands. She rested her head against his hip, and I looked away.

"Let's make dinner, then I'll call her. Or you call her, David, maybe she'd rather see your face first."

Dinner was filled with all of our starts and stops and Rose's desperate efforts to control herself. She could barely eat and hummed the McDonald's theme song over and over again, pausing only to spill her juice down the front of her smock and begin weeping. My father looked at my mother and handed Rose his napkin. She dabbed at herself listlessly, but the tears stopped.

"I want to go to bed. I want to go to bed and be in my head. I want to go to bed and be in my bed and in my head and just wear red. For red is the color that my baby wore and once more, it's true, yes, it is, it's true. Please don't wear red tonight, oh, oh, please don't wear red tonight, for red is the color—"

"Okay, okay, Rose. It's okay. I'll go upstairs with you and you can get ready for bed. Then Mommy will come up and say good night too. It's okay, Rose." My father reached out his hand and Rose grasped it, and they walked out of the dining room together, his long arm around her middle.

My mother sat at the table for a moment, her face in her hands, and then she began clearing the plates. We cleared without talking, my mother humming Schubert's "Schlummerlied," a lullaby about the woods and the river calling to the child to go to sleep. She sang it to us every night when we were small.

My father came into the kitchen and signaled to my mother. They went upstairs and came back down together a few minutes later.

"She's asleep," they said, and we went to sit on the porch and listen to the crickets. I don't remember the rest of the evening, but I remember it as quietly sad, and I remember the rare sight of my parents holding hands, sitting on the picnic table, watching the sunset.

I woke up at three o'clock in the morning, feeling the cool night air through my sheet. I went down the hall for a blanket and looked into Rose's room, for no reason. She wasn't there. I put on my jeans and a sweater and went downstairs. I could feel her absence. I went outside and saw her wide, draggy footprints darkening the wet grass into the woods.

"Rosie," I called, too softly, not wanting to wake my parents, not wanting to startle Rose. "Rosie, it's me. Are you here? Are you all right?"

I almost fell over her. Huge and white in the moonlight, her flowered smock bleached in the light and shadow, her sweatpants now completely wet. Her head was flung back, her white, white neck exposed like a lost Greek column.

"Rosie, Rosie—" Her breathing was very slow, and her lips were not as pink as they usually were. Her eyelids fluttered.

"Closing time," she whispered. I believe that's what she said.

I sat with her, uncovering the bottle of Seconal by her hand, and watched the stars fade.

When the stars were invisible and the sun was warming the air, I went back to the house. My mother was standing on the porch, wrapped in a blanket, watching me. Every step I took overwhelmed me; I could picture my mother slapping me, shooting me for letting her favorite die.

"Warrior queens," she said, wrapping her thin strong arms around me. "I raised warrior queens." She kissed me fiercely and went into the woods by herself.

Later in the morning she woke my father, who could not go into the woods, and still later she called the police and the funeral parlor. She hung up the phone, lay down, and didn't get back out of bed until the day of the funeral. My father fed us both and called the people who needed to be called and picked out Rose's coffin by himself.

My mother played the piano and Addie sang her pure gold notes and I closed my eyes and saw my sister, fourteen years old, lion's mane thrown back and eyes tightly closed against the glare of the parking lot lights. That sweet sound held us tight, flowing around us, eddying through our hearts, rising, still rising.

IN MY NEXT LIFE ●

pam houston

THIS IS A love story. Although Abby and I were never lovers. That's an odd thing for me to have to say about another woman, because I've never had a woman lover, and yet with Abby it would have been possible. Of course with Abby anything was possible, and I often wonder if she hadn't gotten sick if we would have been lovers: one day our holding and touching and hugging slipping quietly into something more. It would have been beside the point and redundant, our lovemaking, but it might have been wonderful all the same.

That was the summer I was organic gardening for a living, and I had a small but steady clientele who came to me for their produce and kept me financially afloat. I had a trade going with Carver's Bakery, tomatoes for bread, and another with the farmers' market in Salt Lake City, fresh herbs for chicken and groceries. I grew wheat grass for my landlord Thomas and his lover, who both had AIDS. I traded Larry, at the Purina Mill, all the corn his kids could eat for all the grain I needed for my mare. She was half wild and the other half stubborn, and I should have turned her out to pasture like most of my friends said, or shot her like the rest recommended, but I had an idea that she and I could be great together if we ever both felt good on the same day.

Abby had long black hair she wore in a single braid and eyes the color of polished jade. Her shoulders were rounded like a swimmer's, although she was afraid of the water, and her hands were quick and graceful and yet seemed to be capable of incredible strength.

I met her at a horse-handling clinic she was teaching in Salt Lake that I'd gone to with my crazy mare.

"There are no problem horses," Abby said. "Someone has taught her to be that way."

In the middle of explaining to her that it wasn't me who taught my horse her bad habits, I realized it could have been. Abby had a way of looking at me, of looking into me, that made everything I said seem like the opposite of the truth.

"There are three things to remember when working with horses," Abby said to the women who had gathered for the class. "Ask, Receive, Give." She said each word slowly, and separated them by breaths. "Now what could be simpler than that?"

I rode as hard as I knew how that day at the clinic. Abby was calm, certain, full of images. "Your arms and hands are running water," she said. "Let the water pour over your horse. Let the buttons on your shirt come undone. Let your body melt like ice cream and dribble out the bottom of your bones."

My mare responded to the combination of my signals and Abby's words. She was moving with confidence, bending underneath me, her back rounded, her rhythm steady and strong.

"Catch the energy as if you were cradling a baby." Abby said. "Grow your fingers out to the sky. Fly with your horse. Feel that you are dancing." She turned from one woman to another. "Appeal to the great spirit," she said. "Become aware, inhibit, allow."

At the end of the day while we were walking out the horses Abby said, "You are a lovely, lovely woman. Tell me what else you do."

I told her I played the banjo, which was the other thing I was doing at the time, with a group that was only marginally popular with people my age but a big hit with the older folks in the Fallen Arches Square Dance Club.

Abby told me she had always been intimidated by musicians.

She told me I had medieval hair.

On the first day after the clinic that Abby and I spent together I told her that meeting her was going to change my whole life. She seemed neither threatened nor surprised by this information; if anything, she was mildly pleased. "Life gives us what we need when we need it," she said. "Receiving what it gives us is a whole other thing."

We were both involved with unavailable men, one by drugs, one by alcohol, both by nature. There were some differences. She lived with her boyfriend, whose name was Roy. I lived alone. Roy was kind, at least, and faithful, and my man, whose name was Hardin, was not.

I said to Thomas, "I have met a woman who, if she were a man, I would be in love with." But of course Abby could have never been a man, and I fell in love anyway. It's not the kind of definition Abby would have gotten mired in, but I think she may also have been a little in love with me.

Once, on the phone, when we weren't sure if the conversation was over, when we weren't sure if we had actually said goodbye, we both held our receivers, breathing silently, till finally she had the guts to say, "Are you still there?"

"We are a couple of silly women," she said, when we had finally stopped laughing. "A couple of silly women who want so badly to be friends."

Although only one-sixteenth Cherokee, and even that undocumented, Abby was a believer in Native American medicine. Shamanic healing, specifically, is what she practiced. The healing involved in shamanic work happens in mind journeys a patient takes with the aid of a continuous drumbeat, into the lower or upper world, accompanied by his or her power animal. The power animal serves as the patient's interpreter, guardian, and all number of other things. The animals take pity on us, it is believed, because of the confusion with which we surround ourselves. The learning takes place in the energy field where the animal and the human being meet.

A guided tour into the lower world with a buffalo is not the kind of thing a white girl from New Jersey would discover on her own, but for me, everything that came from Abby's mouth was magic. If she had told me the world was flat, I'd have found a way to make it true.

When Abby taught me the methods of shamanic healing I started to try to journey too. Abby played the drum for me. She shook the rattle around my body and blew power into my breastbone and into the top of my skull. The drumming altered my mental state, that was for certain, but I couldn't make myself see anything I could define. If I pressed my arm hard enough against my eyeballs I could start to see light swirling. But a tunnel? another world? Animals and spirits I couldn't muster.

"People have different amounts of spiritual potential," she said, "and for some people it takes a while. Don't be discouraged by a slow start."

So I would try again and again to make forms out of the shapes inside my eyelids, and I'd stretch the truth of what I saw in the reporting. I wanted to go all of the places that Abby could go. I was afraid she might find another friend with more spiritual potential than me.

"You're seeing in a way you've never seen before," Abby said. "You just don't know how to recognize it. It isn't like cartoons on your eyelids. It's not like a big-screen TV."

Finally, my mind would make logical connections out of the things I was seeing. "It was a bear," I would say, "running away and then return-ing." Abby's green eyes never let mine falter. "A big white bear that could run on two legs." As I said the words, it seemed, I made it so. "It was

turning somersaults, too, and rolling in the blueberries." It didn't feel like I
was lying, but it also didn't feel like the truth.

One thing was certain. I believed what Abby saw. If she said she rose
into the stars and followed them to South Africa, if she danced on the
rooftops of Paris with her ancestors, if she and her power animal made
love in the Siberian snow, I believed her. I still believe her. Abby didn't lie.

But it wasn't only the magic. Abby was gentle and funny and talked
mostly with her hands. She made great mashed potatoes. She had advanced degrees in botany, biology, and art history. And the horses, Abby
loved her horses more than any power animal her imagination could
conjure up.

"The Indians don't believe in imagination," she told me. "They don't
even have a word for it. Once you understand that fully this all becomes
much easier."

We had climbed the mountain behind my house, way above the silver
mine, and were lying in a meadow the moon made bright. Abby threw
handfuls of cornmeal on the ground. "I'm feeding my power animal," she
said. "When I do this he knows that I need him around."

I made Abby batches of fresh salsa, pesto, and spaghetti sauce. I
brought her squash blossoms, red peppers, and Indian corn to make a
necklace her power animal told her to wear.

She told me about her college roommate, Tracy, her best friend, she
said, before me. Tracy's marriage had broken up, she said, because Tracy
had been having an affair with a woman, and her husband, Steve,
couldn't handle it. They had tried going to therapy together, but Tracy
eventually chose the woman over Steve.

"She said she never expected to have an affair with a woman," Abby
said, "but then they just fell in love."

I thought about my friend Thomas, about how he gets so angry
whenever anybody says that they respect his sexual choice. "Choice has
nothing to do with it," I can hear him saying. "Why would I ever have done
this if I had had a choice?"

But I wonder if it's not a question of choice for a woman. Aren't there
women who wake up tired of trying to bridge the unbridgeable gap,
who wake up ready to hold and be held by somebody who knows what
it means?

"In my next life," Thomas was famous for saying, "I'm coming back as
a lesbian."

"That's what I did," my friend of five years, Joanne, said, when I asked
her opinion, as if her lesbian affair was something I'd known about all
along, "with Isabelle. And it was wonderful, for a while. But what hap-

pens too often is that somewhere down the line you are attracted to a man and want to go back, and then it's a whole new kind of guilt to deal with. You're hurting somebody who's on your team, who really knows you, who really is you, I suppose, if you stop and think."

"There are so many more interesting things to do than fall in love," Abby said. "If Roy and I split up, I want to live in a house full of women, old women and young women, teenagers and babies. Doesn't falling in love sound boring, compared to that?"

I had to admit, it didn't. We were both fighting our way out of codependency. I wasn't as far as she was yet.

"The problem with codependency," Abby said, "is that what you have to do to be codependent, and what you have to do to not be codependent, turn out so often to be the same thing."

"So what would you do about sex, in this house full of women?" I said. We were sitting sideways on her sofa like kids on a Flexible Flyer. She was braiding and unbraiding my medieval hair.

"Frankly," she said, "that's the least of my concerns."

"That's what you say now," I said, "but I think after a few years without, you would start to feel differently."

"Yeah, maybe you're right," she said, giving the short hairs at the nape of my neck a tug. "Maybe sex would turn out to be the big snafu."

It was only the third or fourth time we were together when Abby told me about the lump in her breast. "It's been there a long time," she said, "about two years, I guess, but my power animal says it's not cancer, and besides it gets bigger and smaller with my period. Cancer never does that."

Even the doctor, when she finally did go, said he was ninety-nine percent sure that the lump was not a "malignancy" (doctors apparently had stopped using the "C" word), but he wanted to take it out anyway, just to make sure.

On the night before Abby's biopsy, I made her favorite thing: three kinds of baked squash, butternut, buttercup, and acorn.

"Sometimes I'm jealous of Hardin," I said. "He lives right on the surface and he's happy there. Who am I to tell him how to live his life? I should be that happy in all my depth."

"I had a friend in grade school named Margaret Hitzrot," Abby said. "Once on our way to a day of skiing we were the first car in a twenty-one-vehicle pile up. Our car spun to a stop, unharmed against the snowbank, but facing back the way we had come, and we watched station wagons, delivery trucks, VW buses, collide and crash, spin and smash together. Mrs. Hitzrot said, 'Margaret, do you think we should wait for the police?' And Margaret said, 'If we don't get to the ski area before the lift opens the whole day will be ruined,' so we got in our car and drove away."

"It's not the worst way to live," I said.

"The problem with the surface," Abby said, "is that it's so slippery. Once you get bumped off, it's impossible to climb back on."

Abby's arms bore scars on the white underside, nearly up to the elbows, thin and delicate, like an oriental script. "It was a long, long time ago," she said. "And I wasn't trying to kill myself either. My stepfather had some serious problems. There was a good bit of sexual abuse. I never even thought about dying. I just wanted to make myself bleed."

After dinner we rode the horses up to our favorite meadow. She had been riding my horse, who had turned to putty in her hands. I was riding one of hers, a big gray gelding who was honest as a stone. We kept saying we were going to switch back, now that my horse had been gentled, but I didn't push the issue. I was afraid my mare would go back to her old habits and Abby would be disappointed. It was something I'd never felt with a woman, this giant fear of looking bad.

I was depressed that night. Hardin was in another state with another woman, and it made me so mad that I cared.

"You have given all your power away to Hardin," Abby said. "You need to do something to get it back."

We sat under the star-filled sky and Abby said she would journey beside me, journey, she said, on my behalf. This was accomplished by our lying on the ground side by side. We touched at the shoulders, the knees, and the hips. We both tied bandannas around our heads, and Abby pulled her Walkman and drumming tape out of the saddlebags.

"Don't feel like you need to journey," she said. "I'll do all the work for you, but if you feel yourself slipping into a journey, go ahead and let it happen."

For a long time I watched the white spots turn on the inside of my bandanna while Abby's breathing quickened, and leveled and slowed. Then I saw a steady light, and reflections below it. It was my first real vision, nothing about it questionable or subject to change. It was moonlight over granite, I think, something shiny, and permanent and hard.

Abby came back slowly, and I turned off the tape.

"Your power source is the moon," she said. "It was a bear who told me. A giant bear that kept getting smaller and smaller. He was multicolored, like light, coming through a prism. The full moon is in five days. You must be out in the moonlight. Drink it in. Let it fill you. Take four stones with you and let them soak the moonlight. This is one of them." She pressed a tiger's-eye into my hand. "It is up to you to find the other three."

I carried flowers with me into the short-stay surgery wing. I saw Abby in a bed at the end of the hall. She was wide awake and waving.

"You brought flowers," she said.

"Store-bought flowers, made to look wild," I said. "How do you feel?"

"Good," Abby said. "Not too bad at all."

The doctor came in and leaned over the bed like an old friend.

"Your lump was a tumor, Abby," he said.

"What kind of tumor?" she said. "What does it mean?"

"It was a malignancy," he said. "A cancer." (Sweet relief.) "I have to tell you, of all the lumps I did today, and I did five, yours was the one I expected least of all to be malignant."

His pager went off and he disappeared through the curtain. It took a few seconds, but Abby turned and met my eyes.

"Cancer, huh?" she said. "My power animal was wrong."

When I had Abby tucked into her own bed I drove home the long way, over the mountain. It was the day that would have been John Lennon's fiftieth birthday, and on the radio was a simulcast, the largest in history, a broadcast reaching more people than any other broadcast had ever done. It was live from the United Nations. Yoko Ono read a poem, and then they played "Imagine." It was the first time I cried for John Lennon.

Abby called me in the middle of the night.

"I know it sounds crazy," she said, "but I can't sleep without my lump. I should have asked the doctor for it. I should have brought it home and put it under my pillow," she said. "Where do you think it has gone?"

Before her second surgery, a double mastectomy and lymph-node exploration, I took Abby down to southern Utah, to the piece of land I'd bought in the middle of nowhere because I loved it there and because having it seemed a little bit like security. My six acres is in the high desert, where it never rains except too much and more often it snows and freezes cherry blossoms or hails hard enough to make bruises on uncovered flesh. It was sage and juniper mostly, a few cacti.

Abby put her feet into the ground like she was planting them. Two ravens flew overhead in pursuit of a smaller bird, gray and blue. There was squawking, the rustle of wings, and then a clump of feathers floated down and landed at Abby's feet. Three feathers stuck together, and on each tip, a drop of blood.

Abby started singing and dancing, a song she made up as she went along, directed toward the east.

"Why do you sing and dance?" she'd once asked me. "To raise your spirits, right?" she laughed. "That is also why I sing and dance," she said. "Precisely."

She sang the same song to each of the four horizons, and danced the same steps to each with the gray bird's feathers in her hair. The words elude me now, half-English, half-Navajo. It was about light, I remember, and red dirt, and joy. When she finished dancing and turned back toward the eastern horizon the full moon rose right into her hands.

• • •

Abby looked tiny and alone in the giant white bed and among the machines she was hooked to.

"How are you?" I said.

"Not bad," she said. "A little weak. In the shamanic tradition," she said, "there is a certain amount of soul loss associated with anesthesia. Airplane travel too," she said. "Your soul can't fly fast enough to keep up. How are you?" she said. "How's Hardin?"

"He left for the Canadian Rockies this morning," I said. "He'll be gone six weeks. I asked him if he wanted to make love. He was just lying there, you know, staring at the ceiling. He said, 'I was just trying to decide whether to do that or go to Ace Hardware.' "

"I don't want you to break up with him because he would say something like that," Abby said. "I want you to break up with him because he'd say something like that and not think it was funny."

The doctor came in and started to say words like "chemotherapy," like "bone scan" and "brain scan," procedures certain to involve soul loss of one kind or another.

Simply because there was no one, I called Hardin in Canada. "That's too bad," he said, when I told him the cancer was extensive in the lymph nodes. And as usual, he was right.

The nights were getting colder, and the day after Abby got out of the hospital we picked about a thousand green tomatoes to pickle in Ball jars.

"I don't know where I want Roy to be in all of this," she said. "I know it would be too much to ask him for things like support and nurturance, so I thought about asking for things he would understand. I'd like him to stop smoking around me. I'd like him to keep our driveway free of snow."

"Those sound like good, concrete things," I said.

"I love him very much, you know," she said.

And God help me, I was jealous.

We took a walk, up towards the Uintas, where the aspen leaves had already fallen, making a carpet under our feet.

"You know," I said, "if you want to go anywhere, this year, I'll come up with the money and we'll go. It's just credit cards," I said. "I can make it happen."

"I know why my power animal lied," Abby said. "It was the intent of my question. Even though I said 'Do I have cancer?' what I meant was 'Am I going to die?' That's what I was really asking, and the answer was no."

"I'm glad you worked that out," I said.

"I've made a decision," she said. "I'm going to stop seeing the doctors."

Something that felt like a small bomb exploded in my ribs. "What do you mean?" I said.

"I'm not going to have the chemotherapy," she said. "Or any more of the tests. My power animal said I don't need them, they could even be *detrimental*, is what he said."

The sound of the dead leaves under my boots became too loud for me to bear. "Is that what he really said, Abby?" I faced her on the trail. "Did he open his mouth and say those words?"

She walked around me and went on down the trail. "You won't leave me," she said after a while. "Even if things get real bad."

I leaned over and kissed her, softly, on the head.

"I want to support her decision," I told Thomas. "I even want to believe in her magic, but she's ignoring hundreds of years of medical research. This ugly thing is consuming her and she's not doing anything to stop it."

We were walking in the moonlight on our way up to the old silver mine not far above my house. It was the harvest moon, and so bright you could see the color in the changing leaves, the red maple, the orange scrub oak, the yellow aspen. You could even tell the difference in the aspen that were yellow tinged with brown, and the ones that were yellow and still holding green.

"She is doing something," Thomas said. "She's just not doing what you want her to do."

"What, listening to her power animal?" I said. "Waiting for the spirits from the lower world to take the cancer away? How can that mean anything to me? How can I make that leap?"

"You love Abby," he said.

"Yeah," I said. The bright leaves against the dark evergreens in the moonlight were like an hallucination.

"And she loves you," he said.

"Yeah," I said.

"That's," he said, "how you make the leap."

I don't want to talk about the next few months, the way the cancer ambushed her body with more and more powerful attacks. The way she sank into her own shadow, the darkness enveloping what was left of her hair and skin. Her vitality slipping. Maybe I do want to talk about it, but not right now.

With no doctor to supply the forecasts and explanations, watching Abby's deterioration was like reading a book without a narrator, or seeing a movie in another language. Just when you thought you knew what was going on, the plot would thicken illogically.

When it all got to be too much for Roy, he moved out and I moved in. I even thought about trying to find some old ladies and teenagers, of calling some of the ladies from the Fallen Arches, thinking I could create the household Abby had wished for. It wasn't really as pathetic as it sounds. We ate a lot of good food. We saw a lot of good movies. I played my banjo and Abby sang. We laughed a lot those last days. More, I'll bet, than most people could imagine.

Abby finally even refused to eat. The world had taken everything from her she was going to let it take, and she died softly in her room one day, looking out the window at her horses.

Once I hit a rabbit in the highway, just barely hit it, I was almost able to swerve out of its way. It was nighttime, and very cold, and I stopped the car on the side of the road and walked back to where it lay dying. The humane thing, I'm told, would have been to shoot it or hit it in the head with the tire jack or run over it again. But I picked it up and held it under my coat until it died, it was only a few minutes, and it was the strangest sensation I know of, when the life all at once, it seemed, slipped away.

Abby and I didn't talk at all the day she died. She offered me no last words I could use to make an ending, to carry on with, to change my life. I held her hands for the last few hours, and then after that till they got colder than hell.

I sat with her body most of the night, without really knowing what I was looking for. An eagle, I guess, or a raven, some great huge bird bursting in a shimmer of starlight out of her chest. But if something rose out of Abby at the end, it was in a form I didn't recognize. Cartoons, she would have said, are what I wanted. Disneyland and special effects.

For two days after her death I was immobile. There was so much to be done, busy work, really, and thank goodness there were others there to do it. The neighbors, her relatives, my friends. Her stepfather and I exchanged glances several times, and then finally a hug, though I don't know if he knew who I was, or if he knew that I knew the truth about him. Her mother was the one I was really mad at, although that may have been unfair, and she and I walked circles around the house just to avoid each other, and it worked until they went back to Santa Cruz.

The third day was the full moon, and I knew I had to go outside in it, just in case Abby could see me from wherever she was. I saddled my mare for the first time in over a year and we walked up high, to the place where Abby and I had lain together under our first full moon not even a year before. My mare was quiet, even though the wind was squirrelly and we could hear the occasional footsteps of deer. She was so well behaved, in fact, that it made me wish I'd ridden her with Abby, made me hope that Abby could see us, and then I wondered why, against all indications, I still thought that Abby was somebody who had given me something to prove. *Your seat feels like a soft glove*, Abby would have said, *your horse fills it.*

I dismounted and spread some cornmeal on the ground. *Become aware, inhibit, allow.* I laid my stones so they pointed at each of the four horizons. Jade to the west, smoky quartz to the north, hematite to the south, and to the east, Abby's tiger's-eye. *Ask, receive, give.* I sang a song to the pine trees and danced at the sky. I drank the moonlight. It filled me up.

MANY MOTHERS ●

beverley daurio

One

ONCE THE GOVERNMENT rerouted the highway around Atherly in order to take a bend out, the main street, King, was more or less deserted. Half the cars passing through were lost; the other half were heading somewhere else. Atherly's six motels, built on posts sunk into blasted rock just outside of town, were closed. Faded signs invited motorists to stop and rest; no one had bothered to board up the broken windows facing the water. Even the pretty lake didn't draw tourists, which Aunt Sally said was a shame. Cellie's mother disagreed. She said it was nice to have the rocks and beach to themselves.

Cellie licked the last bit of ice from her lime popsicle and tasted wood. She listened as the two women talked over tea. Her mother's spoon, stirring sugar into a china cup, Aunt Sally's knife, laid back on the plate after buttering a piece of sourdough bread, did not make a sound. Cellie finished her popsicle and wiped her sticky fingers in the grass.

It would be eleven years before Cellie's mother vanished in the dark green waters of the lake.

Princesses, golden thimbles, castles and trolls: strange things happened in stories before the prince and princess could be married and live happily ever after. Cellie's mother had taught her to read, and she sounded out the words lying on her plain white bed, alone in her room.

For hours at a time, she pored over the drawings of pink lace dresses and diaphanous fairies.

Cellie trailed her hand along the rough cement wall beside the stairs that led down to the root cellar, tugged the cellar door open by the cool iron handle and stepped into darkness. The cellar smelled of soil and apples and potatoes where they kept preserves on shelves and salt pork hanging. They were poor, her mother said, but the vegetable garden at the back of the yard where the light was good would feed them for most of the winter.

Cellie was checking the cellar for treasure. As far as she could tell, taking flat testing steps across the dirt floor in the dimness, the packed earth beneath her feet was undisturbed. She wanted a treasure, and she wanted to be able to tell the story of her mother. Cellie knew that her mother had ridden a white horse as a girl. She had worn a crown as a singing princess on stage, and wings once when she played an angel. Her mother had walked in her sleep. But there weren't any answers in the dark, and Cellie shut the door carefully against the heat before returning to the yard at the top of the stairs.

Yellow sunlight chopped through the trees in slanted afternoon beams. Apart from the pleasant voices of the women drifting from the kitchen, it was quiet. Cellie's sneakered toes poked over the edge of the back verandah as she arranged white and red and black and brown stones on the wide wooden railing, stones the colors of women's hair and warm as live things in the summer heat. Over the course of many trips to the lake, Cellie had carefully fished the stones from shallow water near the shore, then dried them in the sun and polished them with a cloth. The stones she saved had the shapes of heads and nebulous faces carved into their hard surfaces by time and beating water. She told stories to the stones; she whispered to the tiny head in her palm. It glowed with the vermilion of poppies, of sorcerers' hats and velvet shoes. Cellie loved her mother; she loved to be outside by herself while her mother's voice floated through the wood-framed screen door. As she spoke to the little stones, her miniature mothers, and picked them up one by one to see if they had anything to say, she felt greedy and guilty: why did she want so many mothers when she had such a good one already? Cellie's right hand made the red stone nod.

All around her, white fences edged the rectangular backyards belonging to her house and to her neighbors'. Her mother's garden shimmered in the hot and rising air, orange tiger lilies and blue delphiniums, bleeding hearts and purple flowering chives, nasturtiums and lily of the valley. The clipped grass was flawless. Cellie replaced the red stone beside the others on the railing. A flapping sound, as of sheets whipping in the wind, made her stiffen and search the backyard for its source.

An enormous black bird with a green breast and a yellow beak tottered on top of the fence above her mother's pink roses. Its ungainly body leaned backwards at the same time as its neck curled forward, awkwardly pointing its head down to gaze into the rosebushes. The bird gathered itself and flung its body stupidly off the fence-top and into her yard. After some rustling, it struggled out of the roses and heaved itself onto the grass, where it stumbled, blinking and disoriented. Mesmerized, Cellie knocked her stones with her arm, and they fell off the railing, clicking. The bird's scaly black feet stopped. Its curved beak opened, its breast feathers shivered. The bird's beady glass-yellow eyes, fixed on Cellie in alarm, demanded that she stay back; it waddled, clumsily and wheezing with effort, in front of the verandah and into the patch of Michaelmas daisies on the other side of the lawn. Cellie watched the bird lunge part way out of the daisies, squawking. It hurled its huge body into the air three times, its lustrous green breast swelling with each breath, stumpy black wings batting furiously, before it surged up onto the fence. The bird jumped down into Aunt Sally's yard and out of Cellie's sight, but she could hear its feathers and its legs ferrying it away.

Cellie scrambled down the wooden steps from the verandah to the grass and hurried to the edge of the flower bed where the bird had blundered up out of the daisies. Trembling, Cellie leaned to straighten a stalk with serrated leaves the bird had damaged in its escape. The slatted white fence was too high for her to climb, and though she pushed the leaves and branches eagerly aside, the garden plants were too thickly clustered to see through. Cellie desperately wanted to find out where the bird was going, but by the time she had circled her house and stood peering over the gate into Aunt Sally's yard, the bird had disappeared.

In the spring Cellie and her mother often hiked beside the lake to gather strawberries. Her mother made tarts and preserves to trade for eggs, butter and milk. Cellie had to be careful not to step on the soft fruit sprouting in the dampness underfoot and to leave the hard, white, bitter fruit to ripen. Later, there were raspberries on long prickly canes that whipped her skin; but Cellie's favorites were the fat blueberries that sprang out of the spindly grey-green bushes growing over the rocks.

One afternoon, they were out in their white cotton hats, picking blueberries into large metal buckets—Cellie, her lips and chin and fingers stained bluish-purple, trying not to eat more than she kept—when a man and a woman came up from the lakeshore and walked over the mossy rocks toward them, holding hands. The strangers' clothes were wet, and they moved as if they were blind, free hands extended a little in front of them. They did not wave or speak, but headed silently, dripping, toward Cellie and her mother. Cellie stood up to say hello, but her mother grabbed

Cellie's hand and hastily pulled her and their clanking buckets through the sumac brush toward the road.

Death had taken Cellie Becker's father young and his flattened face gazed out from frames on side-tables and on the wall, constant and happy. Cellie's mother wore a plain black dress on Sundays when they walked to church. Dave was always gone, but her mother was a kind of portable heaven: she was either there, making tea and rice pudding with cinnamon and raisins, humming—or not there. Her mother could quite easily kneel in the living room, cutting lemon-colored wool according to a printed pattern, her angular dark head bent over the scissors, and not be there at all.

Cellie's story of her mother began, *Once upon a time in a city far from here . . .* but Cellie knew only fragments of her mother's life, and when she tried to string them together into a story they didn't make sense. How did Cellie fit in the part about her mother meeting Dave, her father, when he tried to steal her mother's dog? Or at least her mother thought that he was trying to steal her dog, but really he was getting back on the hockey bus because he played hockey for a living, and the dog liked him and followed him up the bus steps and made the other players laugh. On winter Saturday nights, if Aunt Sally was visiting, her mother let Cellie stay up late and watch hockey on television. It confused her, not least because Cellie had some ideas about things dead people did from her occasional evening talks with Aunt Sally. The dark little men on the ice reminded her of fish in water, and Cellie also thought they might be ghosts of her father; sometimes she suspected that one or another of the hockey players waved to her with a tiny dark hand.

Cellie coughed and coughed. *Get it out of your system,* her mother said patiently. Cellie stood up and coughed, curled in a ball on the floor and coughed until a sharper pain drove from her throat into her chest. Her room smelled of toast, medicinal syrup and damp heat. Beside the bed, on a white cane chair, her mother sat wringing a washcloth with cool water in a basin. When Cellie stopped coughing, her mother helped her into bed and tucked the sheets around her shoulders. She smoothed back Cellie's bangs and softly folded the cloth against her hot forehead.

Cellie had a nightmare. A bird the size of her mother climbed up out of the lake. It could not fly because of the thin mud soaked into its wings. The bird stumbled across the ground, eating pennies and pieces of paper with writing on them. Cellie could see that the bird's craw was swollen with the things it had taken in its beak, and when it swallowed she began to cry.

• • •

The evil stepmother or old witch was missing from her mother's story, and Cellie asked if Aunt Sally was an evil old witch. Her mother sputtered, *Evil old witch*? and snapped off a stem of the arum ivy she was re-potting. Cellie persisted: did her mother know any old witches? Had one perhaps been lingering about when Dave died? Her mother replied that Dave had had enough old witch in himself to do the trick, and that Cellie should go and fetch the hammer from downstairs so they could put up the hooks for the hanging plants.

Cellie's mother unfolded the ironing board in the sewing room and sighed and punched her hands deep into her pockets. Cellie was holding down a cotton skirt, poking the arrow-shaped tip of the iron into a pleat, when she burned the inside of her forearm. She did not cry, but came into the living room to tell her mother what had happened. Cellie stood holding her arm just above the swelling red mark, and said out loud, *I've burned myself*. She said it again, but her mother, lost in the clipping and slow laying of bits of twig on a newspaper folded on the windowsill, ignored her. Her mother's hands clipped with the scissors. Her mother's body was in the living room, but she was gone. Her mother had disappeared somewhere. Cellie wanted to go, too.

After she stopped reading Cellie fairy tales, Cellie's mother read to her out of whatever fat book was at hand, randomly and at any moment that struck her: over breakfast; in the middle of a walk; while she dusted. Cellie understood very little of what she heard, because now her mother read to her in the same way she told stories about herself: one page from a green book; a funny sentence; all the dialogue from one chapter. But Cellie remembered names—Catherine, Penelope, Mrs. Dalloway—and repeated them to herself. Cellie's mother never said so, but Cellie assumed that she was being read to about other mothers and the places that they went.

Cellie's mother had a first name but Cellie didn't know what it was. Her father was dead and even Aunt Sally called her mother *Mrs. Becker*, just as her mother called Aunt Sally *Miss Arnprior*, because they were not related.

Aunt Sally lived next door with a woman Cellie called Aunt Marjory. Cellie didn't like Aunt Marjory. She made bread and cookies burnt black at the edges or with too little sugar in them or hard as mica on her teeth, but expected Cellie to eat everything on her plate. Aunt Marjory, for some reason, was always trying to rid her yard of squirrels, and could sometimes be seen in her small front garden, hitting the oak tree with a baseball bat.

• • •

Occasionally, Aunt Sally came to stay with Cellie when her mother was going out, to a Horticultural Society Meeting, for instance, or to buy a skirt-length from Droozer's. Aunt Sally had a great soft lap, and steel-rimmed spectacles which she allowed Cellie to try on. She wrote historical books, and spoke to the little girl, as her mother did, as if Cellie would understand everything she heard. Aunt Sally was very fond of ghosts and foreign ideas about the dead. She also would drink a glass of sherry after dinner, and sometimes two or three more glasses after Cellie's mother went out, which made her talkative, and her voice as sweet and fuzzy as the smell of her breath. Aunt Sally was writing a book about the lake and the settlements around it. The book's first chapter, Aunt Sally said, concerned the wreck of the *Marsupial*, a ferry which for some years had run across the channel from Atherly to an island at the north end of the lake.

One of the things about our lake, Aunt Sally told her, *is that there is a lot of sand in it, and the sand drifts and piles under water into new shapes which sometimes get in the way of boats and can sink them if they run aground and tip; the bottom has to be constantly re-charted. The day the* Marsupial *went down, my sister was crossing with her fiancé and a crowd of others for a holiday picnic. It was gorgeous weather*, Aunt Sally said, *much like today. I can't remember why I wasn't with them, although I was probably wearing trousers and strutting about being disdainful of their fun. You can imagine the lovely dresses and hats*, Aunt Sally said. *A lot of us on the shore were still waving when the ferry tilted to one side and water poured over the railings—the people on deck got wet and began to scream and wave and cry. For a moment—things always look closer over water than they are—I believed that they would all come swimming back, even as the ferry's bow sank under the waves—anything else with the hot sun shining down seemed impossible. It was several minutes before the rowboats and whatever else was at hand could be launched and hauled by oar or sail across the water to rescue whoever was still afloat, my sister among them, bless her, though it was hard to make sense in the scramble, or even to be grateful when they were already dragging for bodies. Eleven women drowned in their long dresses.* Aunt Sally squinted at the shadows thrown by the lamp in Cellie's living room. *Once I went to the beach late at night, and a man and a woman in party clothes dripping with weeds walked right up out of the depths of the lake, soaked in black mud and green bottom slime from hair to shoes.* Aunt Sally sipped her sherry and looked appraisingly at Cellie. *They were followed out of the water by others, who crooked their muddy fingers and tried to call me to join their party, but they could not talk. When they opened their mouths, black water bubbled out.*

On a windy day in May, Cellie and her mother were hanging the old linens out to air on the line in the backyard: quilts and embroidered pillow cases and creamy woollen blankets normally stored in a cedar-lined closet

upstairs and rarely used. Cellie's mother informed her that she had
decided to marry again, and that Cellie was soon going to meet the man
who would be coming to live with them. Her mother said the man was
named Dave, like her father, and she seemed to find the coincidence
curious, though it was hard for Cellie to be sure because her mother's
mouth was full of clothespins. Cellie handed her the next thing in the
wicker basket, a white lace table cloth large enough for their dining-room
table with the three extra leaves in. Her mother shook out its folds,
checking for stains or holes. The cloth hung down to her feet like a long
white skirt, then gathered up in the wind, covering Cellie's mother in lace,
blowing completely over her body so it appeared that only her mother's
form remained, her face masked by the white cloth under which she had
disappeared. Her mother stood still for what seemed a long time, and the
only sounds were of wind and the linens on the line flapping. Panic welled
up in Cellie—the multi-colored rocks she had knocked off the railing and
forgotten lay scattered on the grass below. With a dreadful and clumsy
slowness, she reached over and pulled at the cloth; her fingers trembled as
the white stuff fell away, unveiling her mother's face. A face that was only
smiling.

When Dave moved in (as Cellie thought, *again*) life became big and
noisy and the house had cigarette smoke in it and voices echoed in the
rooms day and night. Pictures of Cellie's father disappeared from their gilt
frames on the piano and on the nightstand in her mother's room, and
chairs and cabinets were painted brighter colors, as if Dave's loudness
coated and changed everything. He seemed oddly familiar—the way he
held a hammer, yelled at the dog he bought for her, rubbed his chin
coming out of the bathroom after shaving. Cellie assumed that the soul of
her father had been transferred into Dave. Her father's soul had been
preserved, waxy and waiting, until it could be brought back to life. The
front door banged abruptly and sent one or another of them into or out of
the house, and Cellie forgot about stories and the pieces that were missing
from them for a while.

Two

Once the government began dredging the sandy harbor-bottoms regu-
larly, boat and tourist traffic in and around the town increased. Deep and
treacherous at its center, the long lake at Atherly is situated where weather
systems cross. Steamy air from the southwest and icy air from the north
mix to create storms that are exaggerated by their containment within high
shores that are mainly cliffs and rock. Bad weather strikes swiftly; low
bushes on the islands move like animals, tall pines tremble and sway in
roaring gales. Slicing wet winds churn the green-black water into waves

that surge ten feet in height, whitecaps topped with foam like lace blown off a clothesline. The empty blue sky fills with purple-brown cumulonimbus and grey rain pours down.

During such a storm, Dave's cabin cruiser capsized and Cellie's mother disappeared into the lake. Her body was lost. The police told Cellie a man in a boat nearby had tried to shout a warning as he made ready to get back to shore when the storm hit. The man heard voices over the water, a man and a woman screaming, and had just got his motor started when waves crashed over their bow and the keel poked up where the cabin had just been. The police found Dave's little boat three days later, aground on the shore of a lagoon north of town. They drove Cellie there to identify the wreck. She stood trembling in the thistles and Queen Anne's lace, while a blue arm held back a hawthorn branch so she could see water licking at the broken hull.

Cellie lives by herself, in a small upstairs room in a boarding house where the dinner dishes are thick, the lilacs painted on them years before faded by hot dishwater. A place is set for her at the table whether she eats in the dining room or not. She has an iron bed, a bookshelf, and a tinny radio.

Perspiring in the August heat behind the counter at Packham's Drugs where she works as a sales clerk, Cellie sighs. Sunlight chops through orange and red and yellow and brown bottles high on shelves near the window and reflects on the skin of her arms.

She watches the flat black and white clock on the wall and unlocks the front door of the drugstore from the inside, the way she does every morning, Monday to Friday. She counts change with an inattentive care born of repetition, and plunks it into the slots in the open till before she clangs the cash drawer shut. With vinegar and water and crumpled paper towels, she wipes down the front window. She rubs the glass hard and scrapes at a wedge of dirt in the corner of the wooden frame.

From here Cellie can see Atherly's entire downtown, the colored awnings and the quiet stores, the nearly empty street where nothing seems to change except the weather and the mood of the lake.

A number of women in Atherly look like Cellie Becker's mother, and it hurts Cellie to see them with their paper bags of oranges and hamburger, their dry limber walk going in the other direction, like ghosts of her mother leaving her alone. Once when she was very small, she straggled far behind her mother on the sidewalk. She yelled *Mommy!* and many women stopped, their cardigans and flowered skirts swinging as they turned; their troubled eyes studied her in concern.

• • •

At about ten o'clock a woman with straight shoulders gets off the northbound local bus. The woman's black hair is arranged in a loose chignon. Awkwardly, as if it weighs a great deal, she slings an overnight bag of good cowhide up onto the slatted wooden bench that serves as the bus stop. Underneath a black cloth raincoat, she is wearing a green dress.

It is a funny thing for anyone to get off the local bus at the downtown crossing. Cellie Becker, behind the cash register rolling dull copper pennies into paper wrappers, watches the woman peer up and down the street, blinking and disoriented. Still wearing her raincoat, the woman sits on the bench and opens a book as if she were in her own living room.

Across the street, a shadow passes on the white brick wall and disappears.

Cellie squints at the glare and pulls a glossy travel magazine out of the rack to her right. Her hot fingers stick to photographs of white horses, of red skiffs drawn up on sand, of old stone roads and minarets and widows in black veils.

It is shadowy and hot inside the drugstore, airless and silent except for the rippling of ribbons on a small fan humming at the back. Water beads on the panels of the cooler and falls soundlessly onto the wooden floor.

Wishing that the woman would come and buy a treat and give her someone to talk to, Cellie wanders back between the shelves of skin cream, aspirin, and rubber gloves to the pop cooler. She plunges her right hand into the ice and holds it there until cold aches in the small bones of her wrist. She runs her wet palm around the back of her neck under her hair.

A little after eleven o'clock, Mrs. Packham bustles in so that Cellie can take her break. After glancing out to make sure the woman is still on the bench, Cellie hurries to the cooler and scoops up a can of cola and a bottle of grapefruit juice. She presents Mrs. Packham with a two dollar bill and taps her fingernails on the counter.

It isn't any hotter outside than it was in the store, despite the round white sun overhead. Air moving off the lake rustles the dry leaves of junipers planted along the boulevard. Black spots appear on the sidewalk where condensation from the cold drips into the dust.

Holding out the bottle of grapefruit juice, Cellie stops in front of the woman, who is about Aunt Sally's age. Her yellow, pointy face, bent over her book, is framed with shiny black hair. A curious verdant color, her dress is finely tailored; her tiny feet, laced tightly into black boots, tap the sidewalk as she reads. Cellie clears her throat.

I saw you sitting here, Cellie says, *and I thought you might want a cold drink*.

Fixed on Cellie, the woman's dark eyes squint before she sets her book aside and reaches up with crooked bony fingers for the bottle. Cellie goes on:

My name is Cellie Becker and I work at Packham's Drugs over there — she points — *which is why I know you've been out in the heat since the bus left. I lost my mother in that lake,* she says, plunking herself beside the woman on the bench and opening her can of pop with a sharp fizz. The woman unscrews the cap on the bottle and sips, her thin lips puckered as if she finds the taste very strange.

Cellie asks the woman her name. She says, abruptly, *Betty Smith,* edging down the bench away from Cellie, her eyes hooded, lines deepening around her mouth. But Cellie is pleased and replies that it is a very nice name and sounds English, and what is she doing in Atherly?

As Betty Smith hesitates, hot wind rises from the west, riffling the bright banners and flags in the square, teasing the leaves on the silver maples white and green. A small girl throws a stick over the grass and a fat grey dog ambles after it.

I fell in love with a monk out west, Betty says finally. *He didn't love me enough to leave the order. It was what I expected,* she continues, scrutinizing Cellie's face as if she needs to believe that Cellie would have foreseen tragedy, too. *But I didn't think I'd be so devastated.*

Where out west?

Nantikokan, British Columbia, the woman says, *the most beautiful valley in the world. Maybe it was the place I loved really, and not him. You're very sweet,* she adds, patting Cellie's wrist.

Have you been to a lot of places? Cellie asks.

Oh, yes, says Betty Smith, *I've been all over Canada and lived for two years in Moscow. I travelled with the circus at that time; sold fried fish beside the Rhone; spied for the Luddites; ended up doing translations for the government. I learned fluent Czech and Portuguese in Paris, and a smattering of Chinese at the embassy. But my stay with the Inuit on the Antarctic Islands is what I treasure most. I had a radio show,* she says, her voice loud and scratchy as a quill on rough paper. *I lived with a harpist, and we spent our summers doing research for the program, down by the ocean measuring walruses and penguins and observing their habits. He died though, of tuberculosis, and so I took the next boat back to Montreal. That was a sad time.* She closes her eyes.

Water and asphalt glisten in front of Cellie and the woman in the still and silent heat. Betty Smith is speaking in another language now, fast and close and mesmerizing, her old hands gesturing, extended a little in front of her. Shimmering clear waves float in the air; the storefronts across the square appear to alternately melt and harden.

Finally Cellie notices Mrs. Packham under the awning in front of the drugstore window, waving. As she gets up to go, Cellie sees tears in Betty's eyes.

Cellie spends the rest of the afternoon at the counter in the drugstore, looking at the lake. She watches Betty gather her bag and hurry up the steps of the southbound bus, the green front of her dress strained by the long handle of the bag pulling on her shoulder. Her coat is buttoned at the neck and draped loosely like a cape, and its black arms flap as she disappears. Through the bus windows Cellie can see the heads of women, women with red and black and white and brown hair, some of whom look like her mother. Cellie spends the entire afternoon realizing and accepting what she has decided to do, how she will go toward wherever it was her mother often seemed to be before the story went wrong and she was drowned, how she will have to study and scrimp and save and that it will all be extremely difficult. She will not announce her plans until she is ready to leave. Could she explain, for instance, to Mrs. Packham, that a woman named Betty Smith sat beside her on a park bench and, in only an hour, made the rest of the world absolutely real?

SUICIDE ●

mariarosa sclauzero

I'VE BEEN CONFINED by society to this apartment, at the eleventh floor of my consciousness. The cement is the veins of this city, the streets their link. People are the cells of this fat body existing in a permanent constipation for lack of freedom. Its surface, dark and solid, does not permit purification of any kind. I am one of the eight million cells living in a world of great expectations. The only space I can afford is my own cell, in which, like the others, I am waiting to die. People come and go with the speed of light. There is no time to sit and talk about each of us. There is no time to cry or laugh. There is no time to caress someone's flesh and wait for the new day to come, so that I can see the color of his skin. I make love to you at night, in the dark, fast and silent. Don't scream if you are seized by pleasure. Behind the walls of this room someone might hear you and call the police about a murder. You can hear only the scream of the television, that's the only safe scream of pleasure that people trust. Any other kind of scream might be a murder. So, please suck your lover's balls discreetly, don't make a sound—you might scare people with your moment of freedom.

The last time someone screamed with pleasure in my apartment, six policemen came to my door.

"Do you have a guest in your apartment?"

"Should I?"

On a day like this you can see the city crying. Its tears are like mud. The thick gray air comes into your lungs like a black ghost, and you know that many people will die suffocated as in a flood. Through my window I see the rain coming from nowhere, there is neither sky nor clouds, nothing but a greasy cape descending from some far-away heaven like a curse.

Dorian Gray came to this apartment only two hours ago. I've been waiting for him all my life, a voice says. I look around. Nobody is around. I am sitting on my white, fat couch. My black cat sits on the floor staring at me. His look is angry, he flicks his tail nervously. I know he's waiting to jump on me at any moment to bite a leg or an arm, whichever he finds first. In the bedroom Dorian Gray is sleeping. He told me that his heart was in pain. "They are after me. They want me dead," he said in a whisper. He looked at the wide open window.

"Who wants you dead?" I asked, surprised. "Can beauty die?"

"Look, I have a pimple on this side of my nose. The pores of my skin are greasy. I'm losing my hair."

"I wish I had your hair. I've always wanted to have gold hair like yours."

"This is the end. They are following me. Don't tell anyone I am here."

"I won't. Try to sleep. You are very tired. You must sleep. You are full of anxiety."

"It is not anxiety."

"Yes, Dorian, it is anxiety."

"It is not anxiety, Blessy."

"Yes, Dorian, it is anxiety. Do you want a fresh carrot juice?"

"Yes, that will be fine. Thank you. I'm sorry. I didn't want to disturb you."

"You are not. I am very happy that you are here. I've been waiting to meet you for a long time."

All my life, a voice says. I look around. Nobody is around.

I still remember the last time someone screamed with pleasure in my apartment. Six policemen came to my door.

"Do you have a guest in your apartment?"

"Should I?"

I'm sitting on my white and fat couch. My black cat jumps on me, then he runs away, hiding behind the table. Dorian Gray is sleeping.

I didn't know he was not sleeping. I thought he was sleeping. He is staring at the mirror in front of him. The window is wide-open. His beauty is fading with age. No man with great beauty can live long.

I never gave him the carrot juice. I had no carrots. I never went back to the bedroom. I left him alone because I thought he was sleeping, but instead he was looking at the wide-open window. He was consumed by anxiety. He had pain in his heart. They were following him. Who were they? Wealthy ghosts full of evil, and servants with demonic manners.

The wall of the living room was transparent. I could see his naked body lying in bed. He had a gold chain around his neck. It was full of memories.

Enchanted by his undefined beauty, I said: If you become a ghost before me, you must come into my nightmares of sex and pleasure. I've been waiting for you all my life, a voice says. I look around. Nobody is around. I still remember the last time someone screamed with pleasure in my apartment. Six policemen came to my door. The window was wide-open. It was not a murder. It was a suicide. I look around. The voice is gone.

His body is still warm, lying dead and naked on the sidewalk. This is one of the many streets that encloses New York like an envelope, one of the many streets that unites this ramification of energy, from which the mechanical speed of the machinery, together with the enduring hope of the unexpected, fulfills one's life.

From the eleventh floor of my consciousness I see the ground, a stage where the public and Dorian Gray are performing a moment of the daily life of this city. This is a monster consuming my identity. Tomorrow this event will be forgotten, only the air will recall Dorian's last breath. Perhaps I will still be here at the wide-open window, trying to find memories of his beauty to play with. I will twist my fingers while I claw the air. In this cold and transparent screen my breath in search of love suffocates in the abyss of its polluted energy. Black smoke, which in my lungs becomes a howl of solitude and illness.

Dorian came and went. I went and I came. It was a murder. It was not a suicide. They always follow someone. What else can they do with their wealth and boredom, these few decadents still around with their aristocratic dignity. I feel a mortal disgust for these respectable people and the hypocrisy which seems to be indispensable to them.

Suicides always leave behind guilt and disorder. This is what these decadents like most about such a sinister act. They love to clothe their dead and throw them into the grave with a moral extravaganza. I saw the dear family of Dorian Gray become a bunch of insomniacs. I saw his beloved imbued with the pleasure inflicted by omnivorous pain. I saw Dorian's servants sharing his wealth with joy and hiding it in the slums from which they came.

This brief encounter with Dorian Gray was a blazing moment in my life. I'm looking at the wide-open window, thinking how he got through it and how he felt, if he did feel something, and how he saw the world while he reached the abyss of nothingness.

One day I want to try, I want to fly into the abyss of nothingness. I want to watch the world upside down.

AUTOBIOGRAPHY ●

carol emshwiller

W HEN GERTRUDE STEIN came to Ann
Arbor, my mother said that all she said was, a rose is a rose is a rose is
a rose.

When Dylan Thomas came to Ann Arbor, my father said that he was a
terrible man.

And that was how I was brought up.

June 1973. My mother is still alive.

I love mountains and forests, but I live near the sea in a very flat place. I
like solitude. I live in crowds.

One day Menlo came to work with Ed to learn about films and he was
very nice and the next day Joan came. She came to work, too, but she
brought her guitar and sang songs all afternoon and nobody got any work
done but that didn't matter except that Ron came the next day and played
on Sue's guitar (he wasn't as good as Joan but he draws better than she
does) and nobody got any work done that day, either. Bob and Emery and
Caroline came and danced naked in the living room for Ed to take pictures
of them. The black paper cyc made smudges on the wall and they're still
there. We ate on the floor because the table was full of piles of things and I
thought to myself that I wasn't going to get anything done this week
except feed people (that turned out to be true) and I also thought about not
getting anything done this summer because of taking a trip out West. I
complained about it nicely when people were here and angrily when all

the people left. Then Nam June called up about midnight and I was glad we hadn't started to make love. Ed got up at six to go off somewhere. I was asleep but I think he kissed me good-bye.

Most of my life is spent not writing.

I was ten. I was thirteen, eighteen, twenty-one. (That last was the year I cut my hair off and suddenly everyone noticed me.) I was twenty-eight, thirty, thirty-five, etc. Even my youngest brother must be thirty-five or so by now.

When I was ten I still wet my bed.

When I was two Charley was born and got the room next to Mother's with the big bay window. Charley got my white bed, too. Charley is my favorite brother. He is growing older and has left his second wife. He is the most romantic of my brothers, but the least happy. We went to see him in Binghamton not long ago, but we didn't go on up to Ithaca at that time.

They told me I had a vagina instead of a penis like Charley. They showed me a picture and told me where it was and I looked, but it wasn't there. I didn't tell them.

Mother put me on her lap and sang, "Baby's boat's a silver moon, sailing in the sky."

I was thirty-eight. I was forty.

Two lies about myself:
A. I have very black hair and a straight, aristocratic nose and I have the kind of long, pointed face I've always wanted.
B. I can dance.

A truth: I spent three years in France as a child. I peed into one of those big vats that they take out to spread urine on the fields. They called Charley *"américain, tête de chien,"* and threw stones at him.

I have dreamed that I was stuck headfirst down a hole and could see the sky up by my feet. I think that comes from being born upside down with the cord around your neck like all artists should be. I have dreamed I couldn't move and I panicked and tried to scream but I still couldn't move. I dreamed that I couldn't find the street I lived on, that I lost my keys, that I forgot the combination to my (high school) locker, I lost my ticket, I couldn't remember where I parked my car, I was lost in a strange city, I telephoned home over and over but no one ever answered, I caught sight of you hurrying by with a portfolio and I thought everything would be all right but I lost you in the crowds in the subway. I was glad when I woke up.

I suppose ours is a happy marriage, and there still are a lot of happy marriages: Mrs. Wallace loves George Wallace, I could see that. Mrs.

Nixon loves Nixon. Mrs. Chisholm loves Chisholm. Mrs. Cassius Clay, ditto. Jean Ritchie loves George Pickow. Margaret Mead loves Mr. Bateson. Mrs. Seeger loves Pete Seeger, and with good reason. Mrs. Lester loves Julius Lester (and I would, too, if I had the chance).

Delight in me, husband, when you have time for it. Swing me up to catch hold of tree branches. Throw me over your shoulder, then let me fall gently into the grass without hurting myself. Twirl me around. Did you say I was to be your partner for life?

Happy birthday last month (April). "It'll do you good to be another year older," he said.

Did I mention forty-three and forty-five yet?

We were talking over our lack of religious conviction with our respective mothers-in-law if you call that talking it over. Once in a while we come to a meeting of minds, or rather, once in a while one sees that the other has human qualities that cannot be ignored. (Nick says it's the innocents that make the best audiences, but then there's not much sex in his dance.)

No, Mother, I won't bite my fingernails, I won't hunch my shoulders, I won't walk like a horse and I'll keep combing my hair and washing my neck, but Charley said girls were no good, anyway, no matter what they did. He kept saying it for four years, from ages nine to thirteen. You didn't contradict him, Dad. You didn't even say, "Well, now, they aren't really as bad as all that."

Back in those days I never talked to anyone on the way home from school because I wanted to dream my own daydreams. If anybody I knew came around I crossed the street and pretended I didn't see them so I could keep on thinking. First I was a cowboy in those thoughts and then I was a famous musician, first violinist of the Philadelphia Orchestra, or a pianist playing Chopin, a cellist, oboe player, bassoonist, sometimes Ezio Pinza singing the lowest notes. But I've changed a lot since then. I never daydream. And being a writer is the most exciting, most romantic thing I know of to be or do now, or being a poet. I still tremble every time I think of it, though actually I seem to belong mainly to the wives-and-children category.

(I'm thinking there must be some way to keep on writing after having lost faith in plot and in any manipulation of characters. Even the slice of life begins to look contrived. I think that instead maybe I will manipulate the rhythms, the style, the organization of paragraphs or the words, or maybe sometimes just deal with little bits of fun or little bits of reality.)

Mother played Chopin, but now she has arthritis.

For a long time I was powerless to resist: my father's opinions, marriage and having three children, the lure of music. I should mention that from the ages of twelve to twenty I practiced the violin four or five hours a day and went to orchestra every afternoon, but it was my brother Bob who got to be in the Philadelphia Orchestra.

Daddy held hands with Mommy. Once I saw him touch her breast.

I was thirteen when my breasts began to grow. Then I knew I really was a girl once and for all.

Her work (mine) represents a slow, almost unconscious break with conventional fiction. She was changing her mind one step at a time. She read Jarry.

One time that she (me) thinks was particularly successful was when she was trying to catch the little, quickly suppressed thought. "You see something," she said, "and you might think, wow, that looks phallic and then you may suppress it before you're aware of your own thought." She tried to catch herself in these thoughts before they were gone. Then, of course, there's the problem of finding a form for this sort of thing. Her story that most exemplifies this study is "The Queen of Sleep."
At the end of that story you'll find this paragraph:

But things go along about as well as could be expected and I will keep on with the diary of lost sleep just so long as nobody goes mad or dies or has a baby and if I don't cut my finger off whipping the cream.

She feels this contains something of her philosophy of writing at that time. In her stories nobody will go mad or die or have a baby, but they may cut their finger off whipping the cream and who's to say that that's not as important in a person's life as going mad? (Think of trying to type with it!)

She says: "What's the hardest thing to write (confess) and what's the most significant?" She says: "Is it more dramatic that my grandfather died trying to rescue his niece from drowning while my mother, eight years old then, stood on the banks of the river and watched, than that I've been in the menopause for two years already now and am wondering when it will end while my mother (that same little eight-year-old girl) went through it easily and happily and never felt better in her life? They're different kinds of reality and menopausal adventures we know very little about." (She says: "First I tried vitamin A, then vitamin E, then I had to resort to estrogen, but I cured myself, finally, with Paba.")

She says her stories have become progressively "cooler" in feeling as time goes on. That is because she has done away with the emotionally building line or flow in favor of a more dronelike form.

She says her stories frequently contain within them hints and clues of the theories by which they were written and why. They are often allegories for themselves. (Not this one, though.)

She says: "A story is not an entrance into a dream world. Avoid this with a style that isn't flowing."

She says: "Can you write a story like your favorite Vivaldi concerto? Can you write a story like a bird sounds? Can you write what you hear when you hold a paper cup up to your ear? No. And don't try. Stories are, if sounds at all, the sounds of words.

"Can you, on the other hand, write a story that looks like your mother, gray hair, fairly good figure, osteoporosis showing in her dowager's hump, varicose veins and all? Can you write a story that looks like a Robert Rauschenberg painting? (I wish I could.) Can you write what looks like half a loaf of your own homemade sesame seed bread on a green plate? No, because you have to write a story that looks like words on a piece of paper."

She says: "It's *all* science fiction."

She says: "Stories! I don't believe in them any more than I believe in pictures on the walls."

She says: "So far I have never, ever, written anything directly about my writing except this."

I went to a party for Jonas's new book about film. I got along well with his secretary, Marguerite something-or-other. Across the room Jonas made a motion to me and said something I couldn't hear. I think he was saying that I looked nice. Later, to reciprocate, I asked him if he had published a book of his poetry (but he hadn't except in Lithuania). He has a brown, wartish thing on the end of his nose.

I went to the opening of the women's film festival and that was nice except I was tired and had hurt my back.

Someone should write a history of women. Where were they when George Washington was at Valley Forge with their men? What was Mrs. Bach doing while Bach composed? But we know what the women were doing, and we know what I do most of the time. I keep busy.

Women, put your urine in a little jar for the doctor every six months. "Take off everything but your slip and your shoes." (I'm glad I remembered to wear a slip.) Underwear goes in bottom drawer where they keep tissues for you to wipe off with afterward, and that's how I spent last Tuesday morning. I keep busy.

Emery said he gets his pupils to take a pose that seems to have possibilities and then they have to make a dance based on that pose. I said,

"Why, that's just how I write a lot of times. I improvise until I find a good beginning. Then I improvise along the suggestions in the beginning. I keep what fits and throw away the rest; nine-tenths of it, as a matter of fact. Then I improvise again along the lines of what I have so far and keep what seems to fit (and I like surprises) and throw away most of it and so on. Not in my biographical stories, though." I really didn't say all this to Emery. I only thought it after what he said.

I always wanted to be the one that picked up the guitar and sang "Candy Man" at a party. I wanted to be the one dancing with abandon. I wanted to be the one in the long purple velvet dress reading her own really good poetry. I wanted to be the one with the wonderful sense of humor (but I'm not even going to go out to buy a long purple velvet dress).

Also I would have liked to be the one that married six times and had a child by each husband. I wish one husband had been a famous folk singer who played the banjo and we'd had music every night and one of his friends had come and played old-time fiddle and shown me how to do it, too. And I'd like one of them to have been the publisher of a good poetry magazine and have published some of my things, and one would have sung bass, one would have written novels, one would have been a guru and taken me to India and maybe one would be the husband I have now.

If you come in the house now, you'll see me as I really am, unkempt. I wipe my hands on these jeans. Somebody's old used Band-Aids are in the bathtub, unread newspapers piling up, also old mail, and I'm just sitting here on the bed talking to children, reading to them about the pygmies or some prose poems one page long, my favorites. They are scattering papers about. Their shoes are in the doorway. Their dirty socks under the couch. I keep saying it's not *my* job to pick them up and besides, I'm already worn out from sitting here thinking.

My daughter wants a goat.

As a mother, I have served longer than I expected.

Once a doctor said I'd be 80 percent normal after my back operation. "Guess what, dear, I'll be 80 percent normal!" It's hard to know what 80 percent normal feels like, but I guess that's what I am.

I was forty-six. I was forty-eight, etc., etc. I'll be fifty-five, sixty-two, sixty-eight if nothing unforeseen happens and maybe still walking around in the woods if I can be near a woods sometimes.

If there's a sunset over Brooklyn, we must take beauty where we find it.

Mother wants me to write something nice she can show her friends.

7

RIGHTEOUS RAGE, SCARS AND SURVIVORS

Under the tutelage of Wild Woman we reclaim the ancient, the intuitive and the passionate. When our lives reflect hers, we act cohesively. We carry through, or learn to if we don't already know how. We take the steps to make our ideas manifest in the world. We regain focus when we lose it, attend to personal rhythms, draw closer to friends and mates who are in accordance with wildish and integral rhythms. We choose relationships that nurture our creative and instinctive lives. We reach out to nurture others. And we are willing to teach receptive mates about wildish rhythms if need be.

But there is another aspect to mastery, and that is dealing with what can only be called women's rage. The release of that rage is required. Once women remember the origins of their rage, they feel they may never stop grinding their teeth. Ironically, we also feel very anxious to disperse our rage, for it feels distressing and noxious. We wish to hurry up and do away with it.

But repressing it will not work. It is like trying to put fire into a burlap bag. Neither is it good to scald ourselves or someone else with it. So there we are holding this powerful emotion that we feel came upon us unbidden. It is a little like toxic waste; there it is, no one wants it, but there are few disposal areas for it. One has to travel far in order to find a burial ground.

. . . But, part of the miracle of the wild psyche is that no matter how badly a woman is "killed," no matter how injured, her psychic life continues, and it rises above ground where in soulful circumstances it will sing its way up and out again. Then wrongful harm done is consciously apprehended and the psyche begins a restoration.

. . . Although there are scars, and there may be plenty of them, it is good to remember that in tensile strength and ability to absorb pressure, scar tissue is far stronger than skin alone.

from the chapters, ''Membership in the Scar Clan,''
and ''Marking Territory, The Boundaries of Rage and Forgiveness,''
both from *Women Who Run With the Wolves*

THE GIFT ●

josephine hart

GREAT TRAGEDY HAS great simplicity and demands a certain purity in its telling.

So I will not try to embellish Beth's story in any way. Beth was my mother's sister and she died last week.

I owe my life to her and that fact is the essence of her tragedy.

The Fates—for she did not believe in God—forced her to become through her virtue, the instrument of my salvation and her own destruction.

I do not wish such virtue on my children. For though I know that virtue is its own reward, I believe the reward is bitter. I have two children, Tom and Sarah. She refused to allow me to name my son Peter—or my daughter Beth. Such symbols of remembrance in one case, and of respect and love in the other, held no significance for her. She had the harshness of the saint. Like many who had faced a great truth it had hardened her, and she lacked gentleness.

Once, when I first began to fully understand what she had done, I tried in an agony of half-articulated emotion to thank her.

"Don't ever speak to me of it again," she said. "Just remember, James, I had no choice. There was no other decision available to me. You'd have done the same."

But now that I am a father I do not know that I would. Or, more truthfully, I do not know that I could.

I cannot tell you the story of her secret heart, nor of her thoughts in the years she remained in the same town and watched me grow to manhood.

Perhaps she wondered at the life I chose—at its unambitious quietness and at its seemingly unbroken rhythm with my wife and children in our house by the beach. I am an architect and daily drive the twenty miles to my small practice in the nearest large town. If I have a certain style—I hesitate to make much of this—it is in my love of space and light. I have a need for ceilings that almost soar, a detestation of doors and perhaps an excessive attachment to tall windows. But I am pragmatic and understand that not all of my clients share my taste.

Beth never questioned me about my life. And though sometimes I would catch her looking at me intently, her eyes told me nothing. Her gaze continued and she would not smile or soften in any way the unspoken tension between us. And yet, if I never discerned affection, neither did I ever sense resentment.

Though once, I'm told, on an early winter morning—the first winter after it happened—she walked barefoot through the snow, dressed only in her nightdress, and stood beneath my parents' bedroom window. She threw stones until my mother wakened and came to the window. And she cried out to my mother, "I hate him, Annie. I hate him. Please send him away from here."

But I was never sent away and the incident was not referred to again.

Beth was not the kind of woman who could easily be comforted. The tragedy broke what remained of a weak marriage and she and her husband quietly separated. He went to Canada I believe and eventually they divorced. She made her own way through the valley of grief, alone and unaided. Her single request was for the absence from her life, even for a time, of a face that must have been an agony to look upon. That was the only cry for help she ever made.

She refused to leave the practice she had taken over from her father. His pride in his doctor daughter, and hers in her own achievement, bound her to the town—to its people, to her memories—with the deep satisfaction the virtuous exercise of power yields.

Her love affairs, and there were many, as she was a handsome woman, were recognized but rarely commented upon. One scandalous passion for a married man, who wished to leave his wife and live with her, was, even in that small town, referred to with discretion.

You could say she frightened people. But you would be wrong. She represented to us all the cruel reality of courage, the awful truth of justice, and the daily, silently-borne cross of goodness. She was profound. And we were not. And we had no wish to be.

Now she is dead. And her death bestows upon me a certain freedom, as death always does—an unpalatable truth. This is her story, but it is also mine now. I tell it to you as she would have told it. You may think of it sometimes, during hard days in the crucible.

A woman takes two children—her only son and his cousin, who is one of a family of four children—for a walk on the beach. There is no one else on the beach. It is late September. The children are very happy. They want to make sandcastles in the dunes. She warns them not to go near the water. They are good little boys and she knows they will obey her.

Leaving them screaming with delight at their endeavors, the woman goes for a walk along the shore. After a while she turns to walk back towards the children. She cannot see them. And she cannot hear them. And the sound of the waves seems to mock the terrible human silence.

She starts to run. She knows what has happened. The dune has collapsed and the boys are buried in a golden tomb. She cannot scream and even if she did no one would hear her. When she reaches the high hill of sand, it gives no clue that it hides two children beneath its shimmering beige cloak. No contours of a human form, no red and blue spade or bucket peep from underneath its heavy secret weight.

She throws herself upon it, tearing at the fringes, scrambling up its defiantly dancing surface, digging into its unresisting but ultimately un-yielding fabric.

And then she feels flesh. She feels a child's foot. She pulls and pulls and she sees a leg. Throwing all her strength at its small limpness she wrests a boy from the tightly packed embrace of the sand. The boy is me. And she sees that I am dying.

She does not want to know this.

She throws herself back upon the hill of sand, searching near the place she found me, for her own son, Peter. Her hands encounter nothing human, just sand and more sand, running through her hands and away from her, as though it were laughing at her.

She turns to me again. And she knows, looking at me, that there is almost no time left. She is cursed by this knowledge. One that she fought hard to gain all through the years she studied medicine. It is her fate to have a knowledge that will allow her no escape into hope, or into innocence, or even its despised cousin, ignorance.

So, she kneels beside me and she commences her work.

When I am breathing, she turns to the golden hill, still holding its precious secret and searches again for her treasure. Still she cannot find him.

Strangers have come upon the beach. A wrong turning earlier had led them to the cliffs. Now, at last, they are at the beach. She thinks of how they could have made all the difference. But they have come too late.

The man carries me home and my grandfather completes the rescue his daughter had begun. Finally, Peter is found. But all the knowledge, of all the doctors in the world, cannot bring a boy back from the dead.

Sometimes at night, before I fall asleep, I see my savior in my mind's eye. I see her bending over me—saving me again. Mine, the only life available to save that day. And as I gaze up at her she seems to me to be a goddess. And she is holding in her outstretched arms a great gift. And, as she hands it to me, I see that she is weeping.

LUCRECE ●

janice williamson

Do not stand at my grave and weep,
I am not there. I do not sleep. . . .
Do not stand at my grave and cry,
I am not there. I did not die.

T HE SUICIDAL OMEN began in classical Rome where Lucrece was proclaimed the most virtuous wife in a city-wide competition. Instead of revelling like the other wives in their husband's absence, Lucrece had been discovered at home spinning. Although an unofficial winner of the contest, her husband Collatinus puffed up with pride on the battlefield where his tent was pitched. A few days after the competition, Lucrece was visited by the son of the ruling tyrant, Sextus Tarquinius, who had vowed to "test" her virtue. At midnight, as part of his examination, Sextus crept into the sleeping Lucrece and raped her while she dreamed. The next morning, all Rome percolated with rumors of this violation. Friends, husband, family gathered to console Lucrece, assuring her, "You submitted to a tyrant's lust only when he threatened he was going to cut your throat, murder a servant, and place him nude beside your body."

(To be true to history, we are obliged to reveal that this original Lucrece was no heroine, for her motives remained compromised in the unex-amined privilege of her proclamation, "Unless I kill myself, never will you trust that I preferred to escape infamy than death. Who will ever believe that he terrified me with the killing of the slave and that I feared more the possible disgrace of a slave joined to me than death, unless, by the strength and courage of dying, I will prove it?") With a quick thrust of the knife, she demonstrated what she had always been taught about the necessity of virtue. To avenge her suicide, her husband's friend Brutus cried out "freedom" over Lucrece's unchaste body. The ruling tyrants vanquished in the din of Brutus's growing fame, drown out the long wailing night of Lucrece.

Episodic Memory

Very singular is the art of this invisible art of memory . . . concentrating
its choice on irregular places and avoiding symmetrical orders.
— *Frances Yates*

1. March 29, 1989, at 2:30 am in a half dream state she heard the

whining of truck tires itching for traction and creak crash of wood. Silence for a moment, the sound of a truck shifting gears and position, more tire whines and wood wail. She awoke knowing the sounds were real: someone had demolished her backyard fence. Awake for hours, she talked herself out of what she imagined was a paranoid fantasy. Cold morning light and her fence has disappeared.

2. Before the cop arrived, Lucrece had asked her journal:

"In a reactionary province, how does the Law read my story?"

3. Yup. Sure is vandalism. Ropes and truck and look

at these boot prints. Male. Public mischief. Lady, d'ya have any enemies?
I have no personal life. How can I have enemies?
Wha kinda work d'ya do?
I'm a teacher.
Whad'ya teach?
Writing.
Whad'ya been teaching?
Lesbian love poems.
Thaddle do it.
That's it?
Yep.
(Silent weeping)
No. Now. Don't start that now, little lady. No use cryin about it. If I was you I'd just whip up another one of them creative lectures, git my fence back up, and flush em out. Call 911 and we'll be here in a flash. Ya gotta act like a bear. Bears look real gentle from far off, but git up close and the bear gives ya a swipe and yur dead. Or a rattlesnake—looks quiet in the hot noonday sun. Me, I'm a hunter; they call me the Mad Trapper. Got some of them conibear traps up on the farm. Illegal ya know. If I wuz you, I'd get one of them traps and put them in my back yard. Yep. Public mischief alright. No suspects.

(In recounting this story, Lucrece is almost reassured. She has the numbers to prove it—file number 89-45300 investigated by badge number 638. The interview takes place in his official car and ends when he rummages in his papers to find his card, a hotline number for anxiety counseling as though, he says, she had been raped.)

4. *"I've been thinking since I returned home about the memo I*

sent to you. The tearing down of the fence is a convincing narrative for listeners like the police, but is it a good story? My fence is not a linguistic construct. When my fence ripped apart, the wood moaned and crashed. This wreckage is no mere vulgar displacement: the frat boys did not mistake my house for the domicile of outraged private property preservers. Neither do I imagine that local developers descended to retaliate for my public civic activism, since my criticism was more theoretical than inciting. Nor is it probable that a Muslim fundamentalist retaliated against my support for Salmon Rushdie. Had there been any local violence, surely other balconies would have been ripped off, a gesture blessed with the verticality of transcendence. No, this is the job of urban cowboys, fundamentalists whose city fences belie cattle rustlers and north country homesteads."

5. *This wasn't a story. The story was not a story. The fence*

was down, shattered. The dean, the chair, the colleagues, the corridor-mates, the neighbors, the students had been notified. Every telling apparently increased her anxiety until finally the entire room heard her break down.

6. *The speaking paralysis revealed only this. Lucrece stayed in bed*   `

and did not move in spite of her assured knowledge. She had heard the ice whine under the tires. She stayed in bed. She did nothing. Had she remembered other mid-night violations?

7. *What stands in for intelligence?*

photographic memory?
workaholism?
instant recall?

Local Memory

The Second Captain or the Circular Line is a man in a circle with legs and arms extended. On the places of this man's body we are to remember the four elements and the eleven heavens: earth, feet; water, knee; air, flank;

fire, arm; Luna, right hand; Mercury, fore-arm; Venus, shoulder; Sol, head; Mars, left shoulder; Jupiter, left fore-arm; Saturn, left hand; sphere of fixed stars, left shoulder; christalline sphere, waist; primum mobile, knees; Paradise, under left foot.

—*"The Art of Local Memory"*
Agostino de Riccio (1595)

1. Flank

A knife is only a knife; a dagger, a dagger. Dissolve memory of past violations at the hand of white doctor, professor, male man of the street. You, Doctor, raped me in the cool afternoon sliced thin in the shade of venetian service. This afternoon, white sheets wrap round my mind; yours masked behind a bearded lip. You lift up my sleep and tell me you love me as though at fifteen this is true. As my body slides toward you, your fingers smooth the sheets. You tell me you love me as though this is medical history. Your hands stroke soft across my belly; my nipples pierce your touch. These very eyes watch yours look deep into my body for an answer to my questions: Were my arms held out for a moment too long? Did my shy gaze seduce? I watch you rape me somewhere above these legs leaden over the edge of the table; my arms sear this white paper smock. Flames kick at your thighs oblivious to anything but silence, your accomplice in this examination for discovery.

2. Arm

You raped me on the coast of Casablanca beside the moon you wanted me to love. You pulled me toward you, pretending your desire as mine; a movie projector would have been less mechanically-minded. At nineteen, you raped me on the beach and told me the burnoose-hooded man who answered my screams was a thief. What possessed me to believe you had my best interests at heart? Swirling through the marketplace, the seaside cafe, the grand marble lobby of your hotel, I was "sister" in your alphabet—the waiter, your uncle. Later the family circle widened to hold your widower's tale. In the disco, we danced; ungraceful men lounged with turquoise women who smiled at my orange juice, fresh and sweet. How could I not be lured to the water's edge of farewell promises, the desert moon at our feet? Your muffled sounds of pleasure will be a prelude to my paralytic retreat.

3. Knee

You come again. This time you left your white gown hooked over the back of your office door. This time your skin is black. You knock on the door, call me "friend," visit late in the evening after the bar to show me your photographs. Across the tropic's empty air, you reach toward me; my arms hold out in dramatic jest. The joke's on me. Your powerful hands slap my face wrung out to the floor. I cry and cry out and you tell me what to do as though I knew how stupid I could be in order to plan not plan this occasion when you rape me. I cry out through your long night, voices in the hall so close I make out drunken love whispers. In the morning, I would get up from the bed. I would get up from the bed, in the morning, in the morning would rise up from the bed. In the morning would get up. Would rise over and over in my mind, wash my face, my hands again and again in a shallow sink, wait for a sun to light up this unknown city to shelter me from you the stench of your other disguise. (From beside me on the bed, his eyes look at me with something like affection as though nothing had happened. He remembers, he must remember, yesterday, on the ship's deck, we laughed at the dark oceans between us.) Do you remember the long passage by sea where we met in the unsteady rhythm around Gibraltar? Or the sound of Lanzerote's black lava cave? Tonight, white sands from Agadir's maze sift from our hair as I fall passive to the floor.

I won't name this occasion rape for fifteen years. Instead, this is fear, or first-world envy, or a domestic race war detached from my being. Behind the balcony of this Dakar hotel, the hot yellow of the prairie field is bleached a less violent shade, the color of your lost French lover's hair. Before you hit me, you show me the photograph of your Catherine Deneuve look-alike. There is a delicate shadow on her neck. Was this the hollow heart of her collarbone or a bruise imprinted by her blue knowledge of you? In the confused paralysis of these moments, I became wise about possible endings. You pull me toward you; my voice careens through your seashell ear. Enraged, you stop or look without seeing or simply watch as you move toward me again and again and again. I would not stop writing this story if there were any other ending than my zero of nothing turned liquid sound. Unbound, my flesh leaks across the room under a wooden door toward an elevator open inside the extended middle of pain shuttered through this body this steaming Dakar hotel room called, I can't remember, down the beach from moonlit dance bars called, I can't remember, down the road from Isle St. Louis where no white man was ever imprisoned for violating your sisters.

4. Head

I can't remember.
You raped me in my home. The child in me remembers something without correspondence. A child's feet kick out the rage of a baby girl's white quilt. In something called "bassinet," she dreams lions and tigers escape through cracks in the wood floor. The white lace of her blanket catches in the futile

directions of a top-hatted animal tamer who dies like all the others. Momma. Daddy.
Still, the dark-haired faceless man (a babysitter? a prospector?) remains outlined at the window. His hands strangely turned and moving. Still, her infant legs flail out against the mystery.

5. Paradise, under left foot

Tonight across the roses in this new garden, I call you rapist one by one. Would my questions stir you now from your Albertan or African sun? I wait while you circle over Paris. I wait for you in Moscow. In Montreal, I see you in the street. In London, I wait for your return home. In Washington, in Peking, I wait for your stories of lapses in decorum or ideological privilege. I wait for you in your father's house. I am at home in the world. In cities, my mouth opens to corridors, cries through stairwells and broken bars, smashes locked doors, the shield of a man asleep in the still quiet returned to our bed. My unquiet breast beats inside the rhythms of your pulsed body. Beats unbeaten in your ear.

Semantic Memory

> *I do not imagine anyone could be excused from finding a solution to this mystery.*
>
> —*Nicole Brossard*

1. Lucrece's first words, "oh god oh god oh god," were written

in a twelve-year-old girl hand which struck a match scorched the edges rolled the message scroll in her fingertips as she stood on top of her window sill, the chair, to reach the small ceiling hole where spiders spun and stole her words.

2. But what did Lucrece know about living that was not loss?

That summer his hands played a big part in the picture. The bicycle wheel photograph circled in front of his body slivered into the complexity of slender whirling shade he would become reading so many love letters; pink kisses all over the page. His note to her began "my love." Later, "my love" reappeared in every conversation hinged to a non-equivalent pronoun, the intimate pivot "tu." So easy to hear to not hear the lawn chairs billow inside out this august storm.

3. "If I weren't in love I wouldn't be here.

I wouldn't be—without expressing my love for you."

Misery makes her more cultured.

4. The man who had a heart noted he had probably been the

one to sacrifice "the relationship." He said he must not have wanted her; he planned it that way, the way she left as a result of his pressure for greater "intimacy." She fell into the trap knowing it was no trap. It mattered not. This was the way it was as though she could choose not choose her next move.

5. In her draft of adult life, the preface examines "regret."

Listen for weeping in the verb "to greet."

All the time Lucrece remembered their bodies together—the "ing" words appropriate for her longing. Lucrece missed him. Why? What was it that made her so eager to write the ending? Her arms reached out to embrace and then, muscles tensed, pushed him away. When he began to press her to give up the work she loved, she felt threatened to something like the core of her being. Her being? Her legs were filigreed veins; she would be dead lace in another few decades.

6. Sick of urban spill, Lucrece heads west along the Yellowhead.

Everywhere in Saskatchewan, signs of life stick up like thumbs or something less appealing. She works to develop character here: the car, the fit of the glove along the smooth hollowed surface of the wheel; the car, the hat tipped wildly back to expose unkempt perm; the car, Joan Didion's darling. (If this is Tuesday, take the highway!)

7. OK Tuesday or Friday. Bison along the roadside. Sky:

brilliant blue lanced with sunlight pours dangerously toward pupils the opposite of dilation pin pointed now in her head faced west. Due.

8. OK in the car facing west between her right ear lobe and

temple, a slit opens up the middle of the night, slide of a man framed in white cardboard just like a dream, the man stands in front of a bassinet or changing table, the whiteness of the plastic quilted to embroidered shadow. He is touching the baby somewhere, her genitals and now that she has read *Don't*, the story of incest with numbered paragraphs, she wonders for a moment whether this memory is no more than a lively re-creation of fictive imaginings, a crossover from that elsewhere.

9. OK in the car facing west the projector of her brain, her

mind's eye refocuses, tears vaseline the lens. Like this she says: OK in the car facing west there is a slide. The prospector, the daddy, or maybe any old uncle man. The dark-haired man.

10. OK in the car facing west Lucrece calls momma

momma. Did this happen? No dear. We would never have left you with the men. They wouldn't know what to do with you. We wouldn't not do our job, abandon you to others. In this last sentence no note of speculation tempers momma's voice.

11. Storymaking, the inside outside story

the inside story a sordid affair: the outside story business as usual: between the two, nothing more than two dots dark eyes stare out of baby head: two tiny memories of somewhere else someone else: the body remembers the tender skin pulled inside the thickened pressure of finger tips knuckle deep now and again the thrust is that the word or is it play daddy play stranger or uncle or big bad wolf: the tender slip of a thing legs buck fat broncos: see see said the blind man: she looked again radiant in waves

12. After Lucrece's dream, her body's pain

shifts ground from her vague anxious doubts to various corridors; her vagina aches without reason and all day long she smells shit as though a dog were in every corner, or under the stairs. She smells it here everywhere on her skin. This mixture of mental debris and lived surfaces.

13. Lucrece pretends the story is one thing then another,

imagines herself inside a new ending. It follows. Years later the structure repeats itself. Story. Story. Her heart beat takes these bare bones and tells this. Between her bent knee negotiating the curb and a red light, her breakdown held her up through 1979. Clinging to vision, she dressed up like Margaret Atwood in Spanish. If it hadn't been for the sand between her toes, she might have been on top of the world. No accidental turn of phrase: her bed, sheets of flames.

Don't start again.

14. In the cedar V of the mountains, a hotel had an upper

story window she had imagined herself floating through. Thirty-seven years later, she returned to recognize the view. But which hotel? Was it the

Hume Hotel, now the Heritage with its encrusted long history of stained glass and buried balustrades or ten-foot fireplaces? Or was her sense of connection an inflated memory of her class history? Or did she remember the Old Nelson, formerly the New Grand where ridges of painted-over deco signs had looked across the harbor before three-story buildings interrupted the view? Or was it the Royal Hotel where the reception desk was now closed and hidden behind a sliding door. Drunks in the saloon mimic somber bearded photographs on the wall, mine wood sidewalk memories to live by.

Later on the telephone, her mother confirms they had all lived in the Royal which Pappa had co-owned. Her daughter laughs at the seduction of the old glory Hume and says, "But the Royal's a dive."

"Yes. It always was," confessed Momma, "but the miners were nice and looked after you."

Dive deep down into this "looked after." No blame. Pounding drunk on the door, a man found the two-year-old daughter wrapped in her grandmother's arms. Years later door-banging laughter in hide and seek is her hidden terror.

"The prospectors liked you and always gave you gold nuggets," said Nanna.

"We wouldn't leave you with the men. They wouldn't have known what to do with you," said Momma.

Lucrece Writes

(Writing is a compensation for life, not a substitute, for Lucrece lives full of rich lively pleasures. Writing stands in for nostalgia, takes the place of recovery. Memory on the move in writing stands aside, takes up alphabet postures as though there were a place for "you.")

Hands: regret runs the length of this column ridged a circumference her hands cannot reach round.

Hands: at three o'clock, memory sifts restless; "a writing in black and white, using shadow and light."

Hands: texture slash of ribbons; remind this pebbled concrete.

Hands: lined like small leaves wrenched from aspen in May.

Hands: summer delphiniums purple in the wind while I imagine the past tense of poison pressed between my ribs.

Hands: "let loose your knotted fever, your cancer around my heart."

Lucrece

In the main gallery, the painting of Lucrece leaps from the wall. Her words are etched in blood: *What woman will be safe if Lucrece has been raped? My appropriate desire of chastity did me an injury. The abominable adulterer wanted to assault not my beauty but my chastity. Can I endure anymore in the corrupted body? Pour forth this blood as an omen.*

Green on this gallery's easel, frame now removed, this canvas restores Lucrece to herself. A female actor in history's tragic drama, Lucrece teaches us to read and write ourselves. Her memory is preserved in the domed tip of her headdress resists the frame's chaste borders. Transparent filigreed ribbons tease out the artist's unpainted margin. This veil of lace gathers into questions: How many centuries passed before someone unmasked the pale edges of her body's story? How did Lucrece's "amnesia of the unconscious" make suicide an inevitable choice for her? What thoughts passed through the artist's mind which hid her traces with gilt? To how many women did the verdant drapery of her sleeve refuse to speak? How much of Lucrece is left to my imagination?

Every day for the past week I've returned to this conversation I imagine with Lucrece. Together we rewrite possible endings—futurity without anxiety, history without regret. Earlier I could only revise my way toward a singular alternate ending which imagined her knife thrown toward the rapist's retreat, narrowly missing his heel or his heart. Perhaps she said "fuck off," but it was hard to hear from this distance. In retrospect, even this modest tantrum refuses Lucrece's martyred act. A tantrum, small sign of resistance, an interrupted sentence—no small victory for some women. But surely there is no more to Lucrece's story than negation in triumphant self-willed death. Our long women's memory teaches us pleasures beyond *carpe diem*; the favorite freshman cry never asks which days are worth seizing.

In the bustle of the Belgian gallery, the painting's surfaces refuse to bind Lucrece. Tissue slides open to receive the dagger's sharp edge, her feint driven home. Along her belly, drops of lifeblood slide vertical, an open palm hides their dark journey. Her suicide exceeds this portrait's understanding. Why do her breasts, perfectly round, emerge from behind the gauze blouse to please . . .? The artist? Only her mouth begins to speak in lines set hard with betrayal. Scarlet-rimmed eyes question the rage. Her lips open to the breath of pain grasped.

Song of Lucrece

The boundaries of Lucrece's history are detailed in the pergola's aslant determination. In this obscure light, I write her lace bodice unbuttoned each morning in verbs, invincible. Across this new ending, the amorous arouses exclamatory. Lucrece's bloody veil unstops bliss, sets sail along her belly, this side of lunar reflection. Flesh mends flesh, minds her body's scarred signature . . .

"I did not die."

INTO THE ROOTS ●

janice galloway

$\mathbf{I}$T WAS RAINING and her hair was getting wet. Not a true rain, but a drizzle, layering a blur on individual strands, thickening into fat drops and sliding down to the scalp. She could feel it there already, spreading with the feel of insect feet. Her hair was flattening with the weight, darkening under a dark sky from russet to the vague amberblack of wood resin.

Alice's hair had always been excessive. Even the earliest of her baby-photos showed it, wee face struggling out from under heavy cloud. It had been white. She had been told as much and could see in the pictures it was true; hair matching the color of the starched frills under the dazzle of the studio lights. What was not part of a coxcomb strayed out fuzzily as though the child had been plugged into an electric socket or struck by lightning, accounting for the expression of boggle-eyed terror. No matter how hard she looked, it was impossible to detect eyebrows. She supposed they had been white too.

Ash, strawberry, ginger red.
It got darker and it got longer. Through primary school, she carried the weight of its spine-length tangle, brushed, teased and woven into itself by her mother's efforts of will to a tightbound pleat. Still, it slipped the ribbon to blossom out behind as she ran, shrieking, in the playground.

Evenings had been spent with head bent in contrition at the fireplace, clamped between mammy's knees as she tore out the knots and condemned them, spitting, to the flames. The longer it got, the more wayward it became. Enough was enough.

She had her first salon cut at the age of eleven: a new uniform and a new persona for the big school. She had been taken by the hand to Carrino's and given up to the dresser—mammy had other things to do. It crossed Alice's mind she was feart to watch. In the mirror, she saw the familiar coat retreat, open into a square of light, then cut from view as the door clicked across like a shutter. Alice was left gazing at her solitary self and was suddenly, thrillingly aware that this was the last of something. Last snapshot of childhood. She closed her eyes and heard the scissors slice.

Alice had known at the time, had said so, she would never forget the feeling the first incision had induced: as though her head were rising like a cork from the bottom of a sink of water. The dresser gave her the still-writhing pleat to hold: a thick-ended shaving brush petering away to elasticated nothing. She clutched it during the rest of the cutting as someone else emerged in the mirror. A long neck, very white from lack of sun, had grown up in the dark like a silent mushroom. The face was very pale and wee inside a curling auburn crop. They stood her up and dusted off the trimmings then handed her back. Mammy let her keep the pleat and she took it home to put into a shoebox; keeping it to take out every so often and remember who she had been. Then mammy started calling it *that thing*, brewing a distaste for the precious, matted snake-in-the-box, though when it disappeared, no one admitted having thrown it out. It didn't really matter: it was discovered only years later and by that time, the hair was long again.

That first cut triggered fresh growth. So much that within two years, its mass had taken Carrino's so long to dress she had been late for the school dance. Slipping embarrassed and hair-sprayed stiff into the squeaky gym-hall with its frenetic Grand Old Duke and illicit kisses. She was never a relaxed child but managed to join in. Enjoyed herself, too: looked well in her home-sewn velvet and starched collar, but she went home alone. People couldn't see her eyes through the fringe and were suspicious. Alice liked it that way.

It brought its penalties, too. She remembered those interchangeable small boys who had chased and pulled her pigtail, hoping for a scream that she never gave. Bloodied her lip sometimes, caging in the pain with defiant teeth, determined not to let it show. And there had been a spider trapped in it once, a dark, struggling shape in the red mesh that shook her rigid with fear, numb for what to do. A boy again, this time one with the temerity to approach gently, had come to the rescue. He extricated both the spider and herself into their separate selves again without undue damage to either.

She folded her eyelids into a crease. Was it Charles? She supposed it must have been. Fourth year, so it was more than likely. That was the year she had dyed her hair for fun, two separate occasions and two colors, before letting it go its own way without further chemical intervention. The stripes of dye were visible if you looked hard enough, and he must have looked hard to get the spider. Long red step-ladders, falling in fudgy bands of auburn from a straight white center parting to well past her shoulder-blades. They had all looked the same. She kept a sixth-year photo: an avenue of senior girls with equiparted skulls and peaky faces aloof to the camera. She was there, right in the front row, fashionably sullen and mini-skirted; a leggy book-end with the girl closest. That other girl lived somewhere else now: two weans and no man. That would have wiped the smile off. As for the rest, Alice knew little or nothing; didn't keep up with old acquaintances. It was her mother had done that and it was an easy thing to take for granted when the woman was alive. Just a necessary part of visits home, those tedious chants of births, marriages, turns-up-for-the-books. Scandals. Till she became one herself and moved in with the man, *living in sin* in Charles's flat. Strange now she thought of it. She had never called it hers, for all her work and care there. Always *Charles's flat* or *Charles's* where she had swirled fair beard-clippings from the sink, smoothed sheets, sewed neat cushions and learned to cook. She had never noticed at the time and now was too late.

She promised herself a haircut for the week she left—butcher the whole lot short because he had liked it long. But the break had dealt unkindly with her face and the thought of staring it out in a public mirror appalled her. She stayed in instead, putting paper on her own terrifying walls, in a place she would have to learn to call home. She tested smiles in the sheen of a clean bathroom sink, took pleasure from finding single strands of his blond in the weave of her jerseys. Kept finding them too, for a surprising length of time. Though now, sometimes, they weren't real.

Still raining. Misting down now and seeping across her head like melting syrup. Alice was becoming irritable. This was meaningless, merely making it worse. What did she think she was doing out in this weather? Some idea to lift her depression, take a few photographs: the dull metal lump of the camera nuzzled cold into her palm in the folds of her pocket. The others were way on in front. No, it wasn't helping: she was feeling no better and the continual smirr reinforced her suspicion that in walking alone, she was walking with a fool.

The backs of the people on the road ahead grew neither nearer nor further. One minute, she seemed to be gaining and the next they wavered like slipping frames of cine-film and were again inexplicably as far as before. Blurred vision—just another side-effect to make matters cloudier. Bloody pills. She wondered if she should force herself on, fight the cold denim cloy at her legs and catch up, as though she had fallen behind to tie a shoelace, admire the view. But she deflected the impulse easily. Own company was safest when these moods came.

The decision made her feel much better. Immediately, she stopped walking, stopped trying to make up lost ground and stood still in the middle of the road. Relief rubbed into her shoulders, at the base of her neck, warming affection for the disappearing figures ahead. Let them go.

And this was as it was meant to be. Alice stood and watched the familiar backs retreat as in a mirror. She closed her eyes and heard her heel twist in the gravel of the road; opened them. And there was the broken tree; split and blasted to the sky. Blood rushed to her lips as she smiled. It was a greeting. The tree waited. Alice stepped up onto the banking with one hand stretching and moist eyes. The tree glistened in the rain. Rich red and shrouded in grey. Mushrooming fungus spurted from all its orifices but one and that one she made towards. An eyesocket of a hole, with a swollen lip of bark and moss that only made the wound seem more raw. It would hurt, but had to be done. She steeled the muscles of her arm, flexing with the sound of metal swishing in her ears and cupped one hand ready to receive.

Choking back her fear, Alice thrust out and plunged two clawed fingers into the hole. It was full of hair.

I DO WHAT I CAN AND ●
I AM WHAT I AM

fay weldon

T HERE IS A DRAGON tattoo on the back of Romula's left hand, for all the world to see, and engraved in her heart (as *Calais* was, they say, in Queen Mary's) is the phrase "*I do what I can and I am what I am.*" In Romula's mind dragon and words are interconnected. A tattoo's there for life, and that's that, and Romula doesn't mind one bit, so long as the phrase stays too.

I do what I can and I am what I am.

Let me tell you more about Romula. Last year she won the Miss Skyways Competition. She won against 82 other girls, all cabin crew—air hostesses, as we used to say—on International Skyways. She deserved to win: not just because she was pretty, and smart, and efficient, and friendly, and everyone liked her, but because she loved her job: it never ceased to thrill her: to fly the Airways of the World, to be the girl in the ad: to watch the mountains moving by below, the plains unfolding: sometimes she would catch her breath with the pleasure of it all. It was her gift, never to be blasé. Romula, years into her job, would still look out of the aircraft window on a clear day, when there was nothing else to do—which was not often, granted—and marvel at the miracle of flying. She would go forward into the cockpit with the crew's food—different dishes for everyone, in case of food poisoning—and watch their strong male hands move amongst the instruments, and rejoice at the luck which got her to this place, this point of time, this source of power, this wonderment.

"You *what*?" demanded Liz her mother. "You won *what*? *Miss Skyways*? For God's sake keep quiet about it.

Liz Ellis was a hard-working, hard-drinking, high-thinking feminist. She hadn't worn a skirt since she was pregnant with Romula, and that was twenty-four years ago. She'd stopped Romula playing with dolls, slapped her if she dusted, tried to give her a proper education so she could take a meaningful place in society, and look what happened. *Miss Skyways*. Handing out G and Ts to businessmen. What sort of life was that?

Sometimes, when Romula went forward to the cockpit, she'd catch the eye of the pilot, or the first officer. Of course she did. How could she not? Hotels in far-off places can be lonely: the camaraderie of the air is strong: tension and danger demand relief: excitement smoulders in the sky as well as on the earth: like salt on meat, passing sex brings out the full flavor of a rich life. Sometimes the sex trembled on the edge of love; never quite, for Romula.

I do what I can and I am what I am.

Men would take Romula's small hand, hold it, pass a finger over the lines of the blue, curling, disfiguring dragon and say, "How did you come by that? What happened?" But she never told them. She told me, though, when I met her at breakfast in Singapore, so I'm telling you. Should you come across her, when you travel Skyways, should the little lace half-glove on the hand of the girl who brings your coffee, tongs out the hot towels (Club Class only), slip back to reveal the macho stamp of the dragon, please keep it to yourself. I wouldn't want her to think a confidence had been betrayed. Details have of course been altered to protect her identity. And in a way it is everyone's story: everyone, that is, who doesn't do what their mother wants.

I do what I can and I am what I am.

When she was fourteen, Romula had the prettiest hands: soft but not puffy, delicate but not feeble, slender fingers just right for rings—not so short they looked stubby, not so long they seemed to have a life of their own and were scary, as fingers can be; her nails were healthily pink and almond-shaped: the skin of the hand translucently white—but then she was a natural blonde: blue veins made a faint tracery beneath the skin, and the ones on the back of her hand traveled straight to her heart, she knew they did.

"Romy, stop waving your hands about and get on with your homework! The way out of all this is education." Liz's hands were big, square and rough: they were competent: they made you feel safe: only once had Romy's father raised his fist to Liz and Romy—that was when Romy was three—and Liz had pushed him out the door for ever.

"We'll manage on our own," she said. "No man's better than half a man," and presently she was standing on platforms waving her own big, effective hands about, speaking on the rights of women, while little Romula stood somewhere apart, standing on first one foot, then another.

"When I grow up," said Romula at five, "I'm going to be a nurse."

"No, you're not," said Liz and all her many female friends in chorus. "You're going to be a doctor."

Romula thought that was a perfectly horrid idea and took off her dungarees and borrowed one of Sylvie's party dresses (Sylvie lived next door and Liz wished she didn't) and went straight out and played in the garden like that. She wasn't often so naughty, though. She cried afterwards and told Liz she didn't know why she did it, and it was true, she didn't.

I do what I can but I'm not what I am.

When Romula was crossed in love or unhappy in any way she'd develop a little wart where the top of her thumb rubbed against her forefinger. When she was in love again, happy again, it went away. Men looked at Romula's hands a lot, in a speculative way, which at first vaguely alarmed her. Other girls had legs which got looked at, or necks, or breasts, or eyes—it was Romula's hands which mesmerized, promised, enchanted.

That was what women did to men, Romula believed, at sixteen. Mesmerized, promised, enchanted. Then they married you and you lived happily ever after. She told her mother so.

"What are you *talking* about?" shrieked her mother. "Dear God, what am I going to do with you?"

Romula was struggling with physics, chemistry, biology: her mother had to fight the school's obstinacy, stupidity and sexism to achieve it. And she had. Liz always got what she wanted. Romula was to be a doctor. The pressure of the pen raised a blister on Romula's middle finger. The blister went septic. She couldn't work for months, it hurt so; she failed exams.

I try but I can't and I'm not what I am.

When she was sixteen, a fortune-teller read Romula's palm.

"What pretty hands," she said. Well, everyone said that. But then she said—"You'll grow up to break your mother's heart. See there, the gap between the head line and the life line, where they rise. That's good for the child, bad for the parent. Unbiddable!"

Yet Romula was the sweetest, gentlest thing. Not a scrap of her father in her, that roistering, fornicating, loud-mouthed bully. Liz missed Romula's dad, for all she claimed she didn't. Romula knew it. But when men go, women must make do, and Liz had her pride. Everyone makes a virtue of necessity.

When she was seventeen Romula said to Liz, "I'm going to the fair with Sylvie." Sylvie was still living next door. Sylvie giggled a lot. She had little red raw knuckly hands which were never quiet: "Like her mouth," said Liz. Sylvie had left school: now she did nothing in particular. She wore very short skirts and her hair was yellow-blonde, not natural blonde, like Romula's.

"Why do you have to go with Sylvie?" asked Liz. "Come to that, why do you have to go at all?" There was a reason Liz didn't approve of fairs—something to do with either goldfish or equal opportunities, though Romula couldn't be bothered to remember which. Romula was going to the fair, and that was that. Everyone was going to the fair.

"Who else is there to go with?" said Romula, snarling.

"Jo," said Liz. "Since you insist on being heterosexual." Jo was Liz's friend Evelyn's boy. He was training to be a social worker. He was sensitive and caring, and stuttered.

"I like Sylvie and I don't like Jo," said Romula. "And Jo may be what you see as heterosexual but I don't and nor does Sylvie."

Honestly, she was a misfit: a prawn in a pool of gleaming trout. What her mother had to put up with!

I do what I can but I'm not what I am!

And then Romula had a really big row with her mother. Liz had just read Romula's school report. Romula had a sweet disposition (*Liz: They must be joking!*), a caring nature, was popular with friends and teachers, and tried hard at lessons. She had an A in Housecraft (now a unisex subject after Liz's letters to the school), a D in Biology, and E's in Chemistry and Physics. (*Liz: They're doing it on purpose. They must be!*)

"Romula," said Liz, "you are an embarrassment to me and always have been and that's that!"

"I suppose you wish you'd never had me," said Romula.

"I wouldn't go as far as that," said Liz. "But it might have been easier if you'd been a boy, and I never thought I'd live to hear myself say that. I should have groaned when you came out, not cheered. Go to the fair, if that's what you want, and good riddance."

Romula gelled her hair and went to the fair in a short mauve frilly skirt and white lace top borrowed from Sylvie. She had to wear her trainers because that was all she had and she was a size 7 and Sylvie a size 3, but they looked okay. She wore a glass diamond ring on each finger: and, such was the magic of her hands, they didn't look cheap and nasty at all.

It was a warm excited night: honky-tonk tunes and sentimental ballads fought it out between and over the rides, the stalls, the shrieks and screams, the arcade machines. The lights on the ground dimmed the moon into nothingness. The site was crowded, but not so you couldn't move. Romula and Sylvie had paper money in their pockets. Romula felt quite peculiar: elated and ashamed by the last thing she'd said to her mother: for some reason it made her skip about.

"I'd have left you too if I'd been my father."

"He didn't leave, I threw him out."

"I don't believe you," cried Romula in triumph. "You made him feel useless, you made him feel wretched, so he left, and I expect now he's the happiest man in the world. I hope he is!"

That'd teach her! Mother, stony-faced dragon in jeans and a sweatshirt. But she was a good woman too: she worked at the Well Woman Centre, for the love of people (well, women), not money. You had to acknowledge it. Only not just now, just not tonight, the night of the fair.

Sylvie and Romula stopped by the Super Disco Waltzer, and fathers with children on their shoulders brushed by (and Sylvie shrieked because now there was candy floss in her hair). And they wondered if they dared.

I do what I dare and I am what I am.

The floor of the Waltzer rotated, faster and faster round its mirrored central pivot, and from its central mirrored pivot music streamed, and jets of steam which spurted out rainbow fog, and through the fog the murmur of a female voice—"You want to go faster? Scream louder! Scream louder!"— poured like soft liquid over the clutching, shrieking, dizzy riders, and the louder they screamed the faster they spun, for as the floor rotated it rose and fell: and on this moving, surging base the open cars rotated and spun; and disco lights and spotlights swung and danced and raced from the whirling ceiling above: and all of a sudden Romula saw the ride atten- dants, the Princes of the Fair, one for every three cars, the young men who rode the Waltzer for their fairground living, who battled with the surging floor like fishermen in a storm, dancing and leaping to stay in the same place; their task to spin the cars as they passed.

"Fixed orbit satellites," said Romula to Sylvie. (Romula paid attention in Physics whenever the subject left the ground. Above a hundred feet and Romula listened. So our vocations make their presence known in early life.) As for Sylvie, she had no idea what Romula was talking about. How could she?

Romula thought she'd never seen anything so beautiful, so magical as the young men, strong, lithe, muscled, not a brain in their heads, as Liz would have said, and who cared? She thought she would faint. The men lunged and pushed, and round and round them went the cars like crazy things, with the white stunned faces of the riders appearing and disappearing as they spun.

"You're scared," said Sylvie. "Too scared to have a go on the Super Disco Waltzer!"

"I'm not," said Romula, but she was, she was—of her future, her past, of sex, of men, of life, of her mother, of everything. And well she might be. It's terrifying.

I am what I dare but I'm not what I hope.

"Men love women for their future," Romula said to me over breakfast, "women love men for their past." Bad news but true, I thought, though who wants to know it? What enchanted Romula about the Riders was not just what they were but "where they'd been I couldn't go, what they felt I'd never know;" not just the blue tattoos flashing on their strong arms under the disco lights as they spun the cars and leapt like fish over waves to keep their balance—"really they were like dancers"—or the gleam of white teeth and red mouth, or the moving of buttocks beneath tight jeans—all of that yet none of that. Something more.

"I can't explain except to say I loved Ben for his past, and his strangeness, and his newness, not just his muscles or the tattoos on his arm, and the ground which was like waves and his mastery over it."

"I'm not scared one bit," said Romula, and they paid their £2 each (the most expensive ride of the fair, and not surprising) and when the cars finally slowed, and sighed, and stopped, they got in, and Romula's little white hands closed softly around the metal bar. And Ben, top Waltzer Rider, didn't just twist the car but rode the car, bewitched, mesmerized and enchanted by Romula's white hands beside his own strong brown ones. After they'd shrieked their fill he took Romula down by the canal, and Romula would have died if he hadn't.

"Do what you can and be what you are," said Ben to Romula. "Life's simpler than you think. Time you left home, anyway."

"AIDS!" shrieked Liz. "AIDS!" Why did Romula tell her? God knows. Girls shouldn't talk to their mothers as if they were sisters. They're mothers. As you grow up they grow old. They don't like it. More chances for you, fewer chances for them.

But there wasn't anything Liz could do, and she was going away for a seminar anyway, on "Yoga—a replacement for tranquillizers?" and Evelyn and her son Jo were moving in to keep an eye on Romula.

I'll do what I want and be what I am.

So every day that week Romula met Ben and she was quite giddy with love and he was quite giddy with something, but the fair was moving on as fairs will: and besides he was married: but somehow the parting seemed right: the grief that followed healing more things than just Romula losing Ben. Round the cars whizzed on the surging floor, faster and faster, big male hands and little white girl fingers.

And every day that week Romula went into the new tattooist who'd opened up in the High Street—"New needles every customer—free!"— and flourishing the fake passport which was sixth-form common property proved herself over eighteen and had a dragon, like the one on Ben's right buttock, tattooed on the back of her left hand. Amazing how you can keep a left hand out of sight if you try.

But you couldn't hide it from a mother for long and when Liz came home she went mad, and threw Romula out of the house. Only temporarily, of course. Afterwards, in remorse, she took Romula on holiday to Greece, to Lesbos. "I shouldn't have gone away when I did," lamented Liz. "Always looking after other people, neglecting my own child." Friends assured her she was wrong, it wasn't like that at all, and they were right, of course. New advances in cosmetic surgery must surely before long make tattoos removable; the dragon wouldn't be there for life.

But it was, it was: the veins in her hand ran straight to her heart: it was there in her heart for ever.

I do what I can and I am what I am.

The journey to Lesbos was Romula's first air flight. Lesbos was tedious, but Romula, gazing at the dragon on her hand, loving Ben, lost for always, for ever and ever, fell in love with flying, and the men who leapt so high above the waves they could stay in the air for ever. "A conversion experience," was how she described it. The kind of thing, skeptics would say, that sometimes happens when unhappiness is too much to bear. But I don't see it like that. I think she was just born to fly.

Be that as it may, when Romula said she was dropping science and planned to be an air hostess, her mother just said, "Okay. If that's what you really want. Do what you can and be what you are, and good luck to you."

LIGHTNING ROD ●

melanie tem

HER BODY SPASMED. The newspaper
flew in pieces from her hands, and the lamp swayed. She was flung hard
against the wall; amid all the other, surging pain, the impact barely
registered.

Heat sizzled from her fingertips, then shot back through the pathways
of her nervous system. Her eyes teared and her nose stung from the
familiar, bitter odor of her own singeing flesh and hair.

"Mom?"

Kevin was standing by the bed. Instinctively, Emma reached for him.
Then, appalled by her own carelessness and selfish need to heal, she
snatched her hands back. Just in time: she saw electricity spark between
them, but it didn't quite reach Kevin.

"I'm all right," Emma managed to say.

"But what's wrong?"

As the shock subsided, Emma found herself tingling with resentment.
Self-absorbed teenager or not, how could Kevin ask such a question?
Reminding herself that maternal sacrifices often go unnoticed—that, in
fact, in order to work they must go unnoticed—she said only, "I was
missing your father," which, she'd come to understand, was not precisely
true.

"Oh. Still?"

Emma pulled herself up to a shaky sitting position against the hot
pillows and pressed her knuckles against the buzzing in her temples.
Sometimes it seemed to her that, if she could create a complete circuit, the

current travelled more smoothly through her, with less painful arcing. She knew it was dangerous to try to make things easier for herself, but for the moment Kevin seemed safe enough.

"You have another headache, huh?"

Emma nodded. "Not a really bad one, though." It had, in fact, been much worse, and would be again before Kevin was grown.

Kevin hesitated, then reached toward her. "Want me to rub your neck?"

"No!" Emma cried in alarm, then added more gently, "It's already getting better." To keep her son from guessing that the headache still raged, she forced her hands open and to her lap.

Kevin settled himself companionably among the rumpled bedclothes but didn't try to touch her again. From this distance, Emma studied him: downy thighs, cheeks and chest with no hint of hair, Adam's apple as yet apparent only to the touch, iridescent grey eyes so much like Mitchell's before the cancer had flooded them. So far, Emma concluded again, it seemed she was doing her job with this one; at thirteen, Kevin had suffered no real pain in his life.

The thought of Mitchell missing his little boy growing up brought Emma a burning sadness, and she thought about it with deliberate regularity, the only thing left that she could do for her husband. The sorrow of Kevin's fatherlessness was actually heart-stopping. Holly had already been grown and living across town with her grandfather when Mitchell had died, but Emma still had a duty to protect her son from ever understanding how much he'd lost.

"I was thinking about him, too," Kevin said now, dry-eyed, even smiling a little. "But just when I was starting to get really sad, I heard you yelling and I had to come in here and make sure you were okay."

Emma closed her eyes in relief. Disaster averted one more time. This, at least, she could do.

"I don't think about him like you do, though. I never did."

Kevin was regarding her warily. Ears still ringing, vision still blurred, breath still coming short, Emma managed to nod approval.

"Most of the time I'm pretty happy, you know? Even right after he died, a few days or so, I was okay."

Those first few thunderous days, before Emma had been able to get her bearings, she hadn't been able to stop Kevin from crying and vomiting and calling for his father. "That's good, honey," she told him now. "That's what I want for you."

"Or I'm worried about other stuff. Normal stuff, like grades or something."

"But not *too* worried," Emma protested. "You don't worry *too* much, do you?"

"Or girls." He blushed. Emma caught her breath at how beautiful he was, how perfect and innocent and utterly vulnerable without a mother's protection.

"You're too young to worry about girls."

"Is it okay to still be happy even if your father died?"

"That's exactly the way it's supposed to be."

"But my life didn't really change. Don't you think that's weird? It's like he never died. Or never lived."

A slight contraction marred his face; Kevin was sad. Emma's throat prickled, but she was able to say, "You're going on with your life. That's what you're supposed to do."

"But what about you? What about your life?"

"This *is* my life." Emma judged it an acceptable risk now to hug her son. He buried his face childishly against her, rubbing the new wounds on her chest, but she didn't wince.

"I don't miss him! I don't know how, and I want to!" Kevin burst into tears. Confused, Emma held him until the sobbing had stopped, which didn't take long. Almost immediately, he grew restless, sat up, wiped his nose with the back of his hand, and asked, "Are Holly and Grandpa coming over for dinner tonight?"

"Of course.

"Gee, they're here every day. Good thing they live close."

"Holly's only twenty-one. She can't be expected to do everything for him. It's enough that she lives there."

"When I grow up, I'm not gonna take care of anybody."

Emma smiled fondly at her son and said nothing.

"What time are they supposed to get here?"

"About six o'clock." Emma felt the brief surge of panic that always accompanied the realization that she was not ready for her father. "What time is it?"

Kevin shrugged.

"Oh, Kevin, what happened to the brand new watch I just bought you?"

"Lost it, I guess. How come you don't wear a watch?"

"I can't. They stop."

"You used to wear watches. You had that real pretty one with the diamonds that Dad gave you for your anniversary that year." Without warning, the smooth little face registered a slight tremor, and the grey eyes glistened with tears. "Oh, I wish Daddy—"

Emma clenched her teeth. The hair on her arms stood up, and she was hot, then cold. It didn't last long and, when she relaxed from it, all trace of Kevin's own sadness had been overridden by concern for her. "We'd better get dinner started," she told him.

"Spaghetti, right? I'll get the pans out."

He clattered off down the stairs. Emma called after him, "Don't turn the stove on till I get there!" though she knew he wouldn't; he was afraid of the burners, as she intended him to be.

Gingerly, Emma swung her legs over the edge of the bed. For as long as she could remember her body had ached, and the aching had worsened since Mitchell had died, joints stiffening and muscles tearing little by little. She made her way across the room, carefully rolling up her shirt so that, by the time she was standing in front of the full-length mirror on the door, the entire front of her torso was exposed to her own view.

Three new scars twisted among the hardened and raised edges of older ones, bright pink amid darker red and brown and white. One descended along her breastbone for an inch or two; one disappeared into her thinning pubic hair; the largest branched out into the vulnerable pale underside of her left arm. The absorbent flesh around her heart was so thickly patterned that she could neither see nor find by tracing with her fingertips where the new marks began.

Below all the other scars, most of which nested together on her chest like those terrible photos of the backs of slaves after the Civil War, was the birthmark that coiled like a red-brown tail out of her navel. Emma touched it. It didn't hurt. She seemed to remember that it had once, but that couldn't be right; she knew birthmarks didn't hurt. It had always embarrassed her until she'd met Mitchell, who used to kiss it with tender awe.

For just an instant, Emma missed Mitchell. But she pushed it away; there was no room for her own sadness amid the sadness of everyone else.

She hadn't saved Mitchell from the cancer. She thought now that she should have seen it coming, should have known he was in danger before he did, before the doctors had given the danger a name. If she'd been braver or more skilful, she could have taken the disease into her own body.

It gave her some comfort to know that she had been able to absorb much of his pain and his fear of dying. Because of her, he'd been peaceful at the end, while Emma's terror of his leaving her had spread and hardened like scar tissue.

She had stayed in bed with him those last long days and nights. Kevin had brought them his homework and the morning paper. Holly had brought them soup. "Why don't you take a break, Mama? I'll stay with him." But Emma knew better than to leave. If she left him, Mitchell would hurt, and he would be afraid. She could feel the wounding and scarring across her internal organs and in the cavities of her mind and body. Finally the circuit had made itself continuous, a self-perpetuating loop, and she'd felt closer to Mitchell than ever before.

Just before he died, Mitchell had whispered, "Something's wrong. I feel like it's somebody else who's dying." Emma had accepted that as measure of how well she'd done her job.

Emma's father had come to the funeral. He'd never paid much attention to Mitchell, and he didn't seem to be paying much attention now. He was safe this time. He hadn't lost anyone he'd loved.

Emma's father had no name.

She knew he had a given name, of course, and a surname that related him to generations of people besides her, but she never thought of herself as that named man's child. She did her best not to call him anything, to keep him where she could watch him, in direct relationship to her—"my father," and nothing else. On the few occasions that had required some form of address, "Dad" and "Daddy" and "Pa" had frightened her, and always a bad shock and deep scarring had followed. For a long time, Emma hadn't known what the pain was that threatened her father at those times, but she could always feel it gathering.

"We can't let your father be hurt any more." Mama had told her that from as early as she could remember, in lullabies and fairy tales and happy birthday songs. Emma didn't remember what Mama looked like or anything they'd done together, just the two of them, but she remembered the sound of her voice saying that, and the scarring on the older woman's chest and stomach like a blooming thorn tree. Mama had never been shy about letting Emma see her body, and every time it seemed there was a new branch on the scar tree, a new pink flower. "That's what you do when you love somebody like him. You protect him. He can't take any more pain."

Her father's father had died when Emma was six. She'd never met him, and Mama said she never had, either; he lived hundreds of miles away and had been estranged from his son for years. In the car all the way to the funeral, Emma and her mother had cried, and Emma, in the back seat, had watched the occasional twitching of Mama's head, the tensing of her shoulders. Her father hadn't said anything, except that they'd have to stop for gas and wasn't that the juncture of Route 36 where they were supposed to turn? He'd looked at his father's body in the coffin without expression, while Mama had wailed. Without comment and without taking a thing, he'd cleaned out the house he'd grown up in; Mama had by this time been so upset that she couldn't help, and Emma's chest had hurt for days.

"He's been hurt enough."

Emma knew the story, although not from her father. She would have been afraid to hear it from him. Before she'd even existed, before there'd been any need for her, he'd had another family, a wife named Mary-Ellen and two little boys named Joseph and John. They'd all died when their house burned down while he was away at work. Just thinking their names made Emma catch her breath painfully; she tried to remember to think their names every day, and she'd made sure to teach them to Holly.

"Our job is to bring him joy and to keep pain away from him." Mama had still been saying that the day she left; Emma was thirteen, no longer a child.

She'd been awakened in the night by her father's cry, followed almost at once by a flash of lightning that lit her room purple, a fierce thunderclap, the acrid smell of ozone, and a jolt of electricity that pinned her for long moments to her bed. She'd felt the progress of the burn, travelling from the base of her throat to her lower abdomen in split-seconds; she'd cried out, but weakly, and her father hadn't heard. The burn had scarred badly, her first scar, and had formed the trunk and roots for all the other scars to come.

Grief threatened her father constantly that first year, and Emma was terrified that she wasn't good enough, that some of it would get through to him and he'd explode. But she learned. "I'm learning, Mama." Before long, she could sense when he was in danger of being sad even if she was away from him. The school nurse thought she was having seizures; the doctor concurred and gave her medicine, which she pretended to take, afraid that even the pretence of self-protection would make them stop.

Once, not looking, she'd crossed the street too close in front of a speeding car. She'd heard its frantic honking and her father's shouting her name at the same moment, and by the time he'd reached her on the other side of the street Emma had been trembling violently, holding onto a signpost, and panting, "I'm sorry! Oh, I'm so sorry!" But her father had been utterly calm; later, she'd wondered if he'd even realized that she'd been in danger.

The fall of her senior year in high school, her father had been transferred to California. Emma had barely started to think about all she was leaving behind when she'd come upon her father standing desolately in the back yard. "I built this house," he'd told her. She hadn't known that. "I've lived here twenty-three years. Your mother—" Emma had collapsed on the grass. Her father had helped her to her feet. When her head had cleared, they'd finished packing their belongings, and both of them had left the emptied house without a backward glance. Now Emma could not remember how one room had opened into another in that house, or how sunlight had come into the back yard.

Her father reminded her of a sock puppet with no face, a thumb-smoothed lump of modelling clay. Approaching eighty now, he was very nearly featureless. He had no hair left, no residue of moustache or beard. His sparse eyebrows were almost the same color as his flesh. He had no wrinkles. It had been years since Emma had seen him laugh or frown or even yawn and, since the night Mama'd left and she had understood her job, she had never seen him cry.

"We take his pain away. That's why he married me. That's why you were born."

Abruptly Emma stepped closer to the mirror and peered at the birthmark that spun like thin red wire from her navel. She touched it. It didn't hurt, but it once had. This, she suddenly realised, was what connected her to her father. This was her first scar.

Emma lowered her shirt and tried to bring her reflection into focus. Since Mitchell's death she could hardly see herself, but she didn't think any of the scars showed.

The shirt, however, was badly wrinkled, and a faint brownish burn pattern spread like charred twigs across the front. Her father and Kevin wouldn't notice, but Holly would. Emma changed quickly into a clean shirt and ran a comb through her hair without really looking, trying to smooth the static with her palms. Her father would be here soon and, although Holly took care of him now, Emma would have to go downstairs.

Emma kept looking around the dinner table. Again and again she studied each of these people she loved, trying to gauge their shifting mental states. Her taut nerves keened like wires in a hot, mounting wind. She hardly ate; she wasn't hungry, and she dared not divert any attention away from her father, son, daughter, father, son. Again and again she focused on each of them; loving them, she was charged with keeping them safe from pain.

Mitchell should have been sitting at the end of the table. His place had been gutted, as if by fire. Emma should have been able to stop that from happening.

Across the table, Holly was watching, too, and Emma saw how little she ate. Now and then, the glances of mother and daughter crossed like antennae; once, for an instant, they locked, and Emma felt a tiny reverberation of loss, something drained away from her, before she looked away.

"Neat, huh, Grandpa?"

Emma snapped her attention back to her son, afraid she was already too late and he'd already been hurt by her father's blankness. Kevin was leaning sideways in his chair and ducking his head childishly to see up into his grandfather's averted face.

"Mmm," said Emma's father, which was virtually all he seemed to say these days. When he took another forkful of salad, he bent his head even further, and Kevin nearly fell off his chair.

Pain was gathering around her son. Emma readied herself. At a very early age she'd stopped trying to interest her father, seeing how uncomfortable it made him; stopped saying she loved him because it put him in danger. Holly had done the same. But Kevin, oblivious or stubborn,

wouldn't give up. "I love you, Grandpa," he still insisted, and his grandfather, if he said anything, said, "Mmm."

He hadn't yet stopped demanding of her, "Does Grandpa love us?"

"Of course he does."

"Why doesn't he say it? Or act like it?"

"He can't, sweetheart. At first he was too afraid, and now he's forgotten how."

Kevin had just told a joke. Emma had missed most of it, but she smiled
encouragingly at the punchline. Holly chuckled. Kevin was looking expectant and pleased with himself. Emma's father sipped impassively at his
coffee.

"You know any good jokes, Grandpa?" The old man regarded him
flatly and then, minimally, shook his head. His face caught the light like
the surface of an egg.

"Wanna see my turtle?"

Kevin was taking too many chances. Emma intervened. "Kevin. Let
Grandpa finish his meal."

"He's finished! He's just sitting there!"

"Kevin. Stop."

Her son left the table scowling then, close to tears. But before he was
out of the room, the soft spot just below Emma's breastbone tingled, and
she saw Holly flinch. A moment later, Kevin went out the back door
whistling.

"He's okay," Emma found herself saying to Holly, and then for the first
time saw the faint red line emerging from her daughter's open collar.
A scratch, she told herself, or the edge of a sunburn. But she knew what
it was.

Abruptly, Emma stood up and carried her dishes into the kitchen.
Kevin was safely outside; she heard him playing with the dog, whooping
like a much younger child. The others were out of her line of sight, but she
could hear her daughter talking gently to her father, could hear his
silences.

Emma leaned heavily against the counter and sobbed. She pressed her
fingers over her mouth to still the noise, but it burst through like a frantic
Morse code. *I miss Mitchell. I want my mother.* Quite unexpectedly, this was
no one else's grief but her own.

The pain was enormous and exquisite. Emma embraced it, claimed it,
fell with it to her knees.

Then it was gone. As if a switch had been thrown, a current diverted.

"No!" she whispered. "It's mine!"

She raised her head and saw Holly in the doorway, collapsed against
the jamb. Her sturdy young body jerked, and her hair stood out wild
around her head. Emma thought she smelled burning, and her ears rang

as if from a loud close noise. Long red burns were steadily making their way along the undersides of her daughter's outflung arms.

"Holly, don't!"

"Oh, Mama, let me. You always take care of everybody else. Let me take care of you. I know how."

"Give it back to me."

Holly shook her head fiercely, and her hair flew. "I love you. I don't want you to be sad."

"It's *mine!*" Emma cried. "It belongs to *me!*"

She lunged at her daughter and tried to take her in her arms. But Holly was stronger. She forced Emma into her lap and cradled her like a baby. She stroked her, and Emma felt her facial muscles going limp as Holly's fingers twisted and splayed.

"I miss them," she whimpered, but she no longer knew whom she meant. Holly had taken it all.

THE UNSATISFACTORY RAPE ●

bev jafek

Now the people were walking into the lake, sliding; they were lapped and tickled by the dream she dreamt, soaked through. A smile. No. There is unmistakably an elephant glowering in their path. ERRARRHHH! goes the ostentatious nose. Brutish eyes. Mean. Reddish. Puny hairs wave foolishly from its bald, irresistible trunk. Stinks plenty. Don't trust it. Be wary of this elephant. Images unfold and dangle, all luxury, from a dense, polished core; herself the maker. But that elephant was embarrassing. Such discomfort pricked, suffused her like a steady light, and thus time passed before she felt the hand on her arm, the mutter mutter mutter *wake up, lady!* Lady, hah, I'm not lady . . . *I've got a knife!* Good for you. (Never trust an elephant.) A possible: card-game attended by reddish, reeking elephants, all stealing extra cards with whips of their tails. Careful now. Be wary. *A knife, lady!* At once: the lake splashed to glinting particles, the light of morning not more clear but more raw, the clock said 6:30, she turned to the deeply frowning stranger who was naked to the waist down beside her bed (but morning, such shots of raw, wild blood, such dangers tingling to foot) and she slapped that blind, inert penis soundly with her hand, "oddly vulnerable" to mind and a yelp from nowhere. She turned, curled to comfort, and slept again. Now wordless snarling, now vast mutterings. She couldn't get the lake back but there, gleaming droplets, oozeworthy, and the elephant all red and rumpled. Enough . . . *Get up, lady!* She felt her arms and back and buttocks being slapped. *You'll get your slaps, too, dammit!* She turned, puffed with sleep and slaps. Who dares? . . . . That damned red thing again. Intrusive!

Pointy. A slap . . . good idea for the spontaneity and spontaneity's always a good idea. Inevitable flap! and turn to fall, asleep. He cawed, ignored to abuse; grabbed her body, rolled it out of bed. Thump. Bump. Floor. And day; bright and blunt as lava. She yelled, shut up, elephant!

I've got a knife!

So I hear.

I'm on top of this!

She smiled. This man, this headless force, a dinosaur! chose the wrong door to trudge down. She saw the better of him below her armpit, all rage and skinniness, a bald, exacerbated noodle. It struck one: scarlet penis, purplish at the hilt, bulging there like a swollen tropical fruit; awful thing to be saddled with. Pin the tail . . . She said careful you don't cut your thing off, you old baldheaded elephant.

He cut a scratch on the back of her leg. I mean it! And he was desperate, not with longing, but abuse; she knew it. Owch (not spoken).

Well, here we are, she said, dimpling hideously beneath her armpit. He crouched and glared; a vulture hanging over it knows not what. That penis, sleeping fatfruit and overgrown. It led this fool around, made all of him point inward to a soft, engorged center. A thought, should I scream? Absolutely not. Why? Unnecessary. This is trial, after all, an overtly fertile challenge. That doesn't happen very often. Good, good. Do it right. Prove the stuff. This man is delicate, smooth, and simple from abuse. Question: how many sadists can cavort on the head of a penis? Answer: abused pricks engorge themselves endlessly, and we make the best of pricks by deflating them. She said, so what's your way, Prick, standing naked and ugly in my bedroom?

He said, turn over and spread your legs apart, bitch.

Another scratch on the leg. Owch (not spoken). Ho, she thinks, why order me around? That's just as sweet as calling me lady. You're not used to forcing things. You want it slick 'n easy as porn. And she screwed and squelched her face, puckered and displaced all, yet puffed her lips. O, the troll confounds! Thus reddened, thus grotesque, she hooted one long over-ripe indecent howl like nothing ever heard before. His flag went down. Good, good. She said, You're at half-mast, Prick.

To which: he grabbed her round the waist, lifted, twisted the unknown, abrasive quantity to what, he hoped, was up. It was not up but bedeviled level-even. She clutched the leg of the bed in her fist; intransigent and supine, upon her belly. A time for sailing, she thought, from memory, sun and blue: sails, whiteness, water and she slackened out the line of her to wind and floatingthings. To which result, all six feet and 180 lbs. of hotly contested womanflesh adhered, limply and dreamily, to the floor. Could he lift this great, wilted bundle? He could not. He could not again. And again. Good, good. He grunted in painfully controlled, stacatto aspirations, a haunted man. But again around the belly—up, up not so far, down, an unabashed groan. And again: up, up and gagging, swiftly down, and pure exacerbation. Satisfying, perhaps exhilarating; to the wrong party. It went on.

Came to her mind: a huge, unmanageable sack of potatoes carried by a sweating, cursing workman. He falls. Voluptuously, the sack envelops him. It covers his face with shamelessly luxuriant, round bulk. He gasps. Good, good. The effort was now such that his red face rubbed against the back of her neck. Strangely trusting, she decided, as though a man any man working thus, so hard, must always receive sympathy and assistance from a woman any woman, that kind of breast; invisible but roundly assumed. She turned and stuck two fingers up his nostrils, said Don't forget I'm dangerous, Prick. He hacked, he shook his hot hot head, craned neck; those nostrils flared, he looked at her, astonished. Then onward with the ritual of force, for he was steamy red, determined.

No, a sack of dough. It really was a sack of dough, for he was not the kind who saw differences between things: there were holes, there were shapeless masses of bulk, impeding, there were rods, mainly frustrated— that was all of it. Dough: unloaded from a ship. It lies upon the workman's chest, triumphant. You may photograph me, it says, for I have saved 180 lbs. of butter from destruction at the hands of a Mongolian hordesman.

She wondered through sails, if it might be: a kind of place they both wanted, a fluid space, and round with play, malleable and porous; it was the smallest continent and richly, full of cunning—he to thrust and thrust his thorny load, the morning-after of the headless horseman, she to run and bite and bite, a happy fox, to see blood fall upon such strangely even ground.

He sprung up suddenly and tore off the back of her nightgown.

Then he squatted.

Over her back, cautiously, clumsily, all fierce little eyes and glee, hauling his tender equipment into place. One leg easing down, now, on either side of her hips, the baggage there between and a twitch of a smile; he inserted his pendulous glory into the tip of her anus. She tightened her sphincters to the node of a drum; he drummed. A known quantity: her asshole was a nut, simply out of danger. But it was intriguing to her, the squatter's peace of mind. Like watching a staged hallucination. You wondered who was sponsoring, how much it cost. He drummed. She caught a twitchy grin again, or so it seemed. He was, after all, so puckered a thing; it was hard to think of pleasure. Well, well. On he went.

There, she caught it—the rhythm of the man, now peaceful: thrust down, we have here a woman thrust down a woman a woman, after all that ruckus, thrust home; things were corrected, just so. Things were now the man and the woman, thrust forward, the woman in place of the hole and the dough all assembled. Thrust down, fine, fine, excellence preserved. Not like before with the ruckus, things all miasmic and bawling about, a false bottom: not the man and the woman, no thrust, the what? who? what?

Lightly, lightly she loosened her sphincters. And as though he were driving from a great height, the plunge! a frothy laughter of seashores going past, his ecstasy; so deeply he penetrated into her anus. Ha. A trap. She tightened her sphincters again. That hot, delicious coil. He screamed. He grabbed his great redtoy and wrenched it, barely, out, screaming. Screaming! Then silence! These bitches were irresponsible, not to be spoken to. Now he held his toy away from her in his hand, protective, furious, puckered. And outraged. She saw it amidst that red disdain. It asked how she could do this—change the rules, a simple blot, change the players, impossible. Now nothing was what he had thought. This ceaseless odd. He held his redtoy, angry eyes on the floor, until the matter was clarified and resolved.

She got up and walked into the livingroom. Woman to the woman: the big one. The pioneerwoman out pulling, steadfastly, with the oxen; so strong is she of back and arse. She said, Sphincters, eh Prick? In the livingroom, she pressed a small rectangular piece of metal, down, to a click; good enough. She looked at it, frowning—so unnecessary, these things were; Prick would love it. In the bathroom, she closed the door without locking it. Waited. He burst through the door, all furrows, puckers. What're you doing? he yelled.

Dumping, she said. He glared and glared at the awful thing; she couldn't be doing it, not at all. He hunched toward her, the knife stuck out. Now geometry: the red hand, holding knife, then below, the redtoy, on a par, coming closer. He held the point to her stomach and said, I could kill you. You know just how I could kill you.

She said, Cold cunt, Prick. And she screwed her face, thus awry and bent, ideally to convey the dark terror. Lying on top of a corpse and feeling its cold, cold cunt. You didn't come here for that. His face, again, registered astonishment, fear, and above all, the fear of astonishment. In passing: the warm, oozy morsel fell in stages, ker-plop. He stared at her (plop-plop). He turned and stalked out, slammed the door, behind. Good, good.

She stood up and looked into the mirror. That great, malignant moonface. Plumish. Cheeked in mystery: the fat woman knows. The fat woman will get you. She rummaged around the bathroom, picking at things. Picked over: a spoon, 2 magazines, 3 books, a box of cereal, a bottle of ketchup. Must stop eating in the bathtub. A bottle of ketchup! She savagely grinned, yelled, I'm a terrible housekeeper, Prick! She clasped the ketchup like a whiskey bottle; whispered, You'll pay for it.

Out there, a queer silence. What now. Still there, hon'? Oh he was still there. She caught him, at a moment, oddly. He was standing still, expressionless; waiting: a finger, lightly, upon his penis. Silent. It was alright to be quiet, for the moment; how she sensed him. To be resting. Far, far from the ruckus. In the head. Here, in his calm, he seemed to be saying, look at me. Look at my redtruck. Here it is. My finger upon it. Look, look. I'll hold it out to you. We'll both of us look at it. Look, long. It is mysterious. Now she heard him, turned to childsound, a primer.

Look.

Look now, at my redtruck.

Look, Jane. Look, Sally.

Look oh look,

at my redtruck.

She snorted, guffawed, banged the door again; held her mouth with one hand, the ketchup in the other. Resulted, a snorkling-hissing sound. HARGHISS. She looked into the mirror; that evilplum. Opened the ketchup bottle. A spray of red ooze! over the shoulders. Cold and gooey. The fat red lines now eased themselves from the bottle; unfolded all over that rotundly vengeful form, that neck, back, arm, and breast, smudged gently to crimson waves, across the cunt. Good, good. Laughing, ISSSSSS.

She opened the door again, poised body on tiptoe. Extended arms; waved.

Now. Ready: it would have to be perfect. It would have to be the thing he would always remember; else, nothing. On tiptoe she ran, arms roiling about, rough sound from her wet, parted lips; a wilderness in motion. He made a vague gesture to this redhurling body, something like, Don't bother, I don't want to buy, a simple thing he thought would do: to keep it away. That last thing he heard was, "I love you, Prick!" before those red arms encircled his neck, that flush pulled him closer, red breast rubbed against him; before he vomited.

From between his lips: the soft, inarticulated center of the man; the evidence. He looked up at her; squinting, narrow-eyed, a snake of the hour. A rape must succeed. When all points to that angry, exposed center, nothing can turn away. It is rape or pure folly.

Now he would try to kill her.

She walked into her bedroom and picked up the gun, cocked minutes before; walked back. The knife in the air, poised savagely, dropped instantly.

They stared at one another; this ugliest moment of the man and the woman, no truth to their titles. He vomited, again, to her pleasure, for it caused great pleasure. She said, Hello again, Prick, I'm going to kill you.

He blanched nearly down to his penis, the last hold out. She watched him serenely for it was simple, was it not? holding the gun. It was long ago that the enormity had passed over them, leaving only these brief, illuminating bits of strife and flirtation with dominance, with death, and the room was not, had never been, hers; it was the taut skin of the world he entered for plunder; she said, dreamily, I've been waiting for you all my life, Prick.

The gun fires! A monument in foam. A spray of blood, reaching, rushing, becoming the last gush of scarlet, from his chest. Like a samurai. A movie.

No.

It didn't happen. She hadn't fired the gun at all. An awkward pause, in deference to what, awkwardly, had not happened. He continued to blanch to his penis, she continued to point the gun at him; neither, in their respective capacities, firing.

A draw.

His breath suddenly expired. He sagged and puckered to normalcy. She said, You come back here again next year, Prick, and we'll do this right. A tentative truth: she was unable to fire the gun. Pendant, the brief, dry fibers of her failure, gently, twinged.

A draw, dammit. But he didn't know that, yet. A novel strategy: he watched her, cautiously, and reached cautiously for his pants, shook them at her as if to show—nothing hidden, lady!—began to put them on, said O.K. lady, I'll go now, continued to watch her fitfully, and then all that awkwardness zipped up and rushed for the door.

She barked, Come back here, you little fart! He rushed back, awkwardly, faced her, his hands in the air like a cowboy, properly obedient, obediently proper. She barked, again, take 'em off! His eyes grew round with terror; he took off his pants to reveal that astonishingly below, a dreadful sag . . . He eyed the floor, saw the gleaming tip of the knife, eyed his tender sag, thought, Awful business to have this awful woman make connections . . . She smiled, he saw her smile, she'd made connections. He squirmed, whispered, No! You can't! and with the tip of his shoe, he kicked the knife under the bed, safe, ah.

She smiled again. No, not that. Why the hell not? Because she could rape him that's why. R-r-r-rape! A teeter-totter going up going down, she on one side up, up, he on the other down, down, oh the spontaneity.

No.

He'd been flaccid since she pulled out the gun. She felt, again, those gently active fibers of discontent, for it was outrageous it was unsatisfactory it was to be deeply peeved, all for this unkillable, unrapeable idiot standing naked in her bedroom.

A draw, worsening. Perhaps: a way to live with one another? Cold war? Status quo?

The last strategy: he offered it thinking, still, of the knife beneath the bed. You know, lady, he said, you can call the police.

She hissed, the police! My dumping ass I'll call the police! He blanched again, said nothing, and thought of the knife. But the egg was laid. A solution: tall, firm, and aberrant like a tree from which the darkening fruit hung; lightly she plucked.

She grabbed his pants from the floor and shook out the contents of his pockets. She stared at this fallen, minor bundle: a sheaf of money, over $300, two pairs of earrings, a watch, a bracelet, a necklace. A thief's bounty, fit for a lady. She threw his pants out the window and left his bounty on the floor.

A draw? Not likely, she thought. The final score: he would leave, naked, with his pendant glory pointing the way; she would keep his pocket. The goods, divided. She yelled, Now get out of here, you silly ass! Obediently he left; led, indeed, by that finger of his fate.

8

INITIATION, ENDURANCE, THE WORLD OF FEMALE KNOWING

Shadowing means to have such a light touch, such a light tread, that one can move freely through the forest, observing without being observed. A wolf . . . like the wild nature . . . shadows anyone or anything that passes through her territory. It is her way of gathering information. It is the equivalent of manifesting and then becoming like smoke, and then manifesting again.

Wolves can move ever so softly. The sound they make is in the manner of los angelos timidos, the shyest angels. First they fall back and shadow the creature they're curious about. Then, all of a sudden, they appear ahead of the creature, peeking half-face and one golden eye from behind a tree. Abruptly, the wolf turns and vanishes in a blur of white ruff and plumed tail, only to backtrack and pop up behind the stranger again. That is shadowing.

The Wild Woman has been shadowing human women for years. Now we see a glimpse of her. Now she is invisible again. Yet she makes so many appearances in our lives, and in so many different forms, we feel surrounded by her images and urges. She comes to us in dreams and in stories, for she wants to see who we are, and if we are ready to join her yet. If we but look at the shadows we cast, we see that they are not two-legged human shadows, but the lovely shape . . . the unusual and blessed shape of something, of a someone, free and wild.

from the chapter "Shadowing, *Canto Hondo*, The Deep Song"
from *Women Who Run With the Wolves*

HOW I CAME WEST, ●
AND WHY I STAYED

alison baker

IT WAS A LONG, strange trip, over frozen plains and rivers and into the mountains; but when the going got really tough, I'd close my eyes, and there they were: Lisa, in camouflage pants, stalking bears; Debbi, in blaze orange, wheezing out female elk calls till huge bull elk stampeded down the hills, ready to perform.

Now I stood outside the Silver Dollar Saloon, the wind whipping around my collar, my hands like two lumps of ice even in my Thinsulate-lined mittens. The sky was cluttered with stars, but I couldn't stand there staring at them all night. I took a deep breath and pushed my way through the swinging doors.

My glasses steamed up, but I could tell everyone was looking at me by the dead silence that dropped over the room. I took off my glasses and wiped them clean on my neckerchief. Then I put them back on. I'd been right; every head in the bar was turned toward me, and the faces were sort of orange, and puffy looking, in the light from the video games.

I cleared my throat. "I'm looking for cheerleaders," I said.

They looked at each other and then back at me. "What's that?" said an old geezer at the bar.

"I said, I'm looking for cheerleaders," I said.

"That's what I thought you said," the old guy said. He guffawed; and suddenly the whole room erupted in laughter, people pounding each other on the back, slapping their thighs, rolling in the sawdust on the floor. I smiled, glad the ice was broken.

I walked over to the bar and sat down beside the old guy. He was called Ol'Pete. "You cain't never find 'em, not in this weather," he said. The snow had stopped, but the night air was bitter cold. The roads up the pass were closed, with drifts over twenty feet high.

"Haw!" Ol'Pete suddenly guffawed again, and the rest of the heads— hoary, bewhiskered, grizzled—turned back in my direction. "On'y a fool!" he said, and the others grinned and nodded, and chanted, "Fool, fool."

"Buy 'em a round," whispered the bartender as she wiped off the bar in front of me.

"A round on me," I said, and an excited hum swept the room. After the third round the hum broke out into singing, and in the middle of ". . . deer and the antelope play . . ." someone sat down beside me.

"Why you want to go up there, anyway?" she said. I turned and looked her in the eye. She was dark, of indeterminate age, and she wore a buffalo-helmet, complete with gleaming horns. "They wanted you up there, wouldn't they a took you with 'em?"

I nodded. "I can't explain it," I said. "It's just something I have to do."

She nodded, too. "I can understand that," she said. "It's big—bigger than you, maybe. What's your name, stranger?"

"Most folks call me Whitey," I said.

"It won't be easy, Whitey," my companion said. "I can coach you some, but it'll be hard work."

She said her name was Buffalo Gal, and that I could bunk with her. On one wall of her cabin she had a USGS map, all squiggles, with red-headed pins marking the cheerleader near-sightings. I stared at it but could discern no pattern in the scattered red dots.

"They come and go," Buffalo Gal said. "They might as well be Bigfoots."

"Bigfeet," I said.

"Whatever," said Buffalo Gal.

She worked me hard. She never let up, never let me slack off. "Hit 'em again," she'd say, time after time. "Harder, harder." But she was generous in her praise, too. "Go, go, go!" she'd shout as I telemarked through the quakies. I worked harder for Buffalo Gal than I'd ever worked before; there was something about her that made you want to.

And then one evening, as we skiied through a narrow canyon, Buffalo Gal stopped so fast that I crashed into her. "Listen," she said.

"Give me an *A*," the voice came, faint as starlight, distant as the sigh of a bear in her snowbound cave. It was followed by a wailed response from a dozen throats, "*A*." It echoed down the hills and canyons, and up under the trees around us.

"It's them," Buffalo Gal said.

• • •

Saturdays we made the long trek down to the Silver Dollar, just to make contact with human beings, and to have a drink.

"Sure, I heard 'em," Ol'Pete said when I asked him. "Hear 'em all the time."

"Have you seen them?" I said.

"Hell," Ol'Pete said.

When he didn't say any more, I had to ask. "How can I find them, Pete?"

"Haw!" he guffawed, and nods and slow grins spread across the other faces in the room. "Where you from, Whitey?"

"Veedersburg, Indiana," I said.

"Well, then, I'll tell you," Ol'Pete said. "Them cheerleaders is like a poem. You don't go lookin' for a poem; it sort of comes to you, iff'n yer in the right place, doin' the right thing." His rheumy eyes got rheumier, dripping a little, as he watched Lu, the bartender, wiping up some spilled milk. "You cain't predict. You can be out there for days, huntin', trackin' 'em across the range, countin' the buttercups, and you won't see hide nor hair. And then one day you just washed yer hair, or yer mebbe smokin' some weed you saved up from yer last trip south, and there she'll be, standin' afore you, smilin' down at you, her hand stretched out, whisperin', 'Score, Pete, score.' "

"Wow!" I said. "That happened to you?"

"Nope," he said.

Buffalo Gal and I skiied home, heading back out of town and up the canyon through the moonlight. I looked around for shooting stars, and my nose twitched at the smells that skidded across the moonscape toward us: a last whiff of tobacco from the Silver Dollar; the sweet, flowery smell of someone's anti-static sheet from a dryer vent; the mucus-freezing smell of cold air rushing off the mountains. It was just the sort of time I might have seen them, if I'd only known.

In the mountains, in Montana, in winter, time loses its substance; it becomes meaningless. Night ran into day like the Ovaltine that Buffy stirred into our milk in the morning. I knew time was passing by the way the moon grew and shrank; I knew a week had gone by when we headed for the Silver Dollar on Saturday night. But that's all I could tell you.

"That's how it is here," was all Buffalo Gal would say.

One day, up in Avery Pass, we came upon a single, dainty footprint, clear as day, left by a size-seven ripple-bottom gym shoe. I flung myself into the snow beside it. "How could she leave just one?" I cried, and when I put my face next to it, I sniffed just the faintest of odors—rubber? anti-fungal medication?

"You tell me," Buffalo Gal said. With her ice axe she chopped the footprint out of the frozen snow and laid it gently in her helmet. I pulled it along the ground behind me, the horns serving as runners across the snow. We flew down the mountain, down to the lower pass and back to the cabin, and the speed of our passage created a wind that freeze-dried the footprint, sucked the moisture right out of it. It was frozen so solid it would never melt.

We hung the footprint above the front door, hoping it would bring us luck.

I was beginning to understand how important the presence of the cheerleaders was to the local people. They were part of the mountain mythology, feral fauna as significant as the mountain lion, the grizzly, the Rocky Mountain bighorn sheep. And they were not a recent phenomenon; nor were they exotic visitors. The history of cheerleaders in Montana went back for many, many years: as far back as local memory reached.

Ol'Pete had given me a hint of what they meant. What the manatee is to the naturalist in the mangrove swamp, what the race car is to the Hoosier, what the tornado is to the Kansan—that is what the cheerleader is to the Montanan. Cheerleaders are Possibility, they are Chance, they are Fate; they are beauty, and grace, and poetry.

Many had learned the hard way that Ol'Pete was right: you couldn't find a cheerleader. You had to wait, and be ready. Many an expedition, hunters in their red flannel, stocking up their mules or their llamas or their ATVs with two or three weeks' worth of food, had set out determined—come what may!—to find the cheerleaders. They carried guns, too. "Hell," they'd say, if you asked why. Would they shoot a cheerleader? Would they hang a freckled, pink-cheeked face above the fireplace, among the furry heads of grizzlies and mule deer and moose, and the iridescent bodies of stuffed dead pheasants?

The truth was—the truth was that nobody really knew how he or she might react, if he or she actually found them.

And in all the years the cheerleaders had been in those parts, no one *had* found one. There'd been tracks, and signs: bits of pompom here and there, and of course my frozen footprint, and once an old, well-used megaphone, standing on the wide end under a spruce tree.

But many a hunter had returned cold, frostbitten, disappointed. And many a hunter had hung up her gun, and taken up, say, jogging, or tai chi—something that would get her outside, in the woods, on a hilltop—and in solitude, maybe whispering, she'd chant, "S-U-C-C-E-S-S." Just in case, someday, the cheerleaders came to *her*.

"Okay, B.G.," I said one evening, as we stretched like lazy cats before the glowing wood stove, each with her own bowl of popcorn—Buffy liked garlic powder on hers, but I stuck with melted butter. "What gives?"

"Ah," said Buffalo Gal. She smiled, and gazed dreamily at the stove. "Impetuous Youth."

"Youth?" I said. "Buffy, I'm forty-two years old. I'm not exactly Youth.

She shook her head and gave me a look I couldn't interpret. "Whitey, cool your jets. Do you know how long I've been up here?"

"No," I said.

Buffalo Gal leaned over her popcorn bowl and put her face close to mine. "Neither do I," she said.

"But Buffy," I said, "how do I find the cheerleaders?"

"How the hell do I know?" Buffy said. "I've been up here lo, these many moons, and I haven't found them yet."

When Buffalo Gal said that to me—when I realized that, by golly, she never had said she could help me find them—I had to ask. "Why are you up here, Buffalo Gal?" I said.

She smiled. "Whitey," she said, "I used to be a jock. I did every sport you can imagine—field hockey, tennis, jai alai. Seems like every time I turned around, there they were, supporting me all the way. 'Go, Buffy! Yea, rah, Buffy!'" She shook her head. "Guess I just didn't want to go on through life without 'em. Even if it's not me they're cheering for any more. I just want to hear them, once in a while in the night. Just want to know they're there."

I nodded, and stood up. "I'm off," I said.

"See you around," she said.

That's the way it is in Montana. When the time comes to go, you go, and there are no hard feelings.

I don't know how far I skiied that night, or how long. I was thinking as I went, and that's a dangerous thing to do. Thinking distracts you. You can get lost, thinking of something other than where you're going. You can ski right up the mountain and over the top, and you get going so fast that it's already too late when you realize there's nothing under your feet and you have taken off into pure, crystal-clear Montana air. Every now and then in Montana you see it—a skier, flying across the moon like a deformed Canada goose.

I don't know how far I skiied, but when the trail ended, I was right where I knew I'd be: at the door of the Silver Dollar Saloon. I went inside, and when I'd wiped off my glasses, there was Buffy, nodding at me, and Ol'Pete lifted a finger from his glass in greeting.

I had sat down at a little table and ordered a glass of milk when someone spoke. "What are you up to up there, anyway?" she said, across the crowded room.

I knew who it was: Renée, a lean, grim-faced ranch hand, not much older than I was. She'd ridden the rodeo circuit for a while and then come back to Montana to work Ephraim P. Williston's sheep ranch. Somewhere along the line she'd lost her left hand—caught in a lasso and squeezed right off when she was roping a steer—and most Saturday evenings she sat in the Silver Dollar with a chamois rag, rubbing and polishing her elk-antler hook till it gleamed. She was a tough customer, Renée; even the feral dogs stayed away from her flocks.

The room was so still you could hear the chamois rubbing against her hook. She stared at me, her eyes in the shadow of the red crusher she never took off. Her hand, polishing, never stopped moving.

I swallowed the last of my milk. I put down the little glass, and then I looked up and across the room straight at where I figured her eyes were.

"Nothing," I said.

She took off her hat then, and I found myself looking into the hardest eyes I'd ever seen. They were as cold as ice, and dry ice at that; it was hard to believe they'd ever cried, or looked at anything but bleak and wind-swept sagebrush desert.

I'd said the wrong thing.

"Sister," she said, "you just said the wrong thing. You come up here, from God knows where—"

"She's from Veedersburg, Indiana," Ol'Pete interrupted. "She never made no secret of that."

I threw him a grateful look, but Renée shook her head.

"From God knows where," she repeated. "You sit in here and drink with us; you follow Buffalo Gal around the woods like a goddamn puppy dog, sucking up everything she knows; you pry, and eavesdrop, and then you go out and harass our cheerleaders; and when I ask you, in a friendly, innocent manner, what you're doing, you say *Nothing?*"

The silence was so thick you could have cut it with a bowie knife. I didn't know what to say. She was right about part of it: I did come in and drink with them, I did ask questions, I did follow Buffy around. But that part about harassing the cheerleaders was way off the mark.

How could I explain that I was doing this for *all* of us?

"All my life," I began, and I prayed my voice wouldn't shake, "there was nothing I wanted more than to be a cheerleader. All through my childhood my parents held up cheerleaders as role models for me. 'My dream,' my dad used to say, 'is that someday you'll be just like them.' We went to every game. And when I watched the professional games on TV—oh, I burned with the desire to be out there with them, leaping and bending and rolling on national television, and flinging my arms out to embrace the whole world!"

I paused for breath. I looked around the room, and I knew I'd struck a chord. No one was saying a word: all eyes were either on me or were dreamy, looking back to their own youthful aspirations, remembering the cheerleaders from all those little towns they'd left—Moab, Ipswich, Findlay, Kennebunk—and I suspected they'd come for much the same reason I had.

I took a deep breath. "I guess it's an old, old story," I went on. "For years I practiced, twirling my baton, getting in shape with tap lessons. I did so many splits that my legs would hardly stay closed. I memorized the chants, the yells, you name it."

They were nodding; they'd been there, too.

"I never made the squad," I said quietly. "Not even the B squad. I just wasn't good enough."

A sigh rippled across the room; some of those dusty eyes were a little damp.

"You know," I said, "there was nothing in the world I wanted more than to be a cheerleader. I would have sold my soul." I laughed softly, sadly. "I guess it's still for sale."

"Hell," Ol'Pete whispered, "so's mine!"

"Whitey," Renée said, standing up and crossing the room to where I stood, "I misjudged you. I'm sorry." She did a forward lunge and stuck out her hand.

I took it. "Renée, Renée, Renée," I said. "You were right about so many things."

She punched me on the arm with her hook. "Howsabout a turn at the cards?" she said.

"Yeah! Yeah!" The crowd roared its approval, and Ol'Pete actually did a herkie. I grinned with pleasure; this was another Montana tradition. In many a saloon heated discussions came to an end when the cards were pulled out and would-be pugilists resolved their differences with a hand or two of this traditional game of the Old West. It had saved the glassware and bar mirrors of a good many drinking and gaming establishments.

Eight of us sat down around a table, and Ol'Pete dealt the cards. Carol Ann, another shepherd from out at Williston's, held Renée's cards for her—she had trouble managing them with her hook.

It wasn't a long game—these games never are—and one after another the players matched their last card and dropped out. Finally, as fate would have it, Renée and I were face to face. And, friendly as we now were, I was sweating.

I held two cards. Carol Ann was holding one card for Renée, and it was her draw. If she drew the matching card, she'd be out. But if she drew the other, I still had a chance.

Renée kept her eyes on my face and reached. Her hand hesitated above my cards; the tension—friendly tension—in the room was palpable. And then, as Renée's hand descended, she stopped. She lifted her head. "Listen," she said.

I'd heard it, too. A rhythmic clapping, the soft patter of sneaker-shod feet. And then, voices.

"H-O-W-D-Y! Hey-hey! We say Hi!" And through the swinging doors she burst, the first cheerleader the Silver Dollar had ever seen. She popped those doors back and bounced into the room, her hands rolling in front of her, her blond curls cascading over her shoulders. She bounded across the room, right over to our table, and dropped to one knee, one arm flung out to her side and the other straight over her head. "DeeDee!" she cried.

Another cheerleader leaped through the door and sprang over to kneel beside the first. Flinging her arms exactly the same way, she cried, "Kristi!"

And they kept on coming, the doors swinging and banging against the wall, their little rubber-soled feet tap-tapping through the peanut shells that littered the Silver Dollar's floor. "Debbi! Suzi! Lori! Heather! Patti! Mindy! Lisa! Darlene!" They climbed on top of each other till their human pyramid reached the ceiling. They jumped up and landed in splits on the bar.

And in the dim light from the bar we saw that they had changed. Gone were their pleated skirts, the snowy white tennies, the matching panties. Their sweaters were black from the smoke of a thousand campfires and stiff with the arterial blood of dying elk. The dimpled knees were hidden in layers of wool, of heavy-duty twill, of camouflage-pattern neoprene. Their sneakers were gray, worn; their little socks showed through holes in the toes.

And their faces. No longer pink and shiny, their skin was rough from winter winds, wrinkled from the brutal western sun. The blond hair was stringy and sort of greasy, after so long without indoor plumbing.

But their teeth! One after another, they smiled; again and again the gloom of the Silver Dollar was broken as their teeth flashed little reflections of the neon beer signs in the windows. Years of fluoridated water, decay-preventive dentifrices, and orthodonture had done their magic. Whiter than new snow, more uniform than kernels of hybrid corn, brighter than Venus, Jupiter, and Mars in alignment, their teeth alone would have revealed them as the cheerleaders they were.

They stood, and knelt, and sat splayed before us in splendid formation, and then they windmilled their arms and all at once leaped into the air, spreadeagling their limbs toward the four corners of the world, and screamed "Yea! Rah! Team!"

Something warm surged through my body; I looked at Renée, and she was smiling right into my eyes. She reached out and took the card that matched hers.

I was the Old Maid.

The crowd went wild, and the cheerleaders bounced and hugged each other, tears rolling down their leathery cheeks, and they all clustered around Renée and wanted to pat her, and touch her, and have her sign their sneakers. It was Renée's moment of glory.

And I might have felt really bad, if something hadn't happened that warmed my heart all the way to the mitral valve. As everybody pushed over to the bar, the cheerleaders spontaneously stopped, and they all came back and stood around me in a circle, and each one put her left hand on the right shoulder of the next cheerleader. And then they bent their knees, and they stuck out their right hands, and in unison they bobbed up and down, as if they were shaking *my* right hand, and they chanted, "YOU'RE OKAY. YOU'RE ALL RIGHT. YOU PUT UP A DARN GOOD FIGHT! Yea! Rah! Whitey!"

There wasn't a dry eye in the room. "A round on me!" I shouted. And they cheered me again.

In the days that followed, I knew something had changed. I had achieved a goal, a major one, and now—temporarily, anyway—I had nothing to strive for. I was happy, but I felt a little empty, too.

On about Wednesday, I was sitting listlessly in the sun, contemplating the bleak future that stretched ahead of me, when I heard someone coming. I looked around and saw that it was Buffalo Gal, and behind her was Renée.

Buffy got right to the point. "We been huddling," she said. "We want you to stick around."

"I don't know," I said. "I'm not sure I can do this any more."

"Not this," Renée said. "There's an opening on the Williston ranch for another shepherd. Carol Ann's getting hitched."

"I don't know anything about sheep." I said.

"You don't have to," Renée said. "They mill around, and you stand there. Or you sing to 'em sometimes."

"Surely there's others more qualified," I said.

Renée gazed off at the horizon, and rubbed her hook with her mitten. "The thing is, Whitey," she said, "most of us, we never seen a cheerleader since we been here. It's what we came out here for, and we tried to do everything right, and we waited. But they never came until you got here. It's got us hoping again."

"Hoping?" I said.

Hard-bitten, rugged, dry-eyed as she was, she blushed. "We've started practicing again. It's all we really want, still. And we've realized that, even if we'll never be varsity cheerleaders, we can still do the work, learn the new routines. And who knows? Someday they may need a substitute."

I looked at her. There was something in her face I hadn't seen there before, but I recognized it. It was spirit: team spirit. It's something that's hard to find in the West, in Montana, in the wide-open spaces, where women spend most of their time alone. I thought, maybe that's it. It's not the adulation, the cheering, the popularity that we want; it's team spirit.

"I guess I could learn," I said.

So I stayed. I'm still just an assistant shepherd—sort of on the B team—but I'll tell you something: sheep are the best pep club in the world to practice on. You can be out there in front of them walking on your hands, doing triple back flips, and they don't even look at you. They keep on munching the grass, ripping it out of the ground and chewing it up.

But it's in the nature of sheepherding, and of cheerleading, to stick with it, to keep on trying. You realize how hard the cheerleaders have worked to get where they are. That makes you work harder.

Sometimes, of a summer evening—oh, yes; summer finally came—I'll be out there on the range, practicing in front of my sheep. "Give me a P!" I'll shout, and the only response is from a border collie, who obliges on a nearby fencepost. And then the warm summer wind picks up, just as the sun sets, and the sky is all red and purple and pink, and I hear, from miles away, "Two bits!" And maybe a distant figure cartwheels across a hilltop, silhouetted against the place where the sun just disappeared.

And then, from the east where the sky is already dark, I hear "Four bits!" And I know it's Buffalo Gal, calling down from her lonely vigil up on the mountain. And from up at the ranch house, where Renée is loading up supplies to bring out to us the next morning, comes "Six bits!" And I jump up and shout "A dollar!"

And the next voice is so far away the words aren't quite clear—it's up in high pastureland, where the sheep are chewing grass in the dark, and the little lambs are jumping around, or nursing on their moms, and the dogs are lying in the dust after a hard day, sleeping with one eye open, always on the lookout for coyotes. But we all know it's Ol'Pete, yelling, "If you got spirit, stand up and holler!"

And wherever we are, we leap into the sky, and holler for all we're worth. Down in town they probably think it's thunder, but it's us, practicing, ready for when the snow flies in the fall and the cheerleaders come down from the high mountain passes. We'll be ready to go with them, hunting for the Big Game.

OUR BROTHER'S KEEPER ●

lucia berlin

WHEN SOME PEOPLE DIE they just vanish, like pebbles into a pool. Everyday life just smooths back together and goes on as it did before. Other people die but stay around for a long time, either because they have captured the public's imagination, like James Dean, or because their spirit just won't let go, like our friend Sara's.

Sara died ten years ago, but still, anytime her grandchildren say something bright or imperious, everyone will say, "She's just like Sara!" Whenever I see two women driving along and laughing together, really laughing, I always think it's Sara. And of course each spring when I plant I remember the fig tree we got in the garbage bin at PayLess, the bad fight we had over the miniature coral rose bush at East Bay.

Our country has just gone to war, which is why I'm thinking about her now. She could get madder at our politicians, and be more vocal about it, than anybody I know. I want to call her up; she always gave you something to do, made you feel you could do something.

Even though all of us continue to reminisce about her, we stopped talking about the way she died very soon after it happened. She was murdered, brutally, her head bashed in with a "blunt instrument." A lover she had been going with had repeatedly threatened to kill her. She had called the police each time but they said there was nothing they could do. The man was a dentist, an alcoholic, some fifteen years younger than she was. In spite of the threats, and of other times that he had hit her, no weapon was found, no evidence placed him at the scene of the crime. He was never charged.

You know how it is when a friend is in love. Well, I guess I'm talking to women, strong women, older women. (Sara was 60.) We say it's great being our own person, that our lives are full. But we still want it, recognize it. Romance. When Sara spun around my kitchen laughing, "I'm in love. Can you believe it?" I was glad for her. We all were. Leon was attractive. Well-educated, sexy, articulate. He made her happy. Later, as she did, we forgave him. Missed appointments, unkind words, thoughtlessness, a slap. We wanted everything to be OK. We all still wanted to believe in love.

After Sara's death her son Eddie moved into her house. I cleaned his house every Tuesday, so it turned out I was cleaning at Sara's. It was hard, at first, to be in her sunny kitchen with all the plants gone but the memories still there. Gossip, talks about God, our children. The living room was full of Eddie's CDs, radios and computers, two TVs, three telephones. (So much electronic equipment that once when the phone rang I answered it with the TV remote control.) His junky mismatched furniture replaced the huge linen couch where Sara and I would lie facing each other, covered with a quilt, talking, talking. Once one rainy Sunday we were both so low we watched bowling and *Lassie*.

The first time I cleaned the bedroom was terrible. The wall near where her bed used to be was still splattered and caked with her blood. I was sickened. After I cleaned it I went outside into the garden. I smiled to see the azaleas and daffodils and ranunculus we had planted together. We didn't know which end of the ranunculus to plant, so we decided to put in half of them with the point facing down and the other half with the point up. So we still don't know which are the ones that grew.

I went back in to vacuum and make the bed, saw that under Eddie's bed was a revolver and a shotgun. I froze. What if Leon came back? He was crazy. He could kill me too. I took out each of the guns. Hands trembling, I tried to figure out what you did with them. I wanted Leon to come, so I could blow him away.

I vacuumed under the bed and put the weapons back. I was disgusted by my feelings and tried hard to think about something else.

I pretended that I was a TV show. A cleaning lady detective, sort of a female Columbo. Half-witted, gum chewing . . . but while she's feather dusting she's really looking for clues. She always just happens to be cleaning houses where a murder happens. Invisible, she mops the kitchen floor while suspects say incriminating things on the phone a few feet away. She eavesdrops, finds bloody knives in the linen cupboard, is careful not to dust the poker, saving prints . . .

Leon probably killed her with a golf club. That's how they met, at the Claremont Golf Club. I was scrubbing the bathtub when I heard the creak of the garden gate, a chair scraping on the wooden deck. Someone was in the back yard. Leon! My heart pounded. I couldn't see through the stained glass window. I crawled into the bedroom and grabbed the revolver, crawled to the french doors that led to the garden. I peeked out, gun ready, although my hand was shaking so bad I couldn't have shot it.

It was Alexander. Christ. Old Alexander, sitting in an Adirondack chair. Hi, Al! I called out, and went to put the gun away.

He was holding a clay pot of pink freesia that he kept meaning to bring to Sara. He had just felt like coming over to sit in her garden. I went in and poured him a cup of coffee. Sara had coffee going day and night. And good things to eat. Soups or gumbos, good bread and cheese and pastries. Not like the Winchell's donuts and frozen macaroni dinners Eddie kept around.

Alexander was an English professor. He could drone on for hours, Gerard Manley Hopkins gashing gold vermilion. He and Sara had known each other for forty years, had been young idealistic socialists way back when. He had always been in love with her, would plead with her to marry him. Lorena and I used to beg her to do it. "Come on, Sara . . . let him take care of you." He was good. Noble and dependable. But, if a woman says a man is nice it usually means she finds him boring. And, like my mother used to say, "Ever tried being married to a saint?"

And that's just what Alexander was talking about . . .

"I was too boring for her, too predictable. I knew this chap was bad news. I only hoped that I would be around when he left, to help pick up the pieces."

Tears came into his eyes then. "I feel responsible for her death. I knew he had hurt her, would hurt her. I should have interfered some way. All I cared about was my own resentment and jealousy. I am guilty."

I held his hand and tried to cheer him up, and we talked for a while, remembering Sara.

After he had gone I went in to clean the kitchen. Hey, what if Alexander really was guilty? What if he had come over that night, with the pot of freesia, or to see if she wanted to play Scrabble? Maybe he had looked through the curtains on the french doors, seen Sara and Leon making love. He had waited until after Leon left, out the front door, and had gone in, wild with jealousy, and killed her. He was a suspect, for sure.

The next Tuesday the house wasn't as messy as usual so I spent the last hour weeding and replanting in the garden. I was in the potting shed when I heard the bells and tambourine. Hare Hare Hare. Sara's youngest daughter, Rebecca, was dancing and chanting around the swimming pool.

Sara had been upset at first, when she had become a Krishna, but one day we were driving down Telegraph and saw her among a group of them. She looked so beautiful, singing, bobbing around, in her saffron robes. Sara pulled the car over to the curb, just to sit and watch her. She lit a cigarette and smiled. "You know what? She's safe."

I tried to talk to Rebecca, get her to sit down and have some herbal tea or something, but she was spinning, spinning like a dervish, moaning away. Then she was jumping and twirling on the diving board, interrupting her chants with violent outbursts. "Evil begets evil!" She raved on about her mother's smoking and coffee drinking, about her eating red meat, and cheese with retin or something in it. And fornication. She was at the very tip of the diving board now, and every time she hollered "Fornication!" she'd bounce about three feet up into the air.

Suspect number two.

I only cleaned Eddie's once a week, but invariably at least one person came into the back yard. I'm sure people came in every other day as well. Because that's how she was, Sara, her heart and doors open to everyone. She helped in big ways, politically, in the community, but in little ways too, anyone who needed her. She always answered her phone, she never locked her doors. She had always been there for me.

One Tuesday, out of the blue, the biggest, worst suspect of all showed up in the back yard. Clarissa. Eddie's ex-girlfriend. Wow. I don't think she had ever been near Sara's house before, she hated her so much. She had tried to get Eddie to leave his mother's law firm, come live with her in Mendocino and be a full-time writer. She wrote letters to Sara, accusing her of being domineering and possessive, and fought with Eddie all the time about his law career and his mother. Clarissa and I had been friends until finally it came down to choosing between the two women. But not before I heard her say a hundred times, "Oh, how I'd love to murder Sara." And there she was, standing under the lavender wisteria that covered the gate, chewing on the stem of her dark glasses.

"Hi, Clarissa," I said.

She was startled. "Hi. I didn't expect to see anyone. What are you doing here?" (Typical of her . . . when in doubt, attack.)

"I'm cleaning Eddie's house."

"Are you still cleaning houses? That's sick."

"I sure hope you don't talk to your patients like that."

(Clarissa's a psychiatrist, for Lord's sake . . .) I tried hard to think of what questions my cleaning lady detective would ask her. I was at a loss, she was too intimidating. She really was *capable de tout*. How could I prove it, though?

"Where were you the night Sara was killed?" I blurted.

Clarissa laughed. "My dear . . . are you implying that I am guilty of the crime? No. Too late," she said as she turned and walked out of the gate.

As the weeks went by my list of suspects continued to grow, everyone from judges to policemen to window washers.

The only thing about the window washer was the weapon, the pole he carries around with him, along with his bucket. It was scary, seeing his

silhouette through the curtains. A big man, carrying a pole. I had wondered about him for years. He is a homeless young black man who sleeps
at night on Oakland buses and sometimes in the lobby of Alta Bates
Emergency. During the day he goes from door to door asking people
if they want their windows washed. He always has a book with him.
Nathaniel Hawthorne. Jim Thompson. Karl Marx. He has a nice voice and
dresses very well, tennis sweaters, Ralph Lauren T-shirts.

After Sara paid him for washing windows she'd always give him some
god-awful old clothes of Eddie's. He'd say Thank you, ma'am, real polite,
but I used to be sure he threw them in the garbage on his way out. Maybe
she was a symbol or something. A jump suit with a broken zipper the last
straw?

"Hello, Emory, how are you?"

"Just fine, and you? I saw that Miss Sara's son was living here now . . .
wondered if he needed his windows washed."

"No. I'm cleaning for him now, and do the windows too. Why don't
you try at his office, on Prince Street?"

"Good idea. Thanks," he said. He smiled and left.

OK, I said to myself. Pull yourself together and cut this suspect business out right now.

I went in and got some coffee, went back to sit in the garden. Oh. The
Japanese iris were in bloom. Sara, if only you could see them.

She had called me several times that day, telling me about his threats to
her. I was impatient with her about Leon by then . . . why didn't she just
break up with him? I listened to her and I said things like, call the police.
Don't answer your phone.

When she called why didn't I say, "Come right on over to my house"?
Why didn't I say, "Sara, pack your bag . . . Let's get out of town."

I have no alibi for the night of the crime.

indian rubies ●

patti smith

I HAVE ALWAYS POSSESSED a kind of knapsack, if nothing more than a piece of cloth or skin tied in a knot. My sack, worthy companion, produces, when opened, a world defined by its contents—fluxion, unique, beloved.

This uncommon bundle has always been my comfort, my happy burden. Yet I have found it unwise to attach myself to the souvenirs within. For as soon as I focus on a certain object I misplace it or it just disappears.

I had a ruby. Imperfect, beautiful like faceted blood. It came from India where they wash up on the shore. Thousands of them—the beads of sorrow. Little droplets that somehow became gems gathered by beggars who trade them for rice. Whenever I stared into its depths I felt overcome, for caught within my little gem was more misery and hope than one could fathom.

It frightened and inspired, and I kept it in my sack, a waxed yellow packet the size and shape of a razor blade. I'd stop and take it out and look at it. I did this so often it was no longer necessary to see what I was looking at. And because of this I can not say for certain when it disappeared.

I can still see it though. I see it on the foreheads of the women. In the poet's hollow. I see it at the throat of a diva and in the palm of the deserter. Pressing against a wire fence. A drop of blood on a calico dress. I open my bundle and dump the contents in the furrows of the earth. Nothing—an old spoon, a rudder, the remains of a walkie-talkie. Spreading the cloth to rest upon I take breaths as long as the furrows. As if to quell the spirits; hold them from shaking and clanging.

In the ring of the impossible night. Everything elastic. The sky a deep disturbing rose. I can feel the dust of Calcutta, the gone eyes of Bhopal. I can see the prayer flags flapping about like old socks in the warm, ironic wind.

Can I offer you this bell
the whisper merchant
It is extremely valuable
a museum piece, priceless
No thank you, I answer
I do not wish to own
But it is a wonderful bell
a ceremonial piece
a fine bell
My head is a bell
I murmur
between
bandaged fingers
already asleep

KNOWER OF BIRDS ●

rachel pollack

The cards for this story were drawn by myself, as part of the early stages in creating a whole deck. There were only fourteen cards ready when I decided to use them to create my Tarot tale. Following the method suggested for the book, I made no attempt to think of a story before shuffling the cards. When I saw the Emperor the shape of the story became clear. And yet, there was also a card missing. I still have not drawn the Knower of Birds, though the concept has been part of the plan almost since the beginning. From the other cards it became clear that the Knower belonged here as well. Ultimately, a story makes its own rules.

Emperor.

THERE WAS ONCE a woman named Julia who traveled to a far city on the shores of the sea. This city was built around a double mountain which hid the inland streets from the water. Every morning, at dawn, fog would gather itself on the bay, and as the day became brighter it also became darker, for the fog would stream inland, dampening the Sun. Steadily it would climb the hill, one street after another, until it reached the top of the double mountain. There it waited, gathering its strength for the plunge down the other side, into the valley.

One day Julia left the home of her friends and walked several blocks up the hill to where she could catch a bus which would take her to a lecture at an aviary on the other side of town. While she waited at the stop the wind began to rise, and the fog began to push down the mountain. Chilled, Julia stepped back, next to a grey house. Two round pillars of wood framed the doorway. One pillar was painted white, the other dark blue. Julia leaned against the white side, hugging herself against the damp wind. She would have liked to press against the door and let the two pillars shelter her, but it seemed rude. Suppose someone opened the door and she fell inside? Or suppose someone came home and found this shivering woman blocking the entrance? The streets all around her became covered in fog. The wind was picking up, rattling windows and doors, shaking trees in gardens behind the homes. Julia wondered if she should go back to her friends' house. She could still hear traffic but it seemed far away, somewhere on the other side of town. Still, she had promised to go out for the afternoon. Suppose her friends had been looking forward to some privacy? Suppose they were making love, or fighting? And there was a noise that sounded like it might be a bus, a kind of labored rattle pushing its way up the hill. So she waited, while the mist swallowed the houses at the far end of the street. Ten minutes, fifteen minutes, and the engine sound had long disappeared, drowned out by the wind knocking on the houses.

Julia knew she had better get back to her friends. Whatever they were doing, they'd just have to understand. It wasn't safe.

She stepped into the wind. She could hardly breathe. She turned around, putting her back against it. The wind shoved her forward, and she grabbed a mail box to steady herself. When she stood up again, she discovered she couldn't remember which way she was going, which direction meant home. She looked about, but everything lay hidden, some houses dimly visible, others as if nothing existed there but an empty horizon. Sometimes the fog would shift, and a red or a green house would appear out of nothing, hover in the air, and then vanish again. Julia heard crashing noises, broken glass.

She found her way back to the house with the two pillars. Banging on the door she tried to shout for help, but nothing came out of her. The door stayed closed. Maybe she should break a window. She could always claim the wind had done it. She held up her purse; the black leather would protect her hand. Briefly she stood like that, one hand holding the pillar, the other arm stretched out with the hand under the flap of her bag. And then she lowered her arm, remembering her own pain the time she'd come home to find her apartment broken into. Someone on the street must be home, she told herself. Someone would let her in.

A noise like a shout broke the howl of the wind. Down the block a great mass lifted up into the air. Over Julia's head it spun, an entire house, and then it vanished into the mist.

Half crawling, holding on to trees and signposts, Julia pushed towards the place where the house had risen. She found a hole with jagged edges of wood and pipe. Something lay there in the middle, some kind of lump. As Julia climbed down, the wind began to settle, and the fog to lift. It was only when she was standing in damp dirt that she saw that the lump was a man, asleep. Julia stumbled backwards just as the Sun came through a break in the mist. The tight beam seemed to shine only on the man, leaving the rest of the hole in gloom.

He's probably harmless, Julia thought, probably a drunk. He lay curled up, with the collar of his jacket pulled over most of his face. The jacket looked like half of an old pinstripe suit, the kind of thing he'd have found in the Salvation Army. He wore jeans frayed at the seat, and black basket-ball shoes. A pair of twisting wires snaked along the ground from the spot in the dirt where his forehead lay. They looked a little like horns, or maybe diagrams of his dreams.

It was probably safe now to climb out, Julia thought. Instead, curiosity took her a step forward. The man sat up so suddenly that Julia gasped. He was very tall, she realized, with a deep chest and wide shoulders. Dust had matted his long hair into a mass of thick vines. His bloodshot eyes seemed almost entirely red, relieved only by the hard black dots in the center.

In a rasping voice he said, "What does she want?"

It took a moment for Julia to find her breath. "I'm sorry," she said, "I don't think I know who you mean."

"Haven't you come from my wife?"

"I'm sorry. I don't know your wife. I just came down here because of the storm." She became conscious of the Sun shining on her, of sweat on her chest and under her arms, and she wondered if he'd accuse her of lying.

Instead he sat back and let his face fall into his hands. His chest deflated. "I thought you were her lawyer," he said. "I thought you came to tell me her terms." Julia said nothing. "I just want her back. Can't she understand that? I didn't mean it. I was just—I just got crazy. Thought I could run everything myself. I was wrong, okay? Okay?"

Julia glanced up at the top of the hole. It was just too high for her to jump out and run away. She said, "I'm sure your wife will understand. Everybody makes mistakes."

"Then where is she?" he shouted. "Look at this mess." He waved an arm, and Julia didn't know if he meant the cellar or something greater. "I've done my best, I'm just no good at it. She's the one who always ran everything. I don't even like it. I knew that as soon as she left. As soon as she left. Everyone asking me what to do." He began to cry.

Julia moved back against the edge of the hole. Somewhere outside she could hear people talking. She took a deep breath in preparation for spinning around and climbing out. As if to copy her, the man breathed in as well, expanding his chest and bringing up his head, like a bull lifting its horns to the Moon. When he wiped the tears from his face some of the dirt came away as well. His skin showed as streaks of dark gold.

"Will you tell her?" he asked.

"Tell her?"

"That I want her back. That I want her to come home. *I* want to come home."

"I'm sorry," Julia said. "I don't know your wife."

"Then find her!" he boomed. "Sorry," he added immediately. "It's just my old habit. See what happens to me without her?" He smiled suddenly. "Will you find her?" he asked sweetly. "Tell her I need her. Tell her we all need her. I've made such a mess of things." He kept smiling, and staring at her.

"All right," Julia said. She made a noise. Why did she say that?

"Good," the man said, as if approving a child. "Good." He lay down again on the dirt.

"Wait a moment," Julia said. "I can't find your wife. I don't know anything about her. I don't even know her name." No use. He was already asleep. Gingerly she touched his arm, then gave it a shove. He began to snore, a sound like a distant train.

Using a thick board as a step Julia climbed back up to the street. When she reached the corner the bus came. She ignored it and went down the hill to her friends.

In the house that night, some people came over. Over a half gallon of cheap wine they talked about the storm and the rumors of cars flying through the air, and towers of dirt rising into the sky. After an hour the talk shifted to divorce and child care. A man named Tommy didn't know where he would find the extra support money for back-to-school clothes for his daughter by his second wife. Meanwhile, his first wife had vanished, leaving their retarded twelve-year-old son behind. The boy was now with his grandparents until Tommy could work out how to take care of him. And Tommy himself was demanding that his third wife give some support money for their two-year-old. Leaving the boy with Tommy had given her the chance to pursue her career as a corporate color consultant.

Julia's friends described their own scattered children and divorces. Margaret, whom Julia had met years ago in a flea market, had a grown-up daughter who'd dropped out of college to travel to Mexico with her alcoholic father. Margaret's current husband, Michael, also had an adult daughter. She was living at home in between lesbian love affairs. Michael's second wife had just thrown out their teenage son, Jack, who belonged to some cult which involved dressing in drag. Drinking glass after glass of wine Margaret complained about the danger Michael's "perverted" children posed to Margaret's and Michael's three-year-old son.

As soon as it seemed polite Julia went upstairs to the tiny bedroom they'd reserved for her among the house's shifting residents. Despite the warmth she put on a long flannel nightgown and lay down on top of the covers. Why did she make that promise? It didn't really count. She didn't even know the woman's name. Downstairs she could hear a rough weave of angry voices.

High Priestess.

Julia flew home three days later. Leaving the city the plane passed over a series of salt flats, large plots of land, each one a separate color.

The irregular shapes, with black lines swooping across them, resembled ancient drawings of birds.

When she arrived home her little apartment seemed so peaceful. She thought how she could sit for days just staring out the back window at the little pond behind the house. After unpacking, she sat down to watch the news on television. A food shipment to some starving villagers had become contaminated with poison gas. A man in New Jersey had stolen an airplane and crashed it into his wife's house. A woman in prison had died in a hunger strike. Her daughter claimed the guards had force-fed her and she'd choked to death. When Julia went to bed that night she found it hard to breathe. For a while she sat up, reading a book of cartoons. Finally she was able to sleep.

The next day Julia received a new assignment from her temp agency. A private library outside of town needed someone to transfer their card catalogue onto computer. The library turned out to be mostly occult books: seventeenth-century alchemical treatises, rare Tarot decks, diagrams of the human body with strange labels, translations of Hindu beliefs about the universe, and confusing messages from groups of dead people. At first the work went slowly. Julia kept looking around at the floor-to-ceiling cases of forbidden books. She wanted to run from the house before priests in huge cowls would raid the library. After a few days, however, she became fascinated by the descriptions on the cards. The books were so varied, so many different theories. When she thought the owner of the house wouldn't catch her, Julia would search the shelves for some book whose title or description seemed especially enticing. She never really understood any of them. For one thing, most were in foreign languages. And even those in English referred to names and ideas Julia had never heard of. She just liked the feeling they gave her, of life being so much bigger than she'd ever believed.

As she neared the end she tried to work more slowly, doing only a few cards an hour. Finally she couldn't stall any more. She typed in the last entry, about some figure called "the Horned God," and then she went to Mrs. Toth and reported that the catalogue was complete. Mrs. Toth invited Julia for tea. Sitting in a large room with bay windows overlooking a garden, the two women talked about computers and the need to be modern. Suddenly, Mrs. Toth bowed her head and slipped off a chain from around her neck. The chain held a small silver disc incised with a stick figure of a woman in a long skirt, and a pair of birds around her head. "This is for you," she said, and before Julia could say anything the woman had placed it over Julia's head.

When Julia got home that evening she put the disc and chain in her jewelery box. Depressed, she watched television, constantly switching channels to avoid scenes of violence or humiliation. Finally, she went to bed, only to find herself lying awake, exhausted. Every time she began to doze off, she somehow snapped herself back. Abruptly, she got up and put on Mrs. Toth's medallion. In bed again, she smiled at herself. Moments later, she fell asleep. She woke up in mid-morning to the sound of birds.

That afternoon Julia went to an occult bookshop. The store was clean and elegant, with the books carefully arranged on shelves and carousels around a central display of jewelery, crystal balls, Tarot cards, and polished rocks. Julia leafed through several books, hoping she didn't look too much like an amateur. It all seemed wrong, somehow. Too modern. Mrs. Toth's books were mostly bound in thick covers, with leather tooling. These were all paperbacks, with lurid covers showing women dripping moonlight, or cards fanned out like a carnival trick.

When she left the store she began walking aimlessly, unwilling to go home. On a busy street, a white pigeon flew up at her. Julia gasped and put up her hands. Embarrassed, she looked around to see if anyone was laughing at her. Instead, she noticed an old woman standing on the corner, looking confused. The woman was short and slightly bent over, with brittle grey hair. She wore a black cotton dress and worn-out sandals. She was carrying several shopping bags and a large cardboard box. Every time she picked one up another one fell. The woman seemed to want to cross the street but was frightened of the traffic. Behind her people rushed in and out of department stores. When Julia walked closer she saw the woman was crying, from frustration or fear. "Do you need help?" Julia asked.

"Yes," the woman said. "Oh yes, please." She looked a little like Mrs. Toth, a Mrs. Toth without money or a home. Julia picked up the box—it weighed hardly anything—and took one of the bags. With her free hand she held the woman's elbow. It took a while for them to cross the street; the woman walked slowly, and, halfway across, a woman in a silk skirt and running shoes almost knocked them down. They made it across just as the light changed.

"Thank you," the woman said. Julia felt embarrassed. She wished she could walk away, but didn't want to insult the woman, who seemed to be searching for something in one of the bags. "Here," the woman said finally, and held up a filthy brown vial about the size of Julia's little finger. "This is for you."

Julia backed away. "I don't need anything," she said. "I mean, thank you, but—"

Following Julia, the woman said, "My mother always told me to return kindness with kindness." She slipped the vial into Julia's hand and closed her fingers around it. "It'll help against the pain."

"I'm not feeling any pain," Julia said, but the woman hurried away, moving quickly now despite her packages. Julia looked at the bottle. She should throw it away, she knew. It was probably filled with germs. Instead, she dropped it into her bag and headed home.

Death.

That evening Julia cut her finger while peeling potatoes. It was only a small cut, it hardly needed the Band-aid she wrapped around it. Through the evening, however, it hurt more and more. She took off the Band-aid and inspected the wound. It didn't look infected. Not even swollen. Around eleven o'clock Julia's finger hurt so much she couldn't even watch television. She just hoped she could go to sleep.

In bed, she slid her hand under the pillow, as if the soft pressure would contain the throbbing. Just before sleep she thought she heard someone singing outside the house—a clear soprano, singing a folk song, or maybe a spiritual. And then she realized, it was only a bird. Strange, she thought, to hear a bird singing at night. Maybe it was an owl. And with that thought, and no sense of passage, Julia emigrated to the Land of Dream.

She was sitting in the kitchen reading one of Mrs. Toth's books. Across from her the medallion swung from a peg on the back of a chair. She heard a moaning outside the house and walked out through the kitchen door to see what it was. Instead of the small backyard with the pond and the trees beyond it, she stood on a kind of ledge, with a plain stretching for miles below her. The dirt was cracked, and the few trees were withered. All about she saw people sitting on the ground with their heads in their hands, or else leaning against the trees and staring at the dirt. Many of them appeared scarred or bruised. Julia herself staggered as if someone had beaten her.

The scene changed: a large box sat on the ground, an old wooden box, like an antique toy chest. From inside it Julia heard moans and weeping. A tall man came walking up to the box. Dressed in an old-fashioned tuxedo, top hat, and patent leather shoes, he placed his white gloved hands on the lid. Immediately the sounds stopped. Though he stood with his back to Julia she could see a corner of his face. The skin gleamed hard and white, like polished bone.

With a grand gesture the tall man flung open the lid of the box. Julia heard a great whoosh of air as colored bits of paper flew up into the sky. High in the air they changed to birds, all singing joyfully as they flew in and out of each other under the sun. Julia's own heart became a bird. At any moment her weightless body would float away into the light.

She woke up with the pain worse than ever. If she didn't look at her finger she could swear it was twice the size of the others. Julia turned on the reading lamp, and at that moment she remembered the old woman with her greasy bottle. She scrambled through her bag until she found it. She looked doubtfully at it until the pain stabbed her again, and then she pulled out the cork. A sweet smell floated up to her, like orange concentrate mixed with mint. Nervously, she touched the cut fingertip into the vial—

And yelped as the sting hit her like a flash of light. Without thinking she jabbed the finger into her mouth.

The pain vanished, taking with it a neck pain and a lower back ache she hadn't even noticed until they left her. She stood up, grinning, and then laughed. For the first time she noticed it was dawn. She slipped on her bathrobe and went out to the backyard.

Knower of Birds.

The sky had that gentle blue of a morning promising a lot of sunshine. The air was cool, the ground still wet with dew. Julia shivered slightly and pulled her bathrobe tighter. She smiled at the trees and the grass. A breeze stirred some branches, as if the nearest tree was smiling back at her. Julia laughed, and bounced up and down slightly on her toes.

Two green and red birds with gold beaks landed on a branch near her. Julia didn't know what kind they were—she'd never learned to recognize things like birds or flowers—but she didn't think she'd seen anything like them before. And indeed, when they started talking to each other, they were discussing trips across mountains and over the sea. Julia found it so natural to understand them that she didn't even think about it at first, and when she did she wondered why she'd never understood birds before. Probably never took the time to listen, she decided, and then forgot about it as she concentrated on the birds' conversation.

Though she knew the words Julia still found it difficult to follow their rather formal style of speaking, a kind of poetic debate. Also—she didn't know how she knew this, she was certainly no expert—they spoke with an accent, like foreigners.

They were discussing what they called "two-legged mating problems." After a while Julia realized this meant human relationships. They didn't seem to think too much of human customs. When they had told stories of romantic love and rejection from different countries, they began talking of someone they called "the master of rage and pain." This man had lived with a woman who ran a farm or a business or some kind of organization. One day the husband threw her out, taking over the business himself. But where everything had gone so well with the two of them, it all became a disaster when the man tried to do it alone. And now that he wanted her back, he didn't know where to find her. The birds seemed to find this funny, repeating it several times.

"Where does she rest?" one asked, and the other answered, "On the glass mountain. Where the three stone rivers meet." And with that, they launched themselves into the sky. Only when they were fading from sight did Julia realize they had been talking about the man she'd met during the storm. For the first time in weeks she remembered her promise to find the man's wife. "Wait a minute," she called. "Come back. How do I find this mountain? Where do I find the three rivers?" If the birds heard her they paid no attention. They vanished among rows of TV satellite dishes growing on the rooftops like mushrooms on the floor of a forest.

Seeker.

Back in the house Julia sat down at the kitchen table. Three rivers. Didn't the Mississippi have branches? Tributaries, that was the word. Tributes brought to the king. As far as she could remember, they didn't all meet in the same place. And she'd never heard of any glass mountains. Anyway, the rivers could be anywhere. The birds were so well-traveled.

Julia walked into the living room, her bathrobe flapping behind her. Mixed in with some magazines under the television she kept an atlas. She checked the Mississippi, the Nile, the Amazon, the Congo, the Danube, the Don, and then leafed through the maps at random. Now and then she found some likely intersection, but never a mountain right at that location.

She dropped the book on the rug. They didn't just say a mountain, they said a *glass* mountain. And stone rivers. What was that supposed to mean? Maybe they meant lava flows. And a volcano. Didn't lava become like glass? She remembered reading about Aztecs and glass knives harder than steel. The atlas told her nothing.

The next morning Julia went to all the different bookshops she knew, looking for studies of volcanoes. Finally she went to the State University and asked to see a professor of geology. The graduate assistant who spoke to her smirked when she asked if he would describe a volcano as a "glass mountain" He laughed out loud when she asked about the meeting of "stone rivers."

Outside the building Julia thought to herself; it's not fair. How was she supposed to know what a couple of birds meant? Why couldn't they be more explicit? And anyway, how was she supposed to climb the glass mountain? "It's easy for them," she said out loud. 'They just have to flap their silly little wings."

On the way back to her car Julia passed a storefront appealing for help for abused children. There were pictures of kids with broken bones, burnt faces—Julia felt faint. Leaning against a tree, she stared up at the sky. Why do we do these things? she wondered. What's wrong with us? It was like— like something got broken, or misconnected. Above her a trio of birds glided on invisible currents. "Help us," Julia whispered. "Please."

A series of loops and swirls brought one of the birds—a gull, she thought—down to rest on the hood of Julia's car. When Julia ran up to it, the bird flapped its wings to rise into the air a few inches, and then plopped down onto the metal. "Oh," Julia said. "I'm sorry about what I said. I was just upset."

"Follow," the bird commanded. It circled over her car until she maneuvred out of the parking spot and then it began leading her down the street. Around corners and into the center of town they traveled, with the bird resting on the roof of the car whenever Julia had to stop for a light. Through town, through rush-hour traffic jams (where Julia worried that the gull would get impatient and strand her), over to the edge of the city, where the city street met the old state highway and Interstate 85. And at that point, on a fence surrounding the construction site for an office building, the bird came to a rest.

Julia jerked the car to a stop and got out, only to have the bird take off again, climbing so quickly Julia couldn't think of chasing it. She looked around, wanting to cry. In front of her the sign proclaimed the glory the new building would bring to the city. Beyond it rose a ziggurat of blue glass. Julia remembered the local news station describing it as a "model of post-modernism." She turned away, looking at the highway. Three roads. Concrete. Stone—

With a shout she turned back to stare at the skyscraper. The glass mountain. At the top the afternoon Sun lit up a row of glass triangles in different colors. On top of each one she saw a speck, a bird, a congress of birds.

Gift of Rivers.

Unfinished, the building stood unguarded as well. Julia discovered a hole in the fence just big enough for her to squeeze through. Inside, she found a single elevator working to carry her up the central shaft, and at the top an open doorway to the roof.

The roof was much bigger than it looked from the street, the glass pyramids higher and more translucent. The afternoon light passing through them made the flat rooftop a quilt of blended colors. Still brighter, however, were the birds. All sizes and all shapes, some with long necks and huge wings, others so small two or three might have fit in Julia's palm. A few circled round their miniature peaks, as if too high strung to sit still. Most simply perched, their claws scratching the glass. "Hello," Julia said softly, and a great flood of welcome crashed over her, from chirps and whistles to deep croaks. Julia laughed and clapped her hands.

Three loud claps answered her from behind. Julia jumped and turned around. An old woman stood near the edge of the roof. She wore a long green dress with short sleeves and a hem that was coming unravelled. The dress hung loosely on her thin body. Instead of having wrinkles, the woman's face was smooth, almost polished, as if everything extreme had worn away with time. Her fine hair moved continually in the wind. A trick of the Sun, or maybe the light filtered through the triangles, gave the hair a quality of shifting colors, gold mixed with brown, red, even green.

Julia shook her head slightly. She'd never expected the woman to be so old. She remembered an aunt who'd married a younger man and how everyone had gossiped about them. Without thinking, she glanced down at the silver medallion hanging between her breasts.

The woman laughed. "An old picture," she said. She walked closer, moving with an efficient grace. "Where did you get that?" she said. "I haven't seen one of those for years."

"Mrs. Toth gave it to me."

The woman smiled, and her teeth seemed to catch the Sun, so that her mouth, for a moment, appeared filled with light. "Good old Mrs. Toth," she said. "How is she?"

"Fine," Julia said. "I guess. She's got a computer."

"Has she? Wonderful. Good for her."

For a while they just stood there, the woman very still, Julia wishing she didn't sound so dumb. The gull who had led her to the building came and circled round her shoulders. "Don't be afraid," it told her in its loud gull voice.

Julia blushed. She said, "I've got a message. From your husband."

The woman shook her head. "I've never married."

"What? Oh. I mean, I'm sorry. I thought—"

"You haven't made a mistake." A smile appeared, then vanished, as if she didn't want Julia to think this old lady was making fun of her.

"But he told me—a big man with red eyes? He said you were married, and he threw you out. And now he wants you back. I had to give you the message."

The woman nodded. "Thank you. You've done well. It's not your fault he told you something that wasn't true. I doubt that he himself knows the truth any more."

"But the birds said—about the man and his wife—"

The woman laughed, the sound riding over the cries and whistles of the birds. She said, "Just because they can fly doesn't mean they always get their stories right."

Settling on the old woman's shoulder the gull said, "We do our best."

The woman stroked him. "You do very well. All of you. I'm very proud of you all."

Julia said, "Then you never lived with him?"

"Oh, we lived together. He came to me—he looked so sweet then, so young and excited, so full of ideas and enthusiasm." She sighed. "And I guess I was curious. To see what he would do. That's always been my great fault, you know. Curiosity."

"And he threw you out?"

The woman laughed again. "Of course not. I left."

"But why?"

"I just told you. Curiosity." The light somehow shifted her face, so that Julia glimpsed a young woman, hard and bright. And then the old woman returned, patient, unmoving.

"He wants you back," Julia said.

"No. He just wants to believe he controls everything. Me, the work, himself. There's really nothing I can do for him. I'm sorry."

"Then what about us?" Julia said. "Do you know what's happening?" She wasn't sure what she meant, only that a great anger had risen up in her. "We need help. You and your damn birds—"

The woman held out her hands. "Come here," she said.

Julia backed away. "What are you going to do?"

"Nothing that will hurt you."

Julia didn't understand the panic that rose up in her. She couldn't breathe, it was like something was pounding on her heart. She looked at the triangles blocking the edge of the roof. She could climb over them, push aside the birds, get away—But what if she couldn't escape? What if something terrible waited for you after you died? She remembered the children in the photos, burned and broken. She walked up and put out her hands for the woman to take them.

At first nothing happened. Julia just stood there, feeling foolish as the fear subsided. And then she began to cry. She cried in a way she'd never known possible, huge whooping noises, her whole body a flood washing away pains she'd never known or else forgotten, pains she'd kept stored away all her life, like treasures hidden from the world. She looked down at the woman, expecting to see her crying as well. Instead, the ancient face looked up at her, impassive. The anger returned; Julia wanted to throw the arrogant old bitch to the ground. She tried to break loose, but the woman held on to her.

Julia didn't know if the pain was gone, but she discovered other treasures. Pleasure—rage—excitement—fear of excitement—thoughts of murder, of being murdered. And above all, desire. She wanted love. More than love itself, she wanted the power to make love happen or take it away, not just for herself, for everyone. It was the power that counted. She wanted to give life and destroy it. She wanted *her* words and *her* hands to make the grass grow, to give the birds their colors, to set the rhythms of the seas.

And then she looked at that face again, bland and empty. All of it—desire, anger, fear—dropped away in a last wrench of tears. When the crying stopped, Julia simply stood there, unmoving in the evening wind.

The old woman was still looking at her. Julia wondered if she should say something. "Thank you," or "I'm sorry." Or maybe just laugh. Instead, she let go of the hands. The woman's arms dropped to her sides.

"It's getting dark," she told Julia. "Maybe you should be heading home."

Julia looked around at the sky, a dark blue, almost purple. She noticed that the birds had left. Her crying must have covered the sound of the wings. She said, "Did they go because of me?" Then she laughed, realizing how silly that sounded. She said, "Can I come back and visit you again?"

"I won't be here long. They'll need to open the building soon."

Julia nodded. She held out her hands once more and the old woman squeezed them briefly. At the door leading downstairs Julia turned around to see the old woman at the roof's edge, looking out past the triangles. In the evening light her hair had turned to silver and black.

When Julia pulled into her driveway the man in the pinstripe jacket was standing by the garage. "Did you find her?" he said, even before Julia had got out of her car. "Is she coming back?"

"I'm sorry," Julia said. "I did what I could."

"What the hell am I supposed to do, come crawling on my knees? What the hell does she want from me?"

Julia took a step towards the house, then stopped. In one gesture, she took off Mrs. Toth's medallion and slipped the chain over the man's head. Angrily he grabbed hold of it, as if to jerk it loose and throw it on the ground. Instead, he held it in his palm. Just before she went inside and closed the door, Julia saw the man with his hand up near his eyes. He was squinting at the disc. Moonlight made the silver sparkle in the night.

THE WILD CHERRIES OF LUST ●
(for Orisis)

andrea dworkin

bERTHA SCHNEIDER had once been a woman and was now an androgyne. as a woman she had lain for 8 years on her back with her legs open as the multitudes passed by leaving gifts of sperm and spit. now as an androgyne her legs were still open but at the same time they ran, jumped, swam, stood up, skipped, and squatted. her mouth was also open and what nestled there with restless fervor also found its way to her armpits, under and between her breasts, to the creases in her neck, to the small of her back as well as the bend of her elbow. not to mention where the bend of her elbow often found itself.

bertha had passed 2 years of celibacy before becoming an androgyne. she had fucked during that time in much the way vegetarians eat hamburgers—sometimes and not proudly. yes, she had been fucked and gutted and ransacked occasionally by sweet young boys who lived on street corners. yes, she had sucked the cunts of brilliant, strong, and worthy women with abandon and no small measure of delight. but all the while she had dreamed herself celibate and had even imagined that she was a virgin again as she once had been—only this time in spirit as well as in body, on purpose instead of by accident.

bertha had changed much in her one short life. as a woman she had often been whipped and had lusted for that agonizing, exquisite humiliation. those who had whipped her were not yr vulgar wife beaters but velvet coated actors and curly haired painters as well as revolutionaries and workers. the whips had been real leather and when her back and ass were shredded and blood began to form puddles on the floor, the whip handle had often as not been stuffed up her cunt or ass. now as an androgyne she had renounced all that. she was proud of the fact that in her soul whips did not speak to her. oh yes, there were occasional fleeting seconds—moments even—of desire that verged on need. yes, sometimes the muscles in the pit of her stomach did tighten and she did lust for the lash of the whip, not to mention the whip handle. but she was secure in her conviction that she who was now an androgyne would not regress to being a mere woman. it would take, she knew, more than one man could offer to make her into a woman again. it would take, she knew, a concert hall filled with thousands of people, her bare-assed naked on stage shackled in wicked chains, being whipped by, dare she say it, Jean-Louis Trintignant, before she would even be tempted in a serious way.

bertha had changed physically as well. as a woman she seemed to be all breasts and ass. indeed, if other parts of her body existed, they went unremarked by the world at large. now as an androgyne her breasts had diminished while her belly had grown. her belly was now a giant luminous mound, glowing, exquisitely sensitive to every touch, even to every thought of touch. a finger on her belly was the instrument of ecstasy and a tongue brought on multiple orgasms that were as vast and as deep as the universe. stars quaked and comets exploded when her belly came into contact with an electric vibrator.

her nose, of course, had grown. it had grown and grown and grown. sometimes it hung, weak, limp, sweet, beautiful. sometimes upon the passing of a gentle wind, a grazing cow, or a wood nymph, her nose would stiffen and enlarge and become engorged with blood. it was not very pleasant when this happened in the company of ordinary men and women with their hidden private parts and endless sources of shame. but when it happened in the presence of other androgynes, she herself would touch and fondle it. limp or stiff, her nose would roll over arms and into armpits, explore ears that opened up like flowers, juicy and moist and yielding, find its way between toes and rub itself against calloused heels, seek out with gentle insistence the backs of knees, immerse itself in puddles of saliva under the tongue and the rich resonances of slick assholes, vibrate and heave, and finally come to rest on a nipple, touching it just barely. then, as bertha lay exhausted, her lover would touch her belly and so they would begin again and continue and replenish and deplete and invent, and then begin again.

berthas hair of course had changed too. as a woman she had violated it without conscience—cut it, lacquered it, straightened it, curled it, even shaved it from her legs and armpits and pulled it out from between her eyes. now as an androgyne her hair rose and fell with the light, the wind, it danced between her legs, it reached toward the sun in rich profusion from every part of her. each hair was an antenna, sensitive, alert. one hair, like a new filling, could send an icy thrilling chill through her whole body or warm her like whiskey and Ben-Gay. her pubic hair flowed, billowing, curling, lustrous, slightly rough and coarse so that when touched by her fingertips electric impulses would tickle her knuckles and cause her palms to swell and sweat. her hair grew on her legs and reached out and touched the wind and met the water and when touched by other flesh sent thrills into the marrow of her bones and turned her almost inside-out with pleasure.

her hands too had changed. her fingers looked now much like her nose, and her fingertips resembled vulvas. her Mount of Venus had thickened and the lines in her hand were deep, almost cavernous. and her ass, which as a woman had been mostly for shitting and occasional rape, had become an interior tunnel into which flesh sometimes flowed, or honey it seemed, or ice cream. in fact, the whole space between her ass and mouth had become a winding energy passage so that any touch or breath in either place caused sweet chills and exquisite tremors.

bertha schneider, once a woman, then a celibate, had become an androgyne — and when I tell you that she lived happily ever after, I hope you will know what I mean.

KEEP YOUR GUTS ●

karen karbo

MY LAST CATTLE CALL takes place on a smoggy day, temperature over one hundred degrees. Every just-starting-out actress in Los Angeles is there, all lined up, all trying for this part, the female lead in a movie directed by Solly Stein. Even I heard of this guy when I am actress in Moscow. He has big reputation for realism. In his last picture, rumor says, he spends over one hundred thousand dollars on authentic Victorian keyholes visible only in long shot.

Standing in front of me are two bony American beauties. One in a halter dress. All the sharp inside parts of her back can be seen from the outside. She is telling her friend about recent operation to enlarge her cheekbones. She tells how the skin under her eyes is slit open and pyramids of silicone tucked in. The friend says she has heard of times when these implants wander around the body. A woman she knew had a breast implant that wound up in her armpit. The girls look about twenty-two years old.

"Stop this!" I yell. "You guys are so gruesome!" I cover my ears with my hands.

Through my fingers I hear the cheekbone one say, "You do what you have to do."

Normally, I believe Los Angeles is not a bad place for Soviet émigrés—those from Moscow especially are used to sprawl and anonymity, and there is large émigré community here—but the heat and craziness can make you sick. I close my eyes. Sharp zots of color whiz around behind my eyelids. I only stay in line because I believe I have a chance. The advertisement said this role called for "a faded Russian beauty, sensual and world-weary." I am her.

Before I left Soviet Union, I am co-star of film called *I Traded My Love for a Barge*. The premise was this: Typical spirited Socialist heroine leaves husband and "self-satisfied" life in Moscow to help make quota at failing shipyards in Sevastopol.

Except for these idiotic movie roles, my Moscow life was not so bad. I was no dissident. Soviet Union had provided me a good education and career as medium-range actress. I had season hockey tickets and beautiful high-ceilinged apartment in old section of town, with new painted walls. The paint was gotten secretly from West Germany by my lover, Valentin. It was melted-sherbet color, this paint, a shade known as Innocent Peach. Valentin and I painted my walls together, then made love against them while they were cool and soft, barely dry. I talked Valentin's head blue about my love of Innocent Peach. You would think it safe, right? Talking to your lover about the color of your walls.

My role in this barge movie was as the lonely, well-groomed confidante who convinces our heroine to drop everything to go help the Motherland. It was a stupid, impossible piece of acting.

"No young wife leaves her husband to build boats in Sevastopol!" I shrieked at Valentin, who was also my director. Outside my apartment, we screamed at one another until our veins threatened to burst. We got into love only because each respected the other's work, but we were otherwise not well suited.

He told me to take it up with Central Script Editorial Administration. Until we received an official response from them, however, I was to put my arm around the heroine's shoulder and sing, sotto voce, the "Internationale" into her ear. I would not. Valentin was furious. I was doing this to him always, he said, trying to Westernize my role. In a fit, he communicated my insolence to those responsible for tapping telephones and breaking car windshields.

I visited a friend's dacha just outside Moscow for two days, hoping to get my mind away. When I arrive back Monday, what do you think I found? No telephone tap. No broken car windshield. No one even trails me. But they had painted my walls. Such trouble they go to. They had broken in and covered Innocent Peach with a mucous brown, color of the glistening muck left behind by snails.

I saw Valentin once more before I left. Our barge movie was complete, and won many awards at Tashkent Film Festival. The awards turned him sweet. He said beauty of my acting raised tears to his eyes every time he saw the picture. I hold no grudges against Valentin. Is impossible not to love a little the person who loves what you create.

At open cattle calls you read for casting director or even assistant casting director. Some harassed-looking girl with big eyeglass frames. But this Solly Stein, he is particular: he wants to see us himself. He arrives perfectly at ten o'clock, driving a sea-green Rolls-Royce. The license plate says REEL. His eyes, I noticed, matched perfectly the color of his car.

The reputation of Solly Stein says he is fat, big-hearted, and meticulous. In truth, he is some form of modern-day holy. I have not had any acting job since I came to Los Angeles one year ago. I have no agent. I have not membership in SAG, AFTRA, those suspiciously initialed, closed organizations to which you must belong to get paying acting jobs. I go only to open cattle calls. Commercials for cold medicine, breakfast cereals. Outer-space pictures in need of exotic alien beauties. I tried, along with eight hundred others, for role of International Tampax Spokeswoman. Just for experience, I took a job as a corpse in a student film production. I was fired when the nineteen-year-old director said I looked too old dead. He said my face sagged when I lay on my side. I am thirty-six.

But this Solly Stein, this heavy, green-eyed man with a thick pink dash on his neck from it looks like a tracheotomy operation, goes through my résumé with a silver mechanical pencil. He underlines. He jots in the margins. In one year, not one Hollywood producer has studied my résumé like this. A silly old feeling comes, which I get always for my directors: I want to make a baby with this Solly Stein.

As he reads and I wait, and all those beautiful actresses sweat outside, and his assistant pushes back her cuticles with eraser of her pencil, I confess to him my Hollywood failure.

"In Soviet Union, all you need is degree from Leningrad Institute of Theater and to be on right side of the Party. Acting parts come like airplanes waiting to land."

"It's hard, no doubt about it," he says. "But one day . . ."

He talks and reads at the same time, something I cannot do, even in Russian. But I feel as good as though he awarded me the part. "When I was coming through Vienna on my way here, I had appointment with a guy from American Embassy. He gave me good tips. One, be on time. Two, have initiative. I think more émigrés do not have this initiative because meaning to them isn't clear. My English is damn near perfect, but even I have to look it up." I admit I play a little the role of a fresh-faced immigrant, but it amuses him. He laughs. It was deep and raspy, his laugh, like full garbage cans dragged over asphalt.

"I see here you did a picture with Elem," he says.

"You know Elem Yeravansky? He is such a brilliant guy! And young! Did you know he is forty-two years only?"

"I just met him briefly at Cannes."

"I work with him on film called *Keep Your Guts*. Is about a woman heavy truck driver, me. Do not confuse with heavy *woman* truck driver—although it was necessary to put on some kilos for the role. I also did my own stunt driving. That title is bad translation. It should be *Keep Your Wits*." I allow a *v* to slip in instead of *w* on "wits." I know better, but I am auditioning for a tantalizing émigré, right?

"*Keep Your Vits*?" He laughs very hard, but except his big face, nothing on him moves. His elegant cream-colored shirt is so starched, so ironed, it holds him in like a girdle. On table behind where he sits he has a Styro-foam cup of black coffee and a can of pink grapefruit juice. He sips first from one, then the other. My mouth shivers at the thought of those tastes together. "Charming," he says. "In fact, perfect. No, wait. I know this." He thinks, running his little finger under the top fold of his ear. "*Ochin khorosho*. Right?"

"Perfect," I say.

"I took two semesters in college," he says.

After my audition I go to meet my friend Claire at Thai Palace in West Los Angeles. She is a girl I know from Slavic Languages Department where I work teaching Russian. When I arrive, I see Thai Palace is demolished. Claire and I ate together there last Wednesday only, but now in its place is a huge hole. At the bottom of the hole sits a yellow tractor machine for lifting dirt.

Just then Claire pulls up. Out passenger window of her car she yells, "Can you believe this? I called last night to see when they opened for lunch, and they told me twelve o'clock." She suggests another restaurant, down the street.

Claire is secretary of Slavic Languages Department, also a screenwriter. She has taken me under her wing about Hollywood. When I first knew her, she was a shy, earnest girl. She dressed all the time in Levi blue jeans. Then she got an affair with our writer in residence, also an émigré. She wrote a screenplay about her and this man, a tender Soviet-American love story, which no one wanted. People loved it, she said, but they did not want it. They said it was beautiful, brilliant, but they would not return her telephone calls. Someone said if she set it in Mexico and added an extraterrestrial, they would certainly want it. It broke her heart to do this, but she did it, then they lost interest completely. They said that Russians had been Done.

Hollywood poisoned her system. She suspects even the menu. "This *says* Australian wild boar. What d'you want to bet they're just pork chops?" When our waitress comes, Claire asks about this.

"The boars are raised in Arkansas but slaughtered here. It comes with an Indonesian mint sauce. I had it yesterday."

"So they aren't really from Australia."

"No, but the breed is."

Claire has an ability to arch one eyebrow only. This eyebrow is an alarm sensitive to any form of deception. It leaps up now under her curly reddish-brown bangs. She orders salad and a banana milk shake. After our waitress leaves, she says, "They can't very well be *wild* if they're *raised* in Arkansas, can they?" She pulls up her foot and sits on it, anxious to hear everything. "Well, is there any reason to hope?"

"There is always reason to hope."

Chastened a little, she looks down at her fork. "I mean, what happened? Did he like you? Tell me from the beginning. You went to the office, and the secretary handed you a clipboard with a pencil attached by a dirty string. . . ." Her hazel eyes make happy crescents over her big cheeks. This is a joke that goes between us. At my first cattle call, many months ago, she demanded to know all details. I mentioned the dirty string tying the pencil to the clipboard. She interpreted this several ways: it was low-budget production; the role for which I was auditioning was unimportant; the secretary was trying to find little ways to irritate the casting director, who was her lover.

"This string was virgin," I say. "I was first one at the audition. There is place on sign-in sheet where you are supposed to write who is your agent. I wrote, 'No agent, but I was famous actress in Moscow.' "

"You're *kidding*," says Claire. "Either they'll think that's really cute or really stupid. No, fresh—they'll say you're fresh. Or a crackpot. What else?"

I tell her all I can remember. You know those people who can stare at you a long time without blinking? She is one. She says nothing is unimportant in decoding the absurdity of Hollywood.

"How does he look? Last year he was in some big car wreck. His car flipped over twice on Mulholland."

"He has scars on his forehead and neck. He is big guy too, out of shape. You know how people on diets look panicky a little? That was him." I tell about the black coffee and grapefruit juice.

Claire laughs. "Maybe you made him nervous. When is the callback sheet up?"

"He said he will get back to me. He said if it wasn't this, then perhaps something else. He called me perfect."

Both Claire's eyebrows shoot up under her bangs. She is astonished. "He said *that*? He said those *exact* words? How did it go? You finished reading and got ready to leave, and what did he say?"

I repeated it. "Do you think it's real?"

"It sounds real. What reason would he have to get your hopes up?" In silence, we thought. Claire says figuring out reasons why Hollywood people do what they do is like trying to count germs in a public toilet.

A week, then two.

My telephone has power; alive but silent. I cup my palm along the gentle beige curve of the receiver, caressing my future. I try to draw a ring from those thin colored wires inside. One hot evening, I stand outside my apartment building, pretending to enjoy a sooty red sunset. I cock my head to the wires, listening, so I can know what a call sounds like going into my apartment. The sun drops behind the houses across the street. The wires chirr, bip, hum with calls for my neighbors.

My own mind whirs, day and night: he was called out of town, he is busy rewriting, the Fourth of July weekend, he is sick, dead, his assistant lost my telephone number, she transposed the numbers by mistake, she dropped it and it became stuck on sole of her shoe. One day I call to make sure his office is still there, then hang up quick when someone answers.

Claire tells me if he calls and I am not home (when am I not home? I never leave my telephone), he will never call back. "You need an answering machine. If you don't have an answering machine, he'll think you're not serious about being an actress."

I sell some Russian amber I managed to sneak through Immigration, to purchase most expensive model in the store. I somehow believe the more money I spend, the bigger sacrifice I make, the more chance I have of a telephone call. I set up the machine and leave. The longer I stay out of my apartment, the more chance Solly Stein has to call. I drive my Datsun around Beverly Hills, race up and down Sunset Boulevard admiring billboards, go to a movie, the laundromat, eat falafels. When I return at night, the cold red eye of my answering machine stares back at me so cruel. No messages.

"I'm not surprised," says Claire. "When he said he'd call, it really meant you should call him. It meant that at least you wouldn't have to go and hang out with everyone else, waiting in the street for the callback sheet to be posted. You've been promoted to a more privileged level of misery."

Slavic Languages Department holds no summer classes, so Claire is alone to tend our office. I come and eat lunch with her almost every day. Pages of her screenplay are spread all over the floor. There is no air-conditioning in our old humanities building, so Claire looks every day dressed for the beach.

"Okay. If I should call, I call."

"Well, not Monday, because that's the beginning of the week, and not Tuesday, because that's when all the *important* people who didn't call Monday call. Wednesday's not bad, but by then he'll already be behind from Monday and Tuesday. Thursday and Friday are out because that's the end of the week." She arches her eyebrow, a little smug with her logic. "In other words, even though you're supposed to call them, it'll always be a bad time."

"You are as rule-bound as any Soviet," I say.

I pull her telephone across the desk to where I sit. While I dial, she says, "It's lunchtime now. No one'll be in the office until after two-thirty at the earliest. Now's the *worst* time to call." She peels open her sandwich, one of those that appear to be meat but are truly mashed-up beans. I watch her pick out the tomatoes and toss them into garbage can beside her desk.

After many rings, a breathless voice answers. "SollyStein'sofficecan-youpleasehold?" She is gone before I can speak, then she's back. "Thanks for holding."

"Mr. Solly Stein, is he there, please?"

"Who may I say is calling?"

"Tanya Zlopak. I au—"

"One moment, please."

She goes. I perspire all over. My scalp. In between my legs. The receiver is slick in my hand. I smile weakly at Claire. She grins and winks, the mashed bean sandwich poking out her cheek.

"Hiya! How have you been?" This is an unfamiliar voice.

"Excuse me, I wait for Mr. Solly Stein, please."

"Tanya, this is Echo Parchman. I auditioned you with Solly." Ah ha, the assistant.

"Hello, yes. Mr. Stein says he is going to call me, and I was not hearing, so—"

Claire whispers, "Tell them you have another offer and you need to know today." I wave her away.

"Of course!" says Echo Parchman. "This was for . . ."

I am confused. If she remembers auditioning me, doesn't she know what she auditioned me for? "I tried for the role of older but still alluring Russian émigré in his new—"

"Oh, right! Let me see what's happened with that."

I am on hold for some time. Inside the telephone I hear a gentle *tick tick tick*, like a faraway bomb. I stare out the window. A row of palm tree tops rest on the lower ledge. We are on the third floor. They are the strangest trees on earth.

Echo Parchman returns. "Tanya, hiya. Listen, Solly needs to talk to you, but he's tied up right now. When is a good time for him to reach you?"

"Oh, anytime. I have answering machine on my telephone—"

"Does Tuesday the twenty-fourth sound good?"

"July twenty-fourth?" This is three weeks away.

"Terrific. Thanks for checking in, Tanya."

"Uh, thank you."

"Thank *you*."

I hang up. You know the look of people coming off those amusement park rides that go upside down and backwards at eighty miles an hour? That was my look.

Claire reaches over and squeezes my arm. "The thing about this place is that there's always the illusion of things happening when really nothing is happening. Solly Stein's probably sitting in his office right now eating some dietetic gourmet lunch and reading *Variety*. He probably hasn't even *thought* about casting this movie."

Claire was right. He had not thought about it. If he had, he would not have awarded the role of the sensual, worldly Russian émigré, a character whom he described to me at my audition as "an aging beauty born into prerevolutionary-style gentility," to a twenty-three-year-old rock-and-roll singer who has gained her reputation not even singing, but by television commercials for panty hose.

I did not learn I was passed over by receiving a telephone call on Tuesday, July 24. On Tuesday, July 24, I received no telephone call. Not Wednesday, not Thursday either. On Friday I purchased a weekly *Variety* at a newsstand on the corner of Hollywood and Las Palmas. It was on second page, the announcement that this panty hose person wins the role.

I telephoned Solly Stein from Hollywood Boulevard. An anonymous, filthy pay telephone. The receiver was greasy, someone had urinated on the yellow pages. Traffic dragged by. I could hardly hear when I was put through to Echo Parchman. I explain situation. How Solly Stein was going to call me, then didn't, how I read about the role in *Variety*, how he had said there might be something else in the movie if the leading role didn't work out. Echo Parchman said she was surprised he had not called, but he was now on vacation for three weeks. Is it possible he could telephone me in August sometime?

I have never wasted time trying to understand why people do what they do. Is Soviet personality trait. You ask too many questions and you don't get any kind of work, ever, period. I say sure, he can call me whenever. I hang up. I could go right home and lock myself in with the television until I teach again my Russian classes in September, but it would be admitting my immigration was for nothing, that I might have just stayed in Moscow playing forever good-natured Socialist heroines, making love to my vindictive Valentin in my brown-walled apartment.

I force myself back to newspaper stand to buy a *Dramalogue* to see about more cattle calls. The newspaper girl, who has the five-inch fingernails of an old Chinese sage, slips me her copy for free. "You look like you could use some strokes," she says.

From Claire: "He probably *did* really like you. He probably *did* think you were perfect. But this rock singer is hot. She's what they call *bankable*.

She's completely wrong for the part, sure, but they'll rewrite. The studio probably wouldn't let him make the movie unless he cast her. That's where the major-league bullshit comes in. If he wants to make his movie, he's got to cast a bubble-brained cretin from a panty hose ad." She has in her eyes that green-eyed gleam. Her wild eyebrows lurch up and down.

We are having dinner at a restaurant on Third Street where Claire says many Hollywood people eat and perform business. I have held off telling her my unhappy news for almost a month, just to avoid her enthusiastic cynicism. The people here are mostly men, suntanned and overworked, in Levi blue jeans and expensive leather shoes. They eat large salads and scribble on yellow pads anchored under their elbows. Claire says all the waitresses are also actresses. She says perhaps it would be better for me to have a job here instead of teaching Russian. She says I need exposure. I need the right kind of people to notice me. I need a shtick. I need, I need.

I concentrate on looping a green noodle over my fork. My neck is tight. "All I need is opportunity to show my talent."

"It'd be great if it were that simple. I read an article about what it takes to make it in Hollywood. They had a list. Number one, connections; number two, perseverance; three was 'being fun to work with'; and four was talent. Can you believe it?"

I don't answer. I make motions to leave.

"Are we done? Don't you want dessert?"

"No. I would like to go."

"What's wrong? I haven't depressed you, have I? I only want you to know how hard it is. A lot of émigrés think that just because this is America, things'll be easy."

"I know it is hard, Claire. But I am unable to hear it anymore, okay?"

We divide the bill and go outside. On western end of street, the sun slides through streaks of purple and red. Claire and I stand on the curb, waiting for a break in traffic so we can cross. I point at the sky. "Is it true that poisons cause this great beauty?"

Claire turns her head west but doesn't really look. "Probably."

"Now *you* are depressed," I say.

She says nothing. In the silence of people who have argument, we watch the cars pass. The light at the end of the block turns red, halting traffic. We are about to walk, but several cars continue through the intersection. The one in the lane closest to us is a beautiful sea-green Rolls-Royce, license plate REEL.

I feel as though someone has dropped an anvil on me. I want to cower, to run back in the restaurant, to wave and stamp feet. "Solly Stein," I cry to Claire.

"What? Where?"

The Rolls slides toward us, close to the curb. Solly Stein does not see us. He pays no attention to driving. He cranes his head to see whose car is in parking lot of this popular Hollywood restaurant. He is also eating something, madly chewing, madly looking, not at all watching the road.

My opportunity. My connection. It will pass in leather-upholstered, air-conditioned oblivion. I have only several seconds to consider my options. Is it a wonder, being an actress of many years, an actress once well known and well loved in Soviet Union, that I opt for most dramatic one?

I lunge into the street. As I hurl myself down on the asphalt, in the silent, endless instant before screeching of brakes and Claire yelling my name and my shoes skidding off, it comes to my mind that I am dealing in Hollywood. This strange powerful person might just run me over, *thump thump, thump thump*, like driving over a dead piece of shag carpet dropped on the freeway.

But I have faith in this stunt, which I performed myself in *Keep Your Wits*, and somehow, crazy crazy, in my director, Solly Stein. The idea is to act hit before you really are. As I fall, the bottom of the license plate slices into the meaty part of my calf. My skirt scrapes up over my thighs. My legs are good, not muscular but shapely. Sensual and world-weary. The nice legs of a *real* Soviet émigré. I leave the skirt up. I want him to suffer. Twenty-three-year-old panty hose queens! Who can believe this world! My eyes are closed. Heat and wet flow from the leg wound. Claire squeaks out my name. A car door slams. Frantic footsteps, expensive-soled shoes.

"Oh, God. Christ, no." Solly Stein's voice is torn.

This is perfect. Much better than the actor playing opposite me in *Keep Your Wits*, who ordered me brusquely to stand up and continue on for the sake of our Motherland.

Claire kneels next to me, asking about broken bones, spinal injury, wondering aloud if I can be moved. Her purse she has slid under my head, the end of a hairbrush pokes into my scalp. She is so practical now, in what she thinks is an emergency. Why not this practicality about Hollywood?

I open my eyes. I don't want Claire to think I'm in too bad shape. To get a dazed look, I push everything out of focus. Behind her I see the creamy linen mound that is Solly Stein. He stands with his arms limp, utterly useless. An ugly dark mass covers his chest. Blood? How can it be?

Not blood, no. I would feel less bad, less ashamed, if it were. Then it would be only the inside of his body paraded out for all to see, instead of the inside of his mind. It is chocolate, the ghastly smear. His chubby fingers grasp a king-size candy bar. *Now 47% More!* says one edge of the wrapper. A chocolaty clot of nuts and caramel hangs from the lapel of his cream linen jacket.

Some people appear out of the restaurant. They know Solly Stein. Everyone knows Solly Stein. They clap his shoulders. What happened? What happened? Tough going, man. A few look down at me curiously. Is she all right? A little joke goes around, started by a guy I recognize from a popular television series, that the candy bar is the murder weapon. One man slips a card into my hand. He says he's a lawyer.

"A lawyer? Christ." Solly Stein's shoulders heave, his face is weary, tearless but wrecked. "I'm through."

I do not want public humiliation for this man, and certainly not his career to be through. But I have already begun. I have already left Valentin, relinquished my Soviet citizenship, sold my amber. There is nowhere to go. I will persevere. I will be fun to be with.

"Please," I say, "no lawyer. I am all right."

"I'm calling an ambulance," says Claire.

"No, no ambulance," I say, rising on one elbow.

"You need an ambulance," says Solly Stein, not convinced. He moves a few steps toward me.

I take his hand in both of mine and pull him down to me. "Please, I am very poor. I have no moneys. Is embarrassing. I have no insurance for hospital. I be okay."

"Tanya, you have to see a doctor," says Claire. "Look at your leg. You probably need stitches." She stands, wipes her hands, bits of gravel trickling off the heels of her palms. She, of the judgmental dark eyebrow, reader of subtext, expert on Hollywood deception, believes this is an accident. I dare not wink. I dare not whisper, take advantage, mingle with these people, pass to Solly Stein the screenplay I know is stashed in your purse.

"No, I am fine. No ambulance." I wobble a little, hang on Solly Stein's arm as I stand. "My shoes."

One of them was slung into the street, then run over. Solly Stein, grateful for something to do, scoots to retrieve it. He tries to push it back into shape, buffs it on his sleeve.

"We can go to my doctor. He'll take care of the leg," says Solly Stein.

Claire folds her arms. "She should go to the hospital."

"I am all right. This will work." I try to make my eyes communicate to her my trick.

"Please, what did you say your name was? Tawny?"

Solly Stein does not remember. Is just as well. Then I am not the eager émigré he would not call back. I am a new actress. The one who was helpless and foreign, who would not sue him, who gently took the candy bar from his fat paw and threw it into the gutter, who rode away with him in his Rolls-Royce, straight into the shameless Los Angeles sunset.

"Tanya," I say. "Tanya Zlopak."

There is another fact of Hollywood I will use this day to my advantage: in Los Angeles, to drive anywhere is forty-five minutes. Forty-five minutes I have now to speak to Solly Stein. Not of my brilliance, but of his. To speak, actress to director, of his technique, his sensitivity, his ability to extract the most impossible performances. To summon into his sea-green eyes that look I often confuse with love. That look which says, Let us make something together.

BIRDS OF THE MOON ●

lisa tuttle

THE BIRDS WHO LIVE on the moon have heads very like the heads of men; but they are earless, and their faces, which wear no expression, look curiously dead. They fly slowly, heavily, through the airless night and perch alone on bleak rock and in crater walls.

Amalie woke suddenly, as if cold talons had closed about her wrist. Her husband's slow, regular breathing filled the room like moonlight: he slept. She turned her head on the pillow to look at him, and froze at the sight of his open eyes. They were open, but saw only in his dreams.

Before he went to the moon her husband had slept like any man, with eyes closed. Sometimes Amalie knew that her husband had never come back from the moon: as surely as the men who had died up there he had left the most essential part of himself still circling in space. And now his eyes stared perpetually beyond her, at the harsh landscapes of the moon.

Amalie moved on the bed, away from her husband; slid to the edge and got up. He did not stir. She was wide awake, almost alarmingly so. She rarely felt so awake in the daytime, and she wondered if perhaps she were only dreaming she was awake: that would explain the peculiar quality of her awareness.

In the hall she paused before Carmen's door, then opened it quietly. The room was brightly lit by the moon: the curtains were open and the window cranked ajar. Amalie scarcely glanced at Carmen's empty bed; almost without needing to think she had crossed the room and was at the window. She pushed it open and leaned out. The driveway glittered like snow in the moonlight, and the grass that edged it looked black.

And there was Carmen, in a white nightgown that reached to her ankles, her feet bare, her arms outstretched, whirling around on the lawn in a silent dance. Her face was solemn, the dance a ritual of madness. Her mother hesitated, her palms flat against the window sill, ready to climb out after her. Then she turned away and went through the house to the front door.

"Carmen!" Her voice shivered the still air. The little girl turned her face away from the flat, silver face of the moon and stopped dancing. Eyes down, moving like a badly made doll, she went into the house. Her mother tried to touch her, but Carmen shrank away, drawing herself close to the wall, her body repelling human touch. Her mother, knowing this response, let her hands drop like useless wings to her sides.

Her husband had turned over in bed.

"Jim?" she said. The room was silent; she could not hear him breathing. "Jim?"

He started to breathe again, and Amalie let out her own breath. She wondered if he were awake and pretending to sleep. She got back into bed. They slept back to back, a wall of air between them.

The birds who live on the moon are built in a peculiar fashion: large and heavy-bodied with wings small for their size. When at rest their wings fit into their sides and seem to vanish. Their feet are large, ugly and strong: their grip is so powerful that the birds can sleep in any position—upside down, projecting outward—so long as the rock they anchor themselves to is firmly fixed.

Carmen set the table for breakfast, putting down the placemats and the silverware and the napkins, the plates, the cereal bowls, a glass for milk and a smaller glass for juice, and coffee cups in saucers for Mummy and Daddy. Carmen moved in metronomic rhythm, taking the same number of steps on every trip to the table, working out her movements as if they were the steps to a boring but precise dance number.

Amalie scrambled eggs and watched her. Jim came in, dressed for work. She thought she remembered that he had told her he wouldn't have to go in today; that they didn't need him today; but she didn't ask. He would only tell her she was wrong. And did it matter? He could go where he wanted, tell her what he liked.

"Sleep well?" she asked.

"Sure. I'll just have coffee."

She wondered if he would go to the Center today, just as if reporting for work. She wondered if that were where he spent most of his time. Or perhaps he would go into Houston, to the museum with the moon rocks and the capsules scarred by space and re-entry and now outfitted with dummy astronauts. She remembered the first time she and Jim had been taken on a tour of NASA, when he had first been transferred to Houston, before he had even told her there was a possibility he might go to the moon (but she had guessed)—she remembered a field, part of which had been covered for some reason with those chalk-white oyster shells so popular for paving dirt roads and driveways and parking lots.

Their guide, joking, had pointed to this section of field and said it was the simulated moonscape used in training astronauts to walk on the moon. Jim had leaped off the side of the road onto the shells and pulled a stray weed that pushed up through them. "Yes, Houston Control, there *is* life on the moon!"

She thought about it now, that small stretch of dead-white shell and rock surrounded by Texas fields. She thought of Jim standing there and wishing for the moon.

"You should eat breakfast," Amalie said. "Breakfast is the most important meal of the day."

"I know. I'll have coffee."

Carmen was taking Cheerios out of the box in handfuls and layering them into her cereal bowl.

"Carmen, you want some nice scrambled eggs?"

Carmen shook her head three times sharply back and forth and went on with the business of the Cheerios.

Amalie looked at the eggs with dislike. She was never hungry in the morning; Jim rarely wanted anything more than coffee, and Carmen wouldn't be interested in anything else until she had finished preparing and eating her Cheerios—by which time the eggs would be cold. She wondered why she bothered, and scraped the steaming eggs into the disposal.

"Working today?" she asked Jim. He had ignored the place set for him at the table and was leaning against the wall, blowing on his coffee.

"Some stuff to do, yeah," he said. "I may be back for lunch."

"I'll be out with Carmen until two," Amalie poured herself a cup of coffee and watched her daughter bathing the neatly stacked oat circles with milk. "Anything special you want for dinner?"

He shook his head, sipped his coffee.

She went on in the same tone. "You were sleeping with your eyes open again."

"Bullshit."

"Jim, I saw you."

He shook his head.

"I did."

He shrugged and put down his coffee. "Well, so what? I don't believe you, but so what? So I've taken to sleeping with my eyes open—it shouldn't keep *you* awake; it's not like I snored."

"It's eerie."

"It's eerie. I find it even eerier that you should keep waking up and catching me at it." He turned his head, dismissing her. "Daddy's going to work now, baby girl."

"Goodbye, Daddy," said Carmen. She did not look up from her cereal when she spoke, and Amalie felt a deepening of her depression. Every morning she took Carmen's response as a signal of how the day would go—when she looked at her father and spoke it would be a good day. When she did not look at him, it would be a bad day.

"Bye bye," said Amalie listlessly. Her lips and Jim's bumped like passing strangers.

"Bye bye," he said. "Bye bye, Carmen."

The birds who live on the moon are black and white. The moon is black and white, the landscape stark and pure. These birds have no conception of color; they know only darkness and light. The brilliancy of unhindered sunlight; the blackness of a cold night. They sleep in black shadows cast by white rocks. Their black eyes, pupil-less, soulless, have no lids; are always staring.

In the supermarket the colors screamed at her, the bright boxes, jars, cans and bottles seemed to leap off the shelves, daring her, taunting her, begging her to choose, to buy. They strained towards her in the greenish fluorescent light, and the sound of cash registers and muzak, the nearness of other people, scraped at her nerves. She felt the familiar beginning signals of a migraine: the sense of dissociation, the difficulty she had in focusing her eyes to read the names of products, the tingling in her right hand.

She decided to leave without buying anything, to get home to bed before the numbing headache began. Carmen was with the doctor; she had two hours before she had to show up for her part in the day's therapy. She would go home, crawl into darkness and seek out the cool silence of sleep.

"Mrs. Carter." She heard the voice for the first time, but was aware that it had spoken her name once or twice before she heard. She turned and faced a young woman, a stranger with burned-looking eyes and lank, light brown hair. She looked slightly like a babysitter Amalie had once hired, but she did not know this woman.

"You're Mrs. Carter."

"Yes."

"I knew it. I'd seen pictures of you, and I followed you here."

"What do you want?"

"I just want to talk to you—I just want to tell you something you should know."

Amalie had the momentary conviction that this woman did not exist; that this irrationally behaving stranger was only another symptom of her oncoming migraine.

"I have to go," Amalie said vaguely, walking backwards slowly.

"Wait. I'm having an affair with your husband." She looked triumphant. Amalie stopped.

"And I want to tell you that he loves me, and he'd divorce you in a hot second if he wasn't worried about hurting your—his—little girl. But I know I'd be a hundred times better mother to her—she'd be happy with me 'cause I'd love her—and when he realizes that . . . well, I just want to tell you that you've lost your husband and you aren't ever going to get him back, so why don't you just make things easy on all of us and give him a divorce?"

Amalie laughed.

The other woman looked at her, confused, then recovered. "Oh, it's true. Don't you think you can laugh it off. I could tell you things about him so's you'd have to know it's true. We had breakfast this morning at my apartment and then we made love before he went to work. And how about last Wednesday night? When he called and said he was at a poker game in Galveston and since it was so late and he didn't have much gas he was going to spend the night at his buddy's house. Well, let me tell you: he was with me, he wasn't in Galveston at no poker game, he was in Houston sleeping with me at my apartment." Her words tumbled and stumbled over each other and out of her mouth, the pitch of her voice going up, her accent becoming more country, more East Texas. Amalie found the noise as annoying as the insistent golds and yellows and oranges stacked around her, glaring in the evil green light of the supermarket. She had to get out.

She didn't want to laugh any more. She felt too sick for laughter. But the claims of this woman deserved nothing better than ridicule. She didn't doubt that Jim was having an affair with her, but it was unimportant, the woman was no threat—there was nothing to threaten. The fact that she had sought Amalie out must mean that she saw in Amalie, the wife, some danger, but that also was untrue. Amalie could have told her that Jim had been lost, irretrievably lost, years before, to the moon. The moon was his only mistress, his compelling disease.

Amalie walked away from her shopping cart and the woman who loved her husband, and drove home, squinting to see through the pain of her headache and the tiny, glowing moon which hung in the far right corner of her vision.

The birds who live on the moon make no sound—they have no vocal chords—nor do they communicate with each other in any way. Each lives alone, and although groups may cluster together, may roost all together on one wall, each bird knows itself to be forever alone.

Carmen in company with other people was like a young animal placed among the wrong litter, the stranger in the tribe. She kept to herself, she tried to keep herself safe from the importunities of others and remain in communion only with herself, but the effort drained her. Whenever she came home, Carmen always went straight to her room and closed the door. Alone in her room, performing the necessary rituals with her toys, Carmen would calm herself.

Jim called to say that he would not be home for dinner, and Amalie wondered if the woman from the supermarket were standing nearby, feeling triumphant. If tonight she would try to bind Amalie's husband to herself with her flesh and later that night stare hopelessly at his open, dreaming eyes.

Amalie took lamb chops out of the freezer and set them out to defrost. The house was silent. Carmen, who never made any noise, was in her room. But once she had reflected gratefully on the silence of the house, Amalie realised it was not nearly silent enough. Small noises erupted unpredictably, intruding upon the stillness, and there were sounds that went on and on, like the steady buzz of the clock on the wall and the hum of the refrigerator. Outside birds were chirping, all out of harmony with one another, and she could hear the soft wind-rushing sound of cars on the freeway.

The living room was better. When she had shut out the outside world (go, plane, I don't hear you; birds, cars, bugs do not exist) there was nothing to hear, nothing to bother her. Amalie leaned back in a chair and closed her eyes. Now there was nothing but darkness and silence, the way it must be on the moon. Only the sounds of her own body. She had tried to sleep, earlier, but had been unable, and so the migraine, when it passed, left behind a residue, an unpleasant pressure behind her eyes and a rawness to her nerves.

She wondered if Jim had been considering divorce. She wasn't certain if the idea was strange or not. They had not been happy together for a long time, but they had never spoken of separating. They simply went on, not as if they were content, but simply as if there were no other road.

Amalie opened her eyes and realized she had been dozing. The house was unnaturally still. Outside the evening air was greying quickly towards night.

"Carmen?"

The air seemed to wrap itself around the name and absorb the sound. Amalie, ill at ease, stood up. She felt as if the rest of the world had vanished and she had been left here alone.

"Carmen?" Amalie stood outside Carmen's door, hand hesitating in the air before the knob. She let her hand fall against the door, knuckles grazing the wood in a light knock. "Sweetheart? You want to come set the table for dinner?"

No reply. Wondering if Carmen had gone outside, Amalie opened the door.

Carmen was sitting on the floor, within her usual circle of dolls and toys, each one in its assigned place. But around the toys, in a greater circle, stood six strange, large birds. They had big round heads with faces— human faces, not the beaky visages of birds—and ponderous black and white feathered bodies. Standing, they were taller than Carmen sitting in their midst.

Amalie was frozen in the doorway by the sight. The birds did not look at her; Carmen did not move. Amalie broke the tableau with a stumbling run into the room.

"Get! Get!" She shouted harshly, breathlessly, as if she were shooing away ducks or nosy dogs bothering her child. She waved her arms at them, but they did not move, and finally one outswinging arm touched a bird, and she recoiled from the touch. The bird was cold, unnaturally, deadly cold. The bird turned its head and looked at her. Then all of the birds began to move; they fell into file and waddled past her—she drew away— through the door and down the hall. When the last of the birds had left the room Carmen looked up at her mother.

"Is it dinner?" she asked.

Amalie stared at her.

"Is it dinner?"

"Carmen—what—?"

"Is it dinner?" Carmen held out her hand and looked at the Mickey Mouse watch on her wrist. She held one finger to it, taking the pulse of it. "Seven o'clock. Is it dinner?"

Amalie nodded, helpless, and Carmen nodded in turn, then carefully, in order, lifted her toys out of the circle and carried them to the shelves where they belonged.

They were in the living room. Amalie avoided looking in the room as she passed, but she knew they were there. As she broiled the lamb chops and emptied a can of corn into a pot she was as aware of the birds in the living room—dreaming their waking dreams, asleep yet fully conscious— as she was of Carmen, precisely placing three settings at the table a few feet away.

When she went to bed that night the birds were still in the living room, still waiting for whatever they were waiting for. Amalie lay in bed and could not sleep. After a while she heard Jim's car in the driveway, heard him come in and fix himself a drink. Then there was silence for a long time. He didn't say anything, or put on the light, when he came into the bedroom, and she pretended to be asleep. Through her lashes she watched Jim stand by the window and stare out for a long time at the full moon and the quiet street. Then he pulled the curtains to (but they fell apart: a shaft of moonlight spilled across the floor), undressed and climbed in the far side of the bed. Amalie lay still, listening to his breathing become deeper and more even.

She was lying on her side, facing away from Jim, facing the door. Her eyes were open, and so she saw the birds come in. The door was slightly ajar and the lead bird simply pushed it open and then they all filed in.

Amalie began to tremble. The birds walked (silently: there was no sound, as there should have been, of their talons pulling at the carpet) around the bed, to Jim's side, and she knew that there they would arrange themselves in a semi-circle and stand and stare at her husband.

She moved closer to him, trying not to whimper. Her trembling shook him, and she burrowed against his back, wishing away the birds. Jim moved and mumbled. He reached over without turning, patted her, and said, "Sleep, sleep," in an absent way.

She wanted to wake him and make him look at the birds, but she was afraid that if she did he wouldn't see them. And they would still be there.

She must have fallen asleep, for she became aware that the room was darker, the moon no longer shining through the window, but now on the other side of the house.

She sat up and looked across Jim to the other side of the room. The birds were gone: there were no dark shapes crouching there, or at least no dark shapes she could not identify as furniture.

For a moment she felt relief. Then she was more alert than before. Carmen.

Carmen was not in her room. The bed was empty. Again, the window was open. This time Amalie ran to the window and climbed out, scraping a bare leg on the brick of the house.

"Carmen!"

The six birds, grouped closely together, were waiting for Carmen to finish her dance to the moon. They would carry her, said their position, away to the moon where she would be alone and free, where she could pile loose rocks in orderly fashion and no one would bother her, no one would interrupt her rituals. They would be an undemanding family, let her perch among the rocks with them, ask her no questions.

"No!" cried Amalie in anguish. "Don't take her, please."

Carmen danced on, heedless. One bird turned its head and looked at Amalie, and she looked into its dead, chill face, its sphinx's face, and knew that she had misunderstood. They had not come for Carmen, but for her.

Jim had been to the moon and never come back; Carmen had no need to be taken there. Only Amalie longed for the moon and could not attain it.

The birds came to her, and as they drew in closer she felt the cold their bodies gave off the way earth animals gave off heat. They stood close together, in a line before her, and Amalie was reminded of how, in the fairy tale, Snow White sleeps across seven dwarf beds pushed together to take her giant body. Amalie lay down on them and wrapped her arms about one neck.

The birds began to run, and their bodies bumped beneath hers like a line of camels. Just as they left the ground (shifting beneath her like a waterbed) Amalie began to fear that they could not remain together, that they would separate and drop her. She clung tightly.

The birds flew on towards the moon, lifting and lowering their wings dangerously slowly. The birds who live on the moon do not, when they fly, have much gravity to contend with. They fly slowly and glide through breezeless space. The birds who live on the moon are singular and solitary; they depend on no others but themselves; they do not customarily travel in groups, and their rare sense of purpose is never retained long in the minds of more than one at a time.

Flying against the ponderous weight of the earth, with Amalie further weighing them down, the birds lost interest in her and began to separate, beating their wings more strongly now, aiming themselves at the moon, anxious now only to escape the earth's pull.

Amalie clung with all her might, and felt herself falling, as she had fallen so many times in dreams. Her arms ached, as much from the cold of the birds as from the strain of holding on. She was falling, and pulling the bird down with her. It swivelled its head and bit her on the arm with its large, square, hard teeth. She cried out in shock and pain, her grasp loosening, and the bird flew out from under her, and away up towards the moon again, and she fell.

She came to earth on a lonely road, jarred and shattered, face down, broken against the concrete. The moonlight picked out the whiteness of her skin and nightdress and made them glitter as if she were already no more than bones picked clean.

ABOUT THE AUTHORS ●

Meena Alexander (1951–) was born in Allhabad, India. She has taught literature in the U.S., France, and India, and her works include several books of poetry, essays, the short story collection, *Fault Lines*, and the novel, *Nampally Road*.

Isabel Allende (1924–), born in Lima, Peru, grew up in Chile and was later exiled to Venezuela during the military regime of General Pinochet. Her novels include *The House of the Spirits*, *Of Love and Shadows*, *Eva Luna*, and *The Infinite Plan*. She lives in California.

Dorothy Allison (1949–), born in Greenville, South Carolina, has won two Lambda Literary Awards—for best Small Press Book, and best Lesbian Book—for her short story collection *Trash*. Her novel *Bastard Out of Carolina* was nominated for the National Book Award in 1992.

Margaret Atwood (1939–), born in Ottawa, Canada, is a novelist, short story writer, and a poet. Her novels include *The Edible Woman, Surfacing, Life Before Man, The Handmaid's Tale*, and *The Robber Bride Groom*. Her short stories are collected in *Dancing Girls* and *Bluebeard's Egg*.

Alison Baker (1953–) lives in rural Oregon. Her fiction has appeared in the *Atlantic Monthly, Black Warrior Review, Kenyon Review* and other literary magazines. *How I Came West, and Why I Stayed* is her first book.

Lucia Berlin (1936–), born in Alaska, grew up in mining camps in Idaho, Montana, Arizona, and Chile. Her collection of stories *Homesick* won the American Book Award in 1991. Her work includes *Angels Laundromat, Phantom Pain, Safe and Sound,* and *So Long*.

Amy Bloom (1953–) is a practicing psychotherapist in Durham, Connecticut. Her first collection of short stories, *Come to Me,* was a finalist for the 1993 National Book Award.

Leonora Carrington (1917–), a painter and writer, was born in Lancashire, England. In 1937 she met Max Ernst and moved with him to Paris where she became a prominent figure of the Surrealist group. Her paintings and writings reflect an interest in magic, fantasy, and myth. Her books include *The Oval Lady and Other Stories, Six Surreal Stories, The Hearing Trumpet,* and *The House of Fear.*

Angela Carter (1940–1992) traveled and taught widely in Australia and the U.S., but lived in London. She is the author of nine novels including *The Magic Toyshop, Several Perceptions, The Infernal Desire Machines of Dr. Hoffman,* and *Wise Children,* and three collections of short stories. She translated and edited numerous collections of fairy and folk tales and wrote the screenplay for the 1984 film *The Company of Wolves,* based on her short story.

Fiona Cooper lives in Newcastle on Tyne, England. She is the author of *Rotary Spokes, Not the Swiss Family Robinson, Heartbreak, Heartbreak on the High Sierra, The Empress of the Seven Oceans,* and *Jay Loves Lucy.*

Beverley Daurio (1953–) lives in Stratford, Ontario, Canada, where she is editor-in-chief of The Mercury Press. She is the author of *His Dogs, Justice, Next in Line, Hell and Other Novels,* and a collection of poetry, *If Summer Had a Knife,* and the editor of four fiction anthologies.

Andrea Dworkin is the author of *Intercourse, Pornography: Men Possessing Women,* and the novels *Mercy* and *Ice and Fire.* "the wild cherries of lust" is from a collection of short stories, *the new womans broken heart,* published in 1980 by Frog-In-The-Well Press in San Francisco. Ms. Dworkin is the co-author of legislation recognizing pornography as a violation of the civil rights of women.

Debra Earling is a member of the Confederated Salish and Kootenai tribes of the Flathead Reservation. She holds a joint appointment in English and Native American Studies at the University of Montana. Her works include *Gathering Ground,* a book of poetry.

Carol Emshwiller (1921–) was born in Ann Arbor, Michigan. She is the author of *Joy in Our Cause, Verging on the Pertinent, Carmen Dog, The Start of the End of it All* and *Venus Rising*. She currently teaches writing at New York University.

Nina FitzPatrick is of Polish-Irish ancestry and lectures at Stockholm University, Sweden. Her stories are collected in *Fables of the Irish Intelligentsia*, which won the *Irish Times*, Aer Lingus Literature Prize for Fiction, later withdrawn after a dispute over her citizenship. She is the author of the novel, *The Loves of Faustyna*.

Janice Galloway (1956–), born in Kilwinning, Scotland, now lives in Glasgow. Her novel *The Trick is to Keep Breathing*, won the 1990 Book Award from the Scottish Arts Council. Her book *Blood* won the 1991 Scottish Book Award.

Josephine Hart (1942–), was born and educated in Ireland. She was a director of Haymarket Publishing, in London, before going on to produce a number of West End plays, including *The House of Bernarda Alba* by Federico García Lorca and *The Black Prince* by Iris Murdoch. She is the author of the novels *Sin* and *Damage*, which was made into a film directed by Louis Malle.

Diana Hartog (1942–) immigrated to Canada in 1971. Her books include *Matinee Light, Candy From Strangers*, and *Polite to Bees*. She lives in the Slocan Valley in British Columbia.

Bessie Head (1937–1986), born in Pietermaritzburg, South Africa, daughter of a white mother and Zulu father. She moved to Botswana in 1964 and began writing in 1969. Her writings include the novels *When Rain Clouds Gather, Maru, A Question of Power*, and a collection of short fiction, *A Collector of Treasures*.

Pam Houston has been a visiting professor of English at Denison University in Ohio, a part time river guide and a hunting guide. *Cowboys are My Weakness* is her first collection of short fiction.

Keri Hulme (1947–), born in Christchurch, New Zealand, won the New Zealand Book Award for Fiction, the Pegasus Award for Maori literature from Mobil Oil, and the Booker Prize, for her novel *Bone People*. Her other books include *Lost Possessions* and *Te Kaibau/The Windeater*.

Bev Jafek has won numerous awards for her short fiction, ranging from the Pushcart Prize and the Carlos Fuentes Award to inclusion in several volumes of *The Best American Short Stories*. A former Wallace E. Stegner Fellow in Fiction at Stanford University, she now lives in Pelham, New York. Her stories are collected in *The Man Who Took a Bite Out of His Wife and Other Stories*, published by The Overlook Press and shortlisted for the Crawford Award for Best New Fantasy Author of 1994.

Erica Jong (1942–), born in New York City, was a poet and scholar in the field of eighteenth century English literature when *Fear of Flying* catapulted her to fame in 1974. Since then she has written six more novels, including *How to Save Your Own Life* and *Any Woman's Blues*, six volumes of poetry, a book about Henry Miller, and the autobiography, *Fear of Fifty*.

Anna Kavan (1901–1968), born in France, lived, studied, and worked in the U.S. and Europe. Her works include *Ice, A Bright Green Field, Eagles Nest, Julia and the Bazooka, A Scarcity of Love, Asylum Piece*, and *Sleep Has His House*.

Karen Karbo (1957–) was born in Detroit, Michigan. Her first novel, *Trespassers Welcome Here*, won the GE Foundation Younger Writers Award and was nominated for the 1989 Pulitzer Prize. Her most recent novel is *The Diamond Lane* (Overlook/Tusk paperback). She lives in Portland, Oregon.

Evelyn Lau (1970–) is the author of *Runaway: Diary of a Street Kid* and the short story collection, *Fresh Girls*. In 1988 at the age of 18 she received a Canada Council Exploration grant and was judged the most promising writer by the Canadian Author's Association.

Tanith Lee (1947–) has won the World Fantasy Award and the August Derleth Award for her fiction. She has written for television and radio and published over forty books of fiction. Her works include the bestselling *Flat Earth* series and the four volume series *The Secret Books of Paradys*, published by The Overlook Press. She lives in England.

Jill McCorkle (1958–) teaches creative writing at Harvard University. She is the author of four widely acclaimed novels including *Ferris Beach*, and her short fiction has been published in many magazines and literary journals and collected in *Crash Diet*.

Elizabeth McCracken has received grants from the Michener Foundation, National Endowment for the Arts, and the Fine Arts Work Center in Provincetown. Her fiction has been collected in *Here's Your Hat What's Your Hurry*.

Ohba Minako (1930–), born in Tokyo, attended Tsuda College, and later moved with her husband to Alaska. In 1968 her work, *The Three Crabs* received the Gunzo New Writer Prize and the Akutagawa Prize. Her major works include *Funakui Mushi/Ship-Eating Termites*, and *Kiri no Tabi/The Foggy Journey*, for which she received the Women's literature prize.

Kathy Page (1958–), born in London, England, won the Eastern Arts Writer's Bursary in 1989. Her books include *Back in First Person*, *The Unborn Dreams of Clara Riley*, *Island Paradise*, and *As in Music and Other Stories*.

Rachel Pollack (1945–), born in Poughkeepsie, New York, writes both fiction and non-fiction. Her novel *Unquenchable Fire* won the 1988 Arthur C. Clarke Award. Her works include *Shining Woman Tarot*, *The New Tarot*, and *Seventy-Eight Degrees of Wisdom*.

A.N. Roquelaure (Anne Rice, 1941–), was born in New Orleans, Louisiana. She is the author of several novels including *Interview with a Vampire*, *Vampire Lestat*, *Queen of the Damned* and *The Tale of the Body Thief*. She writes erotica under the pen name A.N. Roquelaure.

Lorraine Schein's work has appeared in *The New York Quarterly*, *Semiotext(e)*, *Heresies*, *Women's Glib*, *Terminal Velocities*, and *Asylum Annual*. Her short fiction has been anthologized in *Memories and Visions: Women's Science Fiction* and *Dreams in a Minor Key*.

Mariarosa Sclauzero is the author of *Narcissism and Death* and *Marlene*. She lives in New York City.

Helen Simpson (1957–) was born in Bristol, England. Her collection of short fiction *Four Bare Legs in a Bed* won the Somerset Maugham Prize and the 1990 *Sunday Times* Young Writer of the Year award.

Christine Slater (1960–) was born in Toronto, Canada. She is the author of a collection of short stories, *Stalking the Gilded Boneyard*, and a novel, *The Small Matter of Getting There*.

Patti Smith (1946–), born in New Jersey, is both a poet and performer. Her collections of poetry include *Kodak*, *Seventh Heaven*, and *Witt*. She has received awards from numerous publications including *Creem* for performances in concerts and on recordings.

Darcey Steinke (1962–) is the author of two novels, *Up Through the Water* and *Suicide Blonde*. She lives in Brooklyn, New York.

Melanie Tem lives in Denver, Colorado. Her stories have appeared in such publications as *Isaac Asimov's Science Fiction Magazine, Fantasy Tales* and *Cemetary Dance* and the anthologies *Women of Darkness, Women of the West, Skin of the Soul, Final Shadows* and *Cold Shocks*. She is the author of the novels *Prodigal, Blood Moon*, and *Wilding*.

Sue Thomas is the author of the novel *Correspondence*, which was short-listed for the Heinemann Fiction Award and the Arthur C. Clarke Award, and the novel *Water*, both published by The Overlook Press. She teaches writing at the Nottingham Trent University.

Lisa Tuttle (1956–), born in Houston, Texas, has worked as a newspaper columnist and freelance journalist and has taught at the University of London. Her books include *Windhaven, Familar, Catwitch, Encyclopedia of Feminism, A Spaceship Built of Stone and Other Stories*, and *Heroines: Women Inspired by Women*.

Veronica Vera is the author of hundreds of articles on sex. Her experiences in the sex industry are documented in her video docu-diary "Portrait of a Sexual Evolutionary," which includes her testimony before the Senate Judiciary Committee describing her experiences in pornography. In 1989, she helped organize Prostitutes of New York (P.O.N.Y.) and advocates the decriminalization of prostitution. She is the dean of Ms. Vera's Finishing School for Boys Who Want to be Girls.

Alice Walker (1944–) was born in Mississippi. She has written several books including poetry, essays, short stories and novels. Her novel *The Color Purple* won an American Book Award and the Pulitzer Prize. Her other books include *The Temple of My Familiar* and *You Can't Keep a Good Woman Down*.

Fay Weldon (1933–) was born in England and raised in New Zealand. She has written film and television scripts, plays and fiction. Her novels include *The Hearts and Lives of Men, The Life and Loves of a She-Devil, Life Force* and *Trouble*. She lives in London.

Janice Williamson is Associate Professor in the English Department at the University of Alberta. She is the author of *Tell Tale Signs: Fictions, Altitude X 2*, and *Sounding Differences: Conversations with Seventeen Canadian Women Writers*. The autofiction "Lucrece" was nominated for the Pushcart Prize.